HAMMERTIME

"*Do* something!" Buncan hissed desperately.

"I'm tryin'," said Neena, "but 'e ain't 'elpin' none."

"Wait a minim!" Squill blinked suddenly. The young otter whispered rapidly to his sister. Her expression widened, she nodded and they began to sing once more:

> "Time for the beat, time for the feet.
> Time to get real out on the street.
> Time to Hammer the bad dudes down.
> Time to Hammer 'em right in the ground..."

A glistening argent nimbus materialized above the bushes between the singers and the advancing robbers. The cloud began to congeal into an enormous tool: a hammer of some unidentifiable metal. The hammer shuddered, and then swooshed down with tremendous force. It squashed the first robber as flat as if the singers had dropped a blue whale on him.

The hammer pivoted and began to chase the retreating bandits, repeatedly slamming into the ground, shaking the solid earth...

BOOKS BY
ALAN DEAN FOSTER

Alien
Aliens
The I Inside
Into the Out Of
Krull
The Man Who Used the Universe
Pale Rider
Shadowkeep
Starman

THE SPELLSINGER SERIES:

Spellsinger
The Hour of the Gate
The Day of the Dissonance
The Moment of the Magician
The Paths of the Perambulator
The Time of the Transference
Into the Out Of

Published by
WARNER BOOKS

ALAN DEAN FOSTER

SON OF SPELLSINGER

WARNER BOOKS

A Time Warner Company

WARNER BOOKS EDITION

Questar® is a registered trademark of Warner Books, Inc.

Cover design by Don Puckey
Cover illustration by Tom Hildebrandt
Hand lettering by David Gatti

Warner Books, Inc.
1271 Avenue of the Americas
New York, NY 10020

A Time Warner Company

Printed in the United States of America

First Printing: April, 1993

10 9 8 7 6 5 4 3 2 1

For Carl Roessler,
Friend, shipmate, and good conversationalist,
Above or below the water.

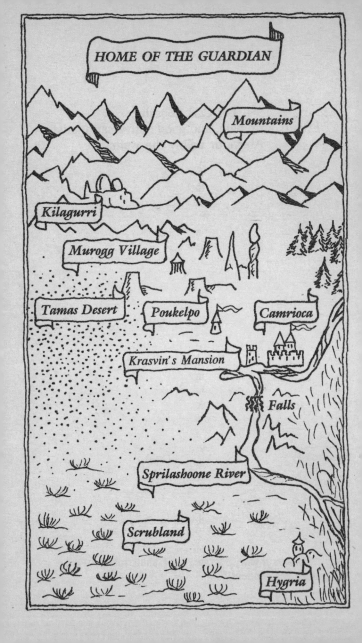

CHAPTER 1

MAYBE NOTHING WOULD HAVE HAPPENED IF TALEA hadn't found the demon in the breadbox.

She'd baked six loaves of fresh humberpine the previous day and had left them in the metal-lined wooden container to cool. It sat on the tiled kitchen counter just to the left of the big oval window cut in the south side of the tree, overlooking the riverbank and the willows that clung there like tipsy spectators at a fishing tournament.

Half a dozen was a lot to make all at once, but thanks to a petite, highly domesticated preserving spell thoughtfully provided by Clothahump, the bread would stay not only fresh but hot for as long as was necessary. It was also more energy-efficient than refrigeration.

When she opened the breadbox to remove some for supper she was startled to see, seated against the nearest loaf, a perfectly formed six-inch-high homunculus. Two curved horns protruded from the sides of his skull, a single smaller one from his forehead. Gossamer rose-hued wings lay folded against his back. He wore long maroon denim pants with matching suspenders, and his clawed feet protruded beyond the ends of thick rubber sandals.

He also owned a hearty appetite. Half the loaf he was seated against had been devoured. She'd caught him red-handed (of course, with demons this was not an especially difficult task).

Startled, he jerked around sharply when she raised the lid of the box, a double-handful of steaming fresh bread clutched in one tiny fist.

"Azmac!" the creature shouted, waving its free hand at her. *"Poreon faytu!* Begone, or I shall make of your life Purgatory resplendent!"

"Get out of my breadbox!" Talea was not in the least intimidated by the baroque threat. Fumbling in a nearby drawer, her fingers wrapped around the handle of a small iron skillet and thrust it toward the loaf.

Dropping its aromatic prize, the demon scrambled toward the back of the box. *"Emarion! Sacarath sanctus!"*

"Never mind that." Reversing the skillet, Talea used the handle to dig at the back of the box. "Get out of my bread!"

Though not very big, Talea was deceptively strong, and the demon, sated on humberpine, was decidedly overfed. There was a loud *poing* as he lost his grip on the rear of the box and went flying, arms and legs akimbo, across the kitchen. He soared neatly over the central butcher block to smack with a slightly wet splat against the rhomboidal window on the far side of the room. There he seemed to hang for an instant, suspended, before sliding down the glass into the dish basin.

Hefting the skillet by its handle, Talea rushed to the sink and peered down among the dirty plates and cups. "What were you doing in my breadbox? Does somebody have it in for me, is that it? I'll bet it's that stuck-up possum Mrs. Genfine up the river. She always stays upside down when we visit." She watched while the dazed demon struggled unsuccessfully to stand. "You're not much of a curse."

Something buzzed loudly past her head and she twisted sideways, the demon in the dishwater momentarily forgotten. This new specter was smaller than the homunculus, with four bright emerald-green wings and a long snaky tail trailing behind it. A face once removed from toad roadkill sneered back at her. From its four hands hung the crystal saltcellar that had been a wedding gift from her mother.

She snatched for it but it darted just out of reach, taunting her with a high-pitched buzz-accompanied version of some cabalistic mantra that sounded very much like "My Darling Clementine."

"*Now* what?" Taking aim with the edge, she swung the skillet. The toadbuzz dodged once, a second time, and then there was a loud bang as the skillet connected. The song faded as the apparition fell on the stove, bounced once, and tumbled off to land on the floor. Unharmed, the saltcellar rolled clear. Ignoring the dazed buzzing of the would-be thief, she knelt to recover it.

"What the hell is going on here?" she mumbled to herself as she put the skillet aside and pulled the big broom from storage. Now, where was the dustpan?

As she bent over to search for it, something smacked her in the rear. Clutching the broom in front of her, she whirled.

It couldn't be called a demon, though it wore a demonic grin. Considerably larger than the pair of intruders she'd already coped with, it squatted before her on thickly muscled, kangaroo-like legs, its flat fish face regarding her blandly. Lavender scales covered the naked body except for the pair of turquoise tentacles that made swimming motions against the air. Sprouting from the top of the head was a bright, rotating blue searchlight.

She hefted the broom and inspected the newcomer. "What are *you* supposed to be?"

"Beeble," it burped. It made another rude body noise and took a tentative hop toward her.

"Keep away from me." She made a threatening gesture with the broom as she started edging sideways, away from the broom closet. "I'm warning you."

The bread demon had recovered and was now busily poking through the kitchen cabinets, looking for something else to eat, its red belly hanging pendulously over its belt line.

"What's going on here?" she muttered. "Jon-Tom!" There was no response. Her husband wasn't due home from work for a while yet. She was isolated in her kitchen. "Somebody! Anybody?"

She dodged as the hop-searchlight took another bound in her direction, extending toward her face a vile and obscene tongue.

"I warned you." She swung the broom and smacked the tongue sideways. The protruding organ whizzed several times around the hopper's head before the tip smacked its owner square in the right eye.

"Ow. Ow, ow, ow!" It hop-retreated, trying to recoil the rebellious organ.

The breadbox demon was in an upper cabinet, scattering her victuals. Broom held high, she charged, shoving the hopper aside. "Damn your demonic ass, get out of my provisions!"

When she reached the cabinet the demon was nowhere to be seen, having sought the depths within. But half a dozen brand-new apparitions flew straight out at her, squealing and screeching. As they circled and darted she swung the broom in frenzied self-defense, fighting to keep them out of her hair.

"Get away from me, get away!"

They were a rainbow of colors and a plethora of shapes, none very pleasing to look upon save for one with iridescent compound eyes. It had the body of an undersize, anorexic macaque attached to the wings of a falcon. They came at her from all directions, forcing her to retreat. "Get away, I'm warning you!" she yelled as she flailed with the broom.

They were pouring out of the woodwork now: emerging from cabinets and drawers, from cracks in the tree floor, from behind bowls, from beneath the sink, and from the doorway that led to the den. Drooling, grinning, gurgling, belching and farting, laughing and hissing as they crawled, slithered, hopped, and flew toward her. They stank and they gibbered, they uttered incomprehensibilities and obscenities, they messed impertinently with her clean dishes, and pawed through her carefully stacked foodstuffs.

Dozens of the creatures filled the kitchen, and more were arriving every minute. There was a translucent winged thing that looked like nothing so much as a vampire butterfly, horrific in aspect save for its decidedly befuddled expression. It kept beating against the skylight as if trying to escape.

Something was tugging at the sandal on her left foot. Looking down, she saw a small bright yellow and pink polka-dotted snake with seven heads.

"Excuse me." The septicephalic slitherer spoke plaintively, its accent unidentifiable. "I seem to have wandered into the wrong mythology. Can you . . . ?"

Talea screamed and jumped backward. "Get out of my kitchen! Get out of my house!" The flailing broom knocked two of the heads senseless, while the other five fell to arguing among themselves.

Something landed on her right shoulder. As she reached up to rip it off, she saw a small fat man with a cherubic expression. He was composed entirely of layers of some resilient white substance that threatened to rub off on her blouse.

"Madame, I don't know what eez going on heere, but I have work to do elsewhere and I reesent most heartily being sucked in with the rest of theeze undeesciplined and unrefined conjurations."

"Don't blame me. I didn't conjure anything." She grabbed the puffy white arm and wrenched. The limb promptly came off in her fingers. There was no blood, only a sort of thick black goo that began to ooze from the ruptured joints.

"Now look what you have done. I will meeze my next assignment."

"Sorry." She handed back the amputated limb.

"Merci." With great dignity the creature jammed the arm back into the vacant shoulder socket. It hopped off her shoulder and bounced across the floor, disappearing into the otherworldly tumult.

The majority of phantasms were not nearly so polite. One tried to take a bite out of her left calf. Using the broom, she smashed it against one leg of the heavy wooden kitchen table. Another leaped at her face, scrabbling at her eyes. All three of its own were missing. She caught it on the rounded end of the broomstick and jammed it hard against the cooler. The big box rattled. *Have to get the coolant spell renewed,* she thought absently.

That was the trouble with being married to a wizard. Or in her case, to a spellsinger. It was all very well and good to go toodling off all the time to save the world or close shattered interdimensional gates or defeat hordes of ravening invaders, oh yes. But try to get something fixed around the house? No way! They never had any time for domestic mundanities.

She picked up the skillet and flung it at another advancing horror. Utilizing all six of its black arms, it plucked the utensil cleanly from the air, studied it intently for a moment, then plunked it down on its already flattened skull, exhibiting an air of considerable satisfaction.

"By the Twelve Crinoline Veils of the Most Repentant Sinner," she bawled irately, "I want you all out of here! *Now!*" Yanking open a drawer, she reached for the large skillet stored inside, only to draw back her hand at the sight of the four tiny imps cavorting within. They wore brightly striped scarves around their necks and nothing else as they skated on the flat metal surface. Tiny wisps of steam rose from beneath their splayed feet.

"Do you mind?" one said, upset at the interruption of his private reverie.

"Do I mind? Get out of my drawer!" She spun around to swing at something that was chewing on the hem of her housedress, then thrust the end of the broomstick at the pan. The skating imps scattered wildly.

Suddenly she felt her feet going out from under her. The broom went flying as she landed on her front, the impact knocking the breath out of her. Looking down and backward, she saw four things that resembled a cross between miniature donkeys and salamanders. Their tack consisted of perfectly fashioned miniature harnesses hooked up to downsized block and tackle, which had been fastened to her ankles.

Seated atop a matching wagon at the back of the alien team was a tiny drover who was mostly long black beard and busy whip. He bellowed orders in a deep, unintelligible mumble as he and his team dragged the frantic Talea toward a gaping, ominous, and hitherto unsuspected cavity beneath the fruit bin. Conflagrant lights alternately flared and faded in the black depths.

She dug at the floor, yelling and screeching, while all around her wee monstrosities and diminutive horrors gibbered contentedly as they reduced her kitchen to rubble.

"That's *enough*!" she roared.

Rolling over, she leaned forward and kicked with both legs as hard as she could. The block and tackle snapped, and both drover and team went flying. Still mumbling and babbling to themselves, they vanished into that abiding black maw.

"My sword," she muttered as she struggled to her feet. "Where'd I store that damn sword?"

Since marrying Jon-Tom she hadn't had much occasion to make use of her old weapon. During holidays it was handy for making spectacularly short work of a big roast. Otherwise it slept in storage, her thieving and fighting days being far behind her. But she hadn't forgotten how to use it.

Was it in with the cutlery? No, not enough room. Behind the stove? No, it would've stuck out there. She finally located it jammed unceremoniously in the back of the broom closet. Except for a light glaze of kitchen grease it was perfectly functional.

Hefting the familiar old grip in both hands, she turned in her housedress to confront the room full of clawing, cawing demons. Pots and dishes were scattered everywhere, food containers had been upturned and their contents dumped on the counters, while piquant liquids pooled on her painstakingly polished floor.

"Chaos repossess all of you, Spawn of Hell!" Swinging the sword in broad, powerful, horizontal arcs, she waded fearlessly into the babble.

Heads, limbs, and interesting other body parts went flying as blood of dissimilar colors spurted, mixing with the spilled honey and milk and household cleansers. She knew it was going to take a heavy, not to mention expensive, housecleaning spell to scrub away the carnage, but she was damned if she was going to clean up this mess manually. Jon-Tom was going to have to drop whatever he was involved with and do something about it.

Squealing and striking out with long, pointed arms, a giant blue spider rushed her on stiltlike legs. Skewering it neatly, she swung the sword and bashed its brains out against the baking counter. Green ichor and pink brains bubbled from the crushed chiton, getting all over the batch of sprinkle-topped cupcakes she'd made just the week before. At that sight her fury knew no bounds, and she laid about the kitchen with a will.

Demonic shapes struck at her, or scrambled to get out of her way, or sought escape in cabinets and drawers. Yet despite her successes, progress eluded her. Mocking her

efforts, fresh furies materialized whenever another was
destroyed. They kept coming at her: oozing up out of the
floor, dropping down from the skylight, spiraling up out of
the sinks—an endless procession of horrors that reinforced
themselves even as she demolished their predecessors.

Gradually she found herself forced to retreat by the sheer
weight of numbers. Backed up against the broom closet, her
sword strokes inevitably grew shorter and weaker as her
assailants pressed their attack.

She'd always envisioned herself perishing on some grand
quest of Jon-Tom's, or at worst while comfortably retired
amongst the widows of the local Thieves and Cutpurses Rest
Home. Not like this, not in her own kitchen, brought down
by a conjuration she'd had no part in and couldn't comprehend.

What had happened to the carefully crafted home protection and insulation spell that usually shielded her sanctum
from nefarious external influences? Admittedly it was pri-
marily designed to vacuum and deodorize, but it should
have restricted the access of demons, gargoyles, and their
ilk as well. That it had failed so spectacularly suggested an
even more powerful sorcery was at work.

Her hair tousled about her, housedress in tatters, she
continued to cut and thrust with the sword. It was just like
old times, except that her arms weren't nearly as responsive
as they used to be, her strokes not quite as economical of
arc.

Just when she thought her trembling legs and arms were
about to give out completely and that the fanged and taloned
mob of necrotic intruders were going to take her down for
the last time, there came the sound of a thump from beyond
the kitchen doorway.

"Hi, honey," boomed a cheery voice, "I'm home!
Clothahump and I finally got the old Toolawhip bridge
braced with a decent suspension spell. Of course, it's only
temporary, but . . ."

Jon-Tom strode around the corner and into the kitchen,
whereupon something compact and violet leaped onto his
chest and thrust a belligerent bulbous blue nose into his
face.

"Youse better stay outta dis if you know what's good for

you, buddy. Da broad givin' us enough trouble as it is, see? We don't need no interference from no kibbitzers, see?''

A startled Jon-Tom clutched the creature by its short, thick neck. It gurgled, and its eyes bulged hugely. Without a word the spellsinger drop-kicked it halfway across the kitchen. It struck a shelf, breaking one of Talea's favorite fairy vases in the process, and fell motionless to the floor.

"What the hell's going on here?" He gaped at the bedlam, eyes wide.

"Don't just stand there." Talea redoubled her efforts, reinvigorated by his appearance. "*Do* something!"

Stunned by the scope of the turmoil, he found himself hesitating. Had he left his duar in the cart? No, he'd brought it in with him. It needed some restringing, but it ought to suffice to deal with this. It had better, he thought, seeing how hard-pressed was Talea.

Racing back to the front hall, he yanked the unique instrument from its slot in the carved umbrella stand and tried to think of an appropriate song as he rushed back to the kitchen. Years of practice under Clothahump's aegis had made him facile. He was infinitely more confident than the awkward young man who'd first found himself transported to this world.

Still, he found himself struggling as he confronted the pandemonium in the kitchen. Historically, the domestic household did not figure prominently in the rock-and-roll lexicon with which he was conversant.

An old ditty by John Mellencamp finally leaped to mind. He began to play, and to sing, his voice and the mellifluous chords of the duar rising strong and pure above the uproar.

From cabinets and vents, from fractures in the floor and the seams around windows, a pink haze began to emerge. Swirling in lazy currents, it picked its way into the kitchen, smelling faintly of pumpernickel and Simellot cheese. There was nothing Jon-Tom could do about the latter. Considering what the miasma could have smelled like, he was rather pleased. Ancillary odors were not his primary concern at the moment.

The slightly moist mist had an immediate effect on the army of invading fiends (or maybe it was the smell). From cabinets and shelves, from pots and pans and dishes, they ceased their activities to stare and sniff. One whiff was sufficient. Shrieking and screaming, they proceeded to get the hell out. Nostrils pinched, mouths puckered, they plunged back into the depths of the cupboards, the floor, the ceiling, returning at breakneck speed to the noxious nexi of their respective existences. In their panicked recision they took with them not so much as a cookie.

The duar pulsed and trembled in Jon-Tom's practiced hands. Unsourced wind caused his iridescent green cape (which was overdue for dry cleaning) to stream out behind him, as though he stood in the forefront of an intense but highly localized squall.

As he strolled deliberately through the kitchen a few of the bolder intruders threw themselves angrily at him, attacking from every direction. The music beat them back, the pink haze forming knots around their necks or club-shaped clouds which smashed them into oblivion.

Her feet and composure regained, Talea warily trailed her husband as far as the sink. She laid the bloody sword lengthwise in the basin, shaking her head. Getting the blade properly clean was going to take a lot of scrubbing. Ichor had a notorious tendency to cling.

Jon-Tom had halted in the middle of the kitchen, his voice quavering. Eighteen years of practice had improved but not perfected the weakest component of his spellsinging. The power of his playing more than compensated, however, for his less than operatic voice.

As she stared, those demons who hadn't been able to escape, or who had foolishly chosen to attack Jon-Tom, began to swell like balloons. They started to rise, bouncing off the cabinets and finally the ceiling. As Jon-Tom brought the song to an end, they began to burst like soap bubbles.

She inhaled despairingly. As if the kitchen wasn't enough a mess already.

Finally nothing remained save swirling pink mist and a powerful scent of cheese and pumpernickel. As Jon-Tom flung his fingers against the double strings of the duar in one last dramatic riff, the mist faded and began to dissipate. Taking a deep, relieved breath, he turned to face her.

"Now, then. Will you please tell me what happened here?" His brows drew slightly together. "Talea, have you been experimenting with thaumaturgical cooking spells again? I told you, I'm not that big on fried foods. Sometimes household shortcuts aren't worth the trouble they cause."

She waggled an admonishing finger in his face. "Don't you lip me, Jon-Tom! I haven't done a damned thing." Moving to the window over the sink, she fought to open it. Coagulating blood and gore caused it to stick. She waved at the remnants of the pink mist, backing away as fresh air sucked it outside. The heavy stink likewise began to disperse, leaving in its wake a faint memory of dill pickle.

She eyed the shattered crockery, the broken crumbs of baked goods over which she'd labored long and lovingly, the disgusting mess which coated everything, the thin rivulets of unidentifiable fluids which dripped from counters to pool noisomely on the floor, and she wanted to scream. Instead she sank tiredly into one of the snakeskin-upholstered chairs in the breakfast nook.

Jon-Tom carefully leaned the warm duar against the cooler, brushed back his long hair, and sat down next to his distraught wife.

"Okay, so you weren't messing with spells." He indicated the kitchen. "How do you explain this?"

She glared at him. "Why ask me? You're the great spellsinger. Someone have a grudge against you?" She sighed. "I'd kill for a cup of tea."

He found a reasonably clean empty cup. "Iced or hot?"

"Oh, no," she said quickly, "no shortcuts!" Rising, she made her way to the stove and checked to make sure that it was set on medium heat. Filling a pot from the sink, she set it on the burner. Beneath, the indentured fire elemental set to work, grumbling audibly. *Have to get him adjusted,* she thought idly. Thoughtfully, she found a second cup before resuming her seat.

Jon-Tom had been pondering her question. "Clothahump and I have some long-term, overdue debtors, but we've never used any strong-arm collection techniques. Nothing that would turn anyone vengeful. At least, I haven't. I can mention it to Clothahump. You know how he can get about money sometimes.''

"The old miser,'' Talea muttered.

"With him it's not the interest. It's the principal of the thing.''

She gestured at the kitchen, her arm shaking slightly. "Jon-Tom, I'm reasonably well versed in the nature of the inhabitants of the Nether Regions. I'd have to be, being married to you. But I didn't recognize half of what materialized here.''

He shrugged. "Other dimensions, other demons. Don't blame yourself. Even the standard references have to be updated every year.''

She leaned toward him, smiling at sudden memories. "Sometimes I think things were easier when you and I were on the road all the time, fighting and slaughtering, living by our wits. Having *fun*.''

"We were a lot younger then, Talea. I didn't have the responsibilities that come with being Clothahump's junior partner. We didn't have a home, or a family.''

"You're forty-one, Jon-Tom. That's hardly old.''

He stiffened slightly. "I didn't say it was. Why, by now Mick Jagger must be . . .'' He changed direction. "Never mind. This doesn't tell us what happened here.''

She shrugged. "Maybe I mixed something wrong. Maybe I whistled a happy tune the wrong way. Maybe some netherworld entity has a grudge against you from some years-old encounter you've long since forgotten.''

"I could check the records,'' he murmured thoughtfully, "but as near as I can remember all old conflicts have been resolved, all numinous debts paid off.''

"You're sure you haven't offended any important deities or spirits recently? Trod on the toes of some easily offended Prince of Darkness?''

"Clothahump and I are careful to observe all protocols. We're very proud of our work habits. Before signing any contracts we run them through half a dozen legal spells and have at least three eternally damned lawyers check them for errors. I'm clean, darling.

"Even if there was a serious problem somewhere, the

provoked entity would take up the quarrel with me, not you.''

"I don't know about that," she countered. "All I know is what went on in my kitchen. Unless you isolate the causality, it could happen again." She shuddered slightly.

"I know that." He put a reassuring arm around her. "Interdimensional manifestations of pure evil don't just happen. There has to be a reason." His lips tightened. "It has to be something I've done. Or haven't done."

They fell silent. After a moment Talea looked up. "Listen."

In the absence of conversation or chaos a faint, rhythmic moaning became audible. A distinctly unpalatable, eerie, pulse-pounding rise and fall of verbalizations that verged on the incomprehensible. The sound issued not from the Nether Regions, but from above. From upstairs.

Jon-Tom followed his wife's gaze. They exchanged a look.

"There it is, then," she told him confidently. "You haven't offended any paranormal princes, and it's not a consequence of random chance. The Plated Folk aren't involved, and neither are the Inimical Outer Guards of Proximate Perdition. It's much, much worse than that." Her gaze rose, tracking the inhuman discord.

"Jon-Tom, you have *got* to do something about that kid."

CHAPTER 2

AS HE MOUNTED THE SPIRAL STAIRCASE CUT INTO THE heart of the interdimensionally expanded tree, the music, if such it could be called, grew steadily louder. Actually, some of what he could hear through the heavy-handed, sound-dampening spell was no worse than borderline awful. The awkwardness of the lyrics, however, made him wince.

Standing just outside the room, he was better able to judge the volume within. He estimated that it fell somewhere between deafening and permanent brain damage. Steeling himself, he hammered on the solid door.

"Buncan! Turn that racket down and open up! I've got to talk to you."

There was no response from within. Either his son couldn't hear him over the din, or else he was pretending not to. The instrumental work wasn't bad, Jon-Tom decided, but as usual Buncan's voice was excruciatingly off-key. In fact, his singing was so bad he made his father sound like a La Scala heldentenor by comparison.

He pounded on the wood afresh. "You hear me, Buncan? Stop that wailing and open this door!"

Something was coming through the barrier. Jon-Tom retreated to the far side of the hall and watched with interest as a two-foot-long white whale emerged, glanced to right and left, then swam off down the hall. It was attached by a thread to a small wooden boat crewed by half a dozen nautically garbed mini-imps wearing tormented expressions. There was barely room in the boat for their tails.

Standing in the bow was a wee fiend with skin the hue of pea soup. His forked tail flicked wildly back and forth, metronoming time for his crew to row by. One leg was fashioned of white ivory, and his expression was suitably demented.

Chanting a plangent tune, he directed his reluctant rowers in pursuit of the retreating mini-whale. They drifted off toward the stairway and disappeared below.

The inevitable scream reached him a moment later, followed by the outraged and angry voice of his wife, who, from the tenor and tone of her voice, he could tell had had it up to the proverbial here.

"Jon-Tom, you make your son quit that *now*!"

This time he kicked the door. "Last chance, Buncan! Open up. Or I'll cast an all-encompassing blanket of silence on your room that'll last for weeks!"

The music within, together with its decidedly unpleasant caterwauling accompaniment, abruptly ceased. With a reluctant creak, the door opened slightly.

Avoiding a cluster of hovering eyeballs that blinked as they looked him over, Jon-Tom pushed his way inside.

"It's all right," said a voice from across the room. "It's just my dad."

Jon-Tom shut the door behind him. "Don't get funny with me, young man. I'm not here on funny business."

Buncan sat up on his bed. "You're right, Dad. Existence is tragic as hell, isn't it?"

Jon-Tom walked over to the single oval window, stared out at the neatly kept grounds and the river beyond. After what he felt was a sufficiently lengthy pause of suitably solemn significance, he turned to regard his son.

Buncan balanced the duar easily in his lap. That had to be the source of the trouble, Jon-Tom knew. Using his own singular duar as a template, with the aid of Lynchbany's finest craftsfolk he and Clothahump had fashioned the new instrument as a gift for Buncan's twelfth birthday. The boy had kept it close at hand ever since. While no match for Jon-Tom's own instrument, it was quite capable of propagating a conjuring nexus at the point where the two sets of strings intersected.

Until recently, however, Buncan had not acquired sufficient skill to do anything other than make music with it. This morning's events showed how drastically that had changed. Making magic with music was one thing. Controlling it, as Jon-Tom probably knew better than anyone else alive, was something else again.

Given Buncan's genuinely appalling voice, it represented a bona fide threat to anyone unlucky enough to come within hearing distance.

Over the years Buncan had added some decorative modifications of his own to the instrument. Instead of the graceful, curving lines of Jon-Tom's duar, his son had grafted on spikes and fake claws. Bright green and red parallel lines gave the instrument the look of a runaway migraine.

But it worked. He could see the nebulous blend of reality and nonreality fading at the stringed nexus even as he spoke. Occasional sparks flared and vanished. Yes, his son's carefully crafted duar functioned like the magical instrument it was.

It was Buncan who didn't always function properly.

Which, since he was only eighteen, was to be expected. After all, Jon-Tom had been considerably older and more experienced when he'd first made the acquaintance of the mysterious duar and its remarkable capabilities.

He left the window and approached the bed, sitting down near the end and promptly sinking clear to the floor. That seemed to rouse Buncan. The boy mumbled a few off-key words and the bed promptly reinflated. Jon-Tom wished he could say the same for his son's attitude.

Buncan was clad entirely in gray with emerald accents. Spiral stripes wound down his pants, as though his legs had been thrust into a pair of green tornadoes. His low-top day boots were bright red.

He was shorter than Jon-Tom, a consequence of his mother's genes, but he retained his father's red hair. It was cut in a short, stiff brush with twin arcs shaved in the sides above and behind each ear. A lanky, almost disjointed build corraled a carefully constructed air of adolescent indolence.

"Look at yourself," muttered Jon-Tom as he considered his progeny.

"Can't do that, Dad. Nearest mirror's in the bathroom."

"There must be a gene for sarcasm. Until now I was sure it was recessive."

Buncan grinned slightly but said nothing. Better not to laugh until he found out what was on his old man's mind.

"And your hair. What's with this short hair? Why can't you wear it a decent shoulder-length like your friends?"

"Caswise wears his short. So does Whickwith."

"Caswise and Whickwith are orang-utans. Orangs are the reverse of humans, follicle-wise. They have naturally short hair on top and long hair everywhere else."

"Maybe I should try and grow long hair everywhere else. I can probably scribe something hairy."

Jon-Tom counted silently, giving up at seven. "I don't suppose you have any knowledge of what just happened downstairs?"

Buncan sat up a little straighter. "No, what?"

"You nearly destroyed your mother's kitchen. Not to mention your mother."

"What are you talking about?"

"You've been spellsinging again, haven't you?" Buncan turned away. "How many times have I told you not to spellsing in the house?"

The younger Meriweather looked frustrated. "Well, where am I supposed to practice?"

"On the riverbank. In the Bellwoods. Outside school. Anywhere but at home. It's dangerous." He softened his tone. "You've got a lot of natural talent, Buncan. You may even be a better duar player than I. But as to spellsinging . . . you've got to work on your lyrics, and your voice. It's taken me eighteen years to learn how to carry a tune adequately. Your pitch, your tonal control, is worse than mine. Sometimes it's nonexistent."

"Thanks, Dad," Buncan replied sardonically. "For the vote of confidence."

"Son, not everyone has the skills necessary to make magic, much less be a spellsinger. It may be that despite your obvious instrumental talents your true vocation lies elsewhere. It's all very well and good to be a brilliant instrumentalist," Buncan perked up at the compliment, "but if the words and phrasing aren't there, you risk unpredictable consequences of a possibly lethal nature."

"Dad, you've been hanging with Clothahump much too long."

"Let me put it another way. You could total yourself." Jon-Tom rose from the end of the bed. "Now come downstairs and take a look at what you did to your mother's kitchen."

Buncan sounded uncertain. "You mean my singing . . . ?"

Jon-Tom nodded. "Demons, devils, imps, inimical sprites, and all manner of nasty conjurations. It's a real mess."

Buncan rose to follow, sarcasm giving way to contrition. "I'm really sorry, Dad. I thought I was being careful. Will you tell Mom I'm sorry?"

"You can tell her yourself." Jon-Tom opened the door and headed down the hall. "This has got to stop, Buncan. You're just not experienced enough to be taking these kinds of chances. Especially in the house. What if you accidentally freed the monster under your bed?"

Buncan followed slowly. "There's no monster under my bed, Dad."

"Shows how much you know. Until they reach their twentieth birthday every kid has a monster under their bed."

His son considered. "Was there one under yours when you were a kid, Dad?"

"I told you, there's one under everybody's. I just didn't know it when I was your age. Mine," he added as they started down the stairs, "was warty and leprous, and wanted to force-feed me eggplant. I hated eggplant. Still do." They reached the den and paused there. "I think it was a Republican.

"No more spellsinging, anytime, anywhere, until your voice improves."

"But, Dad . . . !"

"No buts."

"I hate voice school. Sitting in a chair for hours, listening to that stupid nightingale. I'm not a bird, Dad."

"Mrs. Nellawhistle makes appropriate allowances for the natural limitations of her students. She's very patient." *She has to be*, he thought, *with pupils like Buncan*. "She really can help you with pitch and tone, if you'll let her. Spellsinging takes study and work. Or did you just think you could pick up a duar and successfully manipulate the forces of Otherness? If I hadn't come home when I did, your mother could be lying on the kitchen floor right now, sword in one hand, broom in the other, eviscerated and dismembered."

Buncan chuckled. "Good ol' Mom. That's the way she'd want to go."

"This is *serious*. No more spellsinging until your lyric composition and singing have improved."

"How the hole-in-the-stone can anyone be expected to improve when all they have to work with are these ossified old songs?" Buncan complained bitterly.

Jon-Tom looked shocked. "Those 'ossified old songs' are the classics of my world, Buncan. Good, solid, serious rock. I've made plenty of magic with them. They constitute a fine basis for spellsinging."

"Maybe they do for you, Dad, but I just can't relate to

them. I've tried. Magic or no magic. No wonder I can't keep control. I'm just not into the stuff.''

"You'd better get into it. As for controlling anything, you're eighteen years old, stubborn and bullheaded and inexperienced, notwithstanding you're convinced you know everything. Maybe you ought to take up another instrument."

Buncan glanced sharply at his father. "You can only spellsing with a duar."

"You got it. Then maybe you should take up something else altogether. Woodcarving. I could apprentice you to Genrac the suslik. He'd be glad to teach you. There's no shame in learning a real trade."

"I want to spellsing, Dad. The problem's with the music, not my musicianship."

"Excepting your lamentable singing voice. Frankly, Buncan, you couldn't carry a tune in a bucket. Unless that changes you'll only be a danger to yourself and everyone around you, no matter how well you play the duar. Speaking of which, after Clothahump and Semond and I labored so long and hard over your instrument, I don't see why you couldn't have left it alone."

"I don't just want to play good, Dad. I want to look good, too."

"Then there's these ridiculously subdued outfits you've started to favor."

"Dad, cut me some slack, please? I promise, I won't screw up again. But I'm just not ready to give up on this and go into woodworking or metal husbandry or thieving or any of the other traditional professions yet."

"Okay. I accept your promise. So much for the easy part."

Buncan blinked. "What's the hard part?"

"Keeping your mother from flaying you alive. Follow me."

Preparing himself as best he could, Buncan did so.

At dinner he was sullen and uncommunicative. Not that it was necessarily a corollary to what had transpired earlier. It was the same pose he'd affected for much of the preceding year.

Feeling sorry for the boy, Jon-Tom tried to mediate,

explaining to Talea that it was all just a phase their son was going through. Having been brought up under different circumstances in a very different society from that of her husband, Talea responded that in her clan such phases were usually handled with a sharp knife. Buncan started to say something but wisely thought better of it.

Only after he felt that his mother had vented most of her spleen did he push aside what remained of his vegetables and snake sausage. "Want me to get your sword now, Mom, or should I just take poison after I've finished brushing my teeth?"

"Could we dispense with the sarcasm for five minutes?"

"Hey, what more can I say, Mom? I'm sorry. I didn't do it on purpose. It's not like I turned the stove into a salamander." He hesitated, staring at his father. "All I want is to be like Dad. To do some of the things he's done. To come near to his achievements, have adventures, perform great deeds. I want to rescue beautiful damsels and defeat evil and save the world. Is that too much to ask?"

"Let me tell you something, son." Jon-Tom sliced off a cylinder of sausage and poked it into his mouth, chewing reflectively as he gestured with his fork. "It's true that I helped save the world, and as a full-time occupation I can tell you that it's very overrated. Not to mention highly stressful."

"Actually I think you've saved the world twice, sweetheart." Talea set a fresh bowl of steaming sweet-and-sour potato down alongside the vegetables.

Jon-Tom frowned. "I thought it was just once."

"No, dear," she said firmly. "Twice, at least."

"Really? Anyway," he continued, turning back to his son, "I've been down that road, and it's not half so glamorous as you seem to think it is. A nice, steady, comfortable practice of magic somewhere, executing medicinal spells to help people get well and plastic surgery spells to improve their looks: That's what you want. A good living in a proven profession that's respected and admired."

"But I don't just want to make a living, Dad," Buncan protested. "I want to perform mighty deeds. I want to accomplish great things. I want to see the worlds."

"Better start with this one. You're too young and inexperienced for the rest. Besides, there aren't any great quests at hand presently. I know. I keep a regular check on the 'Q' section in the classifieds. Just for old times' sake," he explained quickly to Talea.

Buncan tried to meet his father halfway. "Are you trying to tell me there are no great quests left in the world?"

"Not at the moment. Not in this part of it, anyway. The Plated Folk have been quiet ever since Clothahump and I kicked their chitonous butts back over the Jo-Troom Pass. Nothing of similar bellicosity has emerged to duplicate the threat they once presented.

"Meanwhile, business is good. I'm not trying to come down hard on you, Buncan. But you can take it from someone who needed more than eighteen years to overcome a bad voice: Right now you aren't close to having what it takes, verbally. And without your duar you sing even worse. Sort of *a crapella*. You need heavy-duty voice training, and plenty of it. It's something you can't fix with magic. I tried that route, and it doesn't work that way. Some things," he finished grimly, "are beyond the reach of even the most powerful forces to fix."

"Clothahump could do it," Buncan muttered. "If he was interested in anybody's problems besides his own."

Talea whacked him on the side of his arc-inscribed head. "Don't speak like that about your goduncle. Even if he is a turtle. He's been very good to your father and me, when he could just as easily have decorporalized us and had done with it, after all the trouble we caused him."

"You have to apply yourself to your studies and your training," Jon-Tom insisted unequivocally. "How can you do that if you're off on a quest somewhere?"

"On-the-job training?" Buncan ventured hopefully.

"Not a good idea where controlling the forces of Otherness are concerned," his father replied. "Anyway, my situation was different. I was trapped in this world and had no choice but to experiment. I did just well enough to stay alive. If it hadn't been for Clothahump . . ."

"That's right," agreed Talea. "Let me tell you, when I

first met your father he was the most wimpy, hopeless, gangly, driveling . . .''

"Hey!" said Jon-Tom.

Buncan pushed himself back from the table. "I know you both mean well, and I promise I'll think about what you've said. But you've fulfilled your dreams, Dad. You've been all over this world and your own. I haven't been any farther than Lynchbany. I've never been beyond the Bellwoods. All I want is what you had." He rose and headed for his room.

"Don't be in such a hurry," his father called after him.

"You haven't finished your snake," his mother added.

Following dinner, Jon-Tom helped Talea with the dishes. "He'll be all right," he assured her. "He's just going through a stage."

"You keep saying that." She handed him a dripping bowl. "Do all the young people in your world go through stages and phases? Personally I think a few good whacks with a stout cane would cure a lot of his problems."

"We don't use that where I come from. We use more enlightened methods, like psychology."

"Does that raise as red a welt as hickory?" She shook her head. "You coddle the boy."

Jon-Tom looked toward the stairs. "I disagree. I think our little talk had quite a profound effect on him. He's a bright kid, and he does play well."

"Yeah, but he sure can't sing worth a copper. He's so bad he makes your voice sound good." She handed him a platter.

He put it on the counter and took her, soapy water and all, in his arms. "You'll pay for that one, Talea."

Something twinkled in her eyes. "There were many who said I should have charged."

For a while they managed to forget all about their obstreperous son.

Later, as they lay on the kitchen floor, Jon-Tom pondered his progeny's future and saw too many potential problems for comfort. After all, Buncan was not what one would call a dedicated student. His academic shortcomings were the bane of his father's existence, Jon-Tom having advanced as far as law school in his own world. It wasn't that the boy couldn't do the work. It was just that his interests lay elsewhere.

Talea was less concerned. "Buncan will never be a solicitor or physician, Jon-Tom. If he has any special talent, it lies in the field of magic."

"But he has to do the minimal schoolwork," he argued. "A basic knowledge of zoology, for example, is critical to the establishment of good business relationships. You need to understand how the needs of a gorilla differ from those of a chimp."

She put her arms around his neck, leaning against him. "You worry too much. Buncan gets along fine with everybody. All his classmates like him."

"Getting along isn't the same as understanding."

CHAPTER 3

BUNCAN DREW BACK HIS FIST, BUT BEFORE HE COULD swing, the heavy-bodied adolescent black bear had a paw on his chest, shoving him back and down. Because he'd inherited some of his father's unusual Otherworld height, Buncan towered over the majority of his fellow students.

But not Fasvunk. The bear came as near as anyone in the school to carrying the mantle of class bully. While no taller than Buncan, he was built far more massively. He adjusted the yellow lizard-skin headband above his eyes, hitched up his matching pants, and beckoned with both paws.

They were surrounded by the rest of Buncan's class. Archmer the badger held the ball they'd been playing pentagon with.

"C'mon, human," Fasvunk growled. "You think you're so special 'cause your sire's a spellsinger. Well, I ain't impressed."

Breathing hard, Buncan confronted the bear squarely. He wasn't afraid of Fasvunk, but neither was this how he'd planned to spend his afternoon.

"I don't want to fight you, Fasvunk. I haven't got the time."

"Sure you do, Buncan." The bear's gaze narrowed. "Way I hear it, you want to fight everybody sooner or later. Why not start with me?" He snorted and kicked at the ground.

"I never said I wanted to fight everybody. I just said that I wanted to deal with everybody. As for my father, you're right about him. If you're not careful he'll—"

"He'll what?" said Fasvunk, interrupting. "Turn me into a fish? Force me down on all fours? I thought you could do that yourself. Or do you have to run to your daddy to perform every little spell?"

"Yeah," came a nasal voice from the surrounding circle. Buncan recognized Othol the anteater. "You're always carrying that duar around so you'll have something to scratch your butt with." A few of the others laughed, but most kept silent, waiting to see the outcome of the confrontation before choosing sides.

Buncan glared. "I'll take care of you next, Othol." The much smaller anteater stubbornly held his ground.

Fasvunk took a ponderous step forward, heavy paws held out in front of him in fighting mode. "You got to get through me first, toad-turd."

Sucking in a breath, Buncan checked to make sure his duar was secure against his back, and adopted a stance. "I can see you're not going to be reasonable about this. Have it your way. No claws, and no biting."

"Why not?" Fasvunk grinned. "So you can make the best use of your height? No restrictions, baldy."

"Suit yourself." Buncan presented his fists. "No death-dealing, though. I don't want you ripping out my throat."

"Hey, would I do that?" The bear opened his right paw, displaying half-inch-long claws. "Just a little nick here and there. Maybe I'll carve my initials in your ass." Several of the spectators giggled.

"And maybe," replied Buncan threateningly, "I'll twist off that stub you call a tail and shove it up your nose."

Fasvunk's smile vanished and he grunted heavily, advancing. "Like to see you try, human."

"No one's going to 'try' anything," said a new voice.

The circle parted quickly to admit Master Washwurn. Not that it would have mattered if they'd tried to hold their ground. The silverback gorilla went where he chose.

Adjusting his thick glasses, his gaze flicked from one antagonist to the other, his white collar stiff against his bull neck. "What's this all about, then? You two at it again?" He glared at Buncan. "I thought I told you no more fighting."

"Hey, he started it!" Buncan gestured at the somnolent black bulk of Fasvunk.

"Wasn't me, sir." The bear sounded appropriately chagrined.

The silverback's nostrils flared. "I have just about had it with both of you. You! Get back to class."

"Yes, sir." Fasvunk turned and beat a hasty retreat back toward the buildings, followed by a wake of relieved onlookers.

"And as for you," the gorilla began, turning his attention back to Buncan.

"You don't like me," Buncan said sharply. "You always side with him, or the others."

"I do not side with anyone, boy," said the silverback with great dignity. "But even you must admit that you are a caution to me."

"If it's about that piece of ensorceled carpet I put in your desk last week, that was intended for reupholstering your old chair. It needs it. I was just trying to do you a good turn."

"It gave me a turn, all right," Washwurn admitted. "Half a week's worth of notes full of interwoven thread; unreadable."

Buncan kicked absently at the dirt. "It was an accident."

The gorilla considered his rambunctious pupil. "You are still intent on following in your father's footsteps, aren't you? If that is the case, you will find a solid academic background invaluable in your intended line of work. It will be especially helpful if it should develop that certain factors preclude your excelling in that difficult profession. Your voice, for example."

"Don't you criticize me too, Master Washwurn. I can *play*."

"That's not enough, a fact I am certain your father has repeatedly pointed out to you. I shall see you back in class. And see if you can't somehow make peace with that unimaginative lump Fasvunk."

Buncan's voice fell to an irritated whisper. "Fasvunk's a wus."

Washwurn pretended not to hear. "And get yourself cleaned up." He turned and with immense self-presence walked back toward the buildings.

Buncan followed him with his eyes. He was alone on the recess ground. His expression tightened as he turned and started running. Not toward the buildings, not after his instructor, but for the line of nearby trees. For the familiar succor of the forest, which did not criticize. For the balm of the Bellwoods, which welcomed without questioning.

He ran aimlessly, the Belltrees tinkling around him. He was a good runner, and it wasn't long before he'd left both the school and the outer fringes of Lynchbany far behind. The same light breeze which stirred the bell leaves cooled him as he ran. Glass butterflies flitted brilliantly through the branches, and in a half-eaten bush coilpillars flashed metallic scales at him as he charged past.

Exhausted, he finally slowed to a walk. Sympathetic or not, Washwurn would still report the incident and his subsequent absence from class to his parents, Buncan knew. It wouldn't be the first time. It meant he'd have to endure another lecture from his father. He'd far rather be beaten, but Jon-Tom was too enlightened for that. If only the old man knew how painfully his words fell on his offspring's ears.

The river lay just ahead. He could follow the big curve around to the far side of Lynchbany and hang out there, with friends who had given up school and even thoughts of apprenticeship. Borgemont the mongoose would be awake soon, and Sissily, human like himself but much prettier, might put in an appearance.

Changing his mind, he headed south, sticking to the forest, heading for the one place where everyone sought answers. What he had in mind would be hard to go through with, perhaps even degrading, but he couldn't go home yet and he couldn't go back to school. It was the only place left.

Tenebrous clouds hung over the gigantic old oak. They didn't worry him, because he knew they were only transitory. The rest of the sky was perfectly clear. It meant that Clothahump was at home and working. From time to time all manner of objects could be seen hovering over his tree: intersecting rainbows, lambent sunshine, tropical downpours, the occasional isolated fragment of befuddled comet. Less wholesome sights ofttimes greeted nocturnal visitors: swarms of dainty dark winged shapes with glowing orange eyes, or ticklish feelers.

Buncan was not afraid of clouds, no matter how threatening. He stepped out of the forest into the neatly mown clearing that surrounded the tree. Immediately a throaty rumble assaulted his ears, and he looked around anxiously.

Dipping out of the center of the boiling clouds was a tightly restrained swirling funnel, the tip of which poked and probed as if feeling for the earth like some necromantic drill.

Buncan's first thought was to run and warn Clothahump. But what if the wizard wasn't home? What if some old enemy was taking advantage of his absence to destroy the turtle's beloved tree?

The duar was heavy against his back. He was completely confident in his playing, but his voice, his lyrics . . . What if he made things worse? What if instead of banishing the apparition he tempted it toward him?

As he equivocated it touched down, corkscrewing across the neatly manicured grounds, sending twigs and leaves and dust flying in all directions. Despite its extensive root system, a bubblebush weed was ripped from the soil to vanish into the howling funnel.

Then the swirling tip touched the tree itself. It grew momentarily darker, denser, before sliding neatly through a half-open upper-story window. He could still hear it, roaring and growling somewhere deep within the irreplaceable bole.

It was time to make a decision. He could race home and relate the tale to his father. Jon-Tom would surely know what to do. Or . . .

He could take action himself. Wasn't that what he'd been wanting all along?

Unlimbering his duar as he walked, he strode purposefully across the meadow that isolated Clothahump's tree from the rest of the forest.

When he reached the door he realized suddenly he had no idea how to proceed. More from reflex than forethought, he knocked.

To his shock and surprise, it was opened from within. A fluttering, hovering shape hung in the air before him. The young great horned owl regarded him disdainfully. It wore a short red vest embroidered in gold and silver thread with unrecognizable cabalistic symbols. Talons clutched a broom in one foot and a dustpan in the other.

"Whoooooo the hell are youuuu? And what doooo youuuu want here?"

"Uh, I need to talk to Clothahump." Buncan tried to see past the hovering owl. He could hear the wailing specter somewhere in the back.

"The Master is busy right now. Come back another time." The owl made as if to shut the door.

"Just a minute. Who're you?"

"Mulwit, his famulus."

Not for the first time it struck Buncan that Clothahump went through famuli the way an echidna went through termites. Using his bulk, he forced his way past the owl.

"This'll just take a minute. My dad's his partner."

"Youuu're Jon-Tom's nestling?" Mulwit looked around uneasily. "It doesn't matter. Youuu have to get out of here. If the Master catches me talking instead of working, it'll go hard on me. But I shouldn't let youuuu in. Not now. Not in the middle."

"Middle of what?" Buncan asked.

"Middle of everything. Go away." With that Mulwit flew off up a side passage, his great wings scraping the walls with each powerful downbeat.

Left alone, Buncan thoughtfully closed the door behind him before starting up the narrow hallway that led into the depths of the interdimensionally expanded tree. Light globes illuminated the way.

Peering into a study filled with scrolls and books, he found it deserted and moved on.

"Clothahump? Master Clothahump?" He came to the workshop and halted.

Suddenly it was right there.

Snarling and thundering, the funnel-shaped storm confronted him. Sticks and chunks of gravel spun wildly within the spiral structure. Instinctively he started to retreat, reaching for his sword.

It was at home, with his dress clothes. Weapons weren't allowed in school.

The stout storm slid behind him and shoved him forward, into the room. He could feel the intensity of the collared winds, the power within. It could as easily have wrenched his head off his shoulders.

At which point Clothahump appeared, peering curiously over his glasses.

"What have we here? Buncan Meriweather, isn't it?"

"Yes. Sir." Buncan turned to stare at the storm, watching in awe as it scooted across the floor, over benches, tiptoeing daintily among delicate equipment. "I was worried about you, sir. I thought maybe this was some theurgic weapon called up by an enemy of yours. I see now that you control it. What hapless unfortunate is to be visited by this irresistible horror?"

"No one. I'm in the midst of my spring cleaning."

Buncan pointed uncertainly at the coiled riot of a storm. "That has to do with spring cleaning?"

"Yes. It's a tornado, albeit a small one. That's your father's name for it. Mine's much longer, and I prefer his. They're very useful meteorologic phenomenons . . . if you can keep them under control. Otherwise they make a total hash of everything." Turning, he uttered a string of phrases which meant nothing to Buncan.

Compliant, the tornado took one last passing swipe at Buncan as it whizzed around the room, sucking the dust from window shelves, poking under carpets, scouring behind furniture, and generally going about the tasks Clothahump had assigned it earlier.

"Quite efficient, actually." Ignoring the tornado, the

wizard put a thick-fingered hand on Buncan's back and eased him out of the workshop, leading him back toward the front study. "Have to renew the spell periodically, though, or it gets irritable. What brings you to the tree, lad?"

Buncan was glancing back over his shoulder. "I think it wanted to eat me."

"Instinct. Don't blame it for that. It's a very effective, not to mention ecologically sound, method of cleaning, especially for those hard-to-reach spots."

"What's 'ecologically'?"

"A term I acquired from your father. Something that sorcery needs to be more concerned with, I'm afraid. Have to stop dumping toxic waste in the third cosmic interstice, things like that. Bright fellow, your father, if a bit impulsive. Of course, he's a human. Shouldn't you be in school?"

Somehow it seemed counterproductive to try to hide anything from the greatest wizard in the world. "I know. I've got problems."

In the study, Clothahump directed his visitor to the couch beneath the wide picture window while taking the stiff-backed chair directly across. "You're eighteen. Of course you've got problems. All the troubles of the world have fallen exclusively on your shoulders, and you haven't the vaguest notion how to cope with them." The wizard glanced to his right. "Mulwit!"

The owl appeared in seconds, a heavily patterned head-band restraining the feathers above its eyes. The broom and dustpan were gone, having been replaced by a rag and a bottle of amber liquid.

"Purebark tea for my visitor and me," the wizard commanded. "Cold or hot?" he inquired of Buncan.

Why is it, he wondered, *that whenever I want to talk about my troubles everyone keeps offering me tea?* "Uh, hot, I suppose."

"Be off!" Clothahump ordered.

The owl shot Buncan an impressively venomous look but soared away to comply. He returned in short order.

"Now then, lad." The wizard adopted a benign tone as he poured himself a cup of the pungent liquid and stirred in a teaspoon of Noworry honey. "Tell me your problem."

"Well, for one thing, the other kids know that my old man's a spellsinger and they're always teasing me about it. It's been that way ever since I started school. I'm sick of academics anyway."

"Your father has mentioned the situation. He seems to believe you might be better off apprenticed to some worthy craftsperson. Or, if you choose to pursue your music, as a member of some larger group. These seem to me worthwhile goals for someone of your age to consider."

"But I want to be a full-fledged spellsinger like Jon-Tom."

"Yes, well," the wizard demurred. He sipped at his tea as he crossed his short, thick-skinned legs. "Not just anyone can be a spellsinger, you know. It's rather more difficult than, say, greengrocering. Your father is an exception. There has to be innate talent present, a special spark."

Buncan tapped the duar strapped to his back. "I've inherited his ability. I know I have!"

"I don't know that such ability is inheritable."

"I can make magic already. I just can't, well, make it do exactly what I want it to every time."

"According to your father, you can't make it do what you want it to any of the time."

"Dad had similar troubles when he was starting out."

"It wasn't as extreme as it seems to be in your case. His voice was merely bad, and he utilized already composed lyrics from his own world. Not liking his music much, you improvise, and from everything I hear it would appear that while your playing may possibly be his equal, your singing is truly excruciating."

Buncan winced. That criticism was becoming a part of him. An unpleasant part. "I'll get better."

"Perhaps. If you don't kill somebody in the meantime."

"So I mussed up the kitchen a little. So what?"

"From what I was told, your would-be spellsinging put your mother at some physical risk."

"*My* mother, at physical risk?" Buncan tried not to laugh. "My mother could disembowel any three of the best swordsmen in Polastrindu before they could land a blade on her. With her balancing arm fastened behind her back."

Clothahump wagged a stubby finger at his visitor. "The

fact remains that you are dabbling in harmonic forces you imperfectly comprehend and cannot control.''

Buncan slumped back in the overpadded couch. ''Why does that sound like a cliché to me?''

''Clichés are merely truths repeated to the point of boredom, lad.''

''Then why don't you teach me? Help me to learn?''

Clothahump sighed. ''Some things cannot be taught. Nor can I cast a spell to improve your voice. At best you might become an accompanist to your father. His fingers are not as fast as they once were.''

''Thanks for your help.'' Barely containing his sarcasm, Buncan rose and headed for the doorway. It was terribly impolite: He should have waited to be dismissed. Clothahump could have restrained him easily with a few choice words. Instead, the wizard simply watched the youth depart, peering down over his beak through his thick glasses.

''You must make your own decisions, lad. You're nearly old enough to do that.''

Buncan whirled. ''What do you mean 'nearly'? I'm going to be a spellsinger and do great deeds. Whether you approve or not, or whether my father approves or not! Now, if you'll excuse me . . .'' He shoved the sputtering, flapping owl out of his way.

''Let him go, Mulwit,'' said Clothahump tiredly. ''After the first hundred years he'll begin to understand. If he lives that long.''

''What was that all about, Master?'' The owl began to gather up the tea service. Clothahump raised a hand.

''Leave it. This spring cleaning exhausts me. As does the impatience of youth.''

''The huuuman vexed youuu, Master?'' Mulwit could not conceal his pleasure.

''We disagreed on the path he has chosen. As do his parents. That's normal, of course. But in the lad's case it could prove truly dangerous.''

''I never disagree with youuu, Master.''

''No. You're as slavishly obsequious a servant as anyone could ask for.''

''Does that mean,'' said Mulwit eagerly, ''that youuu'll

show me the fourth-level aerial spell which enables one tooo fly without breathing?''

"Not just yet. You have other tasks to master first. Like how to get a sink whiter than white."

"But, Master, youuur sink is not white."

"Therein lies the magic. Now behave yourself, or I'll turn you into a kiwi. How'd you like to spend the rest of your apprenticeship flightless, with a long beak and hairy feathers?''

"No, Master! I meant no disrespect. I'll hurry back tooo helping the windstorm with the cleaning." He bounced anxiously off the far wall, like a bug seeking a way through a window.

"See that you do. And keep out of its way while it's at work. There are enough loose feathers around the house as it is."

The owl disappeared. Clothahump finished his tea, then rose with the slowness of great age and stared out the window toward the distant woods. There was no sign of young Meriweather. Clothahump hoped he was on his way home, though that was unlikely.

Well, it wasn't his responsibility. He had other matters to attend to. There were alcoves and storage chambers inside the tree that hadn't been scoured in a hundred years. That's what happened when you put off cleaning for a few decades. Jon-Tom and Talea would have to straighten the lad out by themselves.

Checking the drawers set in his plastron, he trundled off in the direction of his workshop. The tornado ought to be about finished there by now. *Have to make sure and empty it outside,* he reminded himself.

As the wizard suspected, Buncan did not head back toward school or home. Instead he found himself wandering in the direction of the Shortstub, which was itself a tributary of the river Tailaroam, without any particular destination in mind. He was angry at Clothahump both for his summation of Buncan's prospects and for his honesty. Just as he was angry at his schoolmates, his teachers, his parents, and most of the rest of the world, all of which seemed to him engaged in a vast conspiracy to prevent him from doing what he wanted.

In short, he was feeling quite normal for an active eighteen-year-old male.

"So I'm a little off-key," he muttered to himself as he walked. "I can still sing. Dad couldn't sing either when he was first dumped in this world, but he worked on it, and now he manages." Although, Buncan had to admit, Jon-Tom still didn't possess the kind of voice that would sell tickets. "I can get better," he insisted to himself. "I can—"

A sudden sharp sound interrupted his self-pitying reverie and he halted in his tracks, looking around anxiously. The tornado coming after him? Could wind hold a grudge? It was getting late, and it occurred to him that no one knew where he was.

As he gazed nervously into the forest, something hit him from behind and sent him tumbling. He found himself caught up in a flurry of blows and dirt and confusion. But it wasn't the tornado. It was something far more active and a good deal less stratified.

Rolling free of the turmoil, he stood and tried to brush himself off. "Very funny," he murmured.

The nearest of his two assailants was holding his sides, laughing in short, barking yips as he rolled back and forth on the ground. "Well, I thought it was pretty funny, mate!"

His sister sat up and regarded her sibling. "Cor, but it weren't *that* funny, Squill."

"Wot? Why, it were downright hysterical, squinch-face!"

Before Buncan could venture his own commentary the two had fallen to fighting again, locked in each other's arms as they tussled in the grass and dirt. Somehow they managed to keep their clothing intact despite the ferocious level of activity.

Having observed this typical otterish sibling behavior innumerable times before, Buncan simply waited patiently. Another minute or so and it would end. Which was precisely what happened. The two adolescent otters separated, stood, and straightened their attire as they joined him on the horizontal tree root where he was sitting.

Both were full-grown, nearly five feet tall on their short hind legs. Squill was imperceptibly heavier than his sister. He wore a pale-green peaked cap decorated with three feathers, each purchased from a different bird. His vest was a darker shade of green and his short pants brown. A shoulder pouch hung off his neck and across his chest. Both he and his sister carried bows and arrow-filled quivers across their backs and short swords at their sides.

Instead of a hat his sister Neena sported a multihued headband with a thin cabachon of maroon jasper set in the center of her forehead. Bright blue and yellow streaks flowed in waves from the corners of her eyes, running toward the back of her head and up toward her ears. The body paint had been applied with skill and diligence, fur being harder to make up than bare skin. Gold glitter glistened within the paint. Similar designs decorated her short, pro-truding tail. Her shorts were cut to a more feminine pattern than were her brother's, and were pale yellow to match her fuller vest.

As for the wrestling match, it might as well never have happened.

Her tail twitched as she eyed her tall human friend. "Wot are you doin' out 'ere all by your lonesome, Buns?"

"Being angry."

"Oi, we can see that in yer face, mate." With his short, clipped claws Squill dug idly at the root's exposed bark.

How can they see anything in my face? "You can't see anything, fish-breath."

Neena let out an appreciative hysterical bark which resulted in her brother jumping her immediately. Buncan sighed as he watched them brawl, not really interested. A moment later it was all over and they rejoined him as though nothing had happened. Which to their way of thinking was exactly the case. One simply had to tolerate such goings-on when one was in the company of otters. Especially adolescent otters. They had more energy than a shrew on uppers.

For their part, they had to slow down not only their movements but their speech when they chose to share the company of anything as plodding as a human.

Squill carefully straightened the feathers in his cap while his sister adjusted her headband.

"I never see you two in school," Buncan commented. "How do you ever expect to learn anything?"

"Wot," said Squill, "you mean like 'ow to wander about in the woods spittin' into the breeze, like you were doin' just now? Cor, I think I can manage that without stayin' up nights porin' over some manual."

Neena sidled closer to him. "Wot 'appened, Bunky?"

He shrugged. "Got into it with Fasvunk again. Had to take another lecture from Master Washwurn."

She wrinkled her black nose, whiskers arcing. "Sucks, that does."

"It was brief enough. Then I went to see Clothahump."

"No shit?" Squill perked up. "By yourself? That's somethin'. You pick up any spells?"

Buncan shook his head. "Nothing. Just advice. Most of which I didn't want to hear." He aimed a kick at a shelf fungus, knocking the punky growth free of the root.

"Don't surprise me, mate. Me, I don't need advice." Sharp teeth flashed. "I already know everythin'."

His sister made a face. "You don't know anythin', bro'. In fact, I'd opine that you know less than nothin'."

"Yeah? 'Ow about me knowledge o' physics an' engineerin'? Like 'ow I can fit your square 'ead into a round snake 'ole?" He moved toward her.

Buncan held out his hands between them. "Give it a rest, can't you? I'm in agony and all you can do is goof around."

Squill frowned at his friend. "'Ere now, you're really down, ain't you?" He put a short arm around as much of the human's back as he could manage, careful not to disturb the duar.

"It's just that I'm so bored there," Buncan explained. "I want to do great things, to challenge the primary forces of existence. I want to spellsing."

"Uh-oh," muttered Neena, "that again."

"Nothin' personal, mate," said Squill, "but you can't sing well enough to inveigle a deaf dugong, much less a primary force."

"Yeah, well, you can't play a single-stringed bow," Buncan shot back.

Squill raised both paws. "Hey, I know that, mate."

Buncan gazed morosely at the ground. "I keep fooling myself, telling myself I can get better. But deep down I know I'll never be able to sing well enough to make magic."

"At least you can play an instrument," said Neena. "I wish I could play anythin'."

"Same 'ere," her brother confessed.

Buncan slid off the root and turned to face them. "How can I execute spellsongs if I can't sing? How can I save the world and rescue fair maidens if I can't work proper gramarye?"

"Ah!" barked Neena. "Now the truth comes out, it does. You're just like any other male."

He glared at her. "Why do you always have to bring everything down to such a base and common level, Neena?"

She batted her eyes at him enticingly. "Because I'm a base and common sort of lass, Buns."

He turned away from them. "Dammit, I want to do something... something noble and elevating!"

Squill tapped the growth on which he was sitting. "We could climb this 'ere tree."

Exasperated, Buncan whirled on his friend. "Can't you be serious for just a minute?"

The otter considered carefully. "Well now, that's a pretty heavy request, mate." He glanced at his sister. "But since you're about our best friend, we'll make an effort."

"Thank you," said Buncan with exaggerated solemnity. "You know, I can sing well enough to make magic. I just can't sing well enough to control it."

"Don't sound like a very promisin' weapon with which to take on the primal forces." This time Squill didn't smile. "An' I wouldn't rely on your swordwork to get you out o' any scrapes. I've seen you work with a sword."

"You're no match for your father yourself."

"'S'truth, Mudge still wields a quick blade," Neena agreed. "Even if ol' Daddy-whiskers is gettin' a bit wide in the gut."

"You'd better not let him hear you say that," Buncan warned her. "He'll blister your butt." He walked over and rested both hands on the root. "I can do this. I can spellsing. If I could only find a way to improve my vocalizations."

Neena tickled him, and he jumped. "Well, you'd best be careful with it, Bunkle. Like me brother says, you're about the best non-otter friend we 'ave. You kill yourself and we won't 'ave no one better to tease." She exchanged a glance with Squill. "Want to see somethin' really interestin'?"

"What?" He tried not to sound too indifferent, knowing she was doing her best to try to cheer him up.

From a pocket in the lower part of her vest she extracted a flat, squarish black box. A small transparent window was set in the slightly domed top. Intrigued, Buncan took a closer look. His eyes widened as soon as he recognized it.

"Hey, that looks like . . . !"

Neena nodded vigorously. "The CD player your father brought back from his world on his last visit there and gave to Mudge."

Buncan was appalled. "If your parents knew you'd taken that from the den they'd shave you front and back."

Her whiskers twitched. "Bloody right. But they don't know." She winked at her brother. "Mudge didn't teach us all 'is ol' techniques for nothin'."

"They 'ardly ever let us use it," added Squill, "so we just sort of appropriated it for the afternoon."

"The only problem is that we can't get it to work." Neena fingered the black rectangle. "Somethin' about it needin' some magic installed before it'll play. Mudge says it needs 'better days.'"

"'Batteries,'" Buncan corrected her. "I've watched Jon-Tom use them at our tree. They're four little magically charged cylinders that fit in here. See?" He turned the rectangle over and showed them the compartment and the four cylinders nestled like larvae within. "The spell runs down and Dad has to revitalize it before it'll work again. I don't remember the exact words to the spell. Something about a rabbit that keeps going." He shrugged as he resealed the cylinder compartment.

Neena considered. " 'Ere now, Bunco, if you're any kind o' spellsinger at all, you ought to be able to recharge a simple little spell like this."

"Jolly right!" Squill took the player and set it down on the ground. "Get on it, mate."

"Now wait a minute." Buncan looked uneasy. "This involves some serious magic. Electrons and rabbits and all kinds of stuff. I don't know if I should be messing with Mudge's property."

Neena sniffed disdainfully. "An' you want to rescue damsels and battle evil. Right."

"But this is a device from the Otherworld."

"Blimey, give it a try, Buncan," Squill implored his friend. " 'Ow bad can you bung it up?"

"Well . . ." He slid the duar off his back and plucked hesitantly at the double set of strings. A soft golden glow began to coalesce at the place where the strings intersected. "This is risky."

"You think you won't meet any risks on a quest?" Neena challenged him. "Come on, you can do it."

Taking a deep breath, he began to sing. The instrumental accompaniment was exalting, exquisitely rendered, but the words . . . It was a struggle for the otters to keep their paws off their ears.

The CD player twitched a couple of times, but did not otherwise react.

After his best effort drew forth only a brief whine from the device's tiny internal speaker, Buncan let his fingers fall from the duar. "There, you see?" he said angrily. "I told you it wouldn't work."

"You play beautifully, Bunky," Neena told him.

The trio regarded the quiescent player regretfully, until Squill unexpectedly let out a yip of inspiration.

"Oi! I've an idea, I 'ave!"

"Now there's an odd notion," said Neena.

Squill ignored her. "Me sister and me, we 'ave wonderful voices, we do. An' we're bloomin' quick with wordplay." He twirled a whisker. "Otters are quick with everythin'."

"I 'ave to admit that this one time me squish-brained

brother 'appens to be right," Neena agreed. "Though I don't see 'is point."

"Don't you get it?" Squill eyed Buncan eagerly. "Wot if *you* played an' *we* took care o' the singin'?"

"Don't be ridiculous. Spellsinging's not a cooperative enterprise."

"Says who? Don't wizards ofttimes work together to homogenize a big spell?"

"Sure, but that's different." *Isn't it?*

"We've known each other all our lives." Neena enthusiastically took up her brother's suggestion. "We've grown up together. We're personally and emotionally compatible. Lots o' times."

"Being friends is different from making magic together," Buncan argued.

"Bein' friends *is* a kind of magic," she countered. "Much as it pains me deep to admit it, me brother might 'ave somethin' worth pursuin' 'ere." Her eyes shone brightly.

"It's worth a try, mate," Squill added. "Wot's to lose?"

"We can try that new kind of music." A delighted Neena clapped both paws together. "The kind that Jon-Tom brought back from his last visit to the Otherworld, that our parents don't like. That's a *good* reason to use it."

Buncan pondered. "You mean that rap stuff? I don't know if I can play to accompany that."

"Oh, sure you can, mate." Squill exuded confidence. "It's all beat. Just follow us. You can do that, can't you?"

"I suppose." *Who is the spellsinger here?* he found himself wondering.

This wasn't going to work, he told himself. But what else was he going to do? Slink homeward? Time enough for that. Time enough to deal with his parents, and Master Washwurn.

"Okay. I'll suggest some words-of-power I picked up from listening to Dad. You work them into whatever lyrics you improvise, and I'll back you the best I can." He hefted the duar, his fingers hovering over the strings.

The otters looked at each other. "Wot'll we sing about?" Squill asked his sister. "We can't just imitate one o' those Other World songs we've 'eard. It 'as to be specific to the situation."

"To the player." Neena nodded at the black rectangle, which lay motionless on the ground in front of them.

While Buncan waited impatiently they discussed various approaches among themselves. Finally Squill indicated their readiness. Facing each other, the otters commenced . . . to rap. Music flowed from the duar as Buncan matched them chord for word.

"Got no music and we got no sound
Got to hear it clear if we wanna go 'round
Play it loud and play it neat
Play it in the forest 'cause we ain't got no
Street
'Cause we wanna hear the beat
Dig it, wig it, feets for the beat!"

Certainly it was the first rap ever heard in the Bellwoods. The otters were nothing if not enthusiastic and facile improvisers. Buncan was hard-pressed to match their energy with music.

The radiance at the nexus of the duar intensified, darkening from pale pink to a deep rose hue. It expanded to envelop his fingers, then his hands.

The CD player began to quiver.

CHAPTER 4

THE OTTERS CONTINUED TO SING AS THE BLACK REC-tangle bounced on its edges. Bounced in time to the music, Buncan noted. As he looked on, a miniature golden vortex issued from the transparent, domed cover. Music began to emanate from the tiny built-in speaker. He didn't recognize the song: He was too busy playing.

Abruptly the otters ceased their rapping so they could stare. Buncan's fingers stilled.

The player was now floating four feet off the ground, still

jiving and bouncing to the music which issued from within. The words meant nothing to any of them, but that didn't matter. Not now.

"Let's make it louder." Squill was enthralled by his own accomplishment. His sister nodded slowly, her eyes focused on the perambulating player. They resumed their rapping, while Buncan hastened to back them. Or were they backing him? He had no time to wonder.

In response to their efforts the music pouring from the player grew louder. Much louder. The black rectangle was now rotating rapidly on its axis, pierced through from top to bottom by the golden vortex. Around the trio the forest began to vibrate, the Belltrees ringing in time to the rap. Insects and small flying reptiles scattered in panic.

Buncan's initial hesitation had vanished completely, his earlier depression displaced by the ecstasy of pure performance.

"This is great!" He had to shout to make himself heard above the music erupting from the energized CD, the harmonic vibrato of the duar, and the pounding pulse of hitherto never heard otter-rap. Sparks flew from the duar's nexus. They were matched in intensity by bursts of celestial light that were flung off from the golden vortex. He'd been wondering what that was ever since it had first appeared. Now he felt that he knew.

It was music made visible.

And then, as the otters finished off a particularly zesty phrase, the vortex containing the CD player shot straight upward, climbing toward the clouds. Neena squealed in surprise.

At that the player paused, seemed to shudder slightly, and stopped. The vortex hummed energetically as it hovered motionless at treetop level.

The incipient spellsingers gathered beneath it, staring upward and occasionally dodging drizzling shards of effervescent music. As soon as these struck the ground they melted away like ice in a frying pan, notes sinking in descending scale into the music-moistened earth.

"Great." Buncan brushed an errant b-flat from his forehead. "Now what do we do?"

Squill balanced his cap on his head as he craned his neck

to study the player. It showed no inclination to descend from its lofty position.

"Don't ask me, mate. You're the one wot wants to be a spellsinger."

Buncan felt his blood pressure rising. "You two got me into this." He blinked. "Hey, what am I upset for? It's not *my* dad's player."

The otters looked at him. "You can't just leave it like this," said Squill. "You've got to 'elp us."

Buncan shrugged. "That's the way the magic falls."

Neena clutched at his arm. "We've got to get it down, Bunky. If we don't, Mudge will kill us."

"Not to mention wot Mom'll do." Squill tried not to envision Weegee in a rage.

"We sang it up there," Buncan pointed out. "If we try that again, it's liable to vanish completely. But I don't know what else to do."

Squill looked unhappy. "Me neither."

"Of course, we could get some help," Buncan said thoughtfully. "Corander the raven could just fly up and pluck it out of the air."

Squill shook his head doubtfully, the feathers in his cap fluttering. "The bloody thing might take off with 'im, too. That'd be 'ell to try an' explain. No, spellsingin' put it up there, it'd best be spellsingin' we use to try an' get it down."

"You could climb that nearest tree," his sister suggested, "and take a jump at it."

He glared at her. "Wot, am I a flyin' squirrel?" He made an obscene suggestion.

"This isn't getting us anywhere." Buncan plucked at the duar's strings. "Let's get it over with. But you'd better be prepared for it not to work."

"It 'as to work." Neena and her brother backed up slightly and conferenced.

"Get on with it," snapped Buncan after a while. He wasn't impatient so much as he was nervous.

Neena glared at him. "We 'ave to be careful, Bickles. Fok up the first time an' we might not get a second chance, wot?" She brushed glistening notes from her shoulders.

They began to sing, a slow, relaxed rap this time, almost languorous. Caught off guard by the unexpected shift in tempo, it took Buncan a moment to figure out the correct fingering.

"Sounds too high, my oh my
Don' wanna send it up in the sky
Put it down on the ground
Where it can be found
Sound, sound, pound it in the ground
Beats for the feet, feets for the beat!
We've 'ad our treat, now takes a seat."

The duar's nexus pulsed softly, an ethereal pale blue this time. It did not look or feel promising. Indeed, the CD player actually rose another few feet instead of descending. Then it stopped and hovered, seemingly confused.

Still pounding out tracks from the disc spinning within, it commenced a steady regression, descending in time to the otter's slow-paced rap. The golden vortex attenuated, contracting in upon itself, until it was no thicker than a rotating golden pencil. A few random, ersatz notes flaked off, but they were few now and chords between.

As the rap concluded, the player settled to the ground. The supportive vortex vanished utterly. When it had winked out completely, Squill made a dive for the device. It tried to squirt clear of his grasping fingers, but sometimes even magic isn't as quick as an otter. He got one paw on the box, then the other, rolled over and sat up, waving it triumphantly. Exhausted, it didn't so much as quiver in his hands. The music from within ceased.

Neena hurried over for a look. "Is it all right? Is the bloody thing damaged?"

Squill was turning it over in his fingers, careful to keep a firm grip on the plastic in case it was playing dead, waiting for an opportunity to jump free.

"Seems okay to me."

Clutching the duar by its neck, Buncan came over for a look. "Pop the cover."

Squill complied. The motionless silver disc inside was

warm to the touch but otherwise unchanged. Buncan picked out a loose f-sharp and dumped it aside. It landed discordantly near his boots.

The otter snapped the cover shut and shoved the player into his pouch. "That were too bleedin' close. Thought we'd lost it for sure."

Neena's eyes were flashing. "We spellsang! Bugger me if we didn't, Buncan!"

"We did, didn't we?" He eyed the duar thoughtfully. "I wonder why your father never tried singing along with mine."

"Cor', mate," said Squill, " 'ave you ever 'eard Mudge sing? 'Is voice is worse than yours an' Jon-Tom's put together, it is."

"That might explain it," agreed Buncan dryly.

Neena put an arm around her brother. "We got *our* voices from our mum, we did."

"You realize what this means?" Buncan said slowly.

"Yeah," piped Squill. "We can 'ave music anytime we want."

"It means," continued Buncan solemnly, "that while I can spellsing by myself, with your help I can do *serious* magics. I can realize my dreams."

"Wot dreams?" Neena was suddenly wary.

"Save the world. Defeat evil in all its manifestations. Rescue fair damsels in distress."

Squill sauntered back to the arching tree root. "Far be it from me to divert your current, Buncan, but I'm real 'appy swimmin' and eatin' and sleepin'. I ain't got no crawfish on me tail spurrin' me to save the blinkin' world. Let the world take care o' itself, says I." He wore a reflective expression as he lay down on the root. "Though I 'ave to admit the fair damsel part sounds intriguin'."

"Where's your sense of adventure?" Buncan walked over to peer down at his recumbent friend. "Where's your desire to surmount the impossible?"

"Rather surmount a fair damsel." Squill grinned.

"We've 'eard all about that sort o' thing from Mudge," Neena pointed out. "Once you throw out the eighty percent o' 'is stories that's out-an'-out lyin', the rest o' it still sounds unpleasant.''

"Let's try just one more experiment." Buncan walked away from them, toward the riverbank. Exchanging a resigned whistle and a reluctant glance, the two otters followed. "If it doesn't come off, I promise I'll drop the whole business. If it does," he looked back over his shoulder, "you'll agree that not to make use of our combined abilities is a real waste of talent, and that you'll consider coming with me."

"Going with you?" Neena was pacing alongside him. "Going with you where?"

"Why, to . . ." Buncan hesitated. "I haven't figured that part of it out yet."

"Bleedin' precise," muttered Squill. "You've inherited Jon-Tom's sense o' direction as well as his musicianship."

Buncan marched around a bubblebush, ignoring the peach-scented globules that floated out of the mature, oval-mouthed flowers. "Admit it: What we just accomplished was tantalizing."

"Oi, I'll admit to that," agreed Squill. "Been a bloody sight more excitin' if we'd lost Mudge's player. Could've been fatal.''

"We don't have to try anything that extreme this time." Buncan worked to soothe his wary friend. "Something simple, to prove we can do this."

"I thought we just did that," Neena wondered aloud.

Buncan reached out and ruffled the fur on the back of her neck. "That player had previously been activated by one of my dad's spellsongs. We need to do something from scratch, something that's all our own." There was eagerness in his voice. "I'll think of something."

"That's wot worries me," Squill murmured.

Without stopping, Buncan turned, continued walking backward. "Just one spell that's all our own. If it doesn't work I promise I won't bring this subject up again."

"You're a liar, Bunkies." Neena batted her lashes at him. "But I loves you anyway." She glanced at her brother. "Wot 'ave we got to lose, mussel-breath?"

"If a spellsing goes awry?" Squill thrust out his lower

lip. "Not much, I wager. Our fingers, maybe. Our voice boxes. Our 'eads.''

"I'll be careful," Buncan assured him. "If it looks dangerous, I can kill the spell by putting the duar down. Or you can alter your lyrics, or just stop singing. You'll be as much in control as I will."

"Oi, that's right." Squill was still reluctant—he remembered too many of his father's stories—but with both Buncan and his sister egging him on, he finally gave in.

They reached the river and halted. Downstream lay the little aqueous suburb of Twinkle's Bend, home to Squill and Neena, their parents Mudge and Weegee, and a diverse but generally copacetic assortment of riparian citizens: more otters, muskrats, beavers, kingfishers, and other water avi-ans, as well as those locals who simply preferred to live close by running water and the delights it afforded. Pres-ently the river below them was deserted. The Shortstub did not carry anywhere near the volume of commerce of its much larger relative, the Tailaroam, which ran deep and wide all the way down to the Glittergeist Sea.

Buncan had spent many a contented afternoon splashing and diving with his friends in those invigorating waters. They were good about not teasing him, for while he was an excellent swimmer for his kind, no human alive could match the aquatic acrobatics of even the youngest, most inept otter.

It was something other than swimming that was currently on his mind, however.

The bank on which they stood rose some nine feet above the river, falling in a gentle slope to a gravelly beach. At the high-water mark mature trees gave way to weeds and bushes. Sunbeams splashed dappling on the languid water with the ease and skill of a knife spreading butter. Nothing moved in the forest on the far side, though the Belltrees there chorused in counterpoint to those on the other side every time they were agitated by a passing breeze.

Buncan chose a convenient boulder for a seat, plunked himself down, and readied the duar. His legs dangled over a drop of several feet. The otters eyed him expectantly.

"This is your show, mate," said Squill. "Wot'll we sing about?" Neena adjusted her headband, primping.

"You did pretty well before. I thought you two might come up with something."

"Not me. You're the one who wants to save the world. As if it asked you."

It should be profound, Buncan mused. But for the life of him he couldn't think of anything. It was a lovely day, the river was calm, he could not espy any evil sorcerers lurking in the Bellwoods, and no one in the immediate vicinity was screaming for help. Spellsinging in such circumstances seemed suddenly superfluous.

He had to try something. If he waited, given the otters' demonstrated reluctance to participate, they might never again prove so amenable. Especially if either Mudge or Weegee found out what they'd been up to.

"I'm hungry," said Neena unexpectedly.

"We'll be 'avin' supper soon enough," her brother reminded her.

"Cor, but I'm 'ungry *now*." She stared at Buncan. " 'Ow about we try to conjure up some food? We're right on the Shortstub. 'Ow about we spellsing out some nice fish?"

Fish aren't very profound, Buncan reflected. "That's not much of a challenge," he responded dubiously.

Her tail twitched animatedly as she jabbed a short finger in his direction. "You listen to me, Bunkles. It's all very well an' good to want to go off battlin' 'ellish 'ordes an' upliftin' the downtrodden an' all that rot, but a bloke's liable to work up one 'ell of an appetite in the process. So let's see if we can manage a snack first."

"I did say we'd start with something simple," he mumbled.

"Mudge would approve," Neena added.

"Sure 'e would." Squill whistled appreciatively. "Mudge approves o' anythin' 'avin' to do with food."

"Food it is, then." Buncan sighed. "I'm waiting."

Once more the siblings conferenced. When they separated, Neena nodded at Buncan. Three feet tapped out a unified beat.

"Got no gear, got no line.
Still wanna eat, wanna eat what's fine.

Bring it from the bottom, bring it from the depth
Bring up somethin' swimmin' to where we can get it
Bet it, better not let it, better not set it
Down too far, down far away, hey, hey
Wanna eat what's fine but I gots no line."

The otters rapped a nice, relaxed rhythm, one Buncan could follow easily. A satisfyingly bright green nimbus coalesced at the nexus of the duar's strings as the harmonious blend of otterish voices and dual sets of strings drifted out across the placid expanse of the Shortstub.

No fish responded by breaking the opalescent surface to land at their feet. No silver-sided morsels manifested themselves alongside the boulder. The river flowed on undisturbed and indifferent.

Buncan's fingers drifted from the strings. "Come on," he urged them. "You're not putting your hearts into this. I've heard Jon-Tom talk about this a lot. Making magic with music means more than just playing the chords and mouthing the words. You've got to put your whole soul, your deepest feelings, into what you're doing."

"Wot the 'ell do you think we're doin', mate?" snapped Squill.

"Yeah. I mean, I'm really 'ungry, I am," his sister added.

"You have to try harder," Buncan admonished them. "Don't think about spellsinging, don't think about magic. Just think about how hungry you are."

"She's the one who's 'ungry, not me," Squill protested.

Buncan glared at him. "Well, *get* hungry!"

The otter looked thoughtful. "Now that you mention it, all this 'ere work *'as* made me a touch ravenous. Cor, I believes I can feel the pangs workin' in me belly even as I stand 'ere speakin'."

Buncan smiled. "Right, that's the spirit." His fingers returned to the strings. "Let's give it another try. And really put your hearts and your minds into it this time, as well as your stomachs."

The otters put their whiskers together and started over. Buncan could sense the difference immediately. The lyrics

contained the kind of barely constrained energy only a pair
of otters could muster: a nervous, teeth-tingling, edgy con-
centration of adrenaline. Despite his skill, Buncan was
suddenly hard-pressed to keep up with them.

A waxen dark-green mist appeared on the river, palpitat-
ing energy sucked hither from some cabalistic fog bank by
the power of the spellsong. It eddied and intensified, a
curdled haze, shifting about as unpredictably as a cloud
uncertain of where the wind was preparing to blow it
next.

A faint trembling began underfoot as the earth itself grew
nervous. Pebbles jostled and clicked against one another and
blades of grass vibrated, a thousand tiny tuning forks
attuned to an unnatural disturbance of vast potency.

Maybe, Buncan thought, starting to sweat a little, *maybe
this could get out of hand.* The otters rapped on, oblivious
to his concern.

A portion of the bank beneath him collapsed and he half
tumbled, half slid off the boulder, scrambling madly in
search of more solid ground. That he never missed a beat on
the duar was a credit more to his physical than mental
resiliency. On the far side of the Shortstub, cracks appeared
in the hitherto stable bank as soil and sand crumbled into the
water, leaving damp V-shaped scars behind.

Something stupendous was coalescing within the fog.
Something slick of flank and commodious of bulk. A fish,
as Squill and Neena had demanded. A fish, but bigger than
any Buncan had ever seen. Bigger than any he had ever
imagined. He played on mechanically, mesmerized by the
vision, unable to stop.

As it jutted out of the mist, loomed above it, seriously
disturbed the waters beneath, one thing became quickly
apparent.

It was not a fish.

He raised his voice. "Hey! You guys can stop rapping
now." He pointed.

They'd been singing with their backs to the water. Now
they turned, following his gesture. "Sister," Squill murmured
through a long, eloquent whistle, "while I've been on

occasion amazed by your appetite, I didn't realize you were quite this 'ungry.''

The conjuration nearly filled the river from bank to bank. It was twenty times as long as Buncan was tall and must have weighed as much or more than the combined population of Lynchbany, with that of a few outlying farms and maybe a small suburb or two thrown in for good measure. In color it was a light blue on top, a whitish slate-gray underneath. White spots splotched the striated lower jaw. A lurch of its massive tail sent a miniature tidal wave crashing against the far bank. Water plants and fish flew in all directions.

An eye that was small only comparatively located them. The immense skull struggled to turn in their direction, but was constrained by a combination of the green fog and the narrowness of the river channel.

"LET ME GUESS." The voice rumbled and reverberated like a great bell. "YOU THREE WOULDN'T BE RESPONSIBLE FOR MY BEING HERE, WOULD YOU?"

"Ummmm..." Squill jerked a finger in his sister's direction. "It were all '*er* idea."

"*Wot?*" she squeaked, outraged.

"Well, you were the one who were so bleedin' 'ungry!"

Instantly they were clamped in furious internecine combat, rolling about on the now soggy riverbank, flailing and kicking and scratching and biting at one another.

"Otters." Buncan smiled wanly, as though this explained everything.

"I CAN SEE THAT." The grievously displaced blue whale spoke with immense gravity. "THE POINT IS, I SEEM TO BE MISSING AN OCEAN. THERE'S NOT REALLY ENOUGH WATER HERE TO SUPPORT ME, AND I'M ALREADY HAVING A BIT OF DIFFICULTY BREATHING. SO IF YOU DON'T MIND...?"

Buncan swallowed. "Uh, what happens if we can't put you back?"

"WHY, THEN YOU HAVE A VERY LARGE CORPSE TO DISPOSE OF AND A BLOOD FEUD WITH ALL MY BRETHREN."

Since Buncan had from time to time entertained thoughts

of traveling upon the sea, and since this desire might be rendered difficult to fulfill if every great whale upon the waters was made of a mind to kill him, he thought it wise to do his best to prevent that condition from coming about. Preferably as soon as possible.

"It was an accident." He tried to explain, gesturing in Neena's direction. "My friend was hungry and wanted a fish."

"DO I LOOK LIKE A FISH?" inquired the sulphurbottom.

"Only marginally."

"WOULD IT NOT BE INCORRECT OF ME TO AS-SUME THAT MY INVOLUNTARY PLACEMENT IN THIS INSIGNIFICANT ESTUARY IS THE RESULT OF SOR-CERY GONE AWRY?"

"Like I said, it was an accident." Despite the whale's intimidating size and manner, Buncan held his ground. After all, it wasn't likely to burst from the river and come running after them (he hoped).

Certainly, they had to save it by sending it back where it had come from. He couldn't stand the thought of having its death on his hands. His conscience wouldn't stand for it.

Besides, his father might find out.

"Don't worry. We'll send you back. I'm not entirely sure how we brought you here, but we'll send you back. As soon as I can get my friends to stop trying to kill each other."

"I SHOULD APPRECIATE THAT," boomed the whale.

Though it was not unlike trying to unwind a hurricane, Buncan managed to separate the otters. Squill glared at his sister, recovered his precious hat, and taunted her as she struggled to make sense of her makeup.

"Go on," he urged her, "tell our guest 'ow you really wanted to eat 'im."

"Go sit on your face." She looked to Buncan as she brushed dirt and grass from her clothes. " 'Ow do we send this back to the deep ocean, spellsinger?"

Buncan mumbled a reply. "You two came up with the lyrics that brought it here."

"I was 'ungry. I'm inspired when I'm 'ungry. I thought our singin' would get us a little bitty somethin' out o' the river. Not this bloody great mass o' blubber."

"IT IS ASSISTANCE I REQUIRE, NOT FLATTERY."

The otters conferred, finally nodding at Buncan, who began to play with more hope than assurance. Perhaps because they were becoming more confident, or perhaps out of fear of what Mudge would do to them if they failed, they rapped with greater facility than ever before. Buncan's accompaniment was equally accomplished.

The green mist coalesced afresh around the immense bulk, from which eventually issued a relieved sigh of satisfaction. "BE MORE CAREFUL NEXT TIME. AMATEURS," it concluded. Buncan gritted his teeth and offered no comment, not wishing or daring to do anything that might interrupt the flow of the spellsinging.

"Send it back, back
Back to the sea, back to the water, back 'ome
'Ome, 'ome, not the Shortstub to roam
Down in the depths, in the depths, away from 'ere
Steer it clear, steer it free
Don't y'see, free, away from me and away from
Thee."

There was a sharp bang, and a brief but intense gust of green wind knocked the three of them off their feet. Previously dammed up by the whale's bulk, the abruptly released accumulated flow of the Shortstub surged in a towering wave downstream, racing toward its distant juncture with the mighty Tailaroam.

Squill watched the wave recede around the far bend as he levered himself up on his elbows. "I don't know if it 'as occurred to any of you lot yet, but it strikes me that this 'ere sudden spurt o' water 'as the potential to be somewot upsettin' to them wot lives downriver."

"There've been floods on the Shortstub before," his sister pointed out.

"Not this time o' year, fungus-lips." Her brother jabbed a thumb skyward. "Not in this kind o' weather."

"Boats, docks, front porches." Buncan envisioned wholesale downstream destruction as he contemplated the turbulent tributary. "Maybe it would be a good idea if we didn't mention this little episode to anyone for a while?"

"Capital idea." Squill was quick to second the suggestion. "Like maybe, never."

"I think we could leave now." Neena was eyeing her friend and her brother intently. "And get 'ome fast."

There was no need to wait for concurrence.

As they hurried back through the Bellwoods, Buncan couldn't resist nudging the otter nearest him. "It worked, Squill. Maybe not exactly the way we intended, but it worked. We spellsang. We performed great magic."

The otter squinted up at him. "Blimey but you're a 'ard one to convince, Buncan. Next time we're 'alf likely to bring a mountain down on top of us."

"Come on," Buncan prodded his friends. "Aren't you proud of what we just accomplished? Didn't you get a little charge out of it?"

"Well . . . just a flicker, maybe."

"Yeah, right." Buncan was grinning hugely. "We put a little too much into the spell, that's all. With practice we can do better. Modulate, refine. Neena, you want to try for your fish again?"

"I'm not 'ungry anymore, Bunkies. We've got to do some serious thinkin' about this."

"An otter, serious?" he chided her. When she didn't reply, he lowered his tone. "All right. We can talk about it tomorrow. And if anybody asks us about what happened on the river, we don't know anything, right?"

"Bloody right," Squill muttered.

"But we're a team. Don't forget that. Sure I'd like to be able to spellsing like that all by myself, but being part of a team has its advantages, too. I can concentrate all my efforts on the duar."

Neena glared at him. "Oi, and the next time we do somethin' equally stupid we can run away in three different directions and maybe one o' us will survive."

"Don't be so negative. You'd think you'd never seen a whale before."

"Never 'ad," said Squill solemnly, "and neither 'ad you,

except in pictures. Seemed like a right enough bloke, though. Just a bit put out.''

"Think about this, though.'' Buncan was hard put to rein in his enthusiasm. "If we can spellsing up something like that when we're just trying for a fish dinner, imagine what we might do if we take our time and really make an effort to do something serious. We could do better than Jon-Tom, or maybe even Clothahump. We could change the world.''

"Ain't sure I want to change the world, mate.'' Squill spat to one side as he jogged through the woods. " 'Tis a nice day. Maybe if it were blowin' cold I'd try somethin'.''

"Just think about what we've done. That's all I ask.''

All three fell into a contemplative silence as they hurried on through the forest, the Belltrees chiming uneasily around them.

CHAPTER 5

AFTER THE EPISODE IN THE WOODS BUNCAN MADE A show of tending seriously to his studies, but each day he waited for the opportunity to meet with Squill and Neena. They chose a small glade well away from the river in which to practice. Not out of fear of encountering any more polite but irritated cetaceans, but to avoid those angry citizens whose waterfront homes and business establishments had been damaged by the mysterious tidal bore of some days previous.

They sang only small spells, conjuring up nothing they couldn't deal with on a nontheurgic level, practicing and refining their ability to match Buncan's music to the otters' improvised lyrics. Repetition gave rise to confidence as they invented raps for recovering spent arrows or blunting sword points.

Sharpened skills enabled them to turn grass blue, or open sizable holes in the ground without the use of spade or shovel. They spellsang into existence not raw fish but cooked food, and sleeping platforms complete with fresh linen.

Soon they were feeling very good about themselves and their talent. They just couldn't figure out what to do with it. Buncan devoted a good deal of time to the problem, certain that if they just kept their secret and had patience an appropriate situation would present itself.

It was peaceful in the house where the west side of the tree wrapped itself around the dimensionally expanded den. Outside, past the neatly maintained lawn and flowers, the Shortstub flowed tranquil and undisturbed to the south.

Father and son were alone, reading. Buncan had heard Jon-Tom speak of something from his own world called "television," but from his description of it Buncan didn't see how it could better a book for good company and entertainment. It was an evaluation Jon-Tom chose never to dispute.

His mother was finishing up in the kitchen as the door pealed for attention. Buncan barely looked up from his reading as she entered the hall. As he watched he envisioned her wielding the sword she kept in the back of the broom closet instead of the dishcloth she was presently carrying. It was a difficult image to sustain, no matter how many tales he recalled of her early life.

She leaned back to peer into the den. "Dear, there's an owl to see you."

Jon-Tom put down the large book he'd been browsing and rubbed his eyes. He needed glasses, Buncan knew, but insisted on using imperfect vision spells instead. They needed constant adjustment.

Buncan headed for the kitchen on the pretext of getting something to eat. Actually, he rose and moved because it offered a much better view of the front door.

Clothahump's famulus Mulwit stood there, rustling his great wings as he spoke to Jon-Tom, who knelt on one knee to respond to the owl. Talea lingered nearby. Buncan could overhear them without straining.

". . . but the Master declares that youuu have to come *now*," the famulus was saying insistently.

"It's awfully late," Buncan heard his father reply. "And it's chilly out. Why can't it wait until tomorrow?"

"Master Clothahump did not offer explanations," Mulwit hooted. "He says for youuu to come now. Dooo youuu want me tooo go back and tell him you're not coming? If youuu dooo it will go hard on me."

"If it's that urgent . . ." Jon-Tom rose and turned to face Talea. "You heard. I've got to go. I know it's late, but it seems to be important."

Talea stared up at him. "You're not going off on some sort of silly quest or something again, are you?"

He put his hands on her shoulders. "Now look: I told you when you got pregnant that I've done with all that. I've a family and a home to look after, a profitable and respected profession, and they come first. The time when Mudge and I traipsed all over the world getting into all sorts of trouble is history."

"Just so long as you understand that," she responded. "Because by all the imbalances in the Aether, if that hardshell ropes you into some crazy expedition I'll cut off your feet and hide them in the closet before I'll let you go."

"Now, love." Buncan heard the moist echo of a kiss. "Clothahump just wants to network with me." He glanced over his shoulder. "Right, Mulwit?"

"So far as I am permitted to know, Master Jon-Tom. With youuu, and one other."

Jon-Tom's brow furrowed. "There's someone else involved?"

"Not here, not here!" The agitated famulus was flapping his wings as he hopped back and forth from one foot to the other. "Already we have lingered tooo long."

"Just let me get my cloak." Jon-Tom hesitated at the open hall closet. "Do you think I'll need my duar?"

"Wizardry was not spoken of," the famulus responded. "Only talk."

"Good." Jon-Tom swept the iridescent lizard-skin cloak around his shoulders, bestowed another kiss upon Talea, and disappeared into the night in the company of the anxious owl.

As his mother reentered the kitchen, Buncan feigned interest in a piece of cake. "What was that all about?"

Talea stood at the sink, gazing out the oval window in the direction of the dark river. Her demeanor was stiff. "I'll tell you something, boy. If your father gets himself sucked into something dangerous . . ."

"Didn't you used to do dangerous things, Mom?"

She turned to him. "That was different. When I was young I had to do certain things to survive." She attacked the remnants of the innocent dinner dishes, refusing as always to use the cleaning spells stocked in the cupboard under the towels.

"Is there some kind of problem?" The indifference of his query was crafted with admirable skill.

"How the hell should I know? You think they tell me anything? Anyone would think I had no acquaintance with the mysteries of the Universe. I never did trust that turtle completely."

"You can't ever trust wizards, Mom. It's in their nature. They can't help it."

"Every time your father answered one of that aged reptile's calls, it got him into trouble."

Buncan set the cake aside, rose, and stood behind his much shorter mother, resting his hands on her shoulders. "Now, Mom. If Dad said he wasn't going to get involved in anything, then I'm sure he isn't. I just wonder what the ru n is all about."

"Oh, who knows," she muttered irritably. "Some mother wants to change the sex of her unborn two days before it's due, or that fat Mrs. Twogg on the other side of Lynchbany is having digestive troubles again. Emergency!" She assaulted the stewpot with a vigor no mere spell could match.

"Yeah, well, I've pretty much had it, Mom. I'm going on up to bed."

She glanced sideways at him. "Kind of early, isn't it?"

He shrugged. "I've been reading all evening, and I had kind of a rough day at school."

She turned to him and put soapy fingers on his cheek. "You have a good mind, Buncan. Better than mine. You also have talent, but not everyone can be a spellsinger like your father.''

"I know, Mom.''

The outside glowbulbs stayed dark as he slipped out his bedroom window and shinnied down the trunk of the tree, heading northwest across the back lawn. There was hardly enough moon to count as an afterthought, and it was difficult to see the way as he hurried along the secondary path through the woods. The Belltrees were silent, their tinkling blooms closed for the night.

Breathing hard, he still managed to arrive at the edge of the clearing surrounding the wizard's tree just as Mulwit and his father appeared. He waited a suitable interval after they entered. Tethered in the corral out back were a pair of husky dray lizards and the silhouette of a large wagon he didn't recognize.

Normally the wizard kept the clearing alarmed, but those spells would likely remain deactivated until his father departed. With care Buncan thought he could slip inside the tree undetected. He edged forward, advancing noiselessly.

The door was unsealed, and he eased it aside. There was no need to lock it, since anyone not familiar with the way would immediately find themselves confronting an impassable dead end exactly like the burned-out core of an old oak. Remembering from many previous visits the curious twists and turns of the tree's interior, he successfully advanced past the entrance and soon found himself standing in the hallway outside Clothahump's front study. Not too long ago he had sat in that same sanctuary discussing his personal problems with the wizard.

He crept as close as he dared, until he could hear Jon-Tom and Clothahump's conversation clearly. A third voice kept interposing commentary. Not Mulwit, which meant that part of his attention would have to remain on the lookout for the nosy owl. Cautiously Buncan allowed himself a quick peek into the room.

The venerable turtle was seated in his special chair, while Jon-Tom sprawled on the long couch beneath the window. Seated at the other end was a hirsute stranger, a sloth by

tribe. Their kind was uncommon in the Bellwoods, preferring as they did warmer, more southerly climes.

This one wore a thin vest of what looked like metal foil.
Even a hasty glance was enough to show that it was too
flimsy to be any kind of armor. The long-legged pants of
gray cotton were something of a surprise, but the open-toed
sandals seemed appropriate. Though severely trimmed, the
claws on the visitor's hands and feet were still formidable.
Clearly alert and attentive, the visitor nonetheless gave the
appearance of one half asleep, an unfortunate and unavoid-
able characteristic of his kind. His words were carefully
chosen, and no one would mistake his natural slowness of
speech for stupidity.

He wore an extravagant amount of delicate gold jewelry.

Jon-Tom sipped from a goblet while Clothahump leaned
on the sturdy cane he favored lately and scrutinized the
visitor through his thick glasses.

"I have done as you requested, traveler Gragelouth," the
wizard was saying. "I have roused myself from deep
slumber and, since you insisted you would relate your tale
to no fewer than two witnesses of sorceral competence,
caused to be brought hence my junior partner." (Clothahump
always stuck in that "junior," Buncan reflected sourly.) The
wizard leaned slightly but threateningly forward.

"All I have to add is that what you have to say had better
be worth all this inconvenience. After a few hundred years,
one begins to value one's time."

The sloth seemed anxious though unintimidated. "I assure you I would not waste your time, Master." He looked
at Jon-Tom. "As I have informed your colleague, I am a
traveling merchant, dealing mostly in domestic utensils and
household goods."

"Saw your wagon and team out back," Jon-Tom
commented.

Gragelouth nodded. "I buy and sell anything, but that is
my area of specialization."

"Enough personal history," grumbled Clothahump. "Your
story."

"Certainly." The sloth looked thoughtful as he began to
reminisce. "I was far to the north of here, traveling a back

road in the vicinity of L'bor, when a singular sight happened to catch my eye. It appeared to be an injured individual lying forsaken by the side of the road.'' He sniffed.

"You can imagine that I was reluctant to stop. It is a common and well-known ploy of bandits to set out one of their own as bait, decorated to appear damaged, to attract the attention of the naturally solicitous, whereupon when the would-be Samaritan halts to render assistance, the others fall upon and rob him, or worse.

"My outfit, however, is not built for speed, and I would have had little hope of outrunning a band of determined dacoits anyway. As this solitary individual's injuries struck me as quite real, I halted and went to render what assistance I could.''

"That was noble of you.'' Jon-Tom mused privately that the merchant might just as easily have had in mind the same thought as a band of passing robbers.

"His name was Juh Phit, a fox by typus, and his desperate condition was due not to harm suffered in battle but to age, starvation, and exposure. He was still alive when I found him. Weak and exhausted as he was, he still attempted to draw the sword slung at his side when I approached.

"Now, I am no fighter, Masters, and I started to pull back. When he saw that he beckoned me close, and related to me the gist of the tale I now pass on to you.

"He had been long afoot and had come stumbling all that way down out of the high mountains to the northwest of L'bor. Where precisely he had been he could not say, being no geographer or navigator himself. But he had found something up there, and his description of the exact location was marked by the kind of detail one masters when memorizing a field of battle, for I soon found out that he was a mercenary by trade.

"This lifelong professional soldier had encountered something which had frightened him badly. So anxious was he to flee its environs that he lost both his mount and his kit in his rush to escape, and it was only by some miracle that he had half run, half wandered as far southeast as L'bor, shunning all who crossed his path.

"One more day, Masters, and he would have made it to the outskirts of that northern town, which, he confided to me, was his intended destination. But his strength had at last deserted him, his body had played him false, and he had fallen helpless where I encountered him, at which point he was nearer death than L'bor.

"I comforted him and gave him water, but he was too weak to take food."

"So what did he find in the northwestern mountains?" In Jon-Tom's eyes was the hint of an old gleam. "Treasure? Some fabulous forgotten city?"

"Nothing like that," said the merchant. "I do not pretend to understand all that he said. Only that what he found had been compelling and terrifying enough to drive him to that desperate condition. I have discussed this with others whom I knew or encountered on my journey here, and if anything their ignorance on the subject exceeds my own.

"Only one, who had had some minor dealings with matters sorceral, suggested that I seek you out. This I have done because this dead soldier's tale has become something of an obsession with me, and I desire deeply to understand it. Also, it was in a sense all that this unfortunate fox had to bequeath, the only other thing of value left in his possession being his oft-used sword."

"Which you have with you?" Jon-Tom inquired.

The sloth looked away. "Uh, no. I hocked it. I am after all a merchant, and I have to live."

"This thing he encountered?" said Clothahump impatiently.

Gragelouth turned gratefully to the wizard. "He called it 'The Grand Veritable.' "

Over the years Buncan had seen the wizard Clothahump deal with much that was marvelous and inexplicable, from conjuring up entire buildings to transmuting gold into lead (the latter not being a spell that was overmuch in demand, but one which the wizard often performed for practice). In all that time he had never seen the turtle react as he did at that moment.

Clothahump jerked backward so sharply that it snapped the minor retention spell that held his heavy glasses on his beak. With a grunt he picked them off the floor and carefully set them back in place. As for Jon-Tom, he could only look on in bewilderment.

When he had fully recovered, the wizard spoke slowly and with great certitude. "There is no such thing as the Grand Veritable. It's nothing more than a widespread rumor among those of us in the Profession. An old rumor, but a rumor nonetheless. It does not exist. Some wish that it did, but wishing and reality are infrequent companions."

"I know I never heard of it," Jon-Tom added.

Clothahump squinted at him. "You would not, nor is it something you'd be likely to encounter in your spellsinging. It is not a subject to spark casual conversation."

Gragelouth seemed hesitant to comment, perhaps a bit taken aback by the vehemence of the great wizard's reaction. "I do not know whether it exists or not. I only repeat to you the tale of the dying mercenary. Real or not, it cost him his life."

"It's not unknown for individuals weakened by exposure and its consequences to suffer from delusions," Jon-Tom pointed out.

The sloth favored the spellsinger with his inherently mournful expression and perpetually sad eyes. "I may be ignorant in matters thaumaturgical, sir, but I flatter myself that I am a good judge of people. It is a consequence of being a successful trader. Nor have I suffered the companionship, however brief, of many on the verge of death. That confessed, I am convinced those who are about to depart this plane of existence have no reason to lie to a stranger."

Jon-Tom waved off the rationalization. "Okay, so this Juh Phit *believed* he'd encountered something he called the Grand Veritable. That doesn't mean he actually did so."

"I am of course in no position to dispute that." The merchant's voice was as soft as his pelt.

"Even people of good intentions sometimes repeat falsehoods so often they come to think of them as truths," Jon-Tom added. "Real estate brokers, for example."

"I can only say that I received the dying testament of this soldier Juh Phit, and that I believe in what he said."

"Something so dangerous, so insidious, could not exist," Clothahump was mumbling. "When I think of the damage it could cause if it did, the havoc it could wreak, I shudder inside my shell." He leaned back in the chair, the willow springs creaking beneath his weight.

"Just what exactly is this rumor, anyway?" Jon-Tom wanted to know. Out in the hallway Buncan listened motionless, hardly daring to breathe.

"Like all truly great dangers it is at once simple and complex," Clothahump was moved to explain. "To adequately analyze it would require its use, a proposition fiendishly designed to ensnare any who would attempt it. Its attractions would by definition be simultaneously irresistible and invariably fatal." He took a deep breath. "The Grand Veritable, lad, is a notion best avoided by all sensible-thinking folk. Forget about it. Pretend you never heard of it. In the hands of even the most clever, careful, and well-meaning of individuals, it could destroy entire communities, up to and including civilization as we know it.

"Which is why it cannot exist. The mere concept is too terrifying to contemplate." As he delivered this warning the lights inside the tree dimmed until it was black in the hallway and downright murky in the study.

The reduced illumination did not trouble Mulwit, who came flapping into the room through the portal on the side opposite Buncan.

"I didn't call for you," Clothahump admonished the famulus.

Mulwit perched on the back of an empty chair. "Youuu sounded exercised, Master. I thought perhaps youuu might need some assistance."

"Your concern is praiseworthy but misplaced." The turtle harrumphed. "As long as you're here you might as well hang around." He smiled as much as his inflexible beak allowed. "That was an old joke between your predecessor and me." He squinted at the glowbulbs. "Here, this won't do." A quick, arcane sentence restored the study to its previous brightness.

Buncan knew he was pushing his luck by staying. If not Clothahump or his father, the quick-eyed, sharp-eared Mulwit was sure to spot him soon. That would lead to accusatory questions he would be unable to satisfactorily answer. But fascination held him in the hallway.

The Grand Veritable, the merchant Gragelouth had called it. Reality or delusion, it had certainly provoked Clothahump. What could be formidable enough to cause the great wizard to adamantly refuse to acknowledge so much as its possible existence? What could frighten the all-powerful Clothahump that badly?

"The soldier Juh Phit spoke of it in more efficacious terms." Gragelouth dug at a furry ear.

"How like a mercenary," Clothahump murmured.

"He said that possession could make one wealthy beyond imagination. That any desire could be fulfilled if one but learned how to use the Veritable properly."

"The true horrors always bewitch," said Clothahump. "The Grand Veritable does not exist, and if it does, it is best left alone." He stared evenly at his nocturnal visitor. "The fate of your Juh Phit should be proof enough of that. Continue to pursue this rumor and you will surely meet a similar end." He turned abruptly on Jon-Tom, jabbing a finger in his direction.

"As for you, associate, I know how your mind works. Put aside all such thoughts. Besides, your mate would cut you off at the knees if you proposed anything."

"Wasn't going to," Jon-Tom mumbled.

"We have ample work to keep us busy, and I need you here. Even if I did not, I would do everything in my power to stop you from pursuing this dangerous rumor."

"I'm not afraid of rumors." Out in the hall, Buncan felt an unexpected surge of pride. "Talea, however, is another matter." Buncan slumped.

"Deal solely with those nightmares which have been domesticated by sleep," Clothahump advised his human colleagues, "and leave the real ones to the reckless." He turned back to face the sloth. "You have come far to see us, merchant. To what purpose?"

"I think what Juh Phit spoke of as he lay dying in my arms is worthy of further investigation, but I have no experience in matters mystical. I thought to seek assistance.'' The sloth's persistence in the face of Clothahump's daunting skepticism was admirable, Buncan mused.

"You intend to pursue this matter purely in the spirit of intellectual inquiry, of course.'' The wizard stared knowingly at his guest.

"I am a merchant, a trader in goods and stores.'' Gragelouth showed the upturned palms of heavy, clawed hands. "I do not deny that I seek profit alongside elucidation. Tell me: With proper supervision could not this Veritable be a force for good?''

"No, never!'' Clothahump insisted vehemently. "It can only cause divisiveness and disruption, destruction and death. On this the old tales are explicit. I would not trust its possession even to myself.''

"You can at least allow as how someone else might hold a differing opinion.'' The merchant wasn't afraid to defend his ground, Jon-Tom thought approvingly.

"Anyone is entitled to an opinion about hearsay,'' Clothahump grunted. Searching a drawer in his plastron, he removed a small cube of something green and odious, plopped it in his mouth, and chewed reflectively as he slammed the drawer shut. "You'll get no help from me. I'm too old to go chasing after dangerous rumors.''

"You've been 'getting old' for a hundred and fifty years,'' Jon-Tom commented.

The turtle nodded. "And believe me, nothing gets old faster than getting old.'' He sighed heavily. "If you want my advice, traveler, you'll go back to your trading and forget this nonsense. If it's nothing but rumor you'll perish in the seeking of it, and if it's at all for real, you'll perish in the finding of it. I won't charge you for this little conference,'' he said, displaying uncharacteristic generosity. "Disillusionment is costly enough.''

Having tried every ploy he could think of, Gragelouth had nothing more to say. Clothahump shifted in his chair. "Do you have lodging for the night?''

The sloth shrugged wide shoulders, looking even sadder than usual. "Many times have I had to bed down with my wagon and team.''

"It's late, and a ways to Lynchbany,'' the turtle murmured.

"I can make a suitable room for you here. Dimensional expansion. One of my better spells."

The sloth looked up, nodding gratefully. "You are as hospitable as you are discouraging. I accept." He reached for the purse attached to his wide belt. "I will pay—"

"Not now." Clothahump waved magnanimously. "Even absurd tales have their uses. One must balance enlightenment with entertainment. This is fortunate for you, elsewise I might have turned you into a cockroach as penance for interrupting my sleep." The sloth started, sleepy eyes suddenly wide. Jon-Tom was quick to reassure him.

"Clothahump has a unique sense of humor."

The wizard chose not to comment as he rose and lumbered on short, stumpy legs toward the far portal. "Come, traveler, and we'll see to your sleeping arrangements. Your body type would, I think, prefer a particularly soft bed. Or perhaps a low-slung hammock?"

Jon-Tom rose, shaking out his cape behind him. "It's late. I'd better be getting back."

No need to linger to overhear final farewells, Buncan knew. Turning in the darkness, he felt carefully along the wall as he retraced his steps. Soon he was back at the front door, which yielded silently to his touch. Out in the glade then, and moments later safely back among the friendly shadows of the silent Bellwoods. Heading home with the hope that Talea hadn't checked his room in his absence. Even if she had, he'd prepared an elaborate and, he hoped, convincing excuse. In the event of total disbelief, the last thing she would suspect was that he'd been off spying on his father and Clothahump.

His head was awhirl with what he'd just overheard. Too much to contain, it spilled over into ancillary hopes and dreams, washing reality aside. Not to mention common sense.

It was news he had to share with others, and soon.

CHAPTER 6

"SO THIS GARGLEMOUTH—"

"Gragelouth," Buncan corrected him.

"So 'e were a merchant from far away, an' a sloth."
Squill dug his feet into the squishy sand of the riverbank.
"Wot was 'e, besides slothful?"

They were on the beach which struck out into the current
on an upper bend of the Shortstub. Vest and pants bundled
nearby, Neena cavorted in the water, a sliver of brown
sleekness arcing through the silver. Like any other non-
otter, Buncan could only look on enviously.

"Experienced and well-traveled," he told Squill.

"Wealthy?"

"Hard to say. Sloths as a general rule aren't very
forthcoming."

"Don't see many in the Bellwoods."

"This one had a wagon and pair."

"Came a long way, 'e did, to harangue mister hardshell."
Squill evicted a small freshwater crab with a toe, watched it
scurry for the water. "This 'ere Grand Veritable 'e were
prattlin' about. Sounds special."

"Clothahump doesn't think it exists."

Locating a nice palm-sized rock, Squill aimed and attempted
to hit his sister the next time she broke the surface. She
dodged the missile with ease. "Accordin' to wot you're
tellin' me, mate, ol' beak-face spent a lot 'o time listenin'.
Wot do that tell you?"

"That Clothahump is kind to strangers."

"Tell me another! The old bugger's a grump."

Buncan skipped a smooth stone of his own across the
placid surface. He was stronger than Squill, but not as
quick. "Then we're left to consider the alternative, which is
that there was some substance to what the trader was saying."

"Never been to the northwest," Squill murmured thought-fully. "Never been anywheres, really."

Neena had emerged from the water and was shaking herself dry, her dark-brown fur glistening with droplets. "So Clothahump's not gonna check this story out?"

"Doesn't look like it," Buncan told her. "He let this Gragelouth spend the night. I'm sure he's already left."

"Wot about Jon-Tom?" She dug moss from behind one ear.

Buncan regarded the river. "Dad's become . . . settled. You know what Talea would think about him going off on some crazy quest. Or how Weegee would give it to Mudge if he tried the same."

"Old people," groused Squill.

"Better not let Mudge 'ear you say that," Neena warned him as she methodically dried her whiskers.

"Squill's more than half right." Buncan chucked another rock into the water. "They've all gotten tired and lazy, forgotten what adventure's all about. They've become too much a part of the community."

"Well, I ain't part o' no community." Squill rose and adjusted the angle of his cap's feathers. "Me, I says we go after this 'ere Gragelouth and check out 'is story for ourselves. An' if 'e's lyin', we'll be able to bring back proof o' it."

"Right," agreed his sister. "Maybe 'e were just tryin' to extort some money from ol' drawer-guts. Or free 'elp."

"Clothahump doesn't hand out free samples," Buncan murmured.

"Sure, 'e ain't dumb," Squill agreed, nodding. "Just lazy."

"I wonder how far to the northwest this Grand Veritable thing is supposed to lie," Buncan said.

"Don't matter. We got lots o' time." Squill moved nearer. "You said 'e were near L'bor when he found that dyin' mercenary. Did 'e mention if 'e were 'eaded back up that way?"

Buncan tried to remember. "He may have said something along those lines."

"We know where L'bor is." Neena was slipping into her shorts. "We could find our way. This slant-eyed bloke came to Clothahump lookin' for 'elp, did 'e?"

"That's right." Buncan also stood, brushing at the seat of his pants.

"Well, then?" she murmured. The otters exchanged a glance. "Wot are we 'angin' around 'ere for?"

"D'you think he'd take us with him?"

"Cor," she replied, batting her eyelashes at her tall human friend, " 'e's a bleedin' merchant! 'E don't know nothin' about sorceral matters. If its spellsingin' 'elp 'e wants, it's spellsingin' 'elp we'll offer 'im."

"Let's get after 'im." Squill was already heading for the trees. "The farther off 'e gets, the 'arder it'll be for us to catch up with 'im. We'll try the main north-south roads first."

"What, leave right now?" Buncan hurried to catch up to the excited otter. "Without telling our parents?"

"Wot, you want their bloomin' approval?" Neena came up behind him and pinched him on the butt. "We got our clothes, our weapons, your duar. We're bloody well ready for anythin'. We can spellsing a privacy cocoon around us, keep Jon-Tom from spellsingin' us out. That's all we need to worry about. Besides, they're used to us skippin' off for a few days at a time, campin' in the woods. They won't even look for us for a while."

"The more distance we can make before they do," Squill pointed out, "the 'arder it'll be for them to interfere."

"If this Grugletooth—" Neena began.

"Gragelouth," Buncan patiently corrected her.

"If 'e turns out to be nothin' more than some country extortionist, we'll be right back anyways. Clothahump'll be grateful for the confirmation."

"Always wanted to see L'bor," Squill murmured.

"What'll we do for money?" Buncan wanted to know.

"We'll live by our wits, mate. That's wot Mudge always said 'e did."

"Your dad's an inveterate liar."

"I know. It's one o' 'is most endearin' traits. Come on."

"You said this sloth 'ad a team o' two an' a wagon. If it's much o' a team 'e might be movin' fast." Neena was bursting with confidence and energy. "No matter. We'll catch up with 'im some'ow."

Discreet queries revealed that the merchant had indeed passed through Lynchbany that very morning and had been observed heading north out of the town. That meant he was already a day ahead of them.

"We ain't gonna catch a wagon on foot," Squill pointed out. "Bloody 'ell! I was 'oping 'e'd 'ole up 'ere in town for a while."

"We'll 'ave to find transportation." His sister was nodding in agreement.

"How? We have hardly any money," Buncan pointed out.

A twinkle showed in Neena's gaze. "I'm the daughter o' the inimitable Mudge, an' Squill 'ere, sad to say, is me brother. We've spent all our lives listenin' to Mudge's stories. You don't do that an' not pick up a smidgee o' practical information 'ere an' there."

Buncan glanced nervously up and down the busy street on which they stood conversing. "This is awfully close to home. Just being here makes it hard to stay inconspicuous."

"Cor, mate, we 'aven't even started to push things." Squill indicated a comfortable empty half-barrel in a nearby alleyway. "You just 'ave a seat an' wait 'ere. Neena an' I will be back shortly."

"Just don't do anything obvious!" Buncan shouted after them. He doubted that they heard, or if they did, would pay his words any heed.

The pair of four-legged riding lizards the otters found were strong and willing. They left Lynchbany quickly behind and soon found themselves once more among the dense groves of the Bellwoods, heading north at a laudable pace.

Buncan couldn't keep from repeatedly glancing back over his shoulder, but no pursuit appeared on the smooth dirt road behind them. Squill and Neena rode back-to-back on the other animal's saddle.

"If the stable owner catches us first, he'll make hides out of us before we can explain."

"Don't be such an old granny-cakes." Neena smoothed down the fur around her muzzle. "As soon as we catch up with Gragelouth an' 'ire 'ourselves on with 'im we'll let these two skinks go. They'll find their way back, an' their owner'll just think they slipped their bloody tethers."

Clinging to the narrow reins, Buncan considered his horse-sized, yellow-and-blue-striped mount. "I didn't know that skinks had a homing instinct."

Neena waved absently. "Well, they'll find their way back somewhere." Her own mount lurched slightly and she grabbed hold of one of the long saddle's multiple pommels. The saddle was designed to accommodate as wide a variation of backsides as possible. It was not particularly constructed with otters in mind. Or humans.

"Anyway," Squill was saying, "they 'ave to catch us first. If an' when they do, if we ain't got the goods in question in our possession, they can't prove a bleedin' thing. Relax, mate. Nobody saw us."

Buncan did his best to comply.

They rode most of the night, catching a few hours' sleep beneath the branches of a huge old Belltree whose leaves chimed only at the low end of the scale. Like their daytime counterparts the transparent butterflies, glass moths flitted among nocturnal blossoms, the light of the waxing moon shining through their transparent tinted wings and filtering starlight through living stained glass. A pair of owls soared past overhead, making for L'bor. Not searching for him, Buncan mused. Messengers, most likely, or just a young couple looking for a nice empty tree in which to make out.

The otters were up before the sun. Their energy was incredible, though if the mood took them they could also sleep for a day and a half.

By midmorning there was still no sign of pursuit, and Squill had paused to point out fresh ruts in the road.

"See that?" He clutched at his mount's reins, steadying the big lizard. "The merchant's wagon."

"How do you know that?" Buncan asked him. "This is the main road from Lynchbany to L'bor. Plenty of wagons pass this way."

"Ain't seen any," Neena countered. " 'Tis the slow season."

"We'll know right soon." Squill spurred his mount on, and Buncan hurried to follow.

Were their parents missing them yet? he wondered. Following breakfast they'd taken their best shot at a privacy spell. In theory Jon-Tom shouldn't be able to track them now with magic. In theory. He shrugged. There was little more they could do to cover their tracks.

Legend said that his father and Mudge had helped stop the Plated Folk at the Jo-Troom Pass. Hard to believe it was the same person who spent much of his time puttering around the family tree, fixing leaky plumbing and barbecuing fish on the lawn out back. Could that person break through the straightforward solidity of a privacy spell?

He chucked the reins and the big skink hissed slightly, turning its narrow blindered head to look back at him.

"Come on, pick it up," he told the uncomprehending animal. "We want to overtake this merchant before another night falls." With poor grace the lizard increased its pace.

Evening was threatening to make its appearance when Squill suddenly brought his own mount to an abrupt halt. Buncan drew alongside, stopped. "What is it? Something the matter?"

"Don't you 'ear it?"

"I 'ear it." Neena was leaning forward and to one side, trying to see past her brother.

"Well, I don't," snapped Buncan.

"Why not? Your ears are bigger than ours."

"But not as sharp. Above or below the water."

"You're always underwater, mate," Squill told him. But affectionately.

Buncan followed the otters' lead as they dismounted and secured their skinks to a nearby tree. Just as they had for years, they used the undergrowth to conceal their movements as they advanced. Only, Buncan knew that this time Squill and Neena weren't playing. Maybe his hearing wasn't as good as theirs, but he was equally adept at avoiding twigs and dry leaves.

It didn't take long before he, too, could hear what had attracted Squill's attention: many voices shouting and yelling. Only a couple were deep enough to suggest size. The rest were fairly high-pitched.

They came to a place where the forest thinned and they could see the road again. Stopped to one side was the merchant's wagon. Thanks to his well-honed powers of memory and observation, Buncan was able to recognize it instantly from the single brief glimpse he'd had of it parked behind Clothahump's tree.

Also, there was a large spellcharged sign on the side which periodically flashed in bright canary-yellow letters:

GRAGELOUTH—*MERCHANT & TRADER*

The wagon rested on four thick-spoked, brightly painted wooden wheels. A single door interrupted the smooth lines of the stern. There was a built-in ladder which allowed access to the roof, and a pair of stairs bolted beneath the doorway. Pots, pans, and other household goods dangled from hempen and wire leaders like misshapen fruit. Two muscular, squat-bodied dray lizards yoked side by side stood placidly in front of the wagon, scratching at their blinders and sampling the ground with their flattened pink tongues.

Though the wagon faced away from them, they could see the merchant seated on the forebench. Hatless, his thick gray coat showed evidence of recent trimming. The long fur beneath his arms swayed as he argued with those who had surrounded him.

Standing near the front of the team and holding the harness of the lead lizard was a massive masked figure. The mask was natural, for the individual was a spectacled bear. He wore long pants, a dull hazel shirt, and a heavy leather cap. His size made him prominent among the sword- and ax-armed ringtail cats and raccoons who comprised the majority of the gang.

A tall, lithe, rather rakishly clad coatimundi stood nearest the wagon, gesturing animatedly in the merchant's direction with a thin rapier. They could see Gragelouth flinch whenever the blade flicked too close. Brass studs glistened among the coati's attire. Even at a distance Buncan could make out the diamond that sparkled in one of his prominent canines.

"Wot a bleedin' marvelous opportunity!" Neena whispered. "We can rescue the silly sod an' ingratiate ourselves to 'im forever. 'E'll 'ave to take us on." She drew her short sword and took a step forward.

Buncan hastened to restrain her. "Wait a minute!" He raised his eyes above the brush line. "There's . . . half a dozen raccoons and ringtails, the coati, and the bear. There's only three of us, and the bear's a lot bigger than I am."

"Righty-ho, mate," agreed Squill cheerfully. "Them's fair odds, they are."

"Are you crazy? You've inherited Mudge's bravado along with his lack of judgment. If we go charging out there we're gonna get ourselves stomped. Don't lose sight of why we're here." One of the ringtails was now peering curiously in their direction, and Buncan hurriedly ducked back down into the vegetation.

"You're right, Bunkies." Neena sheathed her sword. "We're 'ere to show this merchant 'ow our spellsingin' can 'elp 'im." She rubbed her forepaws together. "So let's get to it."

Squill was less enthusiastic. He fingered his bow. "We might could take two or three of 'em out with arrows before they pinned us. If we try singin' first, we'll give away both our position and the element o' surprise."

Buncan was unlimbering his duar. "Singing might surprise them. Or they might even ignore it. We can always resort to our weapons if it doesn't work. If we don't do something *fast*, they'll kill the merchant and we might as well turn around and slink back home."

The otter considered, then nodded. "Right-o, but 'tis likely we'll only get one chance. Keep your blades 'andy."

Buncan plucked lightly at the duar. A faint globule of pale-blue smoke arose from the nexus. He eyed his companions expectantly.

"Wot'll we sing about?" Squill eyed his sister uncertainly. "Buncan?"

"Don't ask me. You two are the lyricists." He strained to see past them. The discussion at the wagon appeared to be taking a conclusive turn. If they didn't hurry, a sword thrust would render moot whatever effort they expended. "Better get on with it. I have a feeling the hoods are getting tired of Gragelouth's banter."

" 'E must 'ave somethin' worth protecting or 'e'd 'ave

given 'em wot they want by now." Neena leaned over to exchange hurried whispers with her brother.

Buncan waited nervously. If it came to a fight, he was bigger and probably stronger than any of the bandits save the bear, and nothing was quicker in combat than an otter. But there were eight of them, all much more experienced at real fighting than he or his friends. The scarred dandy of a coati in particular looked like a tough customer.

None of which would matter if they could spellsing them aside. Hopefully the otters' wits would prove as quick as their feet.

"How shall I start off?" he muttered.

"Somethin' slow and heavy," Squill advised him. "Like when we called up the whale."

"Okay, but let's try and make this a little more low-key." His fingers hovered above the strings, anxious to begin. "We don't want to kill anyone if we can help it."

"Why not?" Neena regarded him out of bright eyes.

"Because it's messy. We don't want to frighten off the merchant, either."

Squill was staring in the wagon's direction. "That rapier pokes 'im any deeper an' 'e won't be in any condition to do much o' anything." He turned back to his sister. "Ready, mush-mouth? On three. A one, a two, an' a three . . ."

Buncan began to play.

"Rumble in the woods got no place to go
Bangin' in the hood where it ain't no show
Gonna break it up, gonna bring it low, throw
It out, kick it out, stop it now
Stop it before it gets serious. Gets serious?
We're delirious.
Better believe it or you're gonna buy it
Wanna fight our power, better not try it!"

Every one of the bandits surrounding the wagon, from the bear to the slightest raccoon, turned to stare in the direction of the music. Buncan's fingers flew over the duar. He could feel the energy surging from the instrument, felt confidence in the counterpoint he was generating to the otters' rap. The more the three of them performed, the easier it became. He began to feel that with practice and time they might actually become proficient.

Except . . . while the music was invigorating, and sounded fresh, nothing else was happening.

The coati was conversing rapidly with three of the four raccoons. A moment later this heavily armed trio started toward the source of the singing. Two of them wielded axes, and the third a wicked, barb-tipped pike.

"Nothing's happening." Buncan raised his voice over the music. "Something's wrong with your singing, or your choice of lyrics."

"I can't think o' anythin' else," Squill mumbled frantically.

His sister glared at him. "Well, you're the one who's supposed to be so clever!"

"'Ell, don't pick on me! You're always on about 'ow clever you think you are."

"For the Tree's sake," Buncan growled, "don't start fighting *now*!"

The lead raccoon wore a checkered and striped bandanna, while his companion sported an incongruous stovepipe hat decorated with tufts of bird down. The pike wielder shifted a leather beret between his ears. All three readied their weapons as they drew nearer.

"*Do* something!" Buncan hissed desperately.

"I'm tryin'," said Neena, "but 'e ain't 'elping none."

"I just can't think o' nothin' appropriate." Squill glanced anxiously in the direction of the approaching brigands.

"Anything!" A groaning Buncan found himself wondering if he should put down the duar and take up his sword.

"Wait a minim." The otter blinked suddenly. "Remember that one ditty that was on that collection?" He whispered rapidly to his sister. Her expression widened, she nodded, and they began to sing once more, their voices rising in unison above the vegetation.

"Time for the beat, time for the feet
Time to get real out on the street
Time to Hammer the bad dudes down
Time to Hammer 'em right down in the ground

Hammer, Hammer, show 'em who's boss
Show 'em who's the tool that'll waste 'em for a
Loss!''

A glistening argent nimbus materialized above the bushes
between the singers and the advancing robbers. It was
clearly visible to those back by the wagon. The ugly
conversation between the desperate Gragelouth and his increasingly impatient tormentor ceased as both turned to
stare.

The silvery vapor seemed composed of metal fragments.
It was gravid and intimidating, and Buncan instinctively
stumbled away from it until he bumped up against a tree. He
had the presence of mind to keep playing. What they were
conjuring up he didn't know, but so far it was enormously
impressive even in its indistinctness. The otters ducked
slightly but continued to rap. The raccoons clutched their
weapons in front of them and gaped, their advance stalled
by the otherworldly conjuration.

The cloud began to congeal into a crystal the size of a
wine barrel. This was crossed with a much longer cylinder
composed of identical material. Together they formed a
slender T shape that was as long as Gragelouth's wagon.

It was, in point of fact, an enormous tool: a hammer
fashioned of some unidentifiable solid metal. A giant's
hammer. It hung in the air above the bushes and young
trees, vibrating slightly in time to the beat of Buncan's duar.

The raccoons began to edge around it, keeping a wary
eye on the gleaming, highly polished apparition as they did
so.

This wouldn't do, Buncan knew, and he so informed the
otters. Without missing a beat they altered their lyrics
appropriately.

The hammer shuddered. It arced backward, paused briefly
in a vertical position, and then swooshed down with tremendous force. It struck the foremost bandit before he could
dodge and squashed him as flat as if the singers had dumped
a blue whale on him. The denouement was both messy and
noisy. The sight, when the hammer retracted to a position
parallel with the ground, was unpleasant to look upon. It

was sufficiently disagreeable to send the two surviving brigands racing back toward their compatriots, screeching as they threw their useless weapons aside.

Buncan forced himself to look out at the mess the hammerish apparition had created on the otherwise pristine forest floor and felt his stomach engage gears independent of the rest of his system. He was, however, too busy playing to throw up. The otters, delighted, proceeded to ghoulify their lyrics to the utmost extent of their imagination, which was considerable.

The hammer pivoted in midair and began to chase the retreating bandits, repeatedly slamming into the ground behind them and leaving deep, perfectly round impressions in the solid earth. Each time it struck, the ground jumped slightly. Booming thuds echoed through the forest.

Seeing the outrageous device pursuing their panicky companions, the rest of the gang hesitated. At this critical moment the coati bravely scampered forward and made a gallant if misguided effort to rally his dispirited troops. He jabbed at the hammer with his rapier, only to see the blade turned by the smooth astral metal.

The hammer came down on his tail, breaking it in several places.

Letting out a barking scream, the bandit leader keeled over, unconscious. A ringtail and the bear grabbed him under the arms and hustled him away toward the densest cluster of trees while the rest of the gang scattered in every direction. Momentarily confused, the hammer went after all of them at once, missing with predictable but nonetheless intimidating regularity.

Buncan kept playing until the last robber had disappeared around the far bend in the road. He didn't laugh at the sight, because he couldn't. The nearby pulverized bone and expansive bloodstain which had been the unfortunate raccoon was too bright in his eyes, too thick in his nostrils. Instead he settled for a silent cry of thankfulness as he let his fingers relax. The glow at the duar's nexus faded.

"Not bad," he told the otters, who had ceased their singing. "Let's see how our merchant's doing." The trio broke from the underbrush and jogged toward the wagon, carefully avoiding the bloody pulp to their right.

"Wot'll we say to 'im?" Squill wondered as they approached the road.

"I dunno." His sister reflexively tried to smooth her makeup. " 'E looks a bit rattled."

Indeed, Gragelouth was clearly shaken. That was understandable, considering that he'd thus far seen only the homicidal hammer and not its manipulators. When all was explained to him he would doubtless be properly grateful, Buncan mused. After all, they'd just saved his fortune and most probably his life as well.

A loud crash sounded from the tree line, causing Buncan to turn and look behind him. Still flailing about madly, splintering bushes and trees and the occasional small boulder, the hammer reappeared. Having been spellsung into existence, it was not about to simply fade away.

It hesitated as if searching for something new and different to flatten. After a brief pause it aligned itself with the wagon and came thumping directly toward them. From the front seat they could hear Gragelouth moan.

"It's still active!" Squill yelped.

"I can see that." Clutching his duar tightly in both hands, Buncan found himself backing toward the road. "Sing it away."

"Play!" yelled Neena. "You have to play, Buncan!"

Galvanized by her order, he let his fingers drift down to the quiescent strings. The first chords were atonal and ineffective. Meanwhile, the metallic wraith continued its menacing advance.

All three of them retreated in a body, Buncan strumming madly, the otters rapping at maximum speed. They were in the middle of the road now, in front of the wagon, with no cover in sight.

The hammer reached them and hesitated. Paws in the air, Gragelouth cowered back on his bench. The apparition seemed to consider him, then accelerated purposefully in the direction of the somewhat quavering musicians.

"Scatter!" howled Squill at the last possible instant as the head of the hammer plunged toward them. Human and otters broke in three directions as the massive chunk of metal slammed into the earth where they'd been standing, sending gravel and dirt flying.

Buncan yelled as he dodged and played. "Make it go away! Sing something else! Send it back where it came from!"

"Back where it came from?" Squill tried to keep one eye on his friend and the other on the prodigious apparition. "I don't bloody well know where it came from! The bleedin' toolbox o' the gods?" The hammer zigged as he zagged to his left. "You're the damned spellsinger!" He jumped, and the device just missed him.

"You're the singers!" Buncan yelled.

The otters continued to improvise, to no avail. While they were getting tired of trying to dodge and sing at the same time, the remorseless specter gave no indication it was slowing down.

Suddenly the wind increased. Tree limbs and trunks bent toward the road as the breeze rapidly grew into a full-fledged gale. From his seat Gragelouth looked on in fascination.

Leaves and branches thrashed around Buncan. He was tiring fast, having neither the energy nor the agility of the otters. If that thing landed on them . . . The remains of the unlucky bandit were as fresh in his mind as they were on the ground back in the trees.

A flailing branch knocked him down, and he felt the duar slip from his stunned grasp. The pulsing radiance at the nexus of the two sets of strings instantly vanished. Seeing this, the otters ceased their rapping, useless without Buncan's skilled accompaniment.

Lying on his chest, panting, Buncan looked up in time to see the hammer hovering above him, measuring itself for the terminal strike. He closed his eyes.

Instantly the wind died. Two doubled-over trees straightened, their thick trunks catching the hammer on either side of the gleaming head and lifting it upward. They bounced back and forth a couple of times before quivering to a stop, the hammer pinned between them as neatly as on any holder in a carpenter's shop. There the apparition hung motionless, seemingly pacific at last.

Gasping, Buncan rolled over onto his back and regarded the sky. Then he scrambled to his feet and walked over to recover the duar. Some leaves had landed in the active nexus. A couple had simply been fried, while the third had been turned to topaz. He brushed all of them away and examined the instrument anxiously. It appeared intact. He carried spare strings, but if the body had been damaged . . .

A few experimental strums reassured him of its integrity. As he moved to sling it across his back and shoulders, he felt a paw on his arm. It was Squill, gazing up at him with concern.

"You all right, mate?"

Buncan nodded, narrowing his gaze as he looked up at the neatly pinned hammer. "Interesting resolution."

Squill's whiskers twitched. "Couldn't think o' anythin' else except the tools in old man Herton's shop. Worked."

"Wonder how long it'll stay there."

"No tellin'." Neena calmly considered the otherworldly instrument of mass destruction. "Don't like to think of it as puttin' in an appearance some night outside me bedroom window."

"Your bedroom ain't got no window," Squill pointed out.

She sniffed, whiskers rising. "That's right, brother. Just go ahead an' stomp on me reputation."

"Anytime." Squill straightened. "Wot say we go accept the grateful genuflections o' our pitiful fellow traveler?" He started toward the wagon.

"I'll go get the riding lizards," Buncan offered.

Gragelouth sat stiffly on his bench seat, watching them approach. Buncan rejoined his friends momentarily, his expression grim. "Who tethered the skinks?"

"I did," replied Neena.

"Well, they're gone."

"Wot do you mean, they're gone?" Squill turned angrily on his sister. "You snub-tailed twit, you never did learn 'ow to tie a proper knot!"

"Is that so? Want to see me tie one in your whiskers?" She grabbed for his face and the two of them went down, rolling over and over until their scuffling eventually carried them beneath the wagon.

Buncan bent slightly to check on them, then straightened and extended a hand. "Those are my friends, Squill and Neena."

"So I presumed." The sloth shook his head slowly, the dark stripes that began around his eyes and ran down his face giving him a look of perpetual sorrow. "Otters." Holding carefully to the reins of his team with one hand, he took Buncan's with the other. It was warm to the touch. All that heavy fur, Buncan reflected.

"Pleased to meet you. I'm Buncan Meriweather."

The merchant withdrew his hand and placed it over his heart. "I am Gragelouth, trader by profession and inclination. I find that I owe my everything to your timely arrival, young traveler. What I do not understand is why you youngsters," Buncan winced but said nothing, "should intervene on my behalf. You are not, I hope, deranged altruists?"

"Not at all. I'm pleased to tell you that we have a perfectly valid ulterior motive.".

"Ah." Gragelouth smiled, showing surprisingly bright teeth in his broad, flat face. "I am delighted to learn that you are merely foolhardy and not insane." Reaching behind his seat, he rummaged through a large satchel. "You must allow me to reward you for your help. Though I am not wealthy, I am most certainly wealthier thanks to your efforts. I regret only that you did not slay more of those brigands."

Buncan smiled thinly. "Actually, we were trying hard not to hurt anybody. At least, I was."

"Spoken like a true student of the thaumaturgical arts."

"We're still learning."

The merchant straightened and nodded. "That is what life is for. To stop learning is to begin to die." He opened the purse he'd extracted from the satchel and made a show of searching the contents. "I will give you all that I can spare, impossible as it is to put a price on a life. I retain only enough to support me awhile in L'bor, until I can resume my sales."

"We don't want your money." Buncan could hear the tussling otters as they bumped up against the rear wheels.

A grateful Gragelouth sealed his purse with a soft snap. "Something from my stock, perhaps? I maintain quite a diverse inventory. Some fine new weapons to balance your magical skills? Or raiment most excellent, to insinuate you with the female of your choice? Though I carry garments for humans, I am not sure I can fit one of your stature."

"We don't want anything like that."

"What, then, can I do for you?" The sloth spread his hands wide. "An unpaid debt weighs heavy on the soul." His engaging, deceptively lazy smile returned. "No doubt something that involves your aforementioned ulterior motive."

"In point of fact, sir, it involves us doing something more for you."

The sloth sniffed delicately. "Explain yourself, Buncan Meriweather. Your words warm my heart but confuse my brain."

Buncan considered how best to proceed. "It's like this, trader Gragelouth. We're bored."

The sloth grinned. "Ah. The endemic affliction of the incipient adult. I fear it requires a more skilled physician than myself to treat that condition."

"Several nights ago you discussed your travels with my father."

Gragelouth's heavy brows rose. "Your sire is a turtle?"

It was Buncan's turn to smile. "Hardly. But he *is* a master spellsinger."

"How do you know of this?"

"I was there, in the front hall. I heard pretty much everything."

"I see. And you were not discovered. You are a very adroit young human."

"And you're a very intriguing old sloth. I suppose Clothahump could be right and your whole story could be an elaborate ploy to draw attention to yourself, or get some free sorceral help, or whatever, but I happened to think that there was a lot of conviction in your voice."

"The conviction of truth," Gragelouth replied solemnly.

"My friends think so too. Just because Clothahump and Jon-Tom don't feel it's worthwhile to assist you doesn't mean no one does."

Sleepy eyelids rose as realization dawned on the sloth. "You?"

"Why not us?" Squill emerged from beneath the wagon, slapping his hat against his side to knock the dust off. "At least we believe in you. 'Alfway, anyway. We're younger and more resilient than that ol' 'ardback. More important, we're willin' to give you the benefit o' the doubt, we are."

"We're ready and willing," Buncan added.

Gragelouth was silent as he studied his youthful saviors and would-be companions. At last he shook his head slowly, the gray fur rippling.

"I am sorry, but you cannot come with me."

"Why not, guv?" Neena struggled out from beneath the wagon. "Somethin' about our looks you don't like?"

"There is nothing wrong with your appearance, or your enthusiasm. It is your parentage that concerns me. Most especially his." He pointed at Buncan. "You tell me that your sire is the great spellsinger Jon-Tom. I cannot help but feel that since he declined to aid me himself, he would prefer that you did not substitute in his stead. I cannot chance incurring his wrath, much less that of his colleague the wizard Clothahump."

Buncan repositioned the duar against his back. "Yeah, but since he doesn't believe there's any truth to your story, that means he doesn't think there's any danger, either. How can something that doesn't exist pose any threat?"

"The wizard seemed to think that it does. Besides which the journey itself presents many obstacles that will have to be overcome. But you argue like a solicitor. Clearly you have mastered certain skills."

"Like spellsinging," boasted Buncan proudly.

"Oi, that's right enough!" Squill gestured in the direction of the tree-hooked hammer. "Wot did you just think you saw, guv? Unprovoked prestidigitation?" He slipped an arm around Buncan's waist. "Me sister and I does the singin' an' Buncan 'ere the playin'. We're a bloody magic-masterin' trio, we are."

"We saved your bleedin' life," Neena added pugnaciously.

"And nearly lost your own in the bargain. Upon extended

observation it struck me that you have less than complete control over your conjuring."

"Now see 'ere, mate . . . ," Squill began, but Buncan put out a hand to cut him off.

"No, Squill. Let's be honest from the start."

" 'Onest from the start? Me dad would 'ave a fit."

"Nevertheless." Buncan looked back to the merchant. "We don't claim to be masters. There's still a lot we need to learn. But I've spent my whole life watching and studying my father. All I've wanted to do is be like him. I can do some spellsinging on my own, but the otters are in better voice, and the three of us have spent so much time growing up together that we've been a unit of sorts practically since birth. That's why we were able to scatter those bandits the way we did.

"Sure our control isn't perfect, but neither was my father's when he started. Maybe we're not as proficient as him, but we're a damn sight more powerful than anyone else you're likely to encounter. Do you still want the kind of special help we can offer, and if so, how badly do you need it?" He stopped, watching the merchant intently.

Gragelouth sighed. "Your style and sound of spellsinging is entirely new to me. I admit that it frightens me some."

" 'Ell," said Squill, "it bloody well frightens *us* some. Anythin' new is a little bit frightenin', wot? But it works."

"It nearly worked on you."

"That's a risk we're willing to take," said Buncan. "What about you?"

"You espy clearly my desperate situation." The merchant sighed deeply. "Have any of you ever taken a long journey away from your homes?"

"O' course." Squill responded without hesitation. "Wot does we look like to you, mewlin' babes? Why, our sire is Mudge the Stupendous!"

"Mudge the otter, anyway." Gragelouth turned contemplative. "I have heard that name elsewhere, though usually in connection with extensive debts long owed or assorted ingenious moral outrages."

Neena nodded. "That sounds like Dad right enough."

"Yes, I know of his reputation. Mudge the great thief,

Mudge the great drunk, Mudge the great wencher, Mudge the great . . .''

"Well, at least the operative adjective is still 'great,' '' Squill muttered.

"You have daring and guts,'' Gragelouth admitted. "I wonder how extensive is your quotient of courage.''

"As big as any bloody merchant's,'' Squill shot back testily.

"Your inexperience in matters sorceral and otherwise still concerns me,'' he readily admitted, "but as is clearly evident I have no army of wizards clamoring to accompany me. There are occasions when youth can work to an advantage. So . . . I will allow you to accompany me until such time as your presence becomes more of a burden than an asset.''

Buncan couldn't repress a pleased smile. "I hope we never give you reason to regret your decision, merchant.''

"Right, then!'' chirped Neena. '' 'Tis on to L'bor.''

"L'bor?'' Gragelouth made room for Buncan on the bench seat and for the others behind. "We do not go to L'bor.''

Buncan eyed him. "But this is the road to L'bor. That's where you were heading.''

"To seek wizardly aid and advice. I now have, the Great Counter watch over me, you three to supply that. So there is no reason to waste time journeying to L'bor. We will procure final supplies at Timswitty, which is nearer, before striking out northwestward.''

"Northwest.'' Squill's brows scrunched together. "That means crossin' the Muddletup Moors.''

"That is correct.'' Gragelouth was watching him closely. Watching all of them.

Squill spat over the side of the wagon. "Piece o' carp. A little lousy weather, the projected mental murmurin's o' some discontented fungi, maybe an 'umble but interestin' ogre or two. We've 'eard all about the place from Mudge an' Jon-Tom. They made it through. So will we.''

"Bravado is useful when it translates into assurance and not foolhardy overconfidence.'' He glanced at Buncan. "Do you have money of your own?''

"Very little."

The merchant nodded resignedly. "My resources are limited. Now it seems they are to be stretched still further. We will manage somehow. When pressed we have my wagon for shelter, though it will be crowded with four of us." He shuffled the reins in his hands. "We should move on. Great mysteries await resolution." He chucked the reins and the wagon trundled forward. Squill and Neena settled themselves on some cushions behind the bench seat.

"You hope to capture, or acquire, this Grand Veritable?" Buncan asked their host.

"Nothing so estimable," replied the merchant modestly. "I wish merely to ascertain the truth of gallant Juh Phit's story. Yes, when that moment arrives it will be good to have three young, strong companions by my side."

Buncan repressed a grin. "You forget that I overheard the *whole* conversation."

Gragelouth looked slightly abashed. "Well, there would be nothing immoral in making a profit as well."

Tack strained and creaked as the two dray lizards increased their pace, hissing in protest at Gragelouth's insistent reins.

Buncan settled himself as comfortably as he could on the padded wooden seat. They were on their way! This must be how his father used to feel when starting off on one of his inimitable adventures. Though if he and Clothahump were right there wouldn't be any adventure. Just a lot of hard, difficult traveling.

At least it was a journey. At his age that was adventure enough in itself. Everything they saw from now on would be new and different from everything which had been seen before, and therefore exciting. Different if not startling, stimulating if not overawing.

From their excited chatter behind him he could tell that Squill and Neena felt the same way. With the three of them working together he was confident there was nothing they couldn't handle, no obstacle they could fail to overcome.

This was a common enough feeling among young men his age, so he could hardly be faulted for thinking like an idiot.

"Drive on, Gragelouth! We'll find this Grand Veritable, if it exists, and toss it in your wagon like any other piece of goods. Maybe it'll be worth a few gold pieces."

"All things are possible to those whom life has not yet disenchanted," the merchant murmured condescendingly without looking up from his team. "You are not afraid, then?"

"Afraid? Of what?"

"Of meeting Juh Phit's fate. Of horrors and obstacles unknown yet to be overcome. Of what the Grand Veritable itself may be or be capable of."

"It's only a thing," Buncan replied manfully. "I've never yet encountered a *thing* worth fearing. Besides," he finished airily as he crossed his legs and leaned back, "if it gives us any trouble we'll just spellsing it away."

"Bloody right, mate!" Squill barked belligerently behind him. "We'll conjure the bleedin' wotever it is back into thin air! We can do oversize 'ammers. Why not a Grand Veritable?"

"Whatever it is indeed," murmured Gragelouth. "We may hope to survive long enough to find out."

From the undergrowth several pairs of eyes watched the wagon disappear over the next rise in the road. Their owners were exhausted and battered, scratched and torn from their wild flight through the brush, worn out from avoiding the crush of the thaumaturgical hammer. Some studied that apparition warily where it rested high up in the trees. It had not moved for some time, but where the necromantic arts were concerned nothing, absolutely nothing, could be taken for granted.

"Pulp their eyes!" chattered a ringtail. "Who knew the interfering ones were spellsingers?"

"None could have foreseen it," insisted the coati who led them. His eyes flashed almost as brightly as the diamond in his left canine. "Children! Are you all to be put to flight by children?"

"Not me," said another ringtail. "Not by cubs of any species."

One of the assembled raccoons spoke up. "Sorcery invoked by children is still sorcery, and any sensible person fears that."

"They were lucky, that's all." The coati gestured toward the hanging hammer. "Did you not see how after putting us to flight it turned on its conjurers and tried to kill them? They are inexperienced and callow."

"I'm not interested in what it did after it tried to kill us," growled another raccoon. "I saw what it did to poor Jachay. He was my friend. Now he's a smear on the ground."

"Aye," said a ringtail. "That's sorcery of a kind I've no desire to encounter again. Certainly not for what poor swag a humble merchant's wagon might contain."

The coati raged among his followers. "They caught us by surprise, that's all! A little stealth, a little planning next time, and we'll take them before they can sing up so much as a blue wasp!" His voice dropped ominously. "Hard to spellsing with your throat cut."

"And if we fail?" the ringtail wanted to know. "What then? Will assurances and excuses deliver us?"

"Me, I'm not going to chance finding out." Hefting his war ax, one of the reluctant raccoons turned and stalked off toward the road, not in pursuit of the vanished wagon but south, toward Lynchbany.

"Go then, Wrochek!" the coati yelled after him. "Flee to the safety of a Thieves' Hall and a protected bed."

"Sounds good to me," confessed one of the ringtails. He promptly broke into a trot to catch up with the raccoon.

Their impudent departure started a minor rush. Even the spectacled bear lumbered off to join his defecting friends.

"Even you, Sinwahh, put to flight by infants!" The coati's sneers trailed them remorselessly. "All of you 'brave' robbers, terrified by three cubs and some strange music. Cowards, weaklings! Offspring of discount whores! You'll not share in our bounty!"

"Is there any bounty, o revered leader Chamung?" The one raccoon who'd stayed behind was uncertain.

"Aye," wondered the ringtail who'd remained. "The sloth looked like nothing but a simple merchant."

The coati turned violently on his small constituency, all that remained of his once powerful band. "You believe that? Then you're no better than those spineless fools who've fled. What 'simple merchant' merits rescue by three

spellsingers, even young ones? Do you imagine that the
newcomers risked their lives out of the goodness of their
hearts, or from some imagined debt to the trader?'' He spun
'round to glare at the northern stretch of now empty road.

"There's more at stake here than pots and pans. There's
something in that wagon worth dying for. A lifetime's
savings in gold, perhaps, or precious stones garnered in
Glittergeist trade. Or something even more valuable we
cannot imagine. Something worth the concern of young
wizards.'' He turned back to his two anxious companions.

"You are right, Sisarfi. That wagon is not worth the
attention of common thieves. But I am not common, and by
cleaving to me and my leadership you bask in the glory of
my uncommonness."

"Uh, thanks." Though obviously confused, the ringtail
instinctively sensed it would be impolitic to seek further
clarification. He rubbed at the place on his head where his
left ear used to be. It had been sacrificed many years before
in a badly bollixed attempt at robbing a riverboat.

"Those fools." Chamung turned his gaze to the road
leading south. "They'll find no profit in Lynchbany. They'll
starve. It's a town overrun with thieves, and half of them
don't even have Guild cards. All profit entails some risk,
and we're not afraid of a little risk, are we? Come!" He
stalked determinedly toward the road, aiming north. "We'll
have our profit, and revenge for our poor brother Jachay as
well! Already my mind ferments with provocative scenarios
for entertaining disembowelments."

The ringtail and raccoon exchanged a distinctly hesitant
look before following.

CHAPTER 7

THE WAGON WOUND ITS WAY THROUGH THE BELLWOODS
until a barely visible leftward branching in the road that

Buncan would not even have guessed was there drew
Gragelouth to the west. As their new route was not merely
less traveled but practically nonexistent, their progress was
slow. The terrain remained relatively level and firm.

The Bellwoods did not so much meld into the Moors as
give way abruptly. One moment they were traveling among
healthy oaks and sycamores, belltrees and glissando bushes,
accompanied by the singing of crywail lizards and the hum
of insects, and the next found them passing between cinder-
gray groves and the inert hulks of long-dead trees.

These quickly surrendered the soil to an astonishingly
fecund and fevered forest of giant mushrooms, toadstools,
and shelf fungi, an overgrown morass of macabre mycelium
that throbbed with an unwholesome internal phosphores-
cence. The cloud-flecked blue sky of the Bellwoods had
been obliterated by a pervasive gray-green gloom that
disheartened the soul as well as the eye.

Somewhere above the pestilent fog Buncan knew that the
sun still shone brightly, the clouds still collided and coalesced amiably in a blue sea. It was vital to cling to that
image as they plodded through the baleful olive-green twilight.

Water seeped lugubriously from the crowns of gigantic
mushrooms and other fungi. Ghostly white growths loomed
before them, diseased of appearance, loathsome of smell.
Buncan drew his cape a little tighter around his neck. Even
the otters were subdued. The dampness didn't bother them,
but the gloom did. The dour surroundings muted their
irrepressibly cheerful sibling banter as effectively as the
soggy earth hushed the creaky wheels of Gragelouth's
wagon.

"So these are the Muddletup Moors," Buncan commented
uneasily, not because it was necessary but because the
continued silence was unbearable. Peculiar hisses and
squeakings emanated from the undermorass, while phospho-
rescent shapes darted within, hinting at unpleasant horrors
just beyond the range of ready vision. Displaying a subdued
but unshakable sense of assurance (or hope), Gragelouth
picked their way through the intimidating vegetation.

"I've 'eard all about the Moors, I 'ave." Squill knelt on
the cushions behind the driver's bench, peering between

Buncan and Gragelouth. Like his enthusiasm, his smile was forced. Moisture beaded up on the tips of his whiskers. "Mudge talked about 'em a lot. 'E's been through 'ere an' back an' come out tail intact every time."

" 'E just never said wot a really depressin' place it is," Neena added unhelpfully.

"Therein lies the true danger of the Moors." Gragelouth shifted the reins in his thick fingers, his gaze darting nervously to left and then right. "It infiltrates the mind and weakens the will to resist, to go on. Eventually you give up and just stop. Then the spores come, and the white tendrils, and enter your body. They grow in you and on you and use you up, until nothing is left but a collapsed skeleton. That, too, is eventually returned to the muck."

"Glad to see you don't let it bother you," commented Neena dryly.

Squill's expression was sullen. "I 'ave to admit this ain't the 'appiest place I've ever been."

The atmosphere of the Moors was already beginning to get to them, Buncan realized with a start. The all-pervasive aura of depression and hopelessness pressed down relentlessly.

"How about a song?"

"Cor, that's a good idea, Bunkles." Neena levered herself up from the cushions. "Somethin' merry an' 'olesome."

"No spellsinging," Gragelouth admonished them. He eyed Buncan's duar warily. "I thought it was agreed that was only for emergencies. I admit I am depressed, but not mortally so. Not yet."

"No spellsinging," Buncan agreed. "Just something to buoy us up and beat back this gloom."

"That could be useful," the merchant reluctantly conceded.

"Right." Buncan struck the strings, flinging frisky chords into the brooding air like a noble casting gold pieces at an impecunious crowd. Behind him the otters began to harmonize playfully.

"Got no time to be sad today
There's a time to be sad and a time to play
Place to be cryin', place to be dyin'

We're gonna get outta here 'cause we be tryin'
To motivate this wagon on its way."

The music drifted out across the Moors, penetrating and
pushing aside the gloom as if it were a dirty, rotting curtain.
The weight of the oleaginous air they were breathing light-
ened perceptibly, while the nearest sphacelated fungi seemed
to recoil from the unrelenting cheerfulness, a perception that
turned out to be anything but imaginary.

"Will you *stop* playing that music?" pleaded the growth
on their immediate right.

"Blimey, Mudge were right." Neena examined the giant
toadstool. "They can communicate when they want to."

"How can you sing?" declaimed a chorus of shelf fungi
from nearby, "when there's no hope left? When all is
doomed?"

A cluster of mushrooms no higher than a dray lizard's
belly chimed in. "When existence defines itself through
unending misery."

"If you put it like that," Buncan found himself muttering.
A paw came down hard on his shoulder.

"Watch it, mate!" Squill's bright eyes stared into his
own. "Remember that's 'ow they work, the Moors. If the
atmosphere doesn't get you, then they try fatalistic philoso-
phy. That's wot Mudge always told us."

Neena glared challengingly at the rutilant fungi. "There
can't be depression where there's music. Keep playin',
Bunkole."

Buncan looked down at his duar. The polished surface of
the unique instrument seemed dulled, the strings uneven and
fraying. "I don't know if this is doing any good."

This time Squill grabbed him by the shoulders and half
spun him around on the bench. The duar bonged against
Gragelouth's knee. The sloth winced but said nothing,
resolutely tending to his driving.

"Fok your 'don't knows,' mate! This 'ere swamp is the
mother of all indecision. Wake up, and play!"

Buncan nodded, blinking. The effect of the Moors, he
realized, was so insidious you weren't aware of what the
place was doing to you even as it happened. Fortunately,

otters had a *very* strong natural resistance to depression. He directed his attention to the duar with a vengeance.

Immediately the air seemed brighter, clearer. The grim fog rolled back and fungi in the wagon's path crawled or oozed aside. Seeing that the music kept the creeping enervation at bay, even Gragelouth made an attempt to join in the singing.

They were feeling much better when the Moors responded, not with additional intimations of infectious ennui, but with music of its own: a distant, wild baying. It stopped their own singing cold. A prickly clamminess crept down Buncan's back like a rain-soaked centipede.

"Wot were that?" Squill murmured, wide-eyed. "Sounds like somethin' that crawled out o' river-bottom mud." He looked to the merchant.

Gragelouth was sniffing the air. "I do not recognize the sound. Nor do I look forward to encountering its source." As he finished, the noise came again: flagrant, whetted, and definitely closer.

Buncan shook the sloth's arm. "Don't stop now. Not here. Can't we go any faster?"

"My team was bred for endurance and not sprints," the sloth told him. "You can see that for yourself. They are making the best speed they can." He glanced nervously sideways. "There is something about that sound which is more evil than mere depression."

"Penetratin', wotever it is," Neena observed as the wild baying echoed through the morass. It definitely was not the wind: Wind was unknown in the Moors, where even a stray zephyr grew quickly depressed and died. The howling was dark and deep and rich with carnivorous import.

"I see somethin' movin'!" Squill rose and pointed to their left.

A flash of movement among the undergrowth, a glimpse of bright red fireflies; then nothing. Gragelouth sat rigid on the bench. There was nothing he could do to speed his plodding, slow-witted team along the slick, potholed path. His nose twitched.

"I sense many presences."

Buncan eyed him curiously. "You can sense presences?"

"A metaphor, young human. Can't you feel them out there, around us?"

"I don't feel anything except damp depression." He fingered the duar nervously.

"No aura of menace? No overweening sense of incipient doom?"

"No more so than what we've been feeling since we left the Bellwoods." The baying and howling was constant around them now, drowning out the other background sounds of the Moors.

"Then you may be a spellsinger, or half a one, anyway," the sloth murmured, "but your perception leaves much to be desired."

So does your breath, Buncan wanted to say, but he was interrupted by Squill's sudden shout.

"Crikey!" The otter was pointing again.

This time Buncan had no trouble picking out the pair of burning red eyes directly in front of them. They bobbed slightly as they advanced on the wagon. Unable to turn either to right or left, Gragelouth tugged on the reins and brought the cumbersome vehicle to a grinding halt. As he did so, the owner of the fiery gaze appeared out of the mist.

Standing just under five and a half feet tall, the hound had teeth that gleamed in the baleful light. Prominent fangs hung from the upper jaw. The canine specter wore a muckledidun shirt and pants tucked into high boots. Protruding from the trousers, the short tail switched back and forth like a metronome. Or a scythe.

A short sword with an unusually heavy, sharply curved blade hung with studied indifference from one paw. It would take a powerful individual to wield such a weapon with one hand, Buncan knew. His own fingers rested on the duar's strings as he exchanged a meaningful glance with the otters. They nodded understanding, though there was no reason to spellsing yet. While the Moor dweller's aspect was intimidating, he'd made nothing in the way of an overt threat. Yet.

A second pair of eyes materialized out of the mist. Another, and another, and more. All were hounds, though of varying shape, coloration, and size. All were heavily armed.

The one who confronted them had a spiked collar encircling his neck. The spikes had been filed to fine points. None of the others wore anything like formal armor, though Buncan noted an abundance of spiked leg-pieces and wristbands.

Taken in toto they were an altogether disagreeable-looking lot. It was clear they were not out haunting the Moors in search of a casual day's stroll. By the same token, it was difficult to countenance the possibility that they actually lived there, though their appearance suggested a condition and lifestyle even the Moors would be hard-pressed to worsen.

Advancing around the team, the lead hound finally halted to confront the wagon's occupants. As he looked them slowly up and down, Buncan could see the play of muscles across the broad chest and thickly bunched upper arms. As it stared it methodically slapped the heavy blade of its curved sword against an open palm.

"We don't get many travelers out here in the Moors." The voice was a rough, curdled growl, the words crumbling against the heavy palate like gravel in a crusher.

"Not enough," quipped one of the others. Low, ominous laughter came from the rest of the band, which by now had completely surrounded the wagon.

"Where are you headed?" inquired the leader.

"To the northwest." Gragelouth kept his eyes down, avoiding the hound's burning gaze, the reins of his team clutched tightly in his thick, furry fingers.

"That's not very informative. Where to the northwest?"

"Does it matter?"

"No, I suppose not."

Buncan leaned forward. "We've come a long way and have a lot farther to go. If you're bandits, say so now and we'll give you our money." Gragelouth turned sharply to his youthful companion, his pupils widening.

"Can't step anywhere these days without 'avin' to scrape scum off your feet," Squill muttered.

The hound glared up at him. "What was that?"

Squill smiled pleasantly. "I said that it were 'ard to get around these days."

The hound's intensity diminished, but only slightly. "It

certainly is if your destination brings you through the Moors. None come this way who can go otherwise.''

"To go completely around the Moors would have taken too much time,'' Gragelouth mumbled deferentially.

"And yet there are many dangers here.'' Apparently the leader was in a conversational mood.

A hound with a mottled black-and-brown visage edged nearer. A grisly scar ran from the top of his skull down across his face and clear around to the back of his neck. Its pattern and angle suggested a botched attempt at decapitation.

"More dangers than you can imagine,'' he grunted.

"Time is important to us,'' Gragelouth replied lamely.

"We won't delay you long.'' The leader grinned hideously. "Just hand over everything you own.''

Gragelouth swallowed, looking resigned. "I have some money...''

"Oh, we don't just want your money,'' the hound explained. "We'll take your personal effects, too, and your weapons, and your clothes. And I'll personally have that interesting-looking musical device there.'' A clawed finger singled out Buncan's duar. "Also your wagon and team.''

"Don't tell me you need to get somewhere in a hurry, too,'' muttered Neena.

"Not at all.'' The hound stroked the flank of the nearest dray lizard. It bore the caress complacently. "But these look quite savory. You know, there's not a lot for a carnivore to dine on out here in the Moors, and we prefer to avoid the cities. For some mysterious reason town dwellers are shocked by our attitudes and appearance.'' Several of the hounds within hearing range chuckled unpleasantly.

"In fact,'' the creature continued remorselessly, his eyes burning into Buncan's own, "you look quite edible yourselves.''

"Oi,'' Neena husked under her breath, "we've fallen in among a lot of bloody cannibals!''

"And just what is a cannibal, my fuzzy little hors d'oeuvre?'' the hound challenged her. "A term charged with all manner of absurdly sensationalist undertones. There was a time in the far distant past when it was the natural order of things for those with warm blood to devour others of kind. Meat is meat. We who are forced to dwell in the dank depths of the Moors cannot afford to discriminate. Where consumption is concerned we are wholly democratic: We'll eat anyone.'' He was still smiling.

"So we'll have everything you own, and we'll have you as well." He glanced toward the strings of utensils dangling from the rear and sides of the wagon. "It was thoughtful of you to provide the means for your own preparation. At least you will expire in familiar surroundings.''

"We won't go without a fight!" Squill rose sharply behind the driver's bench, an arrow notched in his bow. Neena rose beside him, similarly prepared.

"Oh my, oh dear." The hound tut-tutted as he took a step backward. His companions chortled darkly. "The terror! The fear! Can it be we are surprised?" He caressed the heavy curved blade of his sword. "All of us against three cubs and an old sloth? How ever will we survive? One trifle before we begin, though. I ask the names of those who would provide entertainment before dinner.''

"I'm Squill, son o' Mudge. This 'ere's me sister Neena. That's Mudge the Traveler, Mudge the Conqueror, Mudge the All-Revengin' to you.''

"Never heard of him," the hound responded briskly.

It was Buncan's turn. "I'm Buncan Ottermusk Meriweather. Son of the greatest spellsinger in all of time and space, Jonathan Thomas Meriweather.''

"All those names." The hound snorted. "Never heard of him either. We're not much for celebrity here in the Moors." He glanced to Buncan's right. "And you? Speak up, sloth.''

The merchant flinched. "I am called Gragelouth. A simple barterer in household goods and services.''

"Well, tonight you'll be called supper." Within the hound's jaws, filed teeth gleamed menacingly.

Buncan was whispering to his friends. "Lyrics? Don't you have any lyrics yet? What's keeping you?''

"I can't think o' any songs about 'ounds," Neena hissed. "These 'ere blokes are about the first o' their kind I've ever encountered.''

" 'Ow do you get rid o' 'ounds?" Squill wondered aloud.

"I don't know either, but you'd better think of something

quick. There's too many of them for arrows, and they make the ones who tried to rob Gragelouth back in the Bellwoods look like country bumpkins.'' He turned back to the leader, trying to stall for time.

"Now it's my turn. Who threatens us, with no regard for our ancestry or the revenge that will surely follow if any harm befalls us?''

"Nothing follows into the Moors,'' the hound growled belligerently. "Not kings seeking reluctant subjects nor sorcerers searching for strayed apprentices. Certainly not revenge. This place is the womb of bleakness, and we are its offspring. We who survive here do so only by giving in to woe. It suffuses our very beings. So do not think to appeal to our better nature, because we have none. Though I admit that your presence makes us feel better. It's rare we come across food that has not already begun to rot.''

"That doesn't tell me who you are.'' Behind him, the otters composed frantically.

"We are all hounds here, as you can see.'' The leader gestured expansively. "We are the hounds that haunt your dreams and chase you through your nightmares. We supply the howling you hear in your sleep, the growls that make you toss and turn uneasily, the shrill unexpected barks that you take for those of your neighbor.'' He pointed with his sword.

"There stands the hound of the Mitrevilles, and next to him the hound of the Toonervilles. Off to the left waits the hound of the Cantervilles.'' He went on to identify each member of the band by name.

It granted the travelers a few precious additional minutes. "Anything?'' Buncan whispered to the otters.

"Wot is there to think of?'' Despair had overcome Gragelouth, and the merchant held his woolly head in his paws. "All is lost. These are no ordinary brigands. It will take more than music to overcome them. They have remorse and anguish on their side.'' He sighed heavily. "So much work, a lifetime of struggle, only to end up as a dog's dinner. An inglorious finale. I regret that I have brought you to such a state.''

"We're not there yet," Buncan told him. "My friends will think of *something*."

"Not me, mate," said Squill helplessly.

"Me neither," added Neena. "Wot about you, Buncan? Can't you think of anything?"

"I'm not the singer."

"But you could give us the words!" she pleaded. "A suggestion, a direction we could take. Anythin'!"

"I don't know anything about hounds," he whispered desperately. "I spent all my time learning how to play the duar, not make up—" He broke off, remembering unexpectedly. "There is this old song. I remember Jon-Tom used to sing it to me when I was young. *Real* young. A baby song. It never made any sense to me, but it might fit this situation. A little. It's all I can think of."

"No time for debate," Squill pointed out. "Try it."

Buncan's fingers rested tensely on the duar. "It's no rap," he warned them.

Neena smiled wolfishly. "We'll take care o' that. Just give us some bleedin' words we can work with."

"It goes like this." He proceeded to whisper what he could remember of the saccharine little tune.

Squill looked doubtful. "If you don't mind me sayin' so, the tone ain't exactly sorceral."

"Rap it," he urged them, "and let me play. We've got to try something." He indicated the leader, who was winding up his litany.

". . . And I," the thick-set creature concluded, "am the hound of the Baskervilles."

Buncan frowned. "I may have heard of you."

The hound looked pleased. "So our reputation reaches even beyond the Moors. That is gratifying, but not unexpected. The peculiar mists and winds of the Muddletup transport much that is within without." He raised his sword. "Now that you know who will be dining upon you, we can begin. It is time to substitute butchery for conversation. But tremble not. We are not brutal. We will make this as quick as possible. When you have determined that resistance is not only foolish but painful, simply put down your arms and lay

your heads out parallel to the earth. I will do the honors
myself. My colleagues tend to sloppiness.''

Buncan put up a hand to forestall the hound's approach.
''Wait! A last song before dying. If you would be thought
generous, grant us this one final amusement.''

The hound frowned. ''Music does not do well here. The
air weighs it down. But if you prefer that to battle, have at
it.''

''Oi, thanks,'' said Squill. ''Me, I'd rather go out with a
song.'' He set his bow and arrow aside.

''Be quick about it,'' the hound grumbled. ''My stomach
complains.''

Buncan began to play. Recalling the lyrics he had supplied, the otters joined in, transposing and transforming,
engendering a rap unlike anything they'd tried before.

> '' 'Ow much, 'ow much, 'ow much?
> 'Ow much is that doggie, that one there
> Can't compare, to the one over there
> In the window, dude, in the window, where
> You can't compare any one you knowed
> Before the war, to the one in the window.
> Don't you see; 'ow much is she?''

The hounds looked at once bored and baffled as Buncan
piled chord upon chord, uplifting the strange lyrics, providing them with an irresistible forward thrust that would no
doubt have astonished the composers of the original ditty.

Nothing happened.

No giant otherdimensional carnivorous canine materialized to terrify the hounds into submission, no befanged
beasts oozed up out of the muck to attack them individually.
Nor did the words result in the conjuration of some ensorceled
offensive-minded device like a giant hammer.

''Put your hearts into it!'' Buncan hissed angrily at his
companions. Neena responded with an obscene gesture born
of desperation as much as frustration.

This is it, he thought tiredly to himself. *Not only are we
destined to go no farther, we hardly got started. Put a few
common forest bandits to flight and you think you can take*

on the world. Their demise would be as abrupt as it would be degrading.

A purplish-red mist began to form between the wagon and the leader of the hounds.

The dray lizards started in harness, hissing and spitting wildly, forcing the startled Gragelouth to work his reins to maintain control. The hound hopped backward, thrusting his sword out defensively in front of him. Nervous mutterings sounded from the members of his band.

"Keep singing, no matter what it is, keep singing!" Buncan urged his friends. The otters needed no encouragement, plying variation upon variation on the now fully possessed melody. In their own way they were as entranced as the hounds.

What *was* it they were spellsinging forth?

The mist swirled aimlessly, as if searching for a seed, a core, to fix upon. At last it began to coalesce. Silhouettes appeared, gradually congealing into shapes that boasted both density and weight.

They flashed no armor, wielded no weapons. In fact, they were hardly clad at all, and what they did wear was designed more to flaunt than to conceal. Buncan counted a good dozen of the ghostly figures, precisely one for each member of the voracious circle.

While not all were hounds, each was flatteringly representative of the canine persuasion. Even his inexperienced eyes found their attire of silks and satins provocative.

In addition to which, each and every one of them was fully in heat.

The effect the dozen seductive bitches had on the assembled hounds was nothing short of apocalyptic. Buncan watched as the first let his sword drop from his benumbed fingers. Wearing an utterly stupefied expression, he stumbled forward into the waiting arms of the bitch nearest him. She embraced him with the ease and skill of an experienced professional.

The leader made an effort to save his distracted band, raging among them with words and blows. Then a tall, immaculately coiffed Afghan slunk forward to give him a gentle chuck under his chin. His sword rose but his gaze descended. His nose twitched convulsively, at which point he had no choice but to switch weapons.

"Get moving!" Buncan whispered tersely to the mesmerized merchant without slowing his playing.

Gragelouth looked blank for a moment, then chucked the reins with becoming fervor. Tack creaked and groaned as the lizards picked up their feet. The wagon trundled forward.

No one jumped in their path or made any effort to interfere with them.

Leaning out of the bench seat and looking backward, Buncan thought he saw the hound of the Baskervilles trying to break free of the orgy. The wild-eyed leader went down under the weight of not one but two of the expensive bitches-of-the-evening Buncan and the otters had called forth. He did not reemerge.

As they fled unhindered into the vastness of the Moors the travelers heard one last time the collective baying of the hounds, but that hitherto mournful echo sounded now rather more enthusiastic than threatening.

Only when they were well away did Buncan put his duar aside, wondering as he did so what would happen when the seductive spirits he and the otters had called forth ceased their frenetic ministrations and finally demanded payment for their services. He was certain they would, for the lyrics of the spellsong had been forthright in their mention of price.

Squill clapped him on the back. "That were bloody brilliant, mate! Did you see their faces? Be buggered if I don't envy 'em."

Neena simply shook her head in disgust. "I'm surprised you didn't join in, bro'."

Squill's nose wrinkled. "The timin's 'ardly right. When they finish, that lot's gonna be even 'ungrier than before."

"I didn't have any idea it would work." Buncan protested modestly. "That wasn't exactly the kind of cost-related result I would have expected, either. But it was the only 'hound'-related song I could think of at the time." He shrugged. "That's spellsinging for you. By the way, you two were amazing."

"Well, o' course," Neena agreed without hesitation.

"It was just a baby song," Buncan added.

"Childhood imagery contains much power," Gragelouth commented. "I must apologize."

"For what?" Buncan wanted to know.

"For ever doubting your spellsinging abilities. It is evident now that your youth is not overmuch of a meliorating factor."

"Beg pardon?" said Squill. His sister cuffed him.

"We got lucky," Buncan confessed. "We might just as easily be someone's dinner."

"Do not make light of what you have done. Your talents are undeniable." For the first time since Buncan had set eyes on him, Gragelouth looked almost happy.

" 'E's right, Buncoos." Neena leaned forward and put her short arms around him. Her whiskers tickled the back of his neck. "Ol' Clothabump may be more experienced, and Jon-Tom slicker, but we three are the greatest spellsingin' *team* that ever was."

"Let's not get carried away by a couple of lucky successes," Buncan chided her. But he had to admit he felt good about their prospects.

"So we've proved ourselves to you, droopy-lips?" Neena prodded the merchant.

"We have barely begun." Gragelouth tried to avoid her teasing finger. He didn't like to be touched, Buncan had noticed. "There will doubtless be other dangers to deal with, other confrontations."

"Maybe not," said Squill cheerily. "Maybe it'll be smooth swimmin' all the way to the northwest. 'Ell, we're about through the Moors and we've 'andled not one but two lot o' bandits on the way."

"Perhaps you are right." The merchant sat a little straighter on his bench. "Though it is not in my nature, perhaps I should be more assured."

"Do wonders for your social life, mate." Squill put a paw on the sloth's shoulder. "You just tend to the drivin' and we'll take care o' any nasties that 'ave the nerve to cross us."

Gragelouth nodded slowly. "I only hope that your skills ripen as rapidly as your presumption, river-runner."

CHAPTER 8

FOR A TIME IT SEEMED AS IF SQUILL WAS RIGHT TO BE so confident. The rest of their journey through the Muddletup Moors proceeded without incident, marred only by a damaged wheel that the merchant quickly and efficiently repaired. As they pushed on, Buncan played frequently and the otters sang to keep the enervating atmosphere of the Moors at bay. Of the hounds there was no sign, nor did anything more inimical than a bellicose toadstool attempt to hinder their progress.

Eventually they emerged from the dour surroundings of the Moors onto a wide, lightly vegetated plain that was different from any country Buncan or the otters had ever seen. Having grown up in the lush confines of the Bellwoods, they were immediately intrigued by the stunted trees and dense, dry-leaved bushes and grasses that covered the land.

"Oi, is this the desert?" Neena asked wonderingly as the wagon rattled down the barely visible track. "I've 'eard about the desert, I 'ave." Behind them a low bank of permanent, purulent fog obscured the western reaches of the Moors. Bright sunshine had banished the last psychic echoes of manic-depressive fungi from their minds. It was a pleasure to let down their mental guard.

Pirouetting breezes swept blue-stained dirt into occasional dust devils. Broad-winged flying lizards sculpted predatory patterns in the air, searching for smaller, gravity-bound prey below. Slim, hasty creatures with multiple legs scurried out of the wagon's path to vanish down camouflaged holes and burrows.

"No, this isn't the desert," Gragelouth patiently explained. "There's far too much water present, and the abundance of plants reflects that. I would call this upland scrubland."

He nodded in the direction of high, chapparal-covered

mesas. Where flowing water had eroded the hillsides multi-colored sandstone sparkled in the sun like the layers of a coronation cake. "Pretty, that."

Buncan agreed, and would have enjoyed spending a day or two exploring such country, but they had no time to linger. In any event, the otters did not share his enthusiasm for casual sight-seeing. The absence of running water made them nervous.

The landscape changed little over the next few days. Desert it might not be, but it was more than hot enough for everyone. Fortunately, water in greater quantities soon showed itself in the small streams that ran down from the mesa tops, and in shaded pools deep enough to offer the otters an occasional reinvigorating plunge.

"Doesn't anyone live out here?" Buncan asked the question of their guide on the fourth day out from the Moors. The wagon squeaked in counterpoint to his query.

"There are tales of communities," Gragelouth replied, "but this is little-known country. Civilized folk keep to the Bellwoods, or travel south to the Tailaroam and thence down to the Glittergeist or up the river to Polastrindu."

"Don't see why anyone would choose to live 'ere." Neena sniffed distastefully as she studied the uninviting terrain. "Too dry, too isolated, wot?"

"Some people prefer isolation," the merchant told her. "I have traded with such."

"Each to their own tastes, I suppose."

"This track we're following must run somewhere," her brother observed sagely, "little used though it is."

Sure enough, not another day had passed before they topped a low rise between boulders that gave way to a view of a verdant valley. Two broad streams meandered through well-tended fields, which surrounded a town of surprising dimensions.

Behind a smooth-faced white wall with a curved crest towered buildings of three and four stories, all plastered and painted the same stark, reflective white. Under the midday sun the city shone so brightly that the approaching travelers had to shield their eyes against it. Gragelouth in particular suffered considerably.

Like everything else, the sight only served to inspire the otters. "Where's this, or maybe I should say, wot's this?" Squill's short tail twitched excitedly.

"I do not know," the merchant admitted. "As I have already said, I have never been this way before."

"Sure is well kept-up," Buncan commented as they followed the faint wagon track toward the nearest city gate. He was well aware that the otters were avidly eyeing the nearest of the two main streams. "I don't know about anyone else, but I could do with a swim."

Tentative as always, Gragelouth pursed thick lips as he considered the prospect. "The local farmers may not like people bathing in their irrigation water."

"Chill out," Squill admonished him. "We'll turn off before we reach the city wall and slip in somewhere up-stream. No one'll see us."

"They may not mind. The community looks quite prosperous," Gragelouth had to admit.

As Squill surmised, their brief swim passed unnoticed. All were in high good spirits as they dried themselves in the sun while the merchant drove the wagon back toward the city. There were numerous tracks to follow now. Farmers' wagons, Buncan thought.

As they approached a city gate other vehicles could be seen entering and leaving: wagons piled high with produce or supplies, two-wheeled carts, riders on individual mounts, preoccupied pedestrians. As was typical, Buncan was taller than any of them. His unusual height, he knew, was a gift of his father's otherworldly origins.

It was Squill who first noticed the anomaly.

"Crikey," he exclaimed in surprise as they drew near enough to distinguish individuals. "They're all bloody rodents!"

It was true. The city was populated entirely by rats, mice, squirrels, and their relations. There were no canines, felines, primates, or ungulates; no representatives of any of the other great tribes of the warm-blooded. Such species isolation was unprecedented in their experience. It was almost as if the inhabitants had chosen to segregate themselves. Despite the city's evident prosperity, Buncan knew that such a sequestered population would inevitably make for cultural famine.

Back in the civilized world the representatives of the rodentia had often been looked down upon, until they had helped to turn the tide against the Plated Folk at the battle of the Jo-Troom Pass. So it was most unexpected to find so many of them living like this, isolated from the great and wondrous diversity of the wider world.

Neena was standing on the cushions back of the bench. "Look at them. No expressions o' individuality at all."

Indeed, regardless of tribe everyone they saw was clad entirely in white sheets or robes. These extended in unbroken fashion from head to foot save for slits for ears and tail, and an oval opening for the face. White sandals shod feet regardless of size or shape. Within this all-pervasive whiteness there was room for some variation, with buttons, belts, lace, and other trim of exquisite detail and design providing the only distinctiveness in the absence of color. In addition to their voluminous robes, some additionally wore masks or scarves of embroidered white, perhaps to keep out the dust while working in the fields, Buncan surmised.

More notable even than the unvarying whiteness was the immaculate condition of the city and its citizens. Buncan could not find a spot of mud, a chunk of decaying plaster, or a blighted structure anywhere as they passed through the unbarred gate into the city proper. A pair of squat capybara guards followed the wagon with their eyes but made no move to confront it. Their ceremonial pikes were fashioned of birch wood tipped with blades of sharpened milk quartz.

A warren of structures began immediately inside the gate. Modest or excessive, all were plastered or painted white. Awnings of white cloth shaded small street-side stalls or upper-story windows framed with intricately carved white shutters. The street down which they plodded was cleaner than the tables of most taverns in Lynchbany.

"This whiteness must have religious or social significance," Gragelouth was commenting. "Such uniformity could not persist in the absence of some pressure to conform."

"Foking dull, I calls it," said Squill.

"White reflects the sun and keeps everything cooler,"

Gragelouth pointed out, unintentionally defending the city's inhabitants.

"Wonder what they must be making of us," Buncan mused aloud. "Judging from the stares we've been drawing since we arrived, they don't see many outsiders here."

"Who'd come 'ere," Neena pointed out, "if you 'ad to punch through the Moors first?"

"All this uniformity makes me uncomfortable," said Gragelouth. "It implies a rigidity of thinking inimical to trade. We will linger only long enough to replenish our supplies."

"Be good to sleep in a real bed," Squill commented, "not to mention 'avin' somethin' decent to eat for a change."

Gragelouth brought the wagon to a halt before a two-story structure with no windows in the upper floor. Several other vehicles and their reptiles were tethered nearby. A large, powerful monitor lizard hissed but made room for the newcomers.

"I am a merchant by trade," he responded with some dignity. "Not a cook." He climbed down from the bench seat.

Locals hurrying up and down the street on business stared unabashedly, their snouts and whiskers protruding from their hooded attire. Buncan dismounted to stand next to Gragelouth. He could overhear but not decipher the whispered comments of the passersby.

"Crikey, maybe they're afraid of us." Squill rested one paw on the hilt of his short sword.

"No, I do not get that feeling. It is something else." Gragelouth spoke as he considered the building before them. "I wonder if we are welcome here, or if it might not be better to move on."

"Should be able to find out quickly enough." Buncan placed himself directly in the path of a three-foot-tall mouse with a peculiar bushy tail. It halted uncertainly, gazing up at the towering human.

"What place is this? We're strangers to this city," Buncan hoped he sounded firm but friendly.

The mouse gestured with a tiny hand on which reposed half a dozen exquisitely fashioned rings of white gold.

"Why, this is Hygria of the Plains, primate. Now please, let me pass." He looked anxiously, not at Buncan, but at those of his fellow citizens who had gathered in front of the windowless building to watch.

Buncan didn't move. "A moment of your time, sir. We need to avail ourselves of your city's hospitality. Can you tell us where we might find suitable food and lodging?"

The mouse swallowed, turned. "From this point inward the streets grow narrow. You will have to leave your animals and vehicle here. As to your personal needs, you might try the Inn of the All-Scouring Beatitudes. It sometimes will accommodate travelers. Second avenue on your left." The rodent hesitated. "Though were I you I would not linger here, but would take your wagon and depart soonest."

"Why? We just got here." Buncan's gaze narrowed.

The mouse seemed more anxious than ever to be on his way. "You have broken the law."

Buncan looked to Gragelouth, who shook his head uncomprehendingly. "What law? We haven't been here long enough to break any laws." Those citizens assembled in front of the building were suddenly acting furtive, as if simply hovering in the vicinity of the outlandish visitors constituted in itself a kind of daring complicity in outrages anonymous.

"I have done my courtesy." The mouse abruptly folded both hands beneath its white robe, bowed, and scurried off to his left, dodging before Buncan could again block his path.

"Cor, come 'ave a look!" Turning, Buncan saw the otters standing beneath a canopy across the street. Sauntering over, he saw that they were inspecting the wares of a very nervous jerboa vegetable seller. There were white onions, and white grapes, and a kind of oblong white melon, but there were also peppers and tomatoes and other more familiar produce.

"At least *everythin'* 'ere ain't white," Squill commented.

Neena held up something like a pale-white peppermint-striped cucumber. " 'Ow much for this, madame?"

The jerboa fluttered her paws at them, the tall turban atop

her head threatening to collapse at any moment. "Go 'way, go 'way!" She was peering fretfully down the street.

" 'Ere now, don't be like that," said Neena. "I'm just 'ungry, is all." She presented a fistful of coins. "Ain't none o' this good 'ere?"

"Yes, yes, it's all good." With an air of desperation the jerboa reached out and plucked a couple of minor coins from Neena's hand, practically shoving the vegetable at her. "Now go, go away."

The three nonplussed shoppers rejoined Gragelouth. "Well, they ain't 'ostile." Neena gnawed on the blunt end of the peculiar vegetable. "This ain't 'alf bad. Kind o' a nutty flavor."

"Fits you, then." Squill never missed an opportunity. "No, they're not 'ostile. Just bloomin' antisocial."

Buncan was gazing down the street. "Let's see if we can find that inn." He called back to the vegetable seller. "If we leave our property here, will it be safe?"

The merchant's previous concern became outrage. "Of course! This is Hygria. No one would approach, much less try to plunder, anything so unclean as your belongings."

"Certainly are proud of their cleanliness," Buncan commented as they started down the street.

"Yes," agreed Gragelouth. "One might almost say they make a fetish of it."

"Makes it inviting for visitors."

"Does it?" the merchant murmured. "I wonder."

As they made their way down the narrow avenue, Buncan looked for but was unable to find a spot of garbage, junk, or misplaced dirt. Hygria was without a doubt the cleanest community he had ever seen. By comparison Lynchbany, a comparatively well-kept forest town, was a fetid cesspool.

Gragelouth turned to glance back up the street at where they'd left their wagon. "I think that female was telling the truth. I believe our goods will be safe. Not that you three have anything to worry about. All you brought along you carry with you."

"Wot's this?" Squill's tone was mocking. "Trust? That's not like you, merchant."

The sloth indicated the narrow avenue. "As we were told,

this byway is too narrow for my wagon. There are only pedestrians here. And I found that stall owner's expression of distaste convincing.''

Neena let her gaze wander from structure to structure, each as pristine white as its neighbor. "This place could use a little livenin' up. It's so bleedin' stiff and clean it makes me teeth 'urt.''

They found the inn, its entrance clearly marked by a sign of carved white wood which overhung the street. But before they had a chance to enter, their attention was drawn to a singular entourage approaching from the far end of the street.

A line of half a dozen white-shrouded mice and cavis marching abreast was coming toward them. With fanatical single-mindedness each attacked his or her portion of the avenue with a short-handled, wide-bristled broom. They were followed by a number of mice, pacas, and muskrats armed with wheeled containers and double-handed scoops.

Advancing with the precision of a military drill unit, this furry assemblage was doing everything but polishing the smooth stones that paved the street. Buncan strained but could not see beyond the wispy cloud of dust they raised. Perhaps the polishers, he reflected only half sarcastically, would come later.

"Blimey, would you take a look at that," Squill muttered. "That's carryin' cleanliness too far.''

"No wonder that little jerboa thought us unclean," Buncan added.

Neena couldn't repress a whiskery smirk. "Maybe that's why they call this kind o' country scrubland." She ducked a blow from her brother.

Buncan confronted a well-dressed, slightly corpulent capybara as he emerged from the cool darkness of the inn. His fur was cut in bangs over his forehead.

He eyed Buncan and his companions askance. "Where have you people come from?''

"Out o' the Moors," said Squill proudly.

The capy squinted at him, his blunt muzzle twitching. "I doubt that, but it's obvious you're not from around here.''

Buncan indicated the approaching street sweepers. "How often do they do that?"

"Several times each day, of course." The capy sniffed disdainfully, careful to keep his distance from the tall human. "That's the hygiene patrol."

Squill started to snigger. "Patrol? What do they do when they find dirt? Arrest it?" Gragelouth made anxious silencing motions at the otter, which Squill naturally ignored.

"As strangers here, you self-evidently do not understand. We are proud of our ways." The capy sniffed. "If I were you, I'd get out of sight as soon as possible."

"Why?" Buncan recalled the mouse's warning.

"Because you do not measure up to local standards. Now, if you will excuse me."

Buncan stepped aside and watched the capy waddle away up the street. "Wonder what he meant by that."

"I do not know," said Gragelouth, "but we had better move or we are liable to find ourselves swept up together with the dust and dirt."

They entered into the inn just as the patrol reached them, watched as it literally swept past. Their precision was impressive, Buncan had to admit. As soon as they'd passed he stepped back out into the street, following them with his gaze.

"I think that's it."

A finger tapped him on the shoulder. "Not quite, mate."

Squill nodded down the street. Advancing in the sweepers' wake was a squad of eight pike-armed pacas, squirrels, degus, capys, and assorted others. They marched in two lines, one behind the other, blocking the street from side to side, their white uniforms immaculate. Each wore an inscribed headband beneath his flowing headgear. The insignia of a large rat marching in front gleamed golden.

Buncan met his gaze evenly as the entire squad halted outside the inn. The rat's disgust as he inspected the travelers was almost palpable.

"Strangers," he muttered. "Just arrived?"

"That's right," admitted Buncan. He suddenly sensed Gragelouth trying to fade into the shadows behind him.

A pair of degus stepped inside, squeezing past the otters. "You'll have to come with us," the rat told him.

Buncan frowned. "What for? We were just going to see about a couple of rooms."

"Accommodation will be provided for you." The rat barked an order, and the business ends of seven pikes inclined in their direction.

Buncan put his hand on his sword, felt Gragelouth close beside him. "We are deep within the city. Fighting will do us no good here." As usual, the merchant made sense. Buncan forced himself to relax. "They may only wish to question us," the sloth went on. "Perhaps we will have to pay a fine. Whatever they want, it would be premature to start a ruckus."

"Speak for yourself," said Squill, but he did not reach for his own weapons.

"We haven't done anything." Buncan took a step forward. The three-and-a-half-foot-tall rat retreated instantly from the towering primate, pulling a silver whistle from a pocket and blowing hard. The shrill blast echoed down the street.

Additional soldiers materialized from nowhere, until the travelers were no longer merely surrounded but hemmed in.

"Hey, take it easy!" Like his companions, Buncan was taken aback by the unexpected and overwhelming display of force. Notions of reaching not for his sword but his duar were hindered by the proximity of so many weapons and the edgy attitude of those wielding them. "We'll come with you."

"A wise decision." The rat looked satisfied.

The white-clad troops formed an impenetrable mass both in front of and behind the sullen travelers as they were convoyed down the street. "You still haven't told us what we're supposed to have done," Buncan pressed the rat in command.

"Done?" The commander looked back at him. "You offend by your very presence. Your existence degrades, indeed mocks, all decent community standards."

" 'Ere now, guv," said Squill, "are you implyin' that me and me mates are dirty?"

"No," replied the rat. "I'm saying that your condition is

filthy, execrable, squalid, and unclean. Your odor is rank and your feet defile the ground wherever they make contact. As for your breath, it is of a loathsomeness so lavish that I do not possess terms of sufficient severity with which to describe it.''

Neena leaned close to her brother. "I think 'e's sayin' that we don't quite measure up to the local median, cleanliness-wise.''

"You will have an opportunity to purify yourselves as much as possible prior to your appearance before the Magistrate,'' the rat was telling them as they turned a corner. The street opened onto a landscaped square paved in white limestone. Citizens gathered around the milky marble fountain in the center stared openmouthed as the parade passed.

On the far side of the square they were marched into a large building and made to wait in a spacious chamber while the commandant rat conversed with a colleague behind a desk. Asked to hand over their weapons and personal effects, there was little they could do but comply. To Buncan's chagrin, he was also compelled to turn in his duar. That done, most of their escort departed. The remainder escorted and shoved them, none too gently, down a short corridor and into a large barred vestibule. Even the odd diagonal bars had been painted white.

Jail it might be, but the cell was as spotless as the antechamber outside.

Squill grabbed the bars and yelled after the departing rat and his companion, the chief jailer (a shrew of unpleasant disposition and appearance).

"You'd better not try to keep us 'ere any longer than we're willin' to go along with this! We're powerful sorcerers, we are.''

The rats looked back and grinned thinly. "Of course you are. But tell me: If you're such masters of the arcane arts, why not use your magic to properly cleanse yourselves?''

"We are clean, dammit!'' Gripping the bars, Squill hopped up and down in frustration.

"Not by civilized standards.'' The officers turned a corner and vacated the corridor outside the cells.

Neena took a seat on one of the two benches that hung

suspended from a wall . . . no doubt to make it easier to clean under, Buncan mused.

"Well, we didn't 'ave no trouble findin' a place to spend the night."

Buncan tried to put the best possible light on their situation. "This isn't so bad. Inconvenient, but hardly dangerous. We'll answer their questions and pay their fine, as Gragelouth surmises, and then we'll get the hell out of Hygria as fast as we can replenish our supplies."

"My wagon and team," the merchant mumbled. Buncan eyed him unsympathetically.

"You're the one who said to cooperate."

The sloth regarded him with atypical sharpness. "You saw how many there were. We would have not stood a chance in a close-quarter battle. The intelligent fighter picks the time that best suits him."

"Righty-ho." Squill spread his arms wide. "Why, we're in a much better position to get out o' this compost 'eap now than we were afore."

"At least we're not dead," Gragelouth shot back, showing uncharacteristic pugnacity. "I have watched. You need time to compose your spellsongs. We possessed no such margin for chronological error when we were surrounded."

"We could magic ourselves out o' 'ere," Neena murmured, "except . . ."

"No duar," Buncan finished for her. "We may have to try and clean ourselves up to meet their standards."

"You weren't payin' attention, mate." Squill ran a paw down the diagonal bars. "That'll just get us an audience with the local judge, not out o' 'ere. An' wot 'appens if no matter wot we do we can't never get up to their bleedin' high 'standards'?" He showed bright teeth. "I don't like bein' pushed around."

"They may only want our money," Gragelouth observed.

"Maybe, maybe," Squill murmured softly. "Or they might want everythin' of ours, which they'll confiscate while we rot away in this bleedin' cell."

"They won't let us rot," said his sister. "Wouldn't be a clean thing to do."

"Maybe, but I don't think I want to 'ang around to find out."

Gragelouth rose from where he'd been sitting and gazed up the corridor. "Someone is coming."

It was the rat, flanked by a pair of strangely garbed woodchucks. Their attire was richly embroidered with a plethora of appliquéd arcane symbols.

They halted outside the cell. The nearest woodchuck adjusted bifocal glasses. "What have we here?"

"They claim to be sorcerers." The rat's lips curled in an elegant sneer.

"Look more like vagrants to me," commented the second, slightly taller woodchuck.

His associate nodded. "I am Multhumot, Senior Master of the Hidden Arts for Hygria. I do not believe, but I am willing to be convinced. If you are sorcerers, show me a sample of your skills."

"You mean you're gonna let us?" said Squill. "Right!"

"An effective demonstration will require more than enthusiasm." The woodchuck's tone was dry.

"We are sorry if we have unwillingly given any offense." Gragelouth advanced from the back of the cell to the bars. "If you will but return to us our possessions, we will depart immediately."

"It is too late for that." The commandant was smiling. "You have committed grave offenses and must pay the penalty."

Gragelouth nodded his shaggy head, muttering. "It is as I suspected."

"Oi, you were right, merchant." Neena was staring at the rat. "That's wot they were after all along. Tell me, bald-tail, is your conscience as clean as your butt?"

"I don't know what you mean." By his tone the commandant indicated that he knew exactly what she meant.

"Right." Squill looked eager. "They want proof, let's give 'em some proof."

"Maybe it would be better simply to pay the fine," Gragelouth ventured uneasily.

"Stuff it, sloth," said Squill. "This 'ere's personal now."

"I need my instrument back." Buncan did his best to affect an air of indifference.

"The Master wants to see magic, not music." The rat snorted disdainfully.

Multhumot waved a hand. "Bring what he requests, but first check the interior for weapons and devices." He eyed Buncan appraisingly. "This had best not be a joke, human. Do not think to toy with me."

Buncan kept his expression carefully neutral.

A squirrel appeared with the duar. The cell door was opened and it was passed inside. Buncan cradled it lovingly, checking it thoroughly for damage. It appeared unharmed. Only when he was satisfied did he turn to the otters, who waited expectantly.

"Something simple," he told them. "Just enough for a demonstration."

" 'Ell, I wanted to flatten the 'ole bleedin' city." Squill was unashamedly disappointed.

" 'Ow about we dissolve these bars?" Neena smiled sweetly at the rat. "Would that be adequate proof?" The commandant stiffened slightly. For the first time he looked less than completely confident. By contrast, the two wood-chucks evinced hardly any reaction.

"That would be interesting," Multhumot's associate admitted.

Buncan bowed slightly and commenced to follow the otters' vocal lead.

"Got no freedom in this place
Time to get out an' get on with the race
This place 'ere stinks, this space 'ere winks
Let's waste this fokker and get back to our
Stinks.
Us an' our friends, that's wot we thinks."

The mist that materialized this time was dark and threatening. It coalesced into a compact cumulonimbus cloud which began first to rumble, then to flash ominously. Intrigued, the woodchucks held their ground while the commandant took a couple of steps toward the corridor exit.

Miniature lightning began to run up and down the restraining bars, curling around the metal while seeking the places where the bars were fixed to wall and floor. The strobing light cast the faces of spellsingers and player into barbaric relief. Beyond the corridor, guards and administrators gathered fearfully to listen.

Unperturbed, Multhumot raised both short arms and mumbled laconically. His colleague removed a flask from within his copious robes and began to sprinkle its contents on the bars. The fluid smelled powerfully of lemon and ammonia.

Buncan's nose twitched as the odor struck him, and he knew that the otters, with their more sensitive nostrils, could hardly be missing it.

A second cloud appeared in the corridor. It was an intense, brilliant white, sanctified and fluffy and shot through with silver. Under Multhumot's direction it drifted purposefully toward the cell. Trying to ignore it, Buncan kept playing while the suddenly wary otters rapped on.

The ivory cloud made contact with the one which had spread itself along the bars. Ragged lightning erupted at the confluence, and the air was acrid with the smell of ozone. The dark nimbus Buncan and his friends had conjured began to break apart into tiny, harmless puffs.

There was a bright, actinic flash which caused everyone to blink. The smell of lemon-fresh and otherworldly room deodorizer was strong in the air. Though they sang and played on as determinedly as ever, Buncan and his companions were unable to regenerate the dark cloud.

"So much for your squalid sorcery." Multhumot's associate looked pleased. "We of Hygria can scrub it out of existence, wash it from this dimension, render it impotent through disinfective invocation. From now on this chamber will remain whiter than white and squeaky clean in spite of all your efforts to foul it through your outlander spellsinging." Behind him the commandant, his confidence restored, beamed triumphantly.

" 'Ere, don't let 'em get away with that!" blurted Squill furiously. "Let's 'ave another go, mate."

"I don't know, Squill." Buncan let his tired fingers fall

from the strings. "I don't feel too good right now. Maybe we'd better give it some thought."

"Don't back down on us now, Bunkile," Neena implored him.

He forced himself to straighten. "All right. One more time."

"Let's really give it to the dirty buggers." Squill bent to exchange ideas with his sister. When they had agreed on lyrics, they began to sing.

The vapor that boiled out of the duar this time was a throbbing, angry red that screeched and gibbered. The knife-edged lyrics of the otters were matched by the crimson blades that emerged from the coalescing fog. Seeking eagerly, they hissed up and down, looking for something to slice, as the cloud drifted inexorably toward the cell bars.

CHAPTER 9

THE COMMANDANT'S EXPRESSION FELL AND HE RETREATED to the far end of the corridor, cowering near the portal. Though initially taken aback, the two woodchucks held their ground. As the threatening cloud drifted toward them, they lifted their arms and began to chant in tandem. Grasping arms emerged from the nimbus, reaching outward.

In response to the chant a second white cloud materialized. It was far more active than its predecessor had been, spinning and whirling until it had twisted itself into optimal dust-devil proportions. Buncan gaped as it spun toward the bars.

This time when the two clouds made contact there was no lurid flash of light, no crooked lightning. Only a deep, liquid gurgle. Buncan continued to play, the otters kept singing, and the pair of white-shrouded woodchucks waved their hands and chanted like crazy.

Gragelouth sat at the back of the cell, his gray-furred head resting in his hands, a sour expression on his face.

The cell bars began to vibrate. Soon the walls of the jail joined in sympathetic vibration. Wondering if maybe they hadn't overdone it, Buncan played on. Mortar powdered and flaked off the walls, filling the air with limestone dust.

Angry as the otters' rap was, their combined spellsinging was no match for the cyclonic cleanser the woodchucks had invoked. It tore the red cloud to bits, shredding malformed blades and arms, sweeping them into its central vortex. When the last vestige of crimson had been sucked invisible, the whirlwind shrank in upon itself, growing smaller and smaller until, with a faint puff of compressing air, it popped itself out of existence.

Their throats protesting mightily, the otters were forced to give it up. Buncan finished with a final desultory strum on the duar. The glow at its nexus faded. It was quiet in the cell once more.

And clean. Exceedingly clean.

"You see," said Multhumot, "all the anger and fury in the Netherworld cannot stand against good hygiene, even in sorcery." Perspiration stains were visible beneath his arms.

"We haven't done anything," Buncan argued. "It's wrong to keep us locked up like this."

Multhumot straightened his attire. "Either Kimmilpat or I will be on guard in the antechamber at all times. I warn you not to try anything." He adopted a threatening mien . . . as threatening as a three-foot-high woodchuck could manage, anyway. "Thus far my colleague and I have only countered your necromancy. We have not assaulted you with our own. Rest assured you would not find our serious attentions pleasing. Therefore, I recommend that from now on you behave yourselves."

"You don't scare us, guv." Squill had his face pressed between the bars. He looked back over his shoulder. "C'mon, Buncan; let's give 'em another—"

"No." Buncan put a comforting hand on the otter's shoulder. "No more. Not now. It didn't work, and I'm not ready to try again. Not just yet. If Clothahump were here . . . I saw him use that kind of enchanted wind myself, only it wasn't white." He looked down the row of cells.

"Maybe there's a better way out of here." Another body was standing next to him: Gragelouth.

"What will happen to us?" the merchant asked mournfully of their captors.

"That is the concern of the city magistrate," Multhumot replied. "I suspect you will be fined. To what degree I cannot say. Certainly you will be ordered to dispose of your filthy raiment prior to your court appearance."

"I'm getting real tired of being called filthy," Buncan muttered.

"I ain't goin' nowhere without me shorts," Squill added.

"Wouldn't 'ave bothered Mudge," his sister commented. " 'E spent plenty o' time gaddin' about without 'is pants."

The two plump white-shrouded wizards took their leave of the prisoners. The commandant smirked briefly at his charges before following in the woodchucks' wake.

The evening meal did nothing to lighten the spirits of the incarcerated. It was as sterile and bland as their surroundings.

Squill took a couple of mouthfuls before shoving his bowl aside. "I can't swallow any more o' this swill."

Neena had already reached the same conclusion. "Who could?" Her nose and whiskers twitched.

"It is quite nutritious. I have had worse." Gragelouth seemed to be ingesting the contents of his bowl with no difficulty. The otters watched him in disbelief.

"I guess my stomach's not as strong as yours, merchant." Buncan set his own portion aside as he considered the empty corridor. "Another day of this and we'll be too weak to think of escaping."

"You notice no one said 'ow long we might be stuck in 'ere before we get to see this 'ere bloody magistrate?" Neena pointed out. "It could take weeks."

Squill sat on the floor, leaning against the back wall. "I don't give a shit 'ow bad they torture me: I ain't givin' up me pants."

"There's only one wizard on duty," Buncan murmured. "Maybe if we came up with a different song fast enough . . ."

"I have a feeling his colleague is not far away."

Buncan turned to regard Gragelouth. The sloth spoke patiently. "You have shown your spellsinging ability

convincingly if not overpoweringly. Our overweight opponents may be prepared to call in additional sorceral assistance if they think it necessary. I think we must seek another
way to abet our departure.''

Buncan tried to avoid the odor rising from his food bowl.
''Jon-Tom would know what to sing to get out of this
place.''

'' 'E would that,'' agreed Squill readily, ''or else 'e'd
level the 'ole place tryin'.''

''They're bleedin' fanatics,'' Neena added. ''To them,
anythin' that's different is dirty, so they can't abide us.''

''What kind of spellsong can you use to combat rabid
cleanliness?'' Buncan was thoroughly discouraged.

Squill scratched behind an ear, then a knee, concluding
with his butt. He paused in midscratch to sit up straight.

''Maybe there's another way, like Gragelouth said.''

''Besides spellsingin'?'' His sister eyed him sideways.
''You always was a balmy bro'; now you've gone over the
edge.''

''Not by 'alf, me darlin' sib'. Not by 'alf.'' Squill was on
his feet now, excitement evident in his expression and
gestures. ''Look 'ere: These blokes 'ate anythin' that 'ints
o' dirt or filth or a general mess, right?''

A quick survey told Buncan that he found this no more
enlightening than did any of his companions. Gragelouth in
particular looked especially uncomprehending.

''Your line of reasoning escapes me,'' the merchant
confessed.

''Don't you see? Me sister an' I are experts at makin' a
mess!''

Realization dawned on Neena's face. Her whiskers rose
with her smile. ''Oi, that's right! Otters come by that
natural.''

''An' we learned from the best,'' Squill added, referring
to his much maligned but conveniently absent father.

''I see now where you are leading with this.'' Gragelouth
scratched himself under his chin with a heavy claw. ''There
are risks involved. Such a response may only infuriate our
captors.''

''Bugger 'em!'' snapped Squill. ''They're already mad at

us. Not to mention bein' mad up 'ere.'' He tapped the side of his head, just below one ear. "Wot can they do that they 'aven't already done?"

"Kill us," Gragelouth pointed out quietly.

"Oi, there is that," the otter admitted. "But only if they're able, which I don't 'appen to think they are."

"You presume much." The sloth returned to the rear of the cell and folded his arms. "Perhaps you will be good enough to leave me out of this equation."

"Don't worry, guv," said Neena, completely missing his implication. "Why, you're 'alfway clean. Anyone could see right off that you don't 'ave wot it takes to act like a bona fide slob."

"Thank you," said Gragelouth dryly.

"An' you, Bunkly, you'll just be in the way," she went on. "Go on, off with you. Stand over in the corner with our guide an' let me bro' an' me get on with our work. If we need your 'elp, we'll ask for it."

"Surely there's something I can do." Though Gragelouth was still reluctant to participate, Buncan found himself caught up in the spirit of the enterprise.

Squill was rubbing his hands together as he surveyed the cell. "This ain't goin' to be 'alf work." His eyes fell on the food bowls. "I think I'm about ready for a stomach-churnin' little snack, I am."

Hearing the racket, one of the guards stationed out in the antechamber arrived to check on the disturbance. The sight and sounds that greeted him caused his eyes to widen.

"Stop that! Stop it immediately!" He gestured with his spear as he ran toward the cell.

Weaving unsteadily, Squill staggered over to the bars and proceeded to pee on the paca's immaculate white boots. From the look that came over the guard's face one would have thought he'd been run through, Buncan thought. The paca let out a shriek, dropped his weapon, and ran wildly for the exit. Despite the condition of his stomach, Squill still managed a smile for his companions.

The otters gleefully pursued their methodical degradation of the cell, while Gragelouth and Buncan kept to one marginally unblemished corner. It was at once fascinating and unsettling to watch.

Flanked by a pair of sword-carrying squirrels and the sleepy-eyed commandant, it was Kimmilpat who came waddling down the corridor to confront them. "What is this? What's going on here?" he sputtered as he neared the cell. "All this commotion! It will not go easy on you for having roused me from my sleep when I have only just—"

He halted, openmouthed, as he took in the scene. So did his escort.

Squill and Neena had removed their clothes and scattered them all over the cell. Likewise Buncan and the reluctant Gragelouth, both of whom leaned buck naked against the back wall. It looked as if a laundry cart had blown up.

The cell's single chamber pot had been overturned and its odious contents tossed out into the corridor, save for what had stuck to the now-stained white bars. Fragments of broken dinner bowls lay everywhere, mixed in with the demolished stuffing of the several sleeping pads. Perhaps half the evening's meal lay strewn about. Some of it dripped down the wall opposite the cell, bits of meat and vegetables sliding glaucously down the pristine white surface.

The woodchuck's insides trembled but held steady. "I know what you're trying to do, and it won't work." As he spoke the two guards, their hands clasped to their mouths, turned and fled. To his credit the commandant remained behind, though he was looking exceedingly queasy.

"What won't work, guv?" Tongue lolling, Squill pressed up against the bars and let the drool from his mouth drip down the bars onto the floor outside. The commandant recoiled.

"Some poor citizens are going to have to clean this up," the wizard protested, "after they have been suitably fortified for the task, of course. I warn you to cease this outrage immediately!"

"Wot outrage?" Moving to stand next to her brother, Neena conspicuously picked her nose and flicked the contents out between the bars.

"Agghhhh! You were warned!" Kimmilpat raised both arms and began to chant.

Squill turned to his sister. "Not a bad voice, though a bit 'igh-pitched for me taste." Sticking his head as far between the bars as he could manage, he shoved a furry finger down his throat and commenced to upchuck with astonishing force all over the wizard's impeccable, intricately embroidered gown.

Stunned, Kimmilpat stopped in mid-incantation to look down at himself. At the same time his nostrils conveyed to him the full aroma of the blessing Squill had bestowed upon his august person. Innocent, as it were, of any natural resistance to such effluvia, the dazed wizard promptly whirled and barfed all over the nether regions of the commandant, making an admirably thorough job of it and missing nary a square inch of the glossy white cloth.

By this time utter confusion reigned in the anteroom beyond the cell block as baffled and frightened guards struggled to make sense of what was happening beyond their immediate range of vision. But not, distressingly for them, beyond their range of hearing.

"This . . . this is revolting beyond imagination!" The puce-faced commandant gasped weakly as he struggled to help the overcome wizard back to his feet.

"Why thanks, guv." Spittle dribbled profusely from Squill's lower jaw. "We 'ave a good example to inspire us, we do. 'Ere, let me 'elp clean that up." Taking a huge mouthful of water from the still-intact cell jug, he sprayed every drop of it smack into the face of the unsuspecting Kimmilpat as the stunned wizard stumbled around to face him.

As the overwhelmed woodchuck collapsed for the second time in as many minutes, Squill considered the nearly empty jug. "'Ard to make great art when you don't 'ave sufficient materials to work with. Oi," he shouted to the commandant, "we need another meal in 'ere! We nearly went an' digested that last one, we did."

A cluster of guards tentatively examined the corridor, intent on aiding their commanding officer. The sight and smell turned the ones in front and set them to struggling frantically with those following immediately behind.

Pinching his nostrils with two fingers, Buncan spoke nasally to Gragelouth. "See? Squill was right. Where cleanliness is concerned these people are so used to perfection that they can't handle real filth when confronted with it. They can't cope.''

''They can still kill us.'' The sloth was doing his best to shroud his own much more sensitive proboscis.

''Only at the risk of making another mess.''

''Maybe they have mastered some sterile technique we cannot imagine.''

''When things are tough your optimism's a real comfort, Gragelouth.''

''I am a realist,'' the merchant protested. ''And I have reason to be.'' He pointed.

Forcing his way through the knot of panicked guards was the senior Hygrian wizard, Multhumot, resplendent in a gold-embroidered white gown of office. Indignation colored his broad, furry face and his whiskers were convulsing as he pushed the commandant aside to assist his colleague.

''What is this . . . this corruption?''

''They think to provoke us into letting them go.'' The badly unsettled Kimmilpat was wheezing weakly.

Multhumot glared at the prisoners as he steadied his associate. ''That is not going to happen. Not while I have convicted power left in my body.'' Covering his broad nose as best he was able, he advanced purposefully on the reeking cell, his other hand upraised. Miniature lightning crackled between his spread fingers as he commenced a deep-throated invocation of profound import.

He was barely halfway through the first sentence when Squill, taking unabashed aim and demonstrating extraordinary accuracy even for one so obviously skilled in such matters, proceeded to anoint the wizard with the remaining contents of the water jug via the conduit of his own body. Initially struck square in the face (hard as he strained, Squill couldn't maintain the flow for very long), the wizard stopped dead in his tracks, blinked, realized fully the extent of the ultimate unhygienic act which had been performed upon him, and fainted clean away.

Not the similarly debased Kimmilpat, nor the commandant, nor any of the ordinary guards had the courage to advance to the woodchuck wizard's rescue. Meanwhile the otters, employing the relentless energy and enthusiasm of their kind, did their best to exacerbate the despoiled condition of both their cell and the adjoining corridor. Throwing himself into the spirit of the moment, Buncan participated as best he could. Gragelouth simply could not bring himself to do more than occasionally expectorate on the cell floor. Most of the time he simply kept his face averted from the fray and let out an occasional moan.

Eventually a trio of guards crept down the corridor. Improvised masks covered their mouths and nostrils. They hustled the still-heaving Kimmilpat out of the hallway before returning to drag the comatose mass of his colleague to safety. Pandemonium reigned in the antechamber, clearly audible to those within the cell.

Exhausted but exhilarated, the otters finally took a break from their noxious exertions.

"That ought to give the buggers somethin' to think about," Squill declared with satisfaction. "Wonder 'ow they're goin' to react to our little party."

Buncan was pinching his nose tightly, trying not to inhale any more than was absolutely necessary as he peered up the corridor.

"Whatever they do, I hope they do it soon. It's hot in here and I'm having a tough time maintaining my own equilibrium."

" 'Ere now, Bunkins," said Neena worriedly, "don't you up an' pass out on us."

"I have to confess," came the voice of the distressed merchant from the back of their cell, "that I cannot imagine you spellsinging up anything worse than this." He waved feebly to take in the ravaged cell and hallway.

"Crikey, guv, go easy on the compliments." Squill grinned modestly. "We just improvised as best we could."

"They're coming back." Buncan nodded toward the far end of the corridor.

The commandant was alone, stumbling and hesitating as if he was being urged on (not to say pushed) from behind. The rat's demeanor was as thoroughly disheveled as his previously spotless uniform. Behind the handkerchief he kept tightly pressed to his muzzle, his narrow, pointy face was decidedly green. This was unsurprising given the fact that the city's moist heat had invaded the cell block, the atmosphere of which had already graduated from ripe to rank.

Swaying slightly, he stumbled halfway down the corridor, at which point he could advance no farther. "I am," he emitted a curdled gurgle, fought not to swallow, finally gathered himself, and began afresh, "I am pleased to inform you that a decision has been rendered in your case."

Neena winked at Buncan.

"Is that right?" Squill responded innocently.

"Yes. Through the infinite magnanimity of the Justice Court of Hygria and by special dispensation from the Council of Cleanliness, it has been decided that you will be allowed to recover your worldly possessions and depart unhindered without having to face the formal prosecution you so richly deserve."

Neena leaned against the diagonal bars. "Cor, wot a generous lot o' folks. I almost 'ate to leave. Wot do you think, Bunklewit? Maybe we ought to 'ang around a while longer?"

"No, no." The commandant spoke hastily, before Buncan could comment. "The streets have been cleared for you. This entire borough of the city has been sealed against your presence. Just take your belongings and leave."

Buncan's gaze narrowed as he regarded the trembling rat. "I dunno. I think we're owed something for our trouble, for being accused of something we weren't aware of and for being shut up here while——" He broke off. Gragelouth was shaking him persistently.

"If you do not mind, I would rather not strain our current luck," the merchant hissed. "We should get out while we can."

Buncan smiled and whispered. "I know. I just like to push the envelope."

"A peculiar expression."

"One of my dad's."

Gragelouth stepped past him, waving at the bilious commandant. "Very well. We accept your offer. Now open up! We're ready to leave." He turned to the otters. "While I personally would have opted for a less unconventional means of resistance, I have to admit that the outcome has been congenial. Please try not to puke on anyone as we make our way to freedom.''

"Relax, guv. I don't think I 'ave it in me anymore anyways," Squill informed him. "So to speak.''

Advancing with the pointed toes of a ballet dancer—or a lone scout traversing a mine field—the commandant worked his way down to their cell and fumbled at the lock with a large, ornate key. With more of a metallic clank than a click, the door swung aside. Weaving unsteadily, the rat watched them exit. Buncan almost felt sorry for him.

Squill paused, breathing directly into the rat's face. "Wot about the guards outside?''

"The antech—'' the commandant staggered under the impact of the otter's breath, "the antechamber has been cleared. All doors are open and unbarred to you. Also all windows and every other ventable opening in the building. Now please, go!'' He clung to the cell door for support.

Proving that the rat's declaration was as genuine as his nausea, they found the outer chambers deserted. So was the main boulevard outside, and the square with its intricate fountain. As they hurried along the white paving stones, Buncan sensed eyes following them furtively from cracks in shutters and barely opened windows.

"Would you look at this,'' Squill ventured as they jogged along. "They're bloody terrified of us. I think we could 'ave the run o' the city if we wanted it.''

"Our actions must seem not merely outlandish but incomprehensible to them.'' Gragelouth puffed along in the lead. "We are not free yet. Keep a watch for cocked bows or poised spears.''

"Naw, they wouldn't try anythin' now, guv,'' Squill replied confidently. "Be afraid we might spit on 'em.''

They passed the inn whose hospitality they wouldn't have the opportunity to sample, taking note as they ran past of the barred doors and shuttered windows, and turned up the street leading to the tethering spot where they'd left Gragelouth's wagon. The vegetable seller had deserted her stall, as had all her fellow vendors. After the clamor and

noise which had greeted the travelers upon arrival, they now
found the avenues eerily silent.

Squill and Neena's exertions had made quite an impression on the local authorities.

CHAPTER 10

THEY TOOK THEIR LEAVE OF STERILE, WHITEWASHED
Hygria without regret. No pursuit was mounted once they
were beyond the city walls, not by vengeful guards nor
nauseous sorcerers. It was clear that none of them had, so to
speak, the stomach for it.

Well south of the metropolis, they stopped in a shady
glade of nut trees to bathe in a clear, cool stream. Buncan
relaxed in the shallows while brother and sister otter frol-
icked in deeper waters. Gragelouth used a cloth to daintily
scrub and wash his fur, then set to combing himself out with
a square brush as big as his hand.

When the otters had finally had enough of the water, they
dried themselves and dressed, then helped themselves to a
bushel or so of the ripe nuts; this in lieu of the supplies the
town itself had been so unwilling to furnish. When they had
enough, Gragelouth once again set a course northwestward.

A week passed before the grassy, scrub-flecked plains
gave way to the foothills of a rugged range of unknown
mountains. There were no trails leading within, and they
had to pick their way carefully around boulders and over
rough spots. The dray lizards hissed and jerked violently,
but the merchant kept them under admirable control with
well-chosen tugs on the reins and sharply barked phrases of
command.

"Easier for a mercenary fox on foot than for a vehicle to
get through this way," Buncan commented as they bounced
and rattled through the notch Gragelouth had chosen to
explore.

"I do not know for certain that he came this way," the merchant replied unencouragingly. "Only that this seems to me the only possible avenue through these mountains."

Buncan pursed his lips thoughtfully. "It's your wagon, Gragelouth. So we go your way. What's this range called, anyway?"

"I have no idea." The sloth wrestled with the reins.

"Interestin' name," Neena quipped, but her heart wasn't in it. The path was too rough to inspire ready humor.

As the travelers progressed, the crags overhead clawed more determinedly at the underbellies of the scudding clouds. Their flanks steepened. Unless they chanced upon a formal road or track of some kind, Buncan couldn't see how they were going to wrestle the clumsy wagon through the increasingly rough terrain.

In all this time they encountered no other travelers. If any commerce passed through these mountains, it was by a route different from the one they were traversing. Gragelouth surmised that any such travel probably passed to the east and north. In their case they sought not commerce anyway, but revelation, and the path to that is always more difficult.

Days later the hitherto peaceful atmosphere was interrupted by a steady sussuration. Initially a loud whisper, it intensified with their advance until it had become a roaring in the ears, like a steady gale. It carried with it a becoming freshness to the air which invigorated tired spirits. Even the dray lizards picked up their pace.

The otters recognized it from the first. "Nothin' mysterious or sorceral about that noise, friends." Neena stood behind Buncan, her paws on his shoulders, trying to see into the distance. "'Tis a river, and a big, fast-flowin' one."

"Not as big as the Tailaroam," Squill ventured, "nor maybe even the Shortstub, but steeper o' drop than either. White water!" Clearly the otter relished the prospect.

The narrowing pass they had been following ended at the river, which funneled swiftly but not impassably to the west through a steep gorge. Gragelouth inspected the terrain with a practiced eye.

"It cuts through these mountains more or less in the direction we must take." He pointed downstream. "See, there is a contiguous beach. If it is sufficiently compacted, we can parallel." He chucked the reins, urging his team onward.

As they swung out onto the sand, Buncan uneasily eyed the torrent on their right. "What happens if it rains upstream and the river rises? We'll be trapped in this canyon."

"Better work on your stroke, mate," Squill said cheerily. Buncan was not amused.

The wagon rattled and rocked but did not sink into the firm mixture of sand and gravel. Gragelouth kept a steady eye on the surface ahead, watching for any soft spots. As the canyon closed in around them, Buncan found himself glancing worriedly back the way they'd come. If the river came up the wagon would float . . . until it struck the first submerged boulder.

They hadn't traveled far before the beach spread out to form a shallow plain complete with trees and grass. Just ahead a tributary, slow-moving but too deep and wide to cross, entered the main current from their side. There was no way around it. The beach down which they were traveling, which had looked so promising at first, was a dead end.

Someone, or something, had found the little valley at the junction of the rivers conducive to permanent habitation. Neena pointed out the house and barn, both of which had been fashioned out of river rock and driftwood. The home had a single sharply raked roof facing the main stream.

Behind the barn a corral had been staked out. Its reptilian occupants looked healthy and well-fed. Buncan identified them as a species bred for consumption rather than work. There was also an extensive garden and small orchard, irrigated with water from the tributary by means of two small canals.

Gragelouth indicated the network of stakes in the shallows. "Shellfish farming. Whoever has taken residence here has done well. This is not the abode of traders or transients."

"Not just shellfish." Neena pointed to the double rack of skinned and filleted fish drying in the sun behind the house.

As they drew nearer, several cubs came tumbling out to greet them. They were followed by two adults. No one exhibited any fear or apprehension at the wagon's approach, which suggested that visitors to this place, while probably infrequent, were not unknown.

Buncan had never seen their like before, but Gragelouth recognized them readily enough.

"They are of a tribe called platypi," he informed his companions, "who are noted for their love of privacy."

"Bloody weird-looking, they are." Squill stared at the youngsters, with their grinning, duck-billed faces and slick fur peeping out from beneath their clothing.

"You should have much in common with them. They are as at home in the water as yourselves, though not, I think, quite as quick."

The otter hopped down off the wagon. "If they'll sell or trade us some fresh fish and maybe a cray or two, I'll concede 'em any race."

"They look friendly enough." Buncan climbed down to join his friends. "Think it's a ploy?"

"No," replied the normally suspicious sloth. "There would not be enough traffic through here to make banditry a paying proposition."

Cubs and adults alike jabbered incessantly at the travelers as they escorted them toward the house. As Gragelouth surmised, they didn't get many visitors and were delighted at the prospect of company. Their remarkable bills made them difficult but not impossible to understand.

"Tho you go to the northwetht?" The male of the household addressed them as they all sat on the beach, resting on boulders which had been carved into chairs. His spouse kept the chattering cubs away from the meeting.

The platy put his thumbs through suspenders, nodding downstream. "Your vehicle will never make it through theth mountains. Even if we could raft it across, the beach endth not far downstream."

"We are open to suggestions," Gragelouth told him.

Their host considered. "I have plenty of wood and am experienthed with my handth. Perhapth we can come to an agreement. I could uth a good wagon and team."

"Oh, no," said the sloth. "That wagon is my livelihood. It contains all my goods, all my worldly possessions."

"I wouldn't take your goodth. You could take them

onward with you. I jutht want the wagon and team. Those for a good, thound boat. A fair trade."

"Seems fair to me, it does," said Squill without hesitation.

"Let's do it," his sister added eagerly. "Be grand to travel in a boat for a change. I'm sick of dust and dirt."

Buncan eyed the platy evenly. "Have you actually been downstream? Is it navigable?"

The sloth regarded him approvingly. "Ah. You are learning. I see that being in my company has done you good."

"I've traveled a ways," their host told him. "I have no need to go far." He gestured at the homestead, with its shellfish farm and orchard and garden and animals. "My world ith here. The dethithion ith up to you. I can only tell you with athuranth that you cannot continue to follow the Sprilashoone by land. A boat ith your only real opthion. Unleth you want to go back the way you came and try another route."

"I worry about chancing a heavy load of trade goods on an unknown watercourse," Gragelouth muttered.

"I will thtore them for you," said the platy. "No extra charge. I am a farmer, not a trader. You can return for them whenever you with."

"Rapids?" asked Buncan.

"Not for at leatht two dayth. Farther than that I have not been. And at that point it turnth more to the northwetht, ath you would want. Bethideth, two among you are otterth. Even in the wortht waters they can manage."

"Bloomin' right," Squill agreed expansively.

"If you have trouble with the boat, you have among you two who can go over the thide to fix or recover thingth."

"You've 'andled the land portion of our little sojourn," Neena reassured Gragelouth. "Leave it to me bro' and me to look after things while we're waterborne."

"We might follow the river on foot," the merchant murmured, reluctant to the last, "but the terrain is difficult and becoming more so, and I confess that the prospect of an extended hike does not thrill me with anticipation."

"Then ith thettled." The platy extended a hand.

Buncan had to admit the thought of traveling by water

instead of land was an inviting one. His battered backside and jostled spine certainly approved.

The platy family proved to be excellent hosts, and the travelers spent the most relaxing evening and night in days luxuriating in their hospitality. In exchange for some selections from Gragelouth's stock, the farmer additionally provided them with substantial supplies of dried fish, fruits, crayfish, and freshwater oysters, as well as vegetables from the garden. Even Gragelouth had to admit that the riparian hermits had been more than fair in their dealings. As a result, they did not miss the supplies they had been unable to obtain in Hygria.

The boat was sturdy and larger than expected. There were four sets of oars, which since they were traveling with the current no one expected to have to use save perhaps to fend the craft off the canyon walls should they grow unexpectedly narrow.

The single lateen-rigged mast was stepped solidly into the keep fore of the cabin. Its sail remained furled as they pushed away from the rustic rough-hewn dock and rode the tranquil waters of the tributary into the fast-moving current of the Sprilashoone.

They watched the farm recede behind them until a bend in the river blocked it from their view. The six youngsters ran along the beach, clicking their bills by way of farewell, until they too disappeared from sight.

Buncan found himself wondering if he would ever see the little valley again. Certainly Gragelouth might, in search of what trade goods remained behind.

"This is more like it." He made the comment to no one in particular as he leaned against the bow and watched the canyon slide by. The layered sandstone and granite glistened in the morning sun. Wild lizards and other native inhabitants scrambled in and out of clefts in the rock, pausing occasionally to peer from uncomprehending eyes at the boat drifting past below. Others sped out of the craft's path, their subaqueous activities temporarily disrupted.

"A definite improvement." Having jumped over the side to cool himself, Squill had climbed back aboard over the low stern and now lay on his back on the front deck, soaking up the sun. Gragelouth handled the tiller while Neena hung over the side, trailing a paw in the water.

"To be back on a river." She let out a low, whistling sigh. " 'Tis more than I could've 'oped for."

"I am glad you are pleased."

She turned to look at the merchant. "Don't you ever lighten up, guv? You should try an' be more like me bro' an' I."

"No one can be 'like' an otter except another otter," Gragelouth declaimed firmly. "Your kind possesses the most extraordinary facility for delighting even in unpleasant circumstances."

"Maybe so, pinch-face, but even you 'ave to admit that our present circumstances are 'ardly anythin' but unpleasant."

"I must confess that I am increasingly sanguine about our current situation."

"Crikes, don't overdo your glee. You might strain somethin'."

"I miss the old wagon," Gragelouth continued, "but one must be prepared to make sacrifices in pursuit of great goals." He nudged the tiller slightly to port. "I admit that this method of transportation is both cooler and easier on certain select portions of one's anatomy."

"Bloody well right." She swiped at a surface-swimming fish and missed. "So chill, and try to enjoy yourself."

It required a conscious effort on his part, but by their fourth day on the river the ease of travel and promise of more of the same had even the perpetually dour merchant smiling. The current had increased and the walls of the canyon grown sheer, but they passed through with impunity.

It was midafternoon when a distant hum in the air pricked Squill's ears. He was lounging near Buncan, who was taking his turn at the tiller. Gragelouth and Neena were down in the main cabin, cobbling together a lunch.

"Now there's a sound," the otter murmured, sitting up straight.

"Wot's a sound?" Neena emerged from below, carrying a plate of assorted cold cuts. "Rapids?"

"Probably." Squill helped himself to the food but ate with unaccustomed gravity.

Not much time had passed before the noise had grown noticeably louder. "Big rapids," he muttered as he cleaned his whiskers with his tongue. He walked around the central cabin to stand in the bow, craning forward while sampling the air with nose and ears.

Moments later he shouted back to Buncan. "Oi, mate! We may be comin' up on a bit o' a problem."

"What sort of problem?" Buncan yelled up to him.

" 'Tis the canyon. It seems to disappear just ahead."

Buncan strained to see ahead. "What do you mean, 'it seems to disappear'?"

" 'Ard to tell." Abandoning the bow, the otter scampered monkeylike up the mast and clung to the top, shading his eyes with one paw as he stared forward. Buncan squinted up at him.

"See anything?"

"Not bloomin' much. That's the problem."

Gragelouth's smile had vanished. "I do not like this."

"Didn't the duckbill tell us this river were safe?" Neena murmured.

"He's never been down this far," Buncan reminded her. "He told us that, too. He said there might be rapids." The roar had intensified, progressing from loud to deafening. "Sounds like more than rapids to me." He called to their lookout. "Anything yet, Squill?"

The otter was silent, looking like a large brown comma astride the punctuation of the mast. A moment later he let out a sharp bark and slid down to rejoin them. His eyes were alert as he confronted his tall human friend.

"Ain't no rapids to worry about."

"That is a relief." Gragelouth sighed.

" 'Tis a waterfall. A bloody big one, near as I can tell."

The merchant blinked doe eyes and then turned away to commence a desperate study of the passing banks. By this time the rock walls they were traveling between verged on the perpendicular.

"There is no place to land here. No place at all!" His thick claws dug into the wood of the gunwale. "We are going to go over."

"Just keep calm, everybody," said Neena. "Me bro',

'e's been known to exaggerate. Now Bunkoo, do you recall the tale o' when Mudge an' Jon-Tom 'ad to 'andle a situation like this?"

Buncan thought back to the stories his father had told him. He nodded eagerly as the one she was alluding to leaped to mind. "The Sloomaz-ayor-le-Weentli! The double river."

"Righty-ho. An' remember 'ow they escaped it?"

He nodded vigorously. "Gragelouth, take the tiller. My friends and I have magic to make." Passing control of the boat to the merchant, who was becoming progressively more unglued with each passing moment, Buncan dashed below and returned seconds later with his duar.

"The Sloomaz interdicted four waterfalls at the Earth's Throat," he reminded his companions confidently. "Surely we can spellsing our way down one." Ahead of the boat the now thunderous roaring had given birth to a dense, rising mist.

"We'd better," agreed Squill, "or in a few minutes we're all gonna be mush an' kindlin'."

"Words." Buncan strove to inspire them as he strummed the duar. "Lyrics. Get on it."

Neena stared at her brother. "I don't know anythin' about flyin' over waterfalls."

"Think of *something*." Gragelouth clung to the tiller as though it were some graven wooden talisman, fighting to keep them on a straight course in the grip of the now relentless torrent.

"Floating," Squill mused. "Gently descendin'. That's wot we want."

"I'm going to play." Buncan felt the mist beginning to moisten his skin. They must be very close now. "You two improvise. Fast."

They could see the edge through the fog, a boiling white froth marking the spot where the water plunged to depths unknown. The cascade might be a dozen feet high, or a thousand. *Surely not that much,* he thought as he played.

They were almost to the rim and he was beginning to panic a little himself, when the otters finally began to sing.

"Water rises and water falls
Can't turn away when it beckons and calls
Got to go over, got to see wot's below
But we gots to land gently or we'll sink, don't you
   know?
Wanna set it down light as feather off a crow
Don't blow
It now
Land us gently by the bow."

The otters rapped smooth and easy, and Buncan followed them without effort. The glow at the duar's nexus was concise and clear. None could have hoped for tighter harmony or crisper playing.

None of which was very reassuring when the boat nosed over the thundering edge of the falls and shot straight down, picking up speed rapidly as it fell.

Though they had to cling to the gunwale to keep from sliding down the deck and over the bow, the otters managed to keep singing. Buncan fell back against the rear wall of the central cabin and braced himself with his legs against the fortuitously narrow doorway. He needed to keep both hands on the duar. Thick arms wrapped around the swaying, useless tiller, Gragelouth dangled in midair above the now vertical deck.

They never did learn how tall the waterfall was, but it was high enough to allow the otters to slip in two more verses before they hit bottom. Whether Gragelouth's screaming added to or hindered the spellsong was something else that would remain forever in the province of the unknowable.

Rocks leaped up at them, sparkling strangely silver. Water-saturated wind tore at their skin and clothes and fur.

An instant before they were smashed to bits on the rocks, a pale-green mist enveloped the entire boat. Gragelouth let out a terminal moan and shut his eyes. There was no pain as they struck, though Buncan experienced a sensation as if his entire body had gone to sleep and a million minute splinters briefly pierced his torso.

Boat and bodies shattered on the silver boulders. Through

the mist he thought he could see his friends fly apart, still singing bravely.

He sensed the disparate parts of himself tumbling along underwater, sucked downstream by the inexorable current. Not far away he observed his disjointed hands still playing the miraculously intact duar. One of his eyes turned to look straight at its mate, and he blinked at himself. His mouth floated a few feet away, spinning lazily in the flow. His detached ears picked up the unmistakable and now slightly mystical rap of the otters. He felt no especial desire to try to locate his brain.

Bits of Gragelouth drifted by, the sloth's uncommitted mouth bemoaning its fate in a gurgling litany.

Imperceptibly at first but with increasing speed, the fragmented parts of Buncan and sloth, of otters and boat, began to come together, to realign themselves within the river. He watched the boat re-form from two sides at once, since his separated eyes were momentarily located both to port and starboard. Shattered planks and crushed supplies slowly reconstituted themselves. The process, like the water in which they now drifted, was unnaturally silent.

It was also less than perfect. The cabin was set too far forward, and the tiller reattached itself to the stern upside down. The mast restepped itself at a slight angle. But the result was definitely their boat.

At the same time, he experienced an irresistible tugging sensation as the roaming parts of his body were ineluctably drawn toward each other. Eyes sought out sockets, organs the torso, feet their missing ankles.

It was that final verse, he mused with detachment of a different kind. Not an instant too late, they had finally hit on an effective combination of words and music.

He watched with considerable interest as his various body parts swam toward him, wherever "him" was centered. Fingers, toes, other extremities rejoined the rest of his self near the boat's stern. Gragelouth was becoming a recognizable furry blob proximate to the tiller, complete to his clothing. Squill and Neena re-formed on the bow instead of the stern, where they'd commenced the spellsong.

More than once Buncan had heard Jon-Tom employ the

expression "gone to pieces." Hitherto he had considered it only a metaphor. As the echo of the spellsong brought them together again, it struck him that he was breathing underwater. Or was he?

He took a deep breath and hesitantly felt of himself. He was whole once more, seemingly only a little sore for the experience. Forward, the otters struggled to their feet and hurried to rejoin him. Gragelouth lay slumped on the deck, as wrung out as a used towel in a public bath.

They were sailing along down the Sprilashoone, boat and bodies intact, the river flowing mellow and unthreatening beneath them. Also on either side of them. And overhead. They were in a watery tube, or tunnel. It was noisy as well as impossible.

"More like the Sloomaz than we thought, wot?" Neena examined the watery conduit quietly.

But it was not at all like that fabled river which ran through the northern ranges of Zaryt's Teeth, as they discovered when the boat gave a sudden lurch and sailed *up* the side of the tunnel, continuing its progress until they were cruising along upside down, the original surface of the river directly below them.

Buncan grabbed instinctively for the cabin doorway, then released it when he saw that he wasn't going to plunge headfirst to the water below.

"Nothing in Dad's story said anything about sailing upside down."

Squill came sauntering toward him, hanging on to nothing. "' 'Ere now; you don't look quite yourself, mate.''

Buncan had to strain to hear clearly. Water in his ears, no doubt. He frowned as he considered his friend. "Neither do you." Actually, neither did anyone.

For one thing, Squill's head was protruding not from his neck but from his left side, just beneath his arm. His other arm was waving from where his head ought to have been. Then there was the more subtle problem of his left arm having been swapped for Neena's. The slight difference in length was a clue, the disparity in fur color a dead giveaway. Not that they could compare fur, because Neena, to her utter mortification, was beneath her clothing as bald as a newborn human.

Nor did Gragelouth escape the confusion. Sizable, hairless, naked ears stuck out of the top of his head, whereas Buncan had acquired the sloth's ears: comparatively small, gray-furred flaps of skin. That doubtless explained his current hearing difficulties.

They gathered upside down at the stern to contemplate their physiological disarray. Just as the boat had not re-formed perfectly, neither had they. It was evident that in the process widely scattered body parts had sometimes taken the path of least resistance. In several instances this was not merely comical, it was downright embarrassing.

"Definitely a few kinks in that spellsong," Buncan muttered.

"As kinked as this river," Gragelouth added.

"This simply ain't gonna do." The hand atop Squill's head gestured angrily.

"It certainly ain't." Neena was all but in tears over her condition. "Look at me. Just look at me!" She indicated her furless limbs.

"At least they're in the bloody right places," said her brother from beneath his arm.

Gragelouth's absurd human ears twitched involuntarily. "The solution is clear. You must fix your spellsong and then sing it once again."

"I knew we should have finished stronger," Neena grumbled disconsolately.

"Thank goodness we got our own voices back." Buncan shook the duar lightly. Water droplets fell past his head. A few experimental strums revealed that the instrument had survived the fall and subsequent awkward reintegration unharmed.

"This 'ad better work." Squill leaned against the cabin, bumping his head.

"Don't make it sound like it was my fault." Buncan tilted his head slightly to glare at his friend. "You two were the ones who came up with the lyrics."

"Well, you were responsible for the bleedin' accompaniment."

"Arguing will help none of us." Gragelouth held on to the tiller, more for support than out of any realistic hope of steering the inverted craft. "Please concentrate. I very much want my own ears back."

"Hey, I didn't ask for yours." Buncan strummed his instrument lightly.

The otters conferenced briefly before Neena looked up, her face full of concern. "Wot if we try this again an' it just makes things worse?"

"Wot could be worse than this?" Her brother regarded her from somewhere in the vicinity of his third rib.

"Do you guys remember the words?" Buncan asked them.

Neena smiled wanly. Even her whiskers were missing. "I thought I were goin' to die. When you think you're goin' to die, you remember everythin' right clearly."

He nodded, readied himself. "Let's pick it up near where we left off."

As they rehearsed, the boat slid down one side of the tubular stream, across the bottom, and began to crawl slowly up the other side.

"And let's hurry. I've never sailed on anything like this before, and I think I'm starting to get what Dad calls seasick."

"Oh." Gragelouth examined him with interest. "I thought your present coloration was another consequence of our unfortunate condition."

As the boat described acrobatic loops within the tunnel of the river, they sang and played. A now familiar silvery flame gradually enveloped the entire boat, sweeping over and through each of them with a cold, prickly sensation. It faded with the song.

When his vision cleared, Buncan noted that Squill's head and arm had exchanged places. So had his own ears and Gragelouth's, along with other portions of their anatomy no one had had the courage to discuss in detail. Neena had reacquired her coat of dense, carefully groomed fur, though she didn't relax until she had counted each and every one of her restored whiskers.

Everyone was very much relieved.

"That were 'orrible." Neena preened herself as best she could without a comb. "Imagine goin' through life with no more fur on your body than a 'uman!"

"See," said Gragelouth, pointing. "Your hymn of restorations has rejuvenated our craft as well." Sure enough, the crooked mast had been straightened.

It didn't keep them from twisting and swirling upside down, sideways, and every other which way within the tube that was the river Sprilashoone.

"How do we get clear of this?" Buncan gazed at the hissing, reverberating tunnel of water until he found himself growing dizzy. "How do we find a place to land?"

"How did your fathers free themselves from this other enchanted stream?" Gragelouth prompted him.

Neena scratched her head. "Spellsang 'emselves out, I reckon. Or maybe the river just flattened out. Deuced if I remember."

"At least we are traveling in the right direction." The merchant managed to sound optimistic.

Squill eyed him curiously. "Now 'ow do you know that? I've a brilliant sense o' direction, but upside down and all enclosed like this I'm buggered if I can tell a thing."

Gragelouth did not miss a beat. "Traders who travel as much as I do learn how to judge such matters. Many of my customers live in difficult-to-locate places. It would be bad for business if I were unable to find my way to them." A sudden thought cast a pall of concern over his always melancholy face. "I certainly hope we do not reach a point where this tunnel collapses. Drowning may be a less novel means of perishing than going to pieces, but it is just as decisive."

"We wouldn't let you drown, baggy-eyes." Neena smiled at him. "I'd get lonely for your constant complainin'."

"No signs of any change," Buncan assured the sloth, though he had to admit that the thought worried him. Neither he nor the merchant could hold their breath half as long as the otters.

"Your color has improved," Gragelouth informed him.

"I feel better. I guess I'm getting used to this. As much as it's possible to get used to something like this."

He spoke too soon.

CHAPTER 11

TEN MINUTES DOWNSTREAM THE TUNNEL BEGAN TO WARP and curl in upon itself. It felt as if they were sailing at high speed down the intestines of a gigantic snake in the grip of some wild, dyspeptic dance. Which, for all they actually knew, might in fact be the case.

The tubular river bounced and dove, rose and plunged vertically: rapids inside a corkscrew. All the while the boat clung tenaciously to the surface of the water, while its occupants clung to cabin, tiller, gunwale, mast, or one another. The only thing that helped at all, Buncan discovered, was to close one's eyes tight and concentrate on breathing evenly. Gragelouth had long since give up any attempt at steering, because he wished to devote his full attention to not throwing up. Abandoned, the tiller banged plaintively against the stern.

While human and sloth fought desperately to hang on to various portions of the boat as well as the contents of their stomachs, the inimitable otters amused themselves by leaping overboard and cavorting in the crashing waters that rushed and sang on all sides. They positively reveled in the fervid disruption of natural law, ignoring Buncan's warnings to beware of unexpected whirlpools, or intersecting tributaries that might tunnel away to nowhere.

After all, where else could you swim up the side of a river until you were looking *down* on a boat and your companions, then kick free and dive through the air past them to splash into the water directly alongside?

When the otters came back aboard, Buncan weakly suggested they try spellsinging themselves free of the Sprilashoone's grip. Though the otters improvised and rapped enthusiastically, it did not affect their situation in the slightest.

The fact that Buncan regularly interrupted each attempt with a desperate rush for the boat's railing certainly did nothing to enhance the consistency of their spellsinging.

"Why don't you get out o' those clothes an' join us for a swim, Bunc?" Squill suggested. "Might do you good."

"I can't swim like you." There seemed to be six otters in his field of vision. "You know that."

"We'd keep an eye on you, Bunklo," Neena assured him. "Wouldn't let you drown. Anyways, it's got to be better for you than 'angin' on up 'ere, watchin' this bloomin' water go around an' around as this boat goes up and down, up and down, twistin' an' turnin' and bobbin' an' . . ."

Buncan made a peculiar noise and shuffled hurriedly toward the bow.

"Now see wot you've gone an' done," her brother told her.

"Me?" Neena spread both arms wide, whiskers bristling. "I didn't do nothin', I didn't. 'E were already tryin' for the Bellwoods' all-time upchuck record for 'umans."

"Oi, an' 'e didn't need your 'elp goin' for it. All that chatter about the boat goin' up an' down an' back an' forth an' down through this bleedin' corkscrew . . ."

Unable to ignore this cogent analysis of their present condition, Gragelouth stumbled forward to join his young human companion in misery.

The Sprilashoone had more surprises in store. A corkscrew of water thrust them out into blue sky and open air, only to plunge them down afresh into the watery tunnel which had become their home. When it happened a second time they were prepared for the phenomenon, and by the end of an awful night the river was presenting them to the outside world with increasing frequency.

By the dawn of their third day upon the psychotic watercourse, the tunnel had collapsed completely. No more corkscrews pierced its depths, no integral curls tormented its surface. They found themselves drifting downstream at a modest rate atop a broad stream that seemed determined to act, perhaps by way of compensation for the ordeal they had endured within its upper reaches, in as placid a fashion as possible.

Trees and electric-blue bushes lined both banks, while reeds sprang like unruly green hair from the shallows. As they continued, signs of habitation and farming became visible.

Buncan received this information from his companions with admirable equanimity. He was still too weak to rise from his pallet and look for himself. As for Gragelouth, the merchant seemed to have made a more rapid recovery, which did nothing to improve Buncan's waterlogged self-esteem.

While their friends regained their strength, the otters steered the boat away from the banks and carried out necessary minor repairs and cleanup. When not thus occupied, Squill could be found perched atop the mast, studying the shore while keeping alert for any rocks or snags that might be positioning themselves for ambush.

Though he found the whole notion of food abhorrent, Buncan made an effort to eat. When the first few tentative bites stayed down, he found that both his outlook and condition improved. Subsequent offerings by Neena were consumed gratefully, if not enthusiastically. Sooner than he believed possible, he was once more participating fully in the operation of the boat.

"I don't understand." She stood close to him one afternoon as he took his turn at the tiller. " 'Ow can you get so sick just from watchin' the water go past an' around an'—"

Buncan put a finger to her muzzle. "Not only can that make a human sick, sometimes words alone are enough to set it off."

"Oi, I gets it. Sorry."

"That's all right." He smiled. "Just don't do it anymore, okay?"

She nodded apologetically.

"This is fine country," the sloth observed. "I think soon we will come upon a place to refresh ourselves." He glanced skyward. "In any event, the river seems to have changed course. We have been traveling due east for nearly an entire day now, and if we do not soon find ourselves once more sailing more to the north, we will have to abandon this craft and strike out overland again."

Several large birds soared past overhead, their conversation drifting down to the waterborne travelers. They glanced at the river but chose not to drop down for a chat.

The Sprilashoone continued to flow resolutely eastward. Modest riverbank dwellings began to appear, and people in small boats. Not long thereafter larger vessels manifested themselves, their mixed-species crews seining the deep waters for all manner of seafood.

Gragelouth called out to one such vessel as they passed close inboard its port side. "Hanging aboard! We have been some days upon the river and need to reprovision. Is there a town close downstream where this can be effected?"

Two fisherfolk, a raccoon and a brightly clad muskrat, exchanged a bemused glance before the muskrat leaned out to reply. "Friends, I can't imagine where you've come from not to know of Camrioca, but you'll find all you need there."

"How far?" Buncan shouted as the boats slid past each other.

With one hand the raccoon held on to the net he was splicing and with the other pointed downriver. "At your speed, another half day."

There was no mistaking it when they swung 'round a bend in the Sprilashoone. Camrioca was a city, not a town, a true riverine metropolis that hugged a fine deep-water bay. Hundreds of homes and two-story buildings clustered side by side along the quays, jetties, and beaches, while the central portion of the sprawling connurbation featured a walled inner city filled with structures six and even seven floors high.

After Hygria, it was most reassuring to note that Camrioca's architecture featured incomplete walls and ceilings and a riot of color. Repeated sniffs as they searched for a vacant dock at which to tie up indicated that the town was both earthy and inviting. In other words, comfortingly and typically fetid.

Buncan found himself wondering what his parents must be thinking by now. With the privacy spellsong shielding them, Jon-Tom wouldn't be able to track him through magic. If he and the otters had done their job well, even

Clothahump would be unable to penetrate their tightly woven mask of protection.

He forced himself to concentrate on the bustling, odoriferous quays. Being seasick had been debilitating enough. Now was not the time to surrender to homesickness. He straightened. Let his classmates laugh at him when he returned from *this* adventure.

Assuming he did return, he reminded himself.

Gragelouth was gesturing energetically in the direction of a small, unoccupied wharf. "Put in there."

No sailor, Buncan steered as best he could, and they bumped up against the wooden pilings rather hard. No one in the surging, preoccupied crowd paid them the slightest attention, their indifference serving as further confirmation of Camrioca's cosmopolitanism.

Squill queried Gragelouth as the sloth set about securing their craft to its new mooring. "Say, guv, shouldn't we leave someone 'ere to guard the boat?"

The merchant considered the rabble as he tightened a final knot. "I think it will be all right. There is sufficient foot traffic here to discourage the casual thief." He indicated their worn, battered craft. "Besides, with so many better boats moored here, who would be eager to steal this?"

Squill nodded understandingly and turned to contemplate the town. After their many days of isolation on the river, it felt odd to be around so much activity.

"Doesn't look like another Hygria," Buncan opined.

"Nope," Squill agreed. "Looks like a regular town, she does."

"If we have to head northwestward from here, what are we going to do about overland transportation?" Buncan wondered.

"We have the boat to trade," Gragelouth pointed out, "and I still have my purse." He tapped the bag full of coins which rested against his ribs beneath his shirt. "We will find something."

"Not another bloody wagon." Neena let out a groan.

"Unfortunately, I do not have the resources to hire a

corps of eagles to tow us through the sky," the merchant replied rather stiffly. "Did you think this would get easier?"

"No, I suppose not." She sighed resignedly as they headed into town.

Their initial impression of Camrioca as a sophisticated, wealthy community was reinforced by the appearance and attitude of the individual from whom they sought directions. The marmot was fat, graying, and dressed in a wealth of richly embroidered silks trimmed in soft leather. Buncan admired the outfit, while Neena was positively envious.

Clearly delighted to be back among his own kind, an obeisant Gragelouth put their questions to his fellow merchant. Disinclined to speak with the ragged strangers but desirous of avoiding an argument with two armed otters and a tall human, the marmot politely supplied them with directions to the central marketplace.

Full of hawkers and stalls, street vendors and confusion, rife with argument and pungent with exotic smells, the marketplace lay down the main bay street and immediately inland from the waterfront. Many of the shops were a reflection of their proprietors' prosperity, having been constructed of stone or wood. Here goods from downriver and inland collided in a frenzy of commercial activity.

As if the smell wasn't enough, a query directed them to the livestock pens, where traders haggled over the price of riding snakes and dray lizards, fattened food crawlers and select breeding stock. Bemoaning the loss of his old reliable wagon and team, Gragelouth set about attempting to secure adequate transportation for the journey ahead. A good judge of reptilian flesh, he was unlikely to be cheated, but proper bargaining, he warned his companions, would take some time.

That was all right, Buncan assured him. The marketplace of Camrioca was by far the largest of its type he'd ever visited, and there was much to see. He and Squill and Neena would have no problems entertaining themselves while the sloth set to his . . .

Speaking of Neena, where had she gone and got herself to?

Lizards and snakes hissed and jostled within their pens as

their owners alternately coaxed and cajoled them. A trio of armed city police consisting of two coyotes and a helmeted badger struggled to maintain some semblance of rough order. They ignored the noisy, screeching fight taking place between an insulted margay and a panda certain he had been cheated. The margay had teeth and claws on his side, but the panda had strength. The cops had business elsewhere.

As for Grageloutch, the merchant ignored it all. He was already bargaining intently with a strangely clad, wizened-face little macaque for the use of four bipedal riding lizards. They would not have the endurance or hauling capacity of his old team, but would travel much more swiftly. Squill stood impatiently nearby, looking bored.

Buncan scanned the crowd. Where was Neena?

"Squill, you see your sister?"

"Sure, mate. She's right over..." He blinked, then shrugged disinterestedly. "So she's wandered off, gone bloody shopping. You know 'ow females are."

"Not really. How can she do any shopping? She hasn't got any money with her."

Squill winked. "Old Mudge, 'e can't 'elp teachin' us things Weegee wishes 'e wouldn't."

"If she's off on some crazy stealing spree and she gets caught, we may not be able to get her out. This is a big, well-developed city. I'm sure they have big, well-developed jails. Also, if she gets herself in trouble after everything we've been through and survived, I'll personally pluck her bald all over again myself."

"Good luck at that, mate." Squill was grinning. "She's been plucked before, by better than you."

"It's not funny." He stopped searching over the heads of the crowd and motioned to Grageloutch. Irritated at being interrupted, the merchant excused himself from his haggling.

"What is it, boy? Be quick about it or I'll lose what leverage I've gained."

"Neena seems to have disappeared."

"Otters are always coming and going. It is their manner to be unpredictable and impulsive. I would not worry. She will return soon."

"Probably, but Squill and I are gonna go have a look for her anyway."

"Please yourselves. Try not to be long. I hope not to be long here. Negotiations are proceeding satisfactorily. Oh, and try to stay out of trouble, human."

"I just want to make sure that's what Neena's doing."

The sloth seemed mollified as he returned to his bargaining.

Buncan and Squill made their way through the livestock pens until they were back among the stalls and street vendors. Hours of searching failed to locate the absent otter.

Squill was somewhat less than distressed. "Crikey, I've been tryin' to lose the-mouth-that-swims for years."

"This is serious. Can't you be serious for once?"

" 'Ell of a thing to ask of an otter, mate."

Buncan surveyed the surging crowd. "We have to keep looking."

They finally obtained something more than a curt shake of the head from a mongoose selling copper pots, pans, and other utensils.

"Female you say, about your size?" Squill nodded tersely. "Elaborately streaked and made-up fur? Don't-give-a-damn attitude?"

"That's me sister, all right."

The mongoose looked back down at the saucepan he was hammering out. "Haven't seen her."

Buncan pushed his way past Squill. He towered above the otter, as he did over most of the denizens of the marketplace. The coppersmith eyed him warily.

"Look, I do not want any trouble."

"That was a pretty precise description you just gave of someone you claim not to have seen."

"Well, you see, it is like this." The mongoose's gaze darted in several directions. "It would be worth my life if it were to become known in certain quarters that I voluntarily gave you such information."

Buncan considered. "Correct me if I'm wrong, but what you're saying is that you have some information, but that we're going to have to threaten you to get it?"

"Did I say that? I did not say anything like that."

"Let me beat it out of 'im." Flexing his fingers, Squill

took an eager step forward. The merchant shrank from his approach.

Buncan put a restraining hand on the otter's arm. "I think that's enough of a threat to suffice."

"Oh, yes." The mongoose smiled relievedly. "I am thoroughly intimidated, and therefore no one can blame me for telling you what happened."

"Something happened to Neena?" Buncan's anxiety level doubled.

The vendor fingered the saucepan. "She was asked to spend some time as the guest of a powerful citizen."

Buncan and Squill exchanged a glance. "What citizen?" Buncan finally asked.

"The Baron Koliac Krasvin."

"Never 'eard o' 'im." Squill let out a derisive snort. "But then, up until recently I never 'eard o' this dung'eap either."

"Who is this Baron Krasvin?" Buncan inquired intently.

"A local nobleperson of ignoble repute but substantial fortune," the mongoose informed them. "Please do not torture me anymore."

"Yeah, yeah," said Buncan impatiently. "Get on with it."

"Surrounded by numerous retainers and household guards, he resides in a fortified mansion west of the city and well outside its boundaries. Also its jurisdiction. I cannot stand much more of this pain," he added, rather sedately for one ostensibly in the throes of final torment.

"Why would Neena go with this bloke?" Squill wanted to know.

The trader coughed delicately. "The Baron is not especially well-liked in Camrioca. An expert with both saber and rapier, he has killed several in duels, and there are those who find his presence in the Crescent of Nobles displeasing. But he is the scion of a noble family, and he has money. A difficult combination to abjure."

"Sounds like a real prince," Buncan muttered. "What's this got to do with my friend's sister?"

The mongoose glanced sharply at Squill. "Ah, she is your sister. That is most unfortunate."

For the first time Squill exhibited a semblance of real concern. "Wot are you on about, guv?"

"Besides being a deadly fighter, and powerful and rich, the Baron Krasvin happens to be a mink."

"A mink?" Squill blinked. "Wot's that got to do with . . . Oh. A mink, it is?"

Buncan frowned at his friend. "I guess I'm missing something."

"Did you cut *all* your tribal-classification classes, mate?" Squill peered up at him. "We otters 'ave pretty intense appetites in certain areas."

"Like for fish?"

"I ain't talkin' about food 'ere, Buncan. Otters 'ave extreme longin's for swimmin' and for fun. 'Umans like to argue. Wolves are partial to singin'. Cattle like to stand around an' gossip an' 'orses like to pull things. None o' them can 'elp it. It's all part o' the natural order o' things. Minks like to . . . Let me put it like this. Your average mink would make Mudge look celibate."

"Oh. Oh, *shit*."

Squill was nodding vigorously. "I mean, I never thought o' me own sister as attractive. Kind o' a frump, if you 'appened to ask me. But bein' 'er brother an' all, I suppose from the viewpoint o' another she might possess characteristics that—"

"It would not matter, sir," the mongoose interrupted him. "With the Baron it would become a challenge, a question of honor, were one who happened to catch his eye decide to decline his advances. Would your sister be likely to do that?"

"With a knife, if necessary," Squill readily admitted.

"You're saying you saw this Krasvin ask Neena for a date, or an assignation, or something?" Buncan said.

"Nothing like that. Please stop the pain."

"Come on," Buncan urged the coppersmith. "We're wasting time. What did you see?"

"Please," the vendor hissed at him, "I have to maintain the fiction, or word could get back to the Baron's agents that I helped you willingly."

"All right, all right. I'm beating you to a pulp, see? But try and hurry it up."

"That is precisely what occurred. The Baron was accompanied by a number of his armed retainers. I was sitting right here and saw it all happen. From what I could tell, the young female not only categorically refused his invitation, she laughed at him."

"Uh-oh," Squill muttered.

"Though I did not know her, at that moment I myself feared for her," the mongoose confessed. "I could of course not become involved."

"Of course not," Buncan said dryly.

"The Baron Krasvin is not a mink for a compatible female to laugh at. Especially in a public place. He takes his reputation very seriously. I sensed it was not the sort of insult he could allow to pass. So I continued to watch."

"Your sister," he told Squill, "came down this line of stalls. Down there," he pointed, "is a public lavatory. As she was about to enter, I saw three of the Baron's retainers jump upon her and assault her with clubs. She fought ferociously but, taken by surprise, was quickly overpowered. They placed her in a canvas sack and spirited her away. To the Baron's mansion, I am sure."

"And you didn't try to intervene, or call for help?" Buncan said darkly.

The mongoose was unrepentant. "They would have killed me without a thought, and by the time city police might have arrived they would have been long gone. Besides which, nobles are but infrequently taken to task for their infractions."

"Don't get on 'im, mate," said Squill unexpectedly. " 'E were only protectin' 'imself."

"You think she's been taken to this Krasvin's house," Buncan growled. "Tell us how to get there."

"If you will stop beating me, I will give you directions. Ah, that's better. Perhaps you can make some kind of deal with the Baron, buy her back. He likes money as well as . . ."

"We get the picture," Buncan told him.

The mongoose nodded. "You must of course put any

foolish thoughts of forcibly liberating her out of your minds.''

''Why?'' Buncan wanted to know.

''Because the Baron's abode, within which he lives a life of barbaric ease, is impregnable. While not actually a castle, it would still take a small army to surmount its walls. I myself have seen this residence, and I promise, you would not get past the outer gate.''

''Cor, we *are* a small army.'' Squill jabbed a thumb against his chest. ''An' we 'ave unique weapons at our disposal.''

Do we? Buncan wondered. *Can Squill and I spellsing without the harmonizing of his sister?* He was less than sanguine about the possibilities.

''Don't worry.'' Buncan placed a comforting arm around his friend's shoulders as they made their way back to the livestock pens to fill Gragelouth in on what had transpired. ''We'll get her out.''

''I weren't worryin' about 'er, mate. I was feelin' sorry for this 'ere Krasvin chap. 'E 'asn't a clue wot 'e's got 'imself into.''

''You're not taking this lightly,'' Buncan admonished him. ''Neena's in serious trouble.''

''Maybe. On the other 'and, if we left 'er 'ere she'd probably be all right until we got back, we'd travel faster, and I bet she'd eat better than us.''

Buncan promptly smacked the otter on the side of his head, dislodging his cap. Startled, Squill gazed at his friend in surprise.

''Ow! Wot did you 'it me for?''

''You know damn well what I hit you for! Neena's your sister, your only sibling.''

''You're tellin' me.''

Buncan's voice dropped dangerously. ''Did it ever occur to you that after having his way with her, this Baron could have her killed instead of setting her free? Just for having laughed at him? From what that mongoose told us, this Krasvin sounds capable of that. Maybe if your positions, so to speak, were reversed, you'd be thinking differently.''

''Oh, all right!'' Squill threw up his hands by way of

surrender. "So we'll save 'er or die tryin', just like all brave fools are supposed to. But our jolly merchant will decry the delay."

Sure enough, once he'd heard all the details Gragelouth didn't want any part of their unlikely rescue attempt. If anything, he was less encouraging than the mongoose.

"You are great spellsingers, but you are young and inexperienced, in matters of siege and war no less than in sorcery." He brushed fur away from his mouth. "And I am sure it has occurred to you that with the female component of your spellsinging triumvirate indisposed, you may not be able to work any necromancy at all. Should that be the case, you will be two against a well-defended target. That is not bravery; it is suicide."

"Then we'll have to take the mongoose's suggestion and try and negotiate her release," Buncan said.

"We do not have anywhere near the necessary funds," the merchant reminded him. "We would not even if I canceled the purchase of the riding lizards."

" 'Ow about we sneak inside and kill 'em one at a time?" Squill suggested.

"Oh, that's very good." Buncan smiled sarcastically. "We don't even know what kind of house soldiers Krasvin employs."

Gragelouth let out a long, resigned sigh, half of which emerged via his nostrils. "Perhaps you should leave more of this to me."

Squill eyed him in surprise. "You don't mean you're comin' with us?"

"I need your help if I am ever to ascertain the existence of the Grand Veritable. I cannot imagine encountering again any others as blindly willing and credulous as yourselves."

"Cor, thanks, guv," Squill murmured sardonically.

"We don't go on without Neena. That's understood," Buncan said flatly. Gragelouth nodded tiredly.

"Yes, yes. But we must somehow convince, pay, or trick at least a few soldiers-at-arms into coming with us, or we will surely have less than no chance."

"Righty-ho!" Squill straightened. "Stiff upper whiskers

an' all that. If we're lucky, maybe we can 'ire on a few
more otters.''

"May the god of all honest merchants preserve me from
that," Gragelouth muttered, sufficiently low so that Squill
did not overhear.

CHAPTER **12**

SHE FINALLY BEGAN HER GRADUAL ASCENT FROM THE
bottom of the pool. It was one of the most beautiful pools
she'd ever visited, deep and cool and perfectly circular.
There were no fish, only dark olive-green fronds with
scalloped edges that swayed back and forth in the current.

Sunlight and air beckoned overhead as she spiraled lazily
upward, not swimming at all, carried skyward by a reverse
whirlpool. When she broke the surface, she blinked and
inhaled softly.

Instead of the sun, she found herself staring at a glowbulb
suspended from the nave of a vaulted ceiling decorated with
richly carved dark wood. Turning her head to her left, she
saw a high, narrow window of stained glass. The unknown
artist had used the chromatically colored, intricately shaped
pieces to illustrate a bedroom scene, a scene that . . .

Waking up fast, she rolled over in the expansive, canopied
bed.

There was no refreshing pool, unless one counted the
swirl of fine linen on which she reposed. She was not even
slightly damp. Every strand of her fur had been brushed out,
and her coat radiated a fine, cushy silkiness. Instead of her
familiar shorts and top, she found herself clad in a full-
length dress of pink satin sewn with pearls and semiprecious stones. The sleeves were short and puffed at the
shoulders. Matching slippers shod her feet. Tiny silver bells
had been braided into her tail, and even her whiskers had
been sprayed with pink glitter. They itched.

Her initial reaction was to strip the stones and pearls from the dress and cram them into the first container she could find, but as there was no booty bag handy she spent the time instead yanking off the too-tight slippers while inspecting more of her surroundings.

It was quite the largest bed she had ever seen, with its sweeping crewelwork canopy and line of pillows marching from one side to the other at the top. It could accommodate the most energetic' couple, together with their immediate family as well as assorted aunts, uncles, and distant cousins. No doubt it was a source of continuing delight to its owner.

It suddenly struck her that she might well have been brought to this place to participate in just such entertainment.

Whoever had caused the bed to be fabricated was no giant. It was built low to the floor, and she slipped off easily, heading for the single window. The stained glass lay just out of reach. If she stacked a few things underneath she was sure she could reach the small sill at its base.

As she began her search for suitable objects, she happened to catch sight of herself in a large, oval, freestanding mirror. Her cheerful, brightly hued makeup had been redone exclusively in pink and rose, the stylish streaking running from the corners of her eyes and mouth in waves to the back of her head. Powdered ruby and garnet applied over a base of black specular hematite had been used to create the stunning effect. A glance over her shoulder as she pirouetted revealed that the back of the dress was cut in a sharp V all the way down to the base of her tail.

Blimey, she thought as she stared at her reflection, *I'm bloomin' gorgeous.* Too bad it was a wasted effort on someone's part. She preferred to be asked.

The glowbulb illuminated the entire ceiling, its light supplemented by the pair of tall oil lamps which flanked the bed. She suspected the moderation of its glow was due to intent, not a weakening of the spell which powered it. Someone was striving hard for a particular atmosphere of which she, like the subdued light and the bawdy stained glass and the bed, was merely one more component.

She found a chair and placed it beneath the window. Resuming her search, she passed once more in front of the

mirror and, in spite of herself, stopped to stick out a short
leg. Someone had outdone themselves in fashioning the
dress. Otters were difficult to tailor for, with their short
waists and limbs and long, sinuous bodies. The folds of fine
satin were highly flattering.

"It is better for someone else to admire such a work of
art."

She spun away from the mirror as the speaker shut the
single door behind him. The mink was no taller than she,
and slightly slimmer. His fur was finer and darker. He wore
jeweled sandals with pantaloons and a vest of metallic red
accented with black leather. The vest had a high, stiff collar
which framed his finely formed head. More decoration than
threat, a bejeweled dagger was secured at his waist. A
double earring dangled from his left ear.

Unlike his complimentary tone, the expression on his face
was positively predatory. Not that her situation required
additional explication. Neena was young but hardly naive.
Her elegant attire had been provided for her captor's enjoy-
ment, not hers.

Her pupils dilated sharply. "I know you. You're the
arrogant bastard from the marketplace. You kidnapped me."

"Correct on both counts." The mink had a brusque,
clipped manner of speaking. "I am the Baron Koliac Krasvin,
at your servicing, which I intend to carry out shortly."

"I'll wager 'tis 'shortly,' all right."

His laconic smile vanished. "Your attempt at humor is
ill-timed. I suggest you lighten your attitude instead and it
will be the better for you. You may call me Koliac."

" 'Ow about 'Colon' instead? Or, if you'd prefer a little
more familiarity, Shithead."

One thing for the Baron: He was not easily nonplussed.
"Please, no simple bucolic obscenities. If you are going to
call me names, at least strive for inventiveness."

That sparked an idea. Not a great one, but her options
were pretty limited. "You want to see inventive? I'll show
you inventive." She straightened. "You'd better open that
door right now, or I won't be responsible for the 'orrible
things that'll ensue."

Krasvin took a dainty, measured step forward, grinning unpleasantly. "That's all right. I will."

She retreated from the vicinity of the mirror. "I'm warnin' you; I'm a spellsinger, I am."

His grin widened. "Oh, surely. And you are about to turn me into a newt."

"I mean it. I'll do it."

"You certainly will," Krasvin assured her, "willingly or otherwise. You know, I've never met a spellsinger, but I've heard of them. Do not their mystic conjurations require instrumental accompaniment? I know for a fact that you do not have an instrument on you. At least, not a musical one."

She found herself being backed toward the bed, which was not a preferred line of retreat. "'Ere now, don't you realize that you're a very offensive person?"

"Oh, surely. It's an integral part of my personality. But I've learned to live with it. I noticed that you like your gown. It was originally sewn for a lady mink, but I had it modified especially for you."

"You needn't 'ave bothered."

"No bother."

"Doesn't it trouble you that I'm an otter an' not a mink?"

"On the contrary, I find the differences intriguing rather than disconcerting. Besides which, my tastes are quite broad. As soon as I set eyes on you I knew that an inevitable succession of events was about to commence. These will conclude presently. And I grow tired of talking."

She looked around desperately, but there was only the single high window and the one door. She considered taking a running jump at the stained glass, but it was a foolish notion. Otters were adept at many kinds of physical exertion, but with their short legs running jumps could not be counted among them. If they'd been in the water, now...

The door would surely be guarded. There was no other potential exit, not even a fireplace. Only the bed, several chests full of clothing, the canopy over the bed which was too fragile to support anyone, a couple of chairs, the oval mirror, the cold cut-slate floor, the single glowbulb high above, and the two freestanding oil lamps.

Those were her only potential weapons. But minks were quick. If she threw a lamp and missed, she doubted it would improve his disposition any. And he could always call for help.

She decided to try another tack. "Please, good sir; me friends and I are just passing through this part o' the world. They'll come lookin' for me, don't you know. One o' them is a rich an' powerful merchant."

"Who has to haggle for a bargain in the marketplace." As he advanced she saw that Krasvin's teeth were very white, and very sharp.

She bumped up against the bed frame and started edging sideways. While undeniably beautiful, the dress was a definite hindrance. Perhaps that was the idea.

"Stay away from me."

"On the contrary, I intend to get quite close to you. Bear in mind that I have gone to some trouble and expense to position you in your present circumstances. I have no intention of letting you leave until we have come to know each other much better. So to speak. A number of times."

"I think I know you as well as I want to already." She made it around the foot of the bed, and he followed relentlessly, making no move to rush her, clearly enjoying the athletic foreplay. Eventually she would tire, and there was nowhere else for her to go. They all came to that realization eventually.

"Come now," he chided her. "I'm not such a bad fellow. I assure you from experience that our minor tribal differences will not hinder mutual revelation. Haven't you ever wondered if what they say about minks is true?"

"Not even from an academic standpoint," she shot back.

"You're lying, but that's okay. You're going to get answers to questions you never thought to ask. How old are you, by the way?" His persistent stare was base and clinical. "Not very, I'd wager. Just beginning to bloom. Delightful." Despite his veneer of sophistication, he was all but drooling on the floor.

He was closer now, one paw extended.

"Keep away from me!" She whirled and raced to the other side of the bed.

As Krasvin advanced purposefully, she removed the oil lamp from its metal holder and set the flaming crystal container aside, wielding the metal pole which had formerly supported it like a lance. Krasvin was not intimidated.

"That dress flatters every line of your body, you know."

"No closer!" She gestured warningly with the tip of the lamp pole.

He halted. "Oh, my. You have armed yourself. I fear I must rethink my intentions." He turned his back on her.

She didn't relax even slightly. "Get out. Through the door, go on. I'll just wait in 'ere for me friends."

He peered back over his shoulder, the earring bobbing above his fur. "Anything else you'd like me to do for you? Any other demands? No?" He turned and dropped his eyes momentarily. An instant later he was upon her.

Normally there wasn't a creature alive an agile mink couldn't run down. But despite being slightly stouter of build, otters were nearly as quick. She threw the lamp pole as soon as he made his move. He twisted lithely, knocking it to the floor with both hands. It landed between them, clanging against the stone floor.

As soon as the pole left her fingers, she grabbed up the lamp and heaved it. Again the Baron dodged. The lamp just missed his head, landing a good distance behind him and shattering against the slate. Flaming oil spread along the grout between the stones.

Krasvin glanced at the fire, which would burn itself out harmlessly, before turning back to her. "Don't you find it warm enough in here already? You should save your strength. You're going to need it." He resumed his measured advance. "Has it not occurred to you by now that I have followed this exact scenario through to its inevitable conclusion many times before this, and that I am familiar with anything you might do or try? Much as I enjoy these little games, I don't see any sense in prolonging them. You will not leave this chamber until I say so. Meanwhile, why not give in to reality and make it as easy as possible on yourself?"

Neena seemed to slump. "I guess . . . I guess you're right." She dropped her head, adopting what she imagined to be a conciliatory, complaisant posture.

"That's better," he said curtly. He nodded to his right. "On the bed with you. Or would you like me to throw you there?" He came nearer, stepping over the fallen lamp pole as he reached for her.

As he did so, she advanced submissively toward him. One slippered foot came down on the base of the fallen pole. Hard.

The other end of the pole snapped upward directly between his short legs. His eyes widened sufficiently for her to see the dying oil fire reflected fully in them, while his grin was replaced by another expression entirely as he crumpled to the floor.

She rushed to him and ripped the decorative dagger from his waistband. For some reason he made no move to stop her, perhaps because his hands were presently elsewhere occupied. Nor did he venture any clever *bon mots*.

Skirt swirling around her, she raced for the door and began pounding madly on the heavy wooden barrier. "The Baron," she screamed, "the Baron's 'avin' a heart attack! Someone help, please help us!"

As the door swung wide to reveal a pair of muscular, heavily armed weasels, she stepped aside, holding her hands behind her. While one kept a wary eye on her, the other rushed into the room as soon as he spotted the Baron writhing on the floor. Krasvin was holding himself with one hand and gesturing weakly with the other, his ability to sculpt coherent words still somewhat inhibited.

"No . . . don't . . . ," he was gasping.

His feeble protestations drew the attention of the second guard, at which point Neena brought her arm around fast and hard to thrust the dagger into his side, just beneath his armor. The weasel squealed but managed only a desultory gesture of interference as she sprinted past him.

Only to find an orang-utan clad in black chain mail and spiked helmet blocking the hallway. His long arms extended from one wall to the other, preventing her from dashing past.

"Now where did you think you were going, m'lady?" he growled at her.

"Nowhere," she gasped. " 'Tis just that the Baron 'as been taken suddenly ill an' . . ." She looked back toward the chamber. Through the gaping door she could see the first guard helping Krasvin to his feet. The other had staggered into the room, clutching his side.

Frowning, the orang looked past her. "Looks like he's being helped."

" 'E needs it," she replied, "an' so will you." A lightning strike with the dagger thrust up under the chest armor and into the orang's belly. One long arm groped for her and missed as she withdrew the bloody blade and hurried onward.

Dress flying, she sped down the now empty hallway, searching wildly for any exit. The building she was in seemed endless. As she turned a corner she nearly ran into a pair of spear-carrying rats and a single langur.

There was an open door on her left, and she took it, finding herself in some kind of pantry or kitchen annex. Bundles of dried meat, packages sealed with wax, sacks of flour barred her path as she struggled through. Behind her, voices were rising in counterpoint to the echo of booted and sandaled feet. The household was being alerted to her flight.

She forced open the door on the far side of the vestibule and found herself in a large, open room lit by oil lamps and the single obligatory overhead glowbulb. Fully three walls of the two-story-high chamber were lined with shelves on which reposed more books than she'd ever seen in her life, more books than she imagined even Clothahump must possess. Bindings of wood and metal, of leather and exotic materials, gleamed in the indirect light.

A large double-sided reading table and two matching chairs occupied the center of the room, while a narrow railed walkway ran completely around the library at mezzanine level. A single ladder leaned against an opening in the railing, providing access to the upper shelves. The fourth wall was mostly glass, dark now since it was night outside.

To her right a brace of double doors stood open, revealing a spacious atrium beyond. It also exposed the interior of the library to the outside, which was full of bustling, armed retainers.

One spotted her and pointed. "There she is!"

She looked around frantically. The heavy, beveled windows would open but slowly, if at all. A desperate rush might carry her through . . . at the risk of being cut to bloody shreds.

As the noise outside increased, she grabbed one of the cut-crystal oil lamps, making sure it was at least half full, and scampered up the ladder to the second-level walkway. A pair of armed pacas entered, espied her, and came a-rushing. Setting the lamp down on the landing, she put both hands on the top of the ladder and shoved. It made a satisfying crash as it struck both of them, knocking one to the floor.

A couple of pottos showed up but made no move to resurrect the ladder. They were followed by a hyrax and a trio of stout armadillos. The Baron arrived a moment later, escorted by a single weasel.

"Cheers." She smiled bravely as she clutched the dagger tight. " 'Ow's your ardor? Cooled a bit?"

He grinned back up at her, but it was clearly a strain. "Under different circumstances I might have found the encounter stimulating."

"Cor, you don't say?" She waved the blade. "Come on up 'ere an' I'll be glad to stimulate you some more."

"You're being very tiresome. Come down from there. Now."

"Sorry. I kind o' like it up 'ere. Meanwhile, you can kiss your arse."

He took a deep breath. "I see that ropes and restraints are in order. I had hoped you would come to enjoy my attentions, or at least tolerate them. Now I see that I will have to take a different approach. It will in nowise mitigate my pleasure, but I assure you that you will find it exceedingly uncomfortable." He gestured. There were now a dozen armed retainers in the room.

Two of the armadillos picked up the ladder, while a dexterous gibbon placed his saber between his teeth and prepared to ascend as soon as it had been properly positioned. Seeing that the armadillos intended to set the ladder against the railing on the other side of the room, Neena rushed around the walkway and prepared to confront them.

As the ladder struck home, the climbing gibbon drew his saber and cut at her legs. She hopped lithely over the blow, avoiding a second slash just to show it was no fluke, and sliced the combative primate across his lightly clad chest. Clutching at the wound, the ape lost his balance and fell, rather dramatically, to the floor below. His colleagues thoughtfully scattered, none gallant enough to break their companion's fall.

"Get her down from there, you idiots!" Krasvin raged at his servants. "Get another ladder! Get several." As a number of the retainers rushed to do his bidding, he whirled to glare up at her.

While everyone waited on those who had left, the armadillos raised the single ladder a second time. This time it was a somewhat reluctant rat who cautiously ascended the rungs. As he climbed, he jabbed his long spear in Neena's direction. Retreating, she parried the unwieldy thrusts until the rat was within reach. Then she darted forward beneath the spearpoint and slashed at his hand. The rodent yelped, dropped his spear, and shinnied quickly back down the ladder.

She'd grabbed at the spear but missed, hoping to gain something to hurl at the gaping faces below. It was then she realized that in that regard she was not unequipped.

The first tome she pulled from the shelves was weighty and thickly bound. This satisfying missile struck one of the armadillos square on the forehead. It squealed in pain and let go of the ladder as its companion tried to balance the heavy object.

Additional volumes followed in joyful and rapid succession. They caused plenty of confusion, if no real damage.

A stricken Krasvin stepped hastily to the fore. "Stop that!" He bent to recover a damaged tome, cradling it lovingly. "Don't you realize how valuable this collection is? Do you have any idea what goes into the manufacture of a single book?" He was genuinely distressed.

Neena smiled inwardly. She'd found Krasvin's weak spot.

It seemed he was a collector not only of unwilling young females, but of books. She would not have guessed it.

"No, I don't." She selected an especially beautifully bound volume from the nearest shelf. "You mean it would be really hard to replace this if you did this to it?" Opening the book, she began to rip out pages at random, tossing them over the railing. They fluttered to the floor like stricken moths.

"Don't *do* that!" His fist clenched in a paroxysm of frustration, Krasvin glared at his people. "Where are those other ladders?"

Neena promptly began ripping and flinging fistfuls of pages from volumes chosen at random, until a blizzard of paper and vellum filled the room. Helpless to stop her, Krasvin was suffering more than he had from the lamp pole. Witnessing his agony made Neena feel better than she had in some time.

Wheezing and panting, several retainers finally returned with two more ladders. Gathering along different walls, they prepared to assault her from three directions at once. Quick as she was, she knew she could probably hold them off for a little while. But eventually they would wear her down. Once more in his paws, she knew Krasvin would take steps to see that her escape attempt could not be repeated.

"It's all over." Mink eyes stared ferociously up at her. "Come down right now and maybe, maybe, if you beg me hard enough and long enough, I won't have you killed when I'm finished with you."

"I reckon you're right, mister Baron. It is over. Except for this." Taking the last volume she'd extracted from the shelves, she held it upside down so that the pages dangled loose directly above the open flame of the crystal oil lamp. As soon as it caught, she heaved the flaming folio over the railing. It landed amidst a pile of torn pages, which immediately flared brightly.

"Put that out!" Ripping the cloak from one of his retainers, Krasvin flung it onto the fire and began hopping madly to snuff the flames. Only the quick thinking of the langur, who raced for the kitchen and returned moments later with a pail of water, enabled them to extinguish the blaze before the entire room was engulfed.

When Krasvin was finally able to turn his attention back to his former captive, she already had another pile of irreplaceable kindling ready. Half a dozen other books lay open nearby, soaked with oil from the lamp.

"Righty-ho. Now, do I get out o' 'ere, or does this 'ole blinkin' repository go up in smoke?"

"You'll burn with it."

"I'll take me chances. 'Ow about you?" She was not smiling now.

"You don't get out of here," he spat out. "You never get out of here. Even if you burn down the whole library."

She shrugged. "Suit yourself, guv." She lowered the book she was holding toward the open flame, sure they could smell the oil she'd spread about even on the floor below.

"Wait!" The mink raised both paws. She hesitated. "Let's . . . talk."

She nodded slowly, pursing her lower lip. "That's more like it. I'm always willin' to chat. But I'm pretty tired. Tired o' tryin' to watch everybody."

The Baron gestured. The three ladders were lowered and the retainers backed off, several of them retreating to the atrium outside. Selecting one of the reading chairs, Krasvin sat down facing her. "Better?"

"Bloody right it is. Now I'd like some water."

"How about some fine wine instead?"

She smiled thinly. "I may be young, but I ain't stupid. Just water. Cold. An' somethin' to eat. Fresh fish would be nice."

"Anything else?" he asked tensely.

She didn't flinch from his even, murderous gaze. "If there is, I'll let you know."

He nodded once and relayed the instructions to a servant. The paca vanished through the double doorway. Setting themselves to wait, the remaining retainers put their weapons aside and leaned against the shelves, or sat down on the tiled floor.

Krasvin crossed his arms and continued to watch her.

"You must know that there is no way I'm going to let you leave here without having you first. Especially after what you've done."

"I think you're the one who's been 'ad, Baron." She sat down on the walkway, her back against the shelves.

"What do you think you're going to do after you've eaten and drunk?" he asked her.

"First things first." *There*, she thought. *That's better than confessing that I haven't the slightest idea what I am going to do next.*

"You don't mind if I eat with you?" Something of Krasvin's smile had returned. "All this activity has made me quite hungry." He whispered to another servant.

"'As it, now? I'd 'oped I'd managed to kill your appetite completely."

"No. Only momentarily stun it."

"Too bad I couldn't 'ave used this." She made a gesture with the appropriated dagger. "Instead of just a lamp pole. If my father were 'ere 'e'd slice you up into family souvenirs. An' 'is friend is the greatest spellsinger in all the Warmlands."

Krasvin did not appear impressed. Servants arrived bearing food and drink. She made certain the paca who handed up hers from the top of one ladder was unarmed. When he'd completed the delivery, she kicked the ladder off the walkway. The ever-ready armadillos caught it as it fell.

Krasvin picked daintily at his own victuals. "Unfortunately, none of the individuals of whom you speak are here."

"Me travelin' companions are."

"No, you are wrong. They are in Camrioca. If they haven't already abandoned you. While you . . . are here. With me."

She chewed on the fish and sipped at the water only after carefully smelling of both. If they were drugged, it was with substances beyond her ability to distinguish. She had to chance it.

Besides, from the Baron's point of view there was no need for such subtleties. He could sleep whenever he felt like it, rotating guards as long as was necessary, knowing that exhaustion would eventually overcome her. As they ate she saw other servants coming and going, stocking the library with pails of water to douse any fire as Krasvin sought to prepare for the final assault.

As soon as she'd had enough to drink she poured the rest of the water over her head, soaking the elegant gown and running her makeup. It freshened her, but only, she knew, for a while.

Where in the name of the Ultimate Whirlpool were her friends and that lazy useless ragball of a brother? Not that they were likely to successfully crash this pocket fortress, but surely they were bound to try? She settled herself as best she could, shifting her position on the unyielding wooden walkway.

She was determined to put off the inevitable for as long as possible. If naught else, by the time she finally gave out she might be too exhausted to feel anything.

Krasvin sat watching her, his gaze rarely wavering. His principal adviser, an elderly mandrill, approached and dared to whisper in his ear.

"Why don't we rush her, your lordship? See, she tires already? How many books could she burn before we took her?"

"Fool." The cowled mandrill shrank back. "One more would be too many. Don't you know how precious this library is? How valuable a single volume is in the scheme of existence? How irreplaceable the knowledge it holds, the information it contains within its multitudinous pages? Books are by far the most valuable resource of the Learned. They are the foundation of civilization, the bedrock of society, the source of all that is profound and wise and benign. The loss of a single folio denigrates me, denigrates, you, diminishes all thinking individuals. That is a catastrophe to be avoided at all costs."

"Actually, your lordship, I thought that fornication was more important to you than books."

"I am surprised at you, Byelroeth. You know that this library is my most valued possession. That it is the supreme example of its kind not only in Camrioca, but in all the lands to the south and east. It is the envy of all who visit here. Having seen it, they cannot do else but admire my dedication to erudition and learning, to great literature and to research.''

''Your pardon, your lordship, but may I remind you that this library consists entirely of pornography?''

The mink's gaze narrowed as he regarded his Adviser. ''Are you making fun of me, Byelroeth?''

The mandrill's eyes widened. ''Me? Never, your lordship.''

Krasvin turned away, easing back in his chair and focusing once more on the seated figure of the lady otter on the walkway above.

''Incompetents. I am surrounded by incompetents. No wonder a single female of a tribe not noted for their depth of thinking has been able to outsmart and outfight all of you.''

''Aye. *All* of us, Master,'' came a voice from somewhere behind him.

He whirled furiously. ''Who said that?'' A few startled faces looked back at him. Several shuffled uneasily where they stood. But no one owned up to the comment.

He forced himself to set the matter aside. Now was not the time to go lopping off heads arbitrarily. That could come later. Right now he needed every paw and claw.

''Whoever spoke was right in one sense. She is making fools of us all.''

''We are just not all as frustrated as you, Master,'' said another voice. Krasvin joined in the nervous laughter which followed this sally. *Keep them relaxed and they will put more enthusiasm into their work,* he told himself. Much later, when this episode was concluded, he would administer truth serum to each and every one of them. When the severed heads of the guilty were mounted atop the front gate, he would see to it that they were positioned with smiles on their faces in memory of the untimely quips which had ultimately convicted them.

Fulfillment of his desires had merely been delayed, not thwarted.

The female who was making a fool of him tapped the book she had opened on her lap. It was bound in green snakeskin fore-edged with gold.

''Oi, Baron!'' He said nothing. ''This 'ere could be an educational experience if you weren't so bloody insistent on forcin' yourself on me." She turned a leaf, shook her head at what the next page revealed. "I do believe you're a right nasty-minded little sod, Kraven."

"Krasvin. Will you come down from there?"

"Only if you can figure a way o' assurin' me o' safe passage out o' 'ere, an' promisin' that you won't come huntin' for me and me companions." She looked past him, toward the double doorway. "They should be arrivin' any time now."

He smiled disarmingly. "Your so-called friends seem shy. There has been no sign of any visitors at the gates or on the grounds, save for a single itinerant peddler whom my staff drenched with dirty dishwater and sent packing. Can it be that your erstwhile companions have conceded the reality of your capture and are relaxing in the city, drinking and taking their ease and generally enjoying themselves? That would be the sensible thing for them to do should they have learned what has happened to you. Are they sensible, these friends of yours?"

She nudged the lamp a little nearer to the pile of opened, oil-soaked books just to see him tense up. "I really ought to get this goin'. 'Tis a mite chilly in 'ere."

Below, Krasvin raised a restraining paw. "Don't. These volumes are all unique, all one of a kind."

She tapped the one she was perusing. "I'll bet. I'd 'ate to think there were more than one o' these."

"Judge me if you will, but don't judge my books. All knowledge is valuable."

"Spoken like a scholar. 'Course, that means nothin' to me. I'm just a fun-lovin' sort. So are me friends, as you'll find out when they arrive." At which point, in spite of making a great effort to suppress the reaction, she yawned.

Krasvin's smile returned. "I will put my mind to a method of ensuring your unhindered departure."

"So you've decided to let me go?" She yawned again.

"My library is more important to me than any mere conquest. I will think how to reassure you."

"Now you're bein' smart." As she eyed him uncertainly the book started to slide from her relaxed fingers. Startled, she regripped the covers.

He rose from the chair. "My advisers and I will devise a method to satisfy you. A pity. I admire your spirit as much as your tail. But if it is not to be," he executed an elaborate, theatrical shrug of disappointment, "it is not to be." Turning, he accompanied Byelroeth out to the atrium.

"She tires, your lordship," said the mandrill. "As much pressure as she has been under, surely she cannot remain awake much longer."

"It's nothing compared to the pressure she's going to be under when I get her out of there." Krasvin turned to his Adviser. "I'm going to my chambers for a nap. Make certain the watch on her is rotated regularly and kept fresh. I don't know where she learned to fight like that, but I'm taking no chances. Not with the imbeciles I'm forced to depend on."

"She will doubtless fall asleep before you awaken, your lordship."

"Yes. Then we'll write some pages of our own in a different sort of book. One that's appropriately bound." He stalked off in the direction of his private rooms, his hands clasped behind his back, the fingers kneading one another in anticipation of work to come. The mandrill did not share his Master's peculiar tastes, and he shuddered for the lady in the library.

CHAPTER 13

THE TAVERN WAS SITUATED CLOSE TO BOTH THE CENtral marketplace and the harbor. It was elegant without and spacious within, the sort of establishment where the city's honorable citizens could mix comfortably with less reputable inhabitants and travelers. A good place in which to find both information and aid.

"This mad venture had best not cost overmuch." Gragelouth cautiously considered their intended destination from the outside. "Not that I wouldn't do everything within my power to rescue your sister," he added quickly to Squill, who hovered nearby, "but I cannot forbear from pointing out that our resources are already sorely strained."

Buncan was trying to see through one of the windows into the tavern. It was packed with patrons. There was a wooden piano in back at which a flea-bitten wolf plied his trade. The barmaids came from many tribes, but none looked any less tough or competent than the customers they served. He and Squill followed the merchant inside.

Representatives of dozens of species caroused at booths and tables or harangued the several bartenders. The music was loud, the conversation louder still. Everyone looked . . . used.

"Maybe we'd do better elsewhere," he suggested, having to raise his voice to make himself heard.

"I did some checking." The sloth was ambling toward the entrance. "In a more refined establishment we will not find the kind of help we seek. Indeed, we would run the risk of encountering friends of this Baron." He smiled gently, and not for the first time Buncan found himself wondering what truly lay behind that smile. The smile behind the snout, as it were.

"Anywhere more disreputable and any help we might engage would probably prove unreliable, likely to bolt at the first hint of difficulty or danger. Not that I am hopeful of finding anyone anywhere willing to risk their lives for so little recompense as we can offer."

Buncan nodded his understanding, affecting what he hoped was an air of cosmopolitan insouciance as they sauntered into the main room. They were quickly swept up in the heady, boisterous atmosphere.

While Gragelouth made straight for the bar, Buncan strolled among the tables until his gaze fell on a full-grown, black-maned lion. Standing, the powerful feline would have towered over him. Broad, muscle-slabbed shoulders peered out from beneath iridescent snake-leather armor which was thickly fringed at the edges. It covered shoulders and upper chest only, leaving the flat belly revealed. Matching fringed shorts and high-laced sandals completed the attire. A double-handed sword longer than Squill was tall rested in its scabbard against the side of the round table at which its owner relaxed. Presently, the lion was holding a brass-bound wooden tankard the size of a man's head.

"Now that's just who we need on our side." He headed for the table.

Squill trailed along uncertainly, plucking at his friend's tunic. " 'Ere now, mate, maybe we ought to let the merchant 'ave a go first, wot? 'E's the one with the negotiatin' experience."

Buncan didn't alter his vector. "I'm just going to talk to him. Don't worry, I can handle it."

The nearer they drew, the bigger the lion looked. Squill muttered something under his breath.

The feline was holding court with the oversize, sloshing tankard. His road-toughened companions, a fox and caracal, didn't look like pushovers themselves. The caracal's sharply raked ears turned in Buncan's direction an instant before he spoke.

"Excuse me."

The back of the lion's mane had been combed and tied in a thick ponytail. It rustled as its owner glanced questioningly out of large yellow eyes at the presumptuous young human.

"No," he said without hesitation. His voice was deep and vibrant, as if it rose from the bottom of an old stone well.

Buncan was taken aback. "Sorry?"

A deep rumble issued from the back of the lion's throat. "I mean that I won't excuse you." The tankard rose and beer vanished. A heavy tongue licked subsidiary suds from a tan muzzle. Across the table the fox and caracal shared a meaningful chuckle.

Ignoring Squill's insistent tugs, Buncan regarded the smug trio. "Suit yourself. I guess this means that you're all independently wealthy."

The fox's ears pricked up. "Say again?" The caracal, too, showed sudden interest.

Buncan shifted from one foot to the other, affecting nonchalance. "I said that you must all be independently wealthy. It's clear you don't need any work."

"Who said we didn't need work?" The fox ignored the lion's disapproving glare.

Buncan shrugged. "You're not interested in my offer of employment."

The lion placed a paw on the table, extending all five claws. They dug into the thick wood, which was scarred from similar attention from time and customers immemorial. It was hard not to stare at them.

"Explain yourself, cub."

Buncan bristled but contained himself. "My friend's sister has been abducted."

"What friend?" asked the feline with a low growl.

Buncan turned. Squill was nowhere to be seen. Searching farther afield located him seated at the bar. The otter held a mug in one hand and waved cheerily with the other. With a sigh, Buncan turned back to the table.

"He's over there."

"So his sister's been abducted. It's a tough world. What's that to us?" the caracal muttered.

"Money, and adventure. If you assist us in her rescue."

The smaller feline toyed with his own tankard, which was half the size of the lion's. "Adventure's usually a fool's word for describing discomfort and hardship. If I long for some I can usually find it without having to fight off desperate kidnappers."

"How do you know it'll be like that?" Buncan asked him.

"Because it is a friend who is involved, your interest in this matter is obviously personal," observed the fox. "Ours would not be." He glanced speculatively across the table. "If the fee were right . . ."

"First things first," the lion murmured. "Who's done the kidnapping? Transient thieves? Registered Guild Abductors? Some fool freelancers?" He uttered the last hopefully.

"He's local. A real asshole. Taking off his head would probably gain you the gratitude of everyone in the city."

"We're not after anybody's gratitude," the lion grunted. "As for assholes, you'll have to be more specific. Camrioca boasts a plentiful supply." He gestured with the tankard. "To which local asshole do you happen to be referring?"

"He calls himself a Baron. Koliac Krasvin."

"Krasvin." The lion thrust out his lower lip thoughtfully. "I see. Am I correct in assuming that your friend's sister is being held in the Baron's fortified home?"

"That's what we believe," Buncan told him.

"And you want the three of us," he indicated his silent companions, "to help you extricate this unlucky female from Krasvin's possession?" Buncan indicated the affirmative.

The lion nodded slowly. "Let me tell you something, my furless young friend." He extended a massive paw and tapped Buncan in the sternum with one outthrust finger. Buncan held his ground, refusing to be intimidated.

"First of all, you don't look like you have access to more than a few silver pieces at most. Our services run considerably more than that. Second, Koliac Krasvin is known to keep no fewer than fifty armed retainers by his side at all times, all of whom will fight to the death at his command. Not out of love for their master, who is, as you rightly surmise, widely disliked, but because they know if they don't he'll have their throats slit while they sleep. Krasvin doesn't tolerate disloyalty.

"Thirdly, Krasvin's 'home' is more like a small castle than a large house. The main building is enclosed within a high stone wall that would make any military engineer proud. The windows are barred, the doors and gates reinforced with iron and brass. There's no moat, because one isn't needed. You'll suck no marrow from that bone with the three of us, not even if you somehow managed to cajole ten more into accompanying you. My professional estimate is that you'd need a small army to storm the front entrance, and I don't think you have the money to hire a small army.

"Lastly, despite his well-known wildings and distasteful proclivities, the Baron has friends in Camrioca, some in high places. If word got out that a force of any size was marching on his estate, he'd have time to prepare and rally not only his personal staff but those of his allies. So you'd end up with your small army facing his small army." The thumb stopped prodding and its burly owner leaned back in his chair.

"We're not interested."

"But . . . ," Buncan started to argue.

"I said no. I don't like your proposition, and just incidentally," he added in a low growl that revealed sharp canines, "I don't much care for primates, either."

At that point an older, wiser traveler would have simply taken his leave. Buncan was too young and too frustrated to react sensibly.

"You're not very hospitable to strangers."

Muscles in the fox's neck and arms tensed while the caracal emitted a low, throaty snarl. The lion stiffened slightly but made no move to rise.

"Young human, you're either very brave or very stupid. Since I am big enough to admire the one and forgive the other, I'll simply tell you that I've treated you no differently than anyone else who'd come seeking our assistance. This matter has nothing to do with hospitality. It's business, and I've treated it in a businesslike manner."

"Forget money for a moment," Buncan implored him. The caracal laughed sharply, a sound like sandpaper on velvet. "What about my friend's sister's virtue?"

"I don't know where you're from, cub, but this is Camrioca." The lion gestured expansively. "Virtue is not a particularly valued commodity in these parts. I'm not willing to risk death for my own, much less another's."

"She's being forced."

"If it's gallantry you seek," said the fox sagely, "look to books and cub-tales. If it's muscle and armor, look to your purse. And if it's justice, hope for better in the afterlife." He threw back the remainder of his drink.

Buncan leaned forward. "Please. We've nowhere else to turn."

Looking him hard in the eye, the lion put a massive paw on Buncan's shoulder and gently but irresistibly shoved him away. "Have you tried the door? You humans: Even the young ones will argue you to death. You made your offer; we gave our reply. Leave now, before you upset me."

Buncan wasn't finished, then realized that he was. It would do the unfortunate Neena no good if he got himself slaughtered here in this tavern, much less facing the ramparts of the Baron's home. Disconsolately, he moved to rejoin Squill and Gragelouth.

The merchant made room for him at the bar. He eyed Buncan knowingly as his long tongue lapped liquor from a wide-mouthed, short-stemmed glass. "I could have told you."

"No luck, mate?" Squill asked him.

Buncan replied gruffly. "What do you think?" He rubbed the place on his chest where the lion's thick finger had prodded repeatedly.

The sloth glanced back over a shoulder. "Those were professionals you accosted. A look is enough to brand them as such. Even had they acceded to your request, we would not have had enough money to pay them."

"We could have 'deferred' payment until after Neena's rescue."

Gragelouth scratched at the fur between his eyes. "Now you sound like your otterish friends. An attitude like that will get you killed before you reach your second decade."

"Well, I didn't know what else to do," Buncan replied irritably. "Squill, I don't suppose you've had any better luck?"

The otter gestured to his right. "Actually, mate, I've been chattin' up that squirrelish barmaid over there. The one with the tufts tippin' 'er ears? It's times like these that I wish I'd paid more attention to some o' me dad's stories. The ones 'e's more apt to tell when me mum ain't about."

Buncan looked disgusted. "And with your sister in mortal danger."

"Aw, she ain't in no mortal danger, Buncan." Despite his disclaimer, Squill looked uncomfortable. "I mean, wot's the worst thing that could 'appen to 'er?"

"Put yourself in her position," Buncan told him.

The otter shrugged, but it was halfhearted at best. "See?"

A heavy claw tapped him on the shoulder. "Unlike you and your friend, I may have succeeded in securing us some assistance."

Buncan's surprise must have showed. Squill eyed the sloth admiringly.

"Wondered where you'd got off to," he mumbled.

"I was searching for some solution to our difficult situation. Our fiscal dilemma, you see, is twofold. If we pay for adequate assistance at arms, we will be unable to afford ground transportation with which to continue our journey, and if we choose instead to make arrangements for the latter, we must then go against this Baron without help."

"Why not then try to find one who might, bearing in mind our severely limited resources, serve equally well both needs?"

"Oi, you've gone an' 'ired on a giant!" Squill barked excitedly.

"Though I have heard stories of such creatures, I have never met an actual giant of any tribe."

Buncan gestured in the direction of the lion and his drinking companions. "Black-mane there could pull quite a load, but not the three of us together with supplies, and he's the biggest in the place."

Gragelouth shifted on his chair and leaned closer. "Bipeds fight; quadrupeds carry. That is the natural order of things. Among the intelligent tribes who still walk on all fours, most are inclined to pacific pursuits, with but few inclined to battle. Yet there are always exceptions. I believe I may have found one such."

"A 'eavy 'orse who's willin' to fight," Squill exclaimed. "An' afterward, carry the lot of us swift an' sure away from this place."

"No. Our potential ally is not a member of the equine tribe."

"Where is he?" Buncan asked.

"This is a large establishment. There are numerous stalls and drinking troughs provided out back for customers of four legs."

"Well, if it ain't no 'orse," Squill mumbled bemusedly, "then wot the bloody 'ell is it?"

"Come and see." Gragelouth slid off his chair. "I am convinced the individual in question will work cheap."

"Almost reason enough to hire him right there." Buncan followed the merchant down the length of the bar, toward the rear of the tavern.

" 'E's a fighter, this one?'' Squill was already suspicious of this low-priced avatar.

"The bartender I spoke with knows him, says that he has been in many battles and is a veteran fighter. He is also large enough to transport all of us and a modicum of carefully packed supplies to the northwest. Not quickly or comfortably, perhaps, but efficiently. It will be far better than trying to continue on foot."

"If he'll hire on." Buncan restrained his enthusiasm. "Talea always says that anything which appears to be too good to be true usually is."

"His name," Gragelouth continued, "is Snaugenhutt."

"Don't sound like no poffy lute player," Squill commented approvingly as they exited the rear of the tavern and found themselves in a large circular corral.

A high wooden fence enclosed the grounds, which consisted of packed earth paved with fresh straw. A dozen stalls were arranged in a crescent facing the back of the main structure. Two sets of drinking troughs formed a pair of star patterns on the open ground. Smaller facilities were available within each high-roofed stall, each of which boasted a bed of thicker straw mixed with moss. Lavatory facilities were visible off to the left.

A quartet of horses, two males and two females, stood by one of the star troughs, drinking and chatting amiably. They wore custom-cut blankets and tack, the mares additionally displaying elaborately coiffed manes and tails. One had her hooves painted with blue glitter. The nearest stallion glanced only briefly in the direction of the three bipeds before rejoining the conversation.

The farthest stall to the right was occupied by a pair of merinos, already bedding down for the night. One was naked from the forelegs down, having obviously made a recent sale of wool.

Gragelouth led them toward the center stall. A husky barmaid of the civet tribe was coming toward them, lugging an empty pail. Buncan could smell the tart residue at the bottom of the container as she passed them without a glance.

That odor was quickly overwhelmed by the stink of the

stall itself, which reeked of cheap liquor and musky urine. That he was able to ignore the stench was due to the dominating presence near the back of the shelter of a gigantic, deeply scarred gray mass. It seemed to be facing away from them, though Buncan couldn't be sure.

"That's him, I think," said Gragelouth. "He fits the bartender's description."

"Sure wouldn't mistake 'im for one o' those sleepin' sheep," Squill ventured.

"A rhinoceros. I've never met one of his tribe before. They're bigger than I imagined." A fascinated Buncan slowed as they neared the stall's entrance. "That back's sure big enough to carry all four of us." He took in the scars and wrinkles in the slabs of gray skin. "He looks kind of . . . old."

"Not old, mate, so much as used," Squill corrected his companion. "I mean, this old chap 'as been bad beat up, don't you know?" The otter sniffed pointedly. " 'E's been through the wars, an' I don't mean the fightin' kind."

"He does seem a little the worse for wear." Gragelouth studied the back of their hoped-for savior speculatively.

"Worse for wear me bollocks." Squill took a wary step back from that prodigious and clearly unstable rear end. " 'E's bloomin' swozzled, 'e is. Plastered, smashed, looped, juiced. Drunk on 'is feet." The otter pinched his nose. "Wot's more, 'is taste in spirits stinks worse than 'e does."

At that the great head swung around into view and a single eye regarded them from beneath a drooping, supercilious brow. A horn the length of Buncan's arm tipped the weaving snout, backed by a second half its size. This formidable brace of keratin weapons was darkly stained.

Gragelouth approached tentatively. "Are you the warrior they call Snaugenhutt?"

The reply seemed to come not from the creature's throat but his belly. The accompanying bouquet was overpowering. "What?"

Though staggered by the stench, Gragelouth risked another step. "Snaugenhutt. Are you the warrior . . . ?"

"Oh, yeah." The rhino's voice reminded Buncan of the noises made by the sewer pipes that ran beneath central

Lynchbany. "That's me, isn't it?" The great horned skull bobbed up and down and the eye blinked slowly. "Do I *know* you?"

As the merchant prepared to reply, there emerged from the open mouth a belch of such gargantuan proportions as to register as a seismic disturbance in towns and villages some distance away. This was accompanied by a misty cloud of effluvia noxious enough to burn Buncan's eyes. He stumbled backward several steps, beating frantically at the air in front of his face. How Gragelouth held his ground he couldn't imagine.

As the vapor dissipated, Buncan saw that the rhino had turned to face them. Long, dirty hairs emerged from the inconceivably filthy depths of his shell-like ears.

Buncan took it upon himself to aid Gragelouth. "No, you don't know us, but we've heard of you. We're in real trouble, and we need your help. We want to hire you."

The heavy head swung toward him. "Trouble, eh? What kind of trouble?"

Buncan tried to shield his mouth and nostrils as decorously as possible. It might have been worse. Snaugenhutt might have been a dragon breathing fire.

Come to think of it, that might not be worse.

He indicated Squill, who stood quietly nearby turning a polite shade of pea green. "My friend's sister has been kidnapped by the Baron Koliac Krasvin."

"Krappin, Kraken. *Krasvin*." Snaugenhutt looked pleased with himself at having gotten it right. Each word was a grunt unto itself. "Heard of him. Ermine, isn't he?"

"Weasel," Buncan supplied helpfully.

"Right, weasel. Bad reputation. Bad." The head motivated from side to side.

"Krasvin's holding her at his estate. We're bound to try and rescue her. To do that we need professional help." He glanced at Gragelouth. "You came highly recommended."

"Naturally." The rhino seemed to straighten a little. "I am after all the most experienced fighter in these parts."

"You're certainly the biggest." Buncan intended it as a compliment.

"Yeah, that too, that too." Spittle clung to the heavy

lower lip. "But this Baron, I've heard about his place. Hard to break into. What do you think, Viz?"

A small bird emerged unexpectedly from the fold of the rhino's neck. It plonked itself down between the twitching ears and yawned, its wings stretching wide. A miniature blue beret crowned the feathered head and a matching scarf was wound once around the delicate neck. The bird made tiny smacking sounds with its beak and leaned forward to blink at the visitors.

"I think . . . I think I'm tired." With that it promptly fell over backward, legs in the air, and commenced snoring heavily, sounding rather like a large mosquito.

" 'E's swozzled too," Squill commented in disgust.

"Don't mind Viz." The rhino snorted softly. "He's my tickbird. Been on board for years. But he can't hold his liquor. I've told him that booze and parasites don't mix. All that chiton and green goo and . . ."

Squill made a dash for the lavatory facilities, not caring that they were designed for creatures much larger than he.

Buncan fought to maintain his own stability. The tickbird snored on. "We don't expect charity. I've learned better than to ask for that. We'll pay."

"What we can," Gragelouth put in hastily.

"And after we've saved Neena we'll need your help in getting away from here."

"A rescue, eh?" Snaugenhutt hiccoughed volcanically. "A noble cause. Been a long time since I did anything noble. What do you think, Viz?" The tickbird snored on, oblivious.

"Yeah, I'll help you. When do we start?"

Buncan blinked. "Just like that? Don't you want to know the details?"

"What details? Do I look like the subtle type, human?"

"Uh, no."

"They won't be expecting a frontal assault." Snaugenhutt was murmuring to himself. "I've heard some of the stories about this Krasvin. Thinks he's the greatest thing in fur. We'll surprise him. Bust his tail."

"Sure we will," muttered Buncan. "We'll sneak you inside in a suitcase, dump you out, and let you exhale in the faces of the Baron's soldiers.'' Louder he said, ''You don't drink like this all the time, do you?''

''Certainly not.'' As the rhino swayed on pillarlike legs, a smile creased that slouching jaw. ''Sometimes I drink seriously.''

Buncan turned to Gragelouth. ''Maybe we ought to look elsewhere.''

''What elsewhere?'' The sloth sniffed resignedly. ''I took the best recommendation of the locals I encountered.''

''Another tavern.'' Buncan persisted. ''Maybe down by the waterfront.''

Blinking unsteadily, Snaugenhutt took a ponderous step toward them. ''Something wrong? You don't want my help? You don't want the assistance of the greatest four-legged warrior on the High Plateau?'' His head twisted over and back, gesturing at his flank as best he could with the tall horn.

''Take a look at these scars. See that one on the outside of my rear leg? Got that at the Battle of Muuloden. Scattered twenty big cats all by myself while carrying ten fully armed bipeds into combat. And that one all the way in back, just to the left of my tail? Caught a leg-sized catapult spear right in the butt at the height of the Cabber's Glen Incident. Didn't even slow me down. Had my side hang their battle flag from it.'' He looked momentarily wistful. ''Trampled plenty underhoof in that one, and gored half a dozen more.''

''We have no doubt of your fighting history.'' Gragelouth made placating gestures. ''If you do not mind my inquiring, how long ago did these exploits take place?''

''How long?'' The heavy brow drooped lower still. ''Don't remember. Never was real good with dates.'' He chuckled, and it ended in a rattling cough. As spittle drooled from his mouth, even the dead straw seemed to curl away from it.

Gragelouth gestured with a heavily clawed hand. ''Though our current resources are . . . limited . . . we must have professional help. If you are willing to enter our service for what recompense we can presently offer, we may be able to arrange for some additional payment at a future date.''

Still swaying, Snaugenhutt straightened as much as he was able, staring at the sloth past the tall horn. ''Count me in. Not because of the money, but because a lady's virtue is at stake.''

"She's no quadruped," Buncan reminded him.

One eye considered him haughtily. "Where virtue is concerned, the tribe doesn't matter. There's honor to uphold and gallantry to preserve." With that he hiccoughed again, at least a 7.5 on the hiccough scale, and keeled over sideways. It was akin to watching a great ship slide slowly beneath the waves.

As the vast mass struck the ground with a dull *whomp*, the three travelers hastily backed clear. After satisfying their curiosity, the horses and sheep returned to their respective socializing. Snaugenhutt began to emit Promethean snores.

Having been unceremoniously dumped into the straw, the dazed tickbird picked itself up and fluttered unsteadily to the top of the comatose bulk. Landing atop the half-exposed belly, it curled up in its wings and lapsed back into its momentarily disturbed stupor.

Buncan was not pleased with the picture. "There they are. Our army. Neena's saviors. Cheap at half the price." He turned to the merchant. "Surely we can do better than this, even with as little as we have to offer?"

Gragelouth stared up at the tall human. "I am open to suggestions, my young friend."

"Maybe if we could get the bloated sod sobered up." Squill studied the insensible mass of gray flesh. "If 'e got up to speed, 'e's big enough to do some damage. If 'e 'as any speed left in 'im, that is." He glanced at his friend. "At this point any 'elp's better than no 'elp. We could load the unconscious bugger onto a wagon an' roll it downhill. Might smash in this Krasvin's front door, might not."

"We don't know if there's a hill in front of the Baron's mansion," Buncan pointed out patiently. "I'm not pushing *that* load one stride uphill, and where would we get a wagon, anyway?"

"Steal it." Squill smiled serenely.

"We can do nothing until he sobers up." Gragelouth licked his forehead. "Or, at the very least, awakens."

"What about his companion?" Buncan indicated the softly snoring tickbird.

"I could eat it," Squill suggested.

Buncan eyed him sharply. "Eat another intelligent being?"

The otter sniffed. "Don't look very intelligent to me, mate."

"We're here to get help, not dinner."

"Most every member of Snaugenhutt's tribe lives with a companion tickbird," Gragelouth pointed out. "I do not think our potential ally would look kindly upon your eating his.

"Meanwhile, let me talk to the owner of this establishment. Perhaps he can suggest a potion to both awaken and sober these two."

"You couldn't sober that mass up if you dropped it off a high cliff," Squill riposted.

CHAPTER 14

THE REMEDY GRAGELOUTH ARRANGED FOR ARRIVED IN the form of a brim-full bucket prepared by not one but two mixologists. A good dousing with one of the high-pressure hoses used to keep the corral area clean roused the rhino long enough for Buncan and Squill to sluice half the bucket's contents down his benumbed throat. The operation was repeated with the tickbird, on a much smaller scale. Though there was no evidence of overt sorcery involved, the liquid's contents proved nothing short of magical. The hulking old warrior was on his feet, albeit unsteadily, far sooner than Buncan would have imagined possible.

As Snaugenhutt hadn't the slightest recollection of their previous conversation, they were compelled to repeat both the tale of Neena's abduction and their present dilemma. Viewed in the cooler light of minimal comprehension, the rhino's earlier enthusiasm flagged.

"You don't want my help," he mumbled, turning away. Gragelouth had reluctantly paid for a clean, fresh stall.

Employees of the tavern were still in the process of disinfecting the other. Viz paced between the rhino's ears, hunting for parasites while listening intently. He seemed to be in better shape than his friend. But then, his hangover would be proportionately smaller.

"At this point you are our only hope," Buncan reluctantly admitted. "You're about all we can afford. Time's also important, and so far you're the only one who's indicated a willingness to help."

"Oi," said Squill, "wot were all that rot about preservin' a lady's virtue, an' gallantry, an' 'onor?"

"Did I speak to that?" Snaugenhutt looked thoroughly miserable. He stood with one foreleg crossed over the other, his prehensile upper lip nearly touching the ground.

The tickbird glanced up. "If they say you did, Snaug, I guess you did. I don't remember the discussion myself." He pecked energetically at a particular spot.

Gragelouth sought to energize the quadruped. "Why wouldn't we want your assistance? You are large, powerful, and experienced; clearly no stranger to battle."

The rhino twitched his huge skull. Reflex caused the tickbird to flutter clear and set down without comment as soon as his perch had steadied. "All that was a long time ago," he muttered unhappily. "A very long time ago. Haven't done any fighting . . ." He paused to swallow. "Haven't done much of anything in longer than I can remember."

Buncan picked up on Gragelouth's riff. "You look like you're still in pretty good shape," he lied.

The rhino's head came up a little. "I do the best I can. Frankly, the last few months—the last few years—I've kind of lost direction. Been lapping at the drinking trough now and again, and my reflexes aren't what they used to be. Oh, the underlying muscle tone's still there." He inhaled and seemed to double in size. The effect lasted about five seconds before scarred and wrinkled skin collapsed in on the massive skeleton.

"But that's not enough. I'm out of shape, out of condition. Wouldn't know how to get going. No equipment, anyway." His eyes grew misty. "Used to have full armor and combat equippage. Gilt steel. When I went into battle, the sun rode with me.''

"Where's your gear now?'' Buncan asked thoughtlessly.

Snaugenhutt squinted at him. "Pawned it. Long time ago. Everything was a long time ago, human.'' At which point, to everyone's astonishment, the great beast began to cry.

" 'Ere now, guv.'' Squill moved forward. " 'E didn't mean nothin' personal.''

It did no good. Tears spilled from both eyes as gargantuan sobs wracked the huge form. His perch now shuddering steadily, the tickbird fluttered down to land on Buncan's shoulder. From head to tail he was slightly less than the length of Buncan's forearm. One flexible wingtip adjusted the scarf around his neck.

"It's no use trying to talk to him when he gets like this. You just have to wait for it to pass.'' Unlike Snaugenhutt, the tickbird seemed fully recovered.

"Listen, can I talk to you for a minute?''

"Sure.''

"You two been together for a while?''

"Like Snaug says, a long time,'' the bird chirped.

Buncan nodded slowly. "How much of that stuff he told us about all the battles he's been in is true?''

A wingtip pressed against the side of his head. "Probably all of it, though I don't recall the details. Snaug was a professional long before I hooked up with him. I *can* vouch for the authenticity of his most recent scars.''

"So you've been in battle with him?''

Viz nodded, his beak bobbing. "Lots, though not in some time.'' He examined his bawling companion, whose sobs were finally beginning to lessen. "Snaug, he was the real thing, he was.'' There was tangible pride in the bird's voice. "Wasn't anything or anybody that could stand against him . . . in his prime.'' Feathered shoulders rippled.

"What happened?''

"Isn't it obvious? The liquor trough got him. Sucked him right in. Ate up his money and his life. Not even sure how it got started. I did all I could, but I can't exactly hold my ground in front of him. There was a female. . . . You haven't dealt with life, human, until you've tried to reason with a lovesick rhino in the last throes of unrequited passion.''

"I can imagine,'' said Buncan, not experienced enough to imagine it at all.

"That's when it started to get bad. Snaug could always drink. Have you any idea of the alcoholic capacity of a healthy rhinoceros?''

"Not really.'' Buncan indicated Squill. "I've seen my friend's father put a lot away, but he's only an otter.''

"Try to envision a thirsty abyss. I've guided him through some tough spots, but he's just gotten worse and worse. When he had to hock his armor to pay a bar bill in Hascaparbi, it was the last straw. After that he just gave up. You should have seen his armor: the best steel, some of it inlaid in gold.''

"He might as well have hocked his soul. His self-esteem just crashed. We've been doing the occasional odd towing job ever since, just to make ends meet. Sometimes we beg.'' He winced. "The great warrior Snaugenhutt, reduced to pulling hay carts for feed. One time we even contracted to do plowing.''

Buncan tried to picture the great rhino dragging a plow, furrow after endless furrow, while some ill-tempered farmer trailing behind berated him with orders and curses in equal measure. It wasn't an attractive image.

"Couldn't even hold that job,'' Viz was muttering. "Got plastered one night, had someone hitch him up, went and plowed obscenities into the field. The farmer couldn't see them, but an owl in his employ snitched on us.''

"On 'us'?''

Viz shrugged. "Snaug's strong, but he can't spell worth a damn. When things got real bad I started taking to the sauce a little myself. It helps you forget.''

Buncan scrutinized the rhino, who had finally stopped sobbing. "And there's nothing that can bring him out of this?''

"Sure. Give him back his self-respect.''

"How?''

"How indeed? I've been trying for years. He doesn't listen to me anymore. Of course, the ranker he gets the

better I eat, but there are higher principles at stake here."
He hesitated. "There's one thing that might do it."

"What's that?"

Viz leaned forward, his beak a thumb's length from
Buncan's right eye. "Get him his armor back."

"You've got to be kidding. Gragelouth already told you
we have hardly any money."

The tickbird straightened. "Well, you asked. You know,
if he was rambling on about honor and virtue and gallantry,
he meant every word of it. He's serious about that stuff, and
there isn't a duplicitous bone in that whole enormous body.
When he's sober there isn't a nobler creature on earth."

Buncan studied the immense mass that was Snaugenhutt
and tried to imagine what it would cost to provide armor for
so much sheer bulk. It would be like trying to armor a ship.
Which was rather what the rhino was: a landship on four
legs.

"No way," he told Viz. "Gragelouth doesn't have anywhere near enough funds."

"Too bad. There's no guarantee it would work, anyway."
The tickbird looked wistful. "Though I would like to have
seen it tried." He leaned forward again. "My hearing's
pretty sharp. Did I hear you say something about being a
spellsinger?"

Buncan nodded. "My otterish companions and I. We
work together."

"Then why don't you just spellsing him his armor back?"

"Don't you think that occurred to me?" He shook his
head regretfully. "We only function as a trio. I play the duar
and they rap." At the tickbird's puzzled expression he
added, "It's a type of singing."

"Have you tried it as a duo?"

"Well, not really. It's just been working so well as a trio,
I'm a little nervous about trying anything different. Even if
it's only a little off, spellsinging can produce some weird
effects."

"Try," Viz urged him. "If something goes wrong, we'll
absolve you of any responsibility." The bird lifted both
wings slightly. "It's not like either of us have anything to
lose."

Buncan considered. "All right. Yeah. We'll give it a shot."

Squill was less willing, but the thought of Buncan going it alone and doing some actual singing finally convinced him to participate.

As Buncan played the otter essayed some hesitant lyrics, a sort of wrap rap, which to everyone's surprise actually generated a small cloud around the befuddled Snaugenhutt. It wasn't very intense and it didn't last very long, but the result was decidedly metallic in nature.

When the song concluded, Snaugenhutt stood swathed from head to foot in some shiny, metallic material. Their initial hopes were dashed when it became apparent that even Viz could easily shred the metal "armor" with his beak. The spellsong had worked, but without Neena's harmonizing it had proven less than effective.

"What is this stuff?" The tickbird sputtered as he spit a silvery patch from his mouth. It floated awkwardly to the ground.

Buncan peeled a section from Snaugenhutt's right shoulder. "It looks like something my father brought back from the Otherworld one time. My mother uses it in cooking."

"It's pretty," groused Viz, "but as armor it's a total loss."

"I'm hot," Snaugenhutt moaned. "Get me out of this."

Working together, the discouraged foursome soon had the rhino peeled.

"Right! Now it's my turn." Buncan and the others looked over at an angry Squill. "That is, if you're really set on 'irin' this old sod." He glared at the rhino, who was unable to meet his gaze.

"I don't know." Snaugenhutt was barely audible. "I don't know if I'm any good anymore. With or without armor."

Viz fluttered over to land once more on his companion's skull. "Sure you are, Snaug. The body's intact. It's the spirit that's missing."

The rhino licked thick lips. "Speaking of spirits . . ."

"NO!" Viz hopped forward until he could bend over and

gaze directly into one eye. "No more. As of now, you're on the wagon."

"Don't see no wagon," the rhino mumbled, closing the eye.

"There's a lady in distress in need of rescue, and these good people are relying on us. No one else will help them, so it's up to us. No one else is brave enough to go up against the Baron Krasvin. No one else is stupid enough, dumb enough, foolhardy enough..."

"Oi!" Squill blurted. "Quit encouragin' 'im."

"Can't do it." Snaugenhutt opened the eye halfway. "I need a drink."

"No, dammit!" Viz fluttered up to an ear and plucked a crawling delicacy from amongst the hairs. "Besides, I... I promised. I gave our word."

Snaugenhutt started. "You did *what*?"

"Gave our word of honor. As warriors."

"I'm not a warrior anymore." He struggled to open the eye all the way, failed. "Actually what I am, is tired. Sleepy. Got to... rest."

"No, not now." Viz hovered as his companion settled back on his rear knees, then lowered his front legs. "There are arrangements to be made, agreements to be settled!"

The massive body hit the straw with a dull *boom*. In a minute the rhino was fast asleep.

"This is not promising," Gragelouth declared.

Viz settled down atop his friend's flank. "We have to find him some armor. It's the only chance."

"That's what I was tryin' to tell you about it bein' me turn." They all looked again to Squill. The otter regarded each of them in turn. "I'll take care o' it."

"You?" said Gragelouth.

"How?" Buncan inquired guardedly.

The otter smirked. "'Ow do you think, mate? By usin' the skills Mudge taught me. O' course, it weren't exactly teachin'. 'E just sort o' can't 'elp boastin' a bit when 'e rambles, Mudge can't."

"Even in a city the size of Camrioca, armor for someone like Snaug is going to be hard to find," Viz warned him.

"I'll do the best I can."

"You're going to steal it," Buncan said accusingly.

"Now who said anythin' about theft?" The otter's whiskers twitched in mock outrage. "Mudge told us a lot, 'e did, besides 'ow to steal."

"I'm not giving my approval." Buncan folded his arms across his chest.

"But you won't try an' stop me?"

"Your sister's already in danger. If you want to go and endanger yourself on her behalf, I certainly can't stop you. I know you won't listen to reason."

"Oi; nobly put." The otter glanced at Gragelouth. "Wot about you, droopy-lips?"

"I am a respectable merchant. I might wish at some time in the future to trade in these parts."

"You're a better liar than 'e is, I'll give you that." The otter indicated the stolid-faced Buncan. "I'll just 'ave to take care o' business alone, then."

"Not entirely alone," said a small voice. Viz flew over to land on Squill's shoulder. The otter eyed the tickbird speculatively.

"Might be some trouble."

The bird let out a sharp whistle, gestured backward with a wingtip. "I've been looking out for that ambulating dung factory for five years. A little trouble doesn't scare me. For that matter, jail might be an improvement."

"Righty-ho. 'Avin' an eye in the sky along won't 'urt. You two 'old old Snauggy's 'orn, or wotever. Me an' the bird will take care o' business." With Viz riding his shoulder, Squill scampered off in the direction of the exit.

They did not return that night, nor in the morning. It was well on to midday, when Buncan's concern was starting to give way to real unease, when an oversize wagon drawn by a pair of Percherons came rattling into the corral.

The nearest to Buncan shook his mane as he pawed irritably at the packed earth. "Where you want this stuff?"

Buncan blinked at the heavy horse, trying to see into the slab-sided, tarp-covered wagon. "What stuff?"

The Percheron gave him the once-over. "You're Buncan Meriweather, ain't you?"

"I am. What of it?" Behind him a groggy Gragelouth

was rousing himself from his sleeping pallet, while deeper within the stall Snaugenhutt snored on oblivious.

"Snotty young otter told us we'd find you here," the other Percheron declared gruffly. "Told us to look for a gloomy-lookin' human; tall, overdressed. You fit."

"I guess I do."

"That's all we need to know." He took a half-step forward, raised his right rear leg, and kicked down firmly on an oversize lever. As a spring was released the wagon bed rose and tilted, dumping its contents in a clanging, clattering, tarp-wrapped heap. Gragelouth all but leaped from his bed at the uproar, while Snaugenhutt simply rolled over.

"It's all yours," the other horse announced. Whereupon the two of them turned and clip-clopped back out through the wide, swinging gate, their now empty wagon in tow.

Gragelouth tugged at his vest as he rubbed sleep from his eyes. "What was all that about?"

"Beats me."

Together they approached the irregular-shaped pile and began working on the ropes which held the enveloping tarp in place. When the bindings were undone, Buncan tugged and pulled until the contents lay exposed.

The armor, he found himself thinking. *It has to be.* Not silver or inlaid steel, but massive, square plates of raw black iron that looked as if they had been hastily cast and cobbled together. Hooks, rings, and eyes indicated how the plates were intended to be crudely linked. It wasn't very pretty. Not exactly the epitome of the armorer's art, he thought, though the thick plates looked functional enough.

He hefted one. Though rough-textured and unfinished, it was an immense improvement over the crinkly foil he and Squill had spellsung up.

"Let's get started," he told the merchant.

The sloth blinked at him. "Get started? How can we do that? The rhino still sleeps."

"Then we'll start on that side," he declared with determination.

Wrestling hunks of the armor over to the stall, they began

trying to attach them, starting at the high, rounded backside. Gragelouth protested at the effort required.

By midafternoon they were both exhausted. Snaugenhutt had not helped their efforts by rolling over several times, and they had accomplished very little.

At that point Squill and Viz finally returned, trailed by a huge brown bear clad in light work shirt and pants. A vast multipocketed apron hung from his neck and was secured behind him. His pockets bulged with all manner of tools, as did the thick leather belt that hung from his waist. The smaller, slightly blonder bear who accompanied him was similarly equipped.

"No, no!" The bear rumbled his disapproval as he inspected their coarse handiwork. "Not like zat." Waddling past the startled Gragelouth, the two ursines set to correcting the mistakes Buncan and the merchant had so arduously perpetrated. Their sometimes noisy exertions notwithstanding, Snaugenhutt slept on.

Buncan glared at the otter. "You took your own sweet time. Neena could be in pretty bad shape by now."

"You don't know me sister, mate." But for the first time there was a hint of real concern in Squill's voice. "I admit I thought she'd 'ave broken out o' that place by now."

"Don't undereztimate the Baron," the bear's assistant called back to them. Buncan and his friends walked over to observe the assembly of the armor.

"You know of Krasvin?" Buncan asked him.

The assistant nodded as he worked. "Everybody knowz of ze Baron Krasvin. Camrioca iz a big city, but ze families of noble birth are not zat extenzive."

The larger bear was pounding away with a hammer and a huge pair of pliers. "Finished zoon. He iz going to have to stand zo we can make zure everything fallz properly into place."

"That means waking him up." Viz glided from Squill's shoulder to the slumbering rhino's head. "Might be more difficult than affixing the armor." He rested until the two bears backed off. The larger one nodded.

"Done! Make him ztand."

"Easier said than done." Viz pecked forcefully at an ear.

"Just because we need him awake doesn't mean he'll comply."

The great head rose off the straw. "Need who awake?" Legs began to kick, like a locomotive changing gears.

With a cacophonous rattle and clank, Snaugenhutt struggled to his feet. Drunk he'd still been middling impressive, Buncan thought. Erect and completely clad in the rough black armor, he looked like something out of a serious nightmare. Buncan hoped the Baron's minions would react accordingly.

His old armor had doubtless fit together better. Certainly it must have been more attractive. The blacksmith and his assistant were not armorers and had fashioned the cast-iron gear together out of loose bits of ship armor, battered shields, and whatever other scraps they had been able to scavenge on short notice. Still, their salvage work was mightily impressive.

Snaugenhutt was completely cloaked on all sides. Smaller interlinked plates protected his legs all the way down to the ankles. Sharpened spikes ran in a threatening belt around his equator, while a pair of blades fashioned from oversize swords protruded forward and down from his shoulders.

Hammered arcs of iron shielded his ears and stuck out protectively above each eye, while linked rings protected the rest of his head. Gaps allowed both horns to emerge freely. Concave scutes decorated his spine and not incidentally provided smooth seats for any who might choose to ride there. Welded to the flattened, elongated plate that ran down between his ears toward the shorter horn was a small, raised metal bowl with the back quarter cut out. An iron perch was attached crossways to the interior of the bowl.

Swaying slightly, the rhino now resembled some kind of bizarre alien machine more than any living being. He shook himself uncertainly, producing a sound like a dozen chained skeletons fighting to escape from a dungeon.

"What's all this?" His skull lowered. "Someone's been using my head for an anvil."

Viz fluttered back from the barrel on which he'd been standing and settled into the bowl-enclosed armored perch atop the rhino's forehead.

"Not bad," he told the bear, who accepted the compliment with a grunt. "This'll work fine, if it doesn't get too hot." Hopping clear, he slid down to gaze into his mount's right eye. "What do you think, Snaug?"

"About what?" the rhino moaned.

"He needs a mirror." Viz scanned the stable. "None out here."

"I will find one." Gragelouth disappeared into the main building, returned moments later with a reflective, broken glass oval.

It was enough. Snaugenhutt stared disbelievingly into the mirror. "Is that me? Is that really me?" He turned to and fro, seeking different views.

"No one else 'ere who looks like that, guv," Squill told him. "No one else who smells like it, either."

"Why, I look..." The rhino straightened. Knees locked, armor fell into place. "I took terrifying."

"Oi, right," the otter muttered.

"I look like... my old self. But I'm not my old self."

Uninterested in Snaugenhutt's personal reflections, the bear concluded his circumnavigation of his handiwork. "Zee," he said proudly, "I have finished everyzing zo that ze plates overlap or interlock. He iz completely protected yet ztill able to maneuver freely." He patted one heavy plate affectionately. "Heavier than most zuch armor it may be, but thiz would turn a zhip's ram."

"He can handle it," chirped Viz from his position above Snaugenhutt's eye. "Can't you?"

"I guess so. I am handling it, aren't I?"

"Try a few steps," Buncan suggested.

Advancing carefully, the rhino emerged from the stall. Armor rattled. With each step he also emerged a little bit more from the binge not only of the previous day, but of previous years.

"Head still hurts, but not from the iron," he finally announced.

"That'll pass." Viz hopped back up to his little howdah. "It's going to be like old times."

"Old times," Snaugenhutt echoed, still somewhat dazed.

Buncan came forward and patted one armored shoulder. "There's a damsel in need of rescue, warrior."

"Damsel." Squill rolled his eyes.

"I must admit it is an impressive sight. Obviously there was a great deal of work involved." Gragelouth cocked a querulous eye in Squill's direction. The otter merely grinned back.

"Pennants," Snaugenhutt declared unexpectedly. "I want pennants."

"You want to do penance?" Gragelouth murmured, not understanding.

"No, *pennants*. And ribbons. Lots of ribbons. Bright ones. And paint. This black is intimidating, but I want war paint. Yellow and red flames, yeah! I want to look like hell on the move. Shit, I will *be* hell on the move!" He was fairly trembling with excitement as he turned to face Squill.

"We're gonna rescue your sister, river-runner. By the folds in my skin we will! We'll rescue her and put this Baron to flight. All Camrioca is afraid of him, including his friends. But not I, not I."

Squill smiled back but muttered under his breath. "In a pig's eye."

With a short, curt grunt Snaugenhutt swung his head sharply to the right, knocking a heavy bracing pole clean out of its hole as if it were a toothpick. One corner of the stall ceiling came crashing down.

"Please," Gragelouth implored him, "be careful with the accommodations! We will be asked to pay for that."

The rhino shook his head. "Shoddy construction. I want that war paint! And the pennants, and the ribbons. Trumpets, too, if you can manage it."

Gragelouth mentally consulted his purse. "Trumpets are out of the question, but it may be that we can manage a little of the rest."

Buncan stared in amazement at the rhino. Armored and alert he looked years younger, dynamic and alive. There was fire in his eyes and vigor in his step. It was an astonishing transformation. Clearly the old maxim held true regardless of tribe.

Clothes made the rhino.

He was so excited he'd completely forgotten one small detail. The detail reasserted itself by ambling over to peer down at him.

"It waz good doing businezz with you, young human." The ursine blacksmith rested a heavy paw on Buncan's shoulder. "Thiz iz a worthy enterprise. I know of thiz Krasvin's reputation and have no love for him myself." He turned and headed for the gate, his assistant trailing behind.

"Zee you in one hour," the bear called back over a shoulder.

"An hour." Buncan turned to Squill. Gragelouth and Viz were conversing animatedly with Snaugenhutt. Left to himself, the otter smiled sunnily, flashing sharp white teeth.

Buncan put a comradely arm around his friend's shoulders. "And why, pray tell, are we expected in our friendly blacksmith's quarters in an hour?"

"Why, to sign the papers acceptin' formal delivery o' iron butt's new nightgown, mate."

"I thought you were going to steal something."

"I admit I considered it right off, but the more I got to lookin' at wot were required, the more I decided I couldn't walk out o' no armorer's shop with the necessary gear stuffed in me bloomin' pocket. Even if I could, then I'd 'ave to steal a bloody wagon to 'aul it, an' lizards to pull the wagon. It just got too bleedin' complicated."

Buncan jerked his head in the direction of the now closed gate. "So how did you talk them into making the delivery?"

The otter looked embarrassed. "Don't let this get around among me friends and family, mate, but I sort o' . . . paid for it."

Buncan frowned. "Paid for it? With money? Squill, have you been holding out on us?"

" 'Ere now, mate, I wouldn't never do nothin' like that! It's just that I thought I'd best bring along a few coins in case o' some emergency, an' this 'ere situation struck me as qualifyin'.' "

Buncan's expression grew dark. "Where'd you get any real money?"

The otter looked away. "Well, before we started off I thought we might need somethin' extra, so I sort o' borrowed it from me dad."

Buncan gaped. "You stole from Mudge?"

"Just sort o' borrowed it, Buncan. Mudge, 'e'll understand. 'E did plenty o' borrowin' in 'is time."

"He's going to kill you!"

Squill shrugged. "Got to catch up with me first."

Buncan shook his head in disbelief. "So we've been scrimping this entire journey and you've had money all along?"

"I told you, Buncan, it were for an emergency. Anyway, I got to thinkin' about wot you've been sayin', an' even if she is a worse pest than water lice an' not the kind o' siblin' I'd choose if I 'ad me choice, she is still me only sister."

"I have a feeling you're not exactly the kind of brother she'd opt for, either. How do you expect to pay Mudge back?"

"I kind o' thought we might find some treasure or somethin' along the way. Maybe this Grand Veritable's worth a packet o' gold, or somethin'."

"If it even exists," Buncan reminded him coolly. "Squill, you live in a moral vacuum."

"Oi, that I do." The otter straightened. "Mudge'd be proud." He stepped past his friend. "We got the bleedin' armor, didn't we? We've got an outside shot at bringin' this crazy stunt off, don't we? Ain't that wot matters?"

"I guess so. It's your neck when we get home."

"Bloomin' right it is. So let's find this walkin' beer sump 'is paint and pretties, and get on with it. Besides, if we don't bring this off an' I'm killed, I won't owe Mudge any money."

Once again Buncan was left struck dumb by the inevitability of otter logic.

CHAPTER 15

THEY PLANNED THE ASSAULT FOR MIDNIGHT, HOPING that Neena had somehow remained unsullied thus far by the Baron's attentions.

This was actually the case, though Squill's sister was

growing desperately tired. Having enjoyed a long and restful sleep, Krasvin was now content to bide his time, no longer in any especial hurry. Not wishing to risk a single additional volume from his collection, he had decided to relax until his quarry simply collapsed from exhaustion, which point in time was observably not far off now.

Then, he thought calmly to himself, events would proceed as they ought. He amused himself with elaborate mental preparations.

Buncan and his companions ventured out to sign the blacksmith's papers, leaving Viz to arrange for the war paint and frills his newly energized companion had requested. Unable to rest, they wandered the streets of Camrioca until the sun had set and been replaced by a rising half-moon. Then they returned to the tavern to rejoin the others.

The lion was there, with his two fellow fighters. He made some comment as Buncan and his companions walked past. Buncan saw the fox and caracal laugh uproariously but hardly spared a glance in their direction. They weren't needed, he thought firmly. Snaugenhutt was all they needed.

Save for a pair of deer snuggling in a far bay, the stable area was deserted. They hurried to Snaugenhutt's stall, eager to be on their way.

Which was when disaster, that most uncomely of all possibilities, smiled callously upon them.

Prone in his stall, bright tail pennant stained with urine, ribbons askew, armor slack and anything but intimidating, Snaugenhutt lay snoring sonorously. The thick stench of cheap liquor was overpowering.

Viz sat morosely on the rim of a barrel nearby, his legs hanging over the edge, tiny beret clasped in flexible wingtips, head down. The tickbird was a picture of feathered misery.

"I only went out for a little while. Just a little while."

Buncan sat down in a clean patch of bedding and picked disconsolately at the straw. "What *for*? And why now, of all times?" Angrily he flung a handful of straw at the comatose rhino.

"Disaster most complete." Gragelouth glanced sorrowfully at Squill. "No chance now for your sister."

"I can't believe it." The otter booted an iron scute. It

clinked against another. Snaugenhutt didn't stir. "All 'e 'ad to do was stay sober for 'alf an afternoon. Wot 'appened to his newfound pride, 'is sense o' duty? We 'ad a bleedin' arrangement, we did."

"He was all set to go," Viz mumbled miserably. "Looking forward to it. He was so much like, like his old self. I didn't think there'd be any harm in leaving him for a while."

"Why did you leave him?" Buncan asked testily.

The tickbird couldn't meet the human's gaze. "Tried to arrange a loan. We're over a month behind on our bill here. I meant to tell you later. I was only gone a few hours, but when I got back," he indicated the huge, insensible form, "Snaug was like this. His trough's empty. I was afraid to ask inside how much he'd had."

Squill slumped against the wall, crossing his arms in disgust. "Now wot?"

"We wait until he sleeps it off," Viz told him. "Tomorrow morning, if we're lucky." He gazed at his enormous, presently useless friend. "I don't understand. He was so proud to be embarking on a new campaign."

"How are we going to juice him up a second time?" Buncan muttered. "We can't armor him all over again." He was quiet for several moments. Then he rose and removed not his sword, but a potentially far more powerful weapon.

Squill cocked his head to one side. " 'Ere now, mate, you don't mean to 'ave another go at just the two of us spellsingin'?"

"Got any better ideas?"

"We could do as the bird says an' wait for mornin'."

"Think Neena can hold out another day?"

The otter looked resigned. "This didn't work so well the last time we tried it."

"We've got no choice. Besides, we don't need to conjure up anything solid like armor. All we need to do is rouse this mess and set him on the right path."

"Well . . ." The otter was still dubious. "If we can get 'is bloomin' eyes open maybe the rest'll follow." He stepped away from the wall. "Let me think. Confidentially, Neena's much better at this 'ere business o' lyrics than I am."

"Do your best." Buncan tried to sound encouraging.

Long moments passed, until Buncan could stand it no longer.
"Sing out, Squill. Either it'll have an effect or it won't."
The otter nodded, settled himself, and started in.

"Got a battle up ahead, a battle to be won
Need the 'elp o' one Snaugenhutt, need 'is 'elp by the
ton
Got to get to the Baron's mansion, got to get
there damn fast.
Need to move it out quickly 'cause me sister can't last
Fast, fast, cast it to the winds
Cast it out through the bleedin' sky
Pass it on by, sly, high
C'mon old thing, you gots to try!"

While Gragelouth looked on apprehensively, Buncan coaxed
what he thought was some appropriate underlying bass from
the depths of the duar, from the enigmatic nether regions
where the instrument drew not only its music but its magic.

A silvery mist began to coalesce within the stall.

Squill saw it too and kept rapping even as he backed clear,
hardly daring to believe it was working. Gragelouth retreated
to one side while Viz hastily took wing, abandoning his barrel
perch to hover behind the energetically strumming Buncan.

The argent fog curled into a tight, scintillating whirlpool
directly above the unconscious rhino's head. As it spun it
generated a faint hum. With increased velocity the sound
intensified, until the roaring was so loud Buncan could
barely hear the otter clearly enough to maintain proper
accompaniment.

Small dark clouds formed within the maelstrom. Buncan
and Squill kept their attention focused on the rhino, who
was beginning to stir. Armor clanged softly. The spellsong
was working! Buncan knew it had to work or he'd never be
able to face Mudge and Weegee again, not to mention never
having the chance to unravel the mystery of the Grand
Veritable. It could not *not* work.

Miniature lightning crackled within the diminutive clouds
as Squill's voice rose to a feverish barking. There was a

tremendous reverberating boom as the whirlpool imploded, followed by a flash of light so bright they were all momentarily blinded. Buncan wasn't sure whether he actually ceased playing or not.

When he could see again the stall revealed that Snaugenhutt had rolled over onto his back, all four legs in the air. His armor lay splayed out beneath him, an iron mattress. He looked like a corpse in the last stages of rigor mortis. If anything, his snoring was louder then ever.

Gasping for air, Squill gazed in disgust at the still-recumbent form. "That's it, mate. I can't think o' anythin' else. I've improvised 'til I'm 'oarse." He sucked at the pungent night air.

"Not only didn't it sober him up," Buncan muttered disconsolately, "it didn't even wake him up." He turned toward the merchant. "I guess that's the end of it, Gragelouth. We're finished."

But Gragelouth wasn't looking at him. Nor was he considering Snaugenhutt. His wide-eyed attention was focused instead on something behind the spellsinging duo.

"I wouldn't say that we're finished," proclaimed a surprisingly deep voice.

Buncan whirled. Viz was still behind him. Only, the tickbird wasn't hovering anymore. He was standing. And he'd changed. Grown a little bit, actually. Well, more than a little bit.

When he spread his freshly metamorphosed wings they shaded the entire area.

The frightened deer had buried themselves in the straw of their stall and lay there, shaking. Emerging from the rear of the main building to see what all the noise had been about, the chief bartender, a no-nonsense coyote, took one look at the gigantic winged apparition, let out a strangled squeak, and vanished back inside.

Squill pushed his feathered cap back on his ears and stared up, up at the heavy-beaked, splendiferously plumed skull. "Right spell, wrong subject, mates."

Viz inspected each wing in turn, then his enormous, formidably clawed feet, lastly the broad, spatulate tail. "This is wonderful!"

"Wondrous, at any rate." A stunned Gragelouth ducked as the transformed tickbird turned a slow circle, flattening a protruding chimney across the street.

"No telling how long it'll last," Buncan declared, staring. "Some of our spells don't hold up too well. With just Squill and I executing this one, I wouldn't lay change on its permanence."

"Then we'd better take advantage of this one," the transmogrified tickbird rumbled.

"Wot do you 'ave in mind, guv?" Squill was watching the bird warily.

"Like you've been saying: Time is important. Climb up on my back, all of you." A vast wing dipped until the tip was touching the ground.

Hesitating only mentally, Buncan struggled up the ramp of huge feathers, pulling himself along. Behind him, Gragelouth lingered.

"Come on!" he urged the merchant.

"I . . . I don't know." The sloth's nervous tongue was all over his face. "I am not used to such adventurous exertions. I am only a simple merchant."

Buncan settled into position behind the tickbird's columnar neck. "Don't think about it. With your claws you'll be able to hang on better than any of us."

"Well . . ." Gragelouth glanced down at his powerful fingers. "Having always considered myself permanently earthbound, I suppose it would be a highly educational experience to experience flight." He ambled forward.

Buncan looked past him. "Squill, what are you waiting for?"

"We otters ain't keen on flyin', mate. We like life bloody well close to the ground, and plenty o' time under it."

"It's your sister," Buncan reminded him sternly.

"That's right, smother me in guilt." He shuffled reluctantly forward. "It's only that if I upchuck on Viz's back it might break the spell."

"Anything might break it. Move yourself." Reaching down, Buncan gave his friend a hand up.

"Puke all you want." Viz gleefully tossed his amazing rainbow crest. "It won't bother me. I've lived with *that* for years." He indicated the stagnant, soporific shape of the unconscious rhinoceros.

Gargantuan wings beat the air, driving the cowering deer even deeper into their stall. As the coyote returned with querulous friends, the blast of wind from Viz's wingbeats blew them backward into the tavern.

Two strapping sets of claws reached out and snatched the snoring Snaugenhutt from his stall. The stupefied rhino was a load even for the transmuted tickbird, but with a determined burst of energy he powered his great avian form into the night sky, multiple burden and all.

Banking hard above the towers of languorous Camrioca, an enchanted shape turned sharply westward. Those few citizens abroad on nocturnal strolls who happened to glance upward at a propitious moment did not then nor ever after countenance what their eyes detected at that particular moment.

Viz followed the reflective path of the river, turning inland when the battlements of the Baron's estate became visible off to the north. The half-moon that was playing hide-and-seek with the clouds supplied enough light to show the way.

Buncan dug his fingers tighter into the feathers in front of him as Viz took a wild dip. The tickbird looked back at him, panic in his voice.

"I'm getting weaker already! I can feel it."

"Knew the spell wouldn't last." Squill leaned over, estimating the distance to the trees below, and shut his eyes tight. Beneath the brown fur the muscles of his arms were clenched.

Gragelouth focused his attention on the terrain ahead. "I see no guards on the wall. There are one or two atop the main gate."

"Set us down inside," Buncan instructed their mount. "Right on the roof."

"They'll see us land," Viz argued. "We need something to divert their attention."

"What do you suggest?" The feathers Buncan clutched seemed to be vibrating under his fingers. At any moment, he knew, Viz might contract to his normal size, leaving them all suspended in midair. But only momentarily. In his natural incarnation it would be a struggle for the tickbird to raise a good-sized worm.

"Leave it to me. And hang on!" With that, Viz drew in his great wings and dove straight for the main gate. Ominously, a silvery mist was beginning to collect along the leading edge of his wings.

Hearing the wind that was not wind, one of the guards atop the wall saw the stupendous apparition approaching and let out an involuntary, startled cry. It was enough to alert the evening patrol below, which reacted with impressive lack of decision.

Their yelling was loud enough to reach into the great central hall, where the Baron Krasvin was planning his final assault on the upstart occupier of his precious library. He peered past his courtiers, his expression irritable.

"What's all that noise."

"I'll go and see, Master." Holding his floppy hat onto his head, a woodchuck sprinted for the doorway.

Krasvin grunted at the interruption and returned his attention to his immediate circle. "Now remember: We're going in quietly. Once inside I want all of you to hug the wall. Neiswik and I will go up the ladder first. As soon as we can get the lamp out of her reach we'll toss her down to you. Get on her immediately: She's quick. And don't hurt her." He grinned nastily. "Such pleasures I reserve for myself."

"I can't hold it!" shouted Viz as he plunged lower. "I can feel myself starting to change back."

"Then get the 'ell down!" Squill squealed at him.

"We have to land inside." Buncan tried to estimate the distance remaining to the estate. "We have to!"

At that moment an unearthly shriek split the air rushing past him. It came not from any of his companions but from immediately below. It wasn't surprising that he didn't recognize it. He'd never heard a rhinoceros scream before.

Snaugenhutt had chosen that moment to awaken.

"It's all right." Buncan leaned out and over as far as he could. "We're almost there!"

"Almost wh-wh-where?" Snaugenhutt's words were not slurred, his tone unimpaired. As a representative of a decidedly earthbound tribe, the experience of finding himself suddenly and unexpectedly soaring through the air had done nothing less than shock him sober.

"The gate," their mount shouted. "We're almost upon the gate!"

Though deeply distorted, the tickbird's voice was not unrecognizable. Snaugenhutt's head twisted around and up.

"Viz?"

"Yeah, it's me, you useless old soak. I'm wondering why I bothered to haul you along."

"Sorry. Don't know what happened to me."

"I do. I can't let you out of my sight for a minute without you crapping all over what little reputation we've got left. But that's Krasvin's estate up ahead. You're about to get a chance to redeem yourself. Whether you want to or not."

"What do you mean?"

"I mean that the spell that's done me like this is wearing off fast, we have to get inside that wall unnoticed if possible, and in order to do that we need a diversion. A big diversion."

Snaugenhutt's eyelids shuttered suspiciously. "What kind of 'diversion'?"

At which point there resounded in the night sky above the silent forest west of Camrioca an immortal cry not likely to be repeated in the lifetime of anyone in the immediate vicinity. Or anywhere else, for that matter.

"Rhino awayyyy!"

"Nooooo!" Snaugenhutt howled as those great claws unclenched and Viz released his burden.

As the transformed tickbird soared upward, buoyed by the release, the panicked rhino described an elegant trajectory out and down, plunging horn-first in a great arc straight toward the high, double-doored gateway. On the walkway atop the gate two of Krasvin's household troops witnessed the black-armored, flame-painted monstrosity hurtling toward them out of the half-moon. One fainted dead away on the spot, while the other dove into the courtyard with becoming alacrity.

Pennants and ribbons flying, the cast-iron-clad Snaugenhutt smashed into the center of the gate with stupendous (if decidedly unwilling) force. Planks and cross-braces shattered explosively. His armor banging and clanking like a military band on speed, Snaugenhutt landed in the courtyard, rolled over three times, and ended up on his feet, albeit staggering groggily. Fortunately he did not have to confront any immediate adversaries, the appalled patrol having fled precipitously in all directions.

Watching them abandon their weapons as they vanished into doorways and around corners reassured him as his senses returned. Dust from the devastated gate was still settling as he started forward, trailing broken beams and smashed planks from his broad back.

Confronted by the unimaginably terrifying sight of an armored, flame-scoured, flying (well, falling) rhinoceros, those retainers who arrived to see what had happened beat an immediate and fearful retreat.

"Come back and fight!" Snaugenhutt bellowed defiantly. "Cowards, spineless reptiles! Stand and do battle!" There was so much adrenaline coursing through him that he was hopping up and down on all four feet, making a sound like one of the ore crushers at the fabled Caqueriad Mines.

Not surprisingly, none of Krasvin's minions elected to take him up on his offer.

At that point the Baron himself, trailing retainers like remoras, appeared in the main entrance to the mansion. The sight of the armored, snorting, quadrupedal intruder, eyes bloodshot and nostrils flaring in the moonlight, gave even the belligerent Krasvin pause.

Snaugenhutt took note of the figures crowding awkwardly in the doorway and let out a gratified rumble. "Ahhhh. *Fresh meat!*"

A silken-clad squirrel squealed frantically and vanished back inside. To his credit Krasvin drew his own sword and tried to rally his people.

"Weapons! We'll make a stand here." His saber wasn't as long as the rhino's front horn.

Snaugenhutt wasn't exactly quick out of the blocks, but once he got his great bulk up to speed he could manage a very respectable pace. The Baron held his ground as long as was sensible, then uttered a violent curse and retreated inside, helping to slam the door shut behind him.

Pennants streaming, Snaugenhutt plowed through the portal without breaking stride, sending wood, metal strapping, and fragments of stained glass flying in all directions. Braking with his front feet, he skidded to a stop in the middle of the great hall and immediately began hunting for something else to trample, knock down, or gore. The subjects of his attention ran into, around, and over one another in their haste to avoid his homicidal gaze.

It was a very effective diversion.

CHAPTER 16

RAPIDLY SHRINKING TO HIS NATURAL PROPORTIONS, VIZ just did manage to clear the high wall and land his passengers atop the main building. It was an awkward touchdown, but everyone made it in one piece.

As they climbed to their feet they could hear the yells and screams rising from below, a chorus of confusion and fear.

"It sounds as if our friend Snaugenhutt is doing his job." Gragelouth brushed at his pants. "I was not sure he had it in him."

"Oh, he always had it in him." Viz was skimming back and forth across the roof, searching for a way down for his companions. "It's just that it was always saturated. But that little flight dried him out, rejuvenated him. Downdrafts be damned if it didn't rejuvenate *me*." He paused to hover in front of Buncan. "I enjoyed that little transformation. Think you two could do it again?"

"I don't know. It wasn't what we were trying to do in the first place." Buncan made certain the duar was strapped securely against his back. "Have you found a way down?"

"Afraid not." Viz gestured with a wingtip. "There don't seem to be any stairs leading to this roof. The only openings I was able to find are vents, chimneys, and skylights."

"Fair enough." Squill stood by the edge of one skylight, leaning over to peer through the translucency.

"It'll have to do." Buncan moved to join his friend. "We'll break the glass and climb down the ladder."

Squill frowned at him. "Ladder? Wot ladder?" He put one hand over his eyes and pulled his sword with the other. "We otters are the direct type, mate. You ought to know that by now."

So saying, and before Buncan could make a move to restrain him, he jumped forward as far as his short legs would propel him and plunged through the skylight, sending glass flying in all directions.

"Squill!" Buncan rushed to the opening and peered through. "You idiot!"

Below, the otter was climbing to his feet, brushing glass from his clothing and fur as he examined his surroundings.

" 'Tis a short drop, Buncan. Even old droopy-eyes ought to be able to 'andle it. Looks like servants' quarters. Wot the bloody 'ell are you waitin' for?" He moved out of view.

"Squill! Wait up." Buncan positioned himself as best he could and dropped through. He was followed by Viz, and lastly by Gragelouth, though it took some coaxing to persuade the merchant to make the jump.

No one challenged them as they hurried down the narrow hallway, nor was there anyone coming up the spiral stone staircase to intercept them. The level of noise rising from below suggested total confusion within the Baron's household, if not complete chaos.

Tracking the cacophony led them out onto a narrow mezzanine overlooking a central atrium or hall where a bellowing, defiant Snaugenhutt was holding court, dividing his attention between two groups of Krasvin's retainers. When one would try to flee from behind protective pillars and furniture, he would drive them back. This prompted the members of the other group to try to escape, whereupon the rhino would turn and charge them. Occasionally one fell victim to that thrusting horn, or tripped and went down. If Snaugenhutt happened to step on the prone unfortunate, he did not get up again.

From time to time an arrow shaft or spear would speed the rhino's way, only to bounce harmlessly off his thick, jouncing armor.

Buncan scanned the battleground. "No sign of Neena."

"No doubt she has by now been sequestered in some subterranean dungeon." Gragelouth fingered the knife he carried as his sole form of protection. "We need to find a route that continues to lead downward."

"How do we get past this?" Buncan indicated the chaotic courtyard.

"This way, mates." Squill shouted from the far end of the mezzanine, already two steps down the staircase he'd found.

They were about to descend lower when a shrill, familiar bark halted the otter in his tracks. "She's 'ere!" He looked around furiously. "That way!" Spinning, he charged back up the stairs, bursting past Buncan and Gragelouth. Only Viz was able to keep up with him.

Sword waving, Squill led the charge into the library... and slowed. It was empty, though there was plenty to indicate that it had recently been fully occupied. Food and drink had been abandoned on tables, and lamps still burned dimly.

"They're all busy with Snaugenhutt," Viz opined.

"There's no one here now." Buncan turned a slow circle as he advanced farther into the room.

"Bloody 'eck there ain't, Bunkooch," declared a weak voice from above.

Their attention was drawn to a mezzanine-level walkway, where Neena was trying to rise from amidst an uncomfortable bed of opened books. A single flickering oil lamp disclosed her location.

"Neena!" Buncan searched for a ladder. "Are you all right?"

"Wot the bloody, rotten 'ell took you so long?" She was so tired she had to use the railing just to stand.

"Don't worry, mate. She's right enough." Squill gave Buncan a hand with the ladder he'd found.

"What's this, more guests?"

Standing in the doorway, a lithe figure clad in elegant silks and soft leather gestured with the saber he carried. His attitude as much as his attire marked him as the master of the estate.

Squill leveled his own sword as he advanced on the

Baron. "The game's done, guv. Me sister an' I will be takin' our leave now. We ain't your guests."

"As you wish. I grant you swift departure." The mink's eyes glittered. "Your sibling, however, stays. She and I have unfinished business to conclude."

On the shaky edge of collapse from lack of sleep, Neena still had enough presence of mind to make her way down the ladder Buncan held steady for her.

"Oi, Squill. Lend me your sword an' I'll finish 'is business for 'im, I will."

"Regrett!" It struck Buncan that the Baron was not apologizing, but calling to someone.

Entering behind him and blocking the entire doorway was the ugliest member of the pig tribe Buncan had ever seen. The massive female warthog's huge scythelike tusks had been filed to razor points. Clad entirely in black leather festooned with metal studs and brads, she carried a hooked battle-ax in one hand and a spiked shield in the other.

"I will be damned if I will give her up now," swore Krasvin.

"I certainly hope you will." Buncan slowly drew his own weapon while keeping a wary eye on the hell hog.

"Tell me," Krasvin was saying, "where did you find the horned freak? He's wrecking my home and killing my people."

Viz moved slightly to the fore. "Snaugenhutt's his name and gallantry's our game, twitch-whiskers. We came to rescue the lady in distress."

"I am not hearing this," Krasvin murmured softly. "What sort of irrationality is this? You risk your lives for a female's virtue?"

"If you'd acted like a gentleperson in this matter, Snaugenhutt wouldn't be tearing up your front hall right now," Buncan assured him.

"Ah, well." Krasvin flicked at the air with his saber. "Perhaps it's just as well that you are here. Maybe after she's seen you disposed of she will be more accommodating. Though if you had waited a few hours more it would no longer have mattered."

"Wot's that?" Squill turned to stare at his sister. "You mean you 'aven't been . . . 'e 'asn't . . . ?"

''No, I 'aven't an' 'e 'asn't,'' she assured him brusquely.
''An' now, if you'll do me the favor o' guttin' this bastard
like a trout for the grill, 'e never will anyone else, either.''

Krasvin sighed. ''As the rest of my loyal staff seems
unable to deal with a single intruder, it will be up to you and
me, Regrett, to deal with these three.''

''Four!'' Viz darted toward the Baron and just did dodge
the lightning-fast swipe of his blade. ''Before this night's
out, I'll peck the parasites from your body.''

''I will have you know that I live as cleanly as I kill.''
Krasvin settled his attention on Buncan. ''I am told that
your horned associate flew through the air to smash my
front gate. His tribe possesses no wings. How did you
manage that?''

Buncan immediately swapped the sword for his duar.
''With this. I'm a powerful wizard. A spellsinger, son of a
spellsinger.''

''Really? You look green as a new-sprung twig to me.
The kind my servants chop for kindling.'' The saber flashed.
''I will have your bones burned and the ashes scattered.''

''You really are one first-class disgustin' example of
sentience,'' Squill observed thoughtfully.

''Thank you.'' Krasvin executed a sardonic bow. ''You I
will keep alive long enough to watch what I do to your
sibling. Regrett!''

With (not surprisingly) a deep grunt the huge warthog
lumbered toward them, raising her battle-ax.

''I've 'ad about enough o' this, I 'ave.'' With that, Squill
dashed forward.

''Squill!'' Even Neena was startled by her brother's
unaccustomed bravery... or foolhardiness.

The ax described a vicious arc which, had it connected,
would easily have cleft the otter through at the waist.
Infinitely more agile than the mammoth hog, Squill ducked
under the blow, rolled, and stabbed with his own weapon,
putting all his weight behind the thrust. The point penetrated
between boot and legging to slice the Achilles tendon.
Somewhat surprised at his own success, he sprang to his
feet and backed off.

The warthog shrieked and went down on one knee. Then,

to universal astonishment, she slowly straightened. Though
the wound was clearly visible there was no sign of any
blood, or any indication of damage. As Squill and his
companions gaped she resumed her advance, moving easily
on a leg that ought to have been permanently crippled.

Avoiding blows from the great ax, Squill continued to
harry the monster. Though his thrusts repeatedly struck home,
they had no apparent effect. He continued to avoid retaliation,
but could not do so forever. No one could. And while he
tired, his gargantuan opponent showed no signs of slowing.

"There is sorcery at work here," Gragelouth muttered.
"Dark sorcery."

"Indeed." Krasvin relaxed by the doorway, patiently
awaiting the inevitable. "Regrett is my personal bodyguard,
and the recipient of a very elaborate and expensive restora-
tion spell. Did you think you were the only ones who could
make use of combat thaumaturgy? Her body renews itself
each time it is injured. I doubt any of you can make a
similar claim."

"Eventually she will wear all of you down. Why not
simply surrender now to the inevitable?"

"May you contract a foul disease of the genitals that can
only be treated with lye and sandpaper," said Gragelouth.

Neena gazed at the sloth in astonishment. "Why, you old
slug-a-mug. I didn't think you 'ad it in you!"

The merchant looked embarrassed. "Even I have my
limits, young female."

"Stand still," the warthog growled, "and I will disable
you quickly!" The ax hissed down, striking sparks and
stone chips from the library floor where Squill had been
standing an instant earlier.

The otter continued to brandish his sword. He was as
defiant as ever, but breathing hard now. "Be disabled? By
somethin' as revolting as you? I'd rather throw meself from
the top o' the tallest tree in the Bellwoods."

"I know I am ugly," the warthog rumbled. "Keep
insulting me. It energizes me and gives me strength."

"Squill," Buncan yelled from the far end of the library,
"watch out! She's spell-protected." He put up his sword

and began to play. "Sing! Neena, think of some words to counter this."

"Whuh?" She blinked. "Bunket, I'm so sleepy I can 'ardly keep me eyes open."

"Then sing in your sleep, or you're liable to lose your brother."

She squinted up at him. "Is that supposed to be a threat?"

He glared at her. "Neena! He's risking his life to try and save you."

"Cor, but 'e took 'is own good time about it. Oh, all right."

"Yes, sing, sing." Near the doorway Krasvin started clapping his hands rhythmically. "I'd be delighted to see some genuine spellsinging. Not that such as you are capable of such wonders, your flying behemoth notwithstanding, but I can tell you that it matters not if you are. The most wise and exalted wizard who enchanted Regrett in my service assured me that she is immune to any manner of necromantic interference. So sing out, while you are still able."

Buncan ignored the Baron's taunts. "Squill, you sing too! Try to work with each other."

The ax smashed into the floor so close to Squill that it shaved the hair on his tail by half. "Sing? 'Ow do you expect me to bloody sing, mate? I can't spare the wind."

A sweet, strong alto filled the room. It was Neena, doing her best to improvise while following Buncan's musical lead. Her lyrics resonated in the charged air, snicked off the floor, vibrated the loose pages of open books.

"Got no reason to fight no more
Better mind your manners an' mind the store.
Just ain't right to go around bashin' folks
You don't know, so
You ought to pay more attention to who you are
What's really important ain't that far
From inside you, if you'll just take a look
Take yourself a page out of a kinder book."

Taking note of the immediate consequences of the spellsong, Krasvin soon ceased his clapping. "That's enough. Stop that. *Now*." Which warning naturally inspired Neena to trill that much louder. Hefting his sword, the Baron started toward them.

Viz flew straight at him, landed one nice, solid peck on his forehead, and continued buzzing him, inhibiting his advance. Cursing madly, Krasvin cut and sliced with his saber. The tickbird taunted him too close for Buncan's comfort, but there was nothing he could do about it. He forced himself to concentrate on his playing.

A gray vapor had begun to coalesce around the she-hog. She grunted and swung at it, but neither ax nor shield was effective against what was virtually no more than a dense fog. As Neena sang on, a most remarkable transformation began to take place.

"It can't be," Krasvin howled. "The wizard *shielded* her!"

Indeed, the protective spell was not entirely wiped, for when Squill chose a propitious moment to dart forward and strike afresh, his sword cut readily through crinoline and lace without damaging the flesh beneath.

It was the sudden presence of crinoline and lace that was unexpected.

Squill withdrew his blade and stepped back, gaping, his weapon hanging loose in his hand. Neena ceased her singing and Buncan's suddenly limp fingers strummed in desultory fashion across the duar's strings.

Studs and leather had given way to a sleek dress of lavender and lace. Fine tatting decorated the bodice and sleeves while the multiplicity of petticoats sent the skirt billowing. A pert, matching bonnet was fastened beneath the chin with a satin bow. The battle-ax had metamorphosed into a rather large parasol, the shield into a purse.

With an invigorated roar Regrett swung the purse at Squill, who barely retained sense enough to duck. It smacked against the rear bookshelves and burst open to reveal a flowery interior lined with frills and filled with potpourri.

"What is this?" she bellowed uncomprehendingly. "What's happened?" At that point she caught sight of herself in a rococo mirror mounted nearby among the shelves and gave vent to one of the most horrific shrieks Buncan had ever heard emerge from a female throat.

Tossing aside purse and parasol as though they were made

of burning brimstone, she raced screaming from the library.
This entailed much tripping and crashing to the floor as she
struggled to make the high heels in which her feet were
entrapped function normally. She was last seen vanishing
into the central hallway, her hiked-up skirts rustling around
her thick legs.

Finding himself suddenly outnumbered, with his secret
weapon put to ignominious and utterly unexpected feminine
flight, Baron Koliac Krasvin damned them all with spurious
invective as he bolted for the courtyard.

"NO!" Weaponless, Neena reached for the source of her
preservation and hurled the first oil lamp within reach at the
retreating mink. It missed him and exploded against the
floor. Flaming liquid fountained in all directions. Some of it
caught Krasvin on his tail and right hip. Howling, her
tormentor stumbled wildly through the doorway.

Squill briefly contemplated pursuit before deciding that
his purpose here lay in facilitating escape, not homicide. He
rejoined his companions and watched while Neena planted a
whiskery wet kiss on first Buncan and then a highly
embarrassed Gragelouth.

"Wot, no embrace for your own brother?"

" 'Ow could I forget?" She approached and without
hesitation smacked him upside the head.

"Oi!" He grabbed at his cheek. "Wot were that for?"

"You stupid sod!" She was right up in his face. "Wot
took you so long? Do you 'ave any idea wot that nasty bugger
'ad in mind for me? Do you know wot I nearly went through?"

Squill snarled softly. "Nothin' you ain't gone through
before, luv."

She was on him with a screech, and he fought back
energetically and without hesitation, the two of them joined
in sibling combat as they rolled over and over across the
slate-paved floor. While a distressed Viz looked on, Buncan
considered beating the two of them unreservedly about the
head with the precious duar.

Gragelouth sidled up to him. "We really ought to be
thinking of getting out of here, my young friend. Snaugenhutt
should be able to carry us safely to freedom, if he can be
persuaded to relent in his present exertions."

"I'll handle that." Viz darted for the door and Buncan followed. The two otters had to settle for swapping insults in lieu of blows as they hurried to catch up. It was a marvel, Buncan mused, how any of their clothing managed to survive their exuberant sibling disagreements.

They found Snaugenhutt pawing the floor as he faced the entrance to the kitchen. The great central hall had been thoroughly demolished: furniture reduced to firewood, banners ripped from their lanyards, paintings and sculpture pulverized underfoot. The kitchen door consisted of a metal grille set in a wooden frame. Half a dozen long spears were thrust rather tremulously through the gridwork.

Viz settled onto his iron perch atop his friend's forehead. "Good work, Snaug. Time to call it a night."

Rhinoceran eyes blazed. "No. There's still a few of 'em left alive. Lemme finish 'em off."

"Not necessary. They're only employees." The tickbird stood on the perch and gazed back past his friend's prodigious rump. "Did you see a mink come running through here? Couldn't miss him. His ass was on fire."

"Missed him anyway." Snaugenhutt grunted. "Been busy."

Buncan trotted over to pat the rhino's armored flank. "Take us out of here, Snaugenhutt. You've done all that was asked of you. More than was asked of you."

The great head swung back to peer at him. "But I want to finish 'em off. Please let me finish them off?" His pleading did not pass unnoticed among the anxious contingent cowering in the kitchen. Several spears fell to the floor as their owners made haste to find space elsewhere.

"You are presently engaged in our employ," declared Gragelouth in no-nonsense tones, "and as your employer I demand that you extricate us from this present situation."

"Oh, all right." Bending his front legs, the rhino knelt on the scarred floor. Using the spaces between the iron scutes for steps, they scampered up his flank and settled into the concave metal "seats" along his spine. Buncan took the lead, positioning himself high atop Snaugenhutt's shoulders. He was followed by Squill and Neena, with Gragelouth occupying the space above the rhino's hips.

Clambering back to his feet, Snaugenhutt turned and,

with utter disdain, pointed his rear end at the survivors in
the kitchen as if daring them to respond. It was an offer that
went unrequited. No one made any attempt to inhibit them
as he lumbered out of the mansion, across the wood-strewn
outer courtyard, through the remnants of the main gate, and
out onto the narrow road beyond.

Following Gragelouth's directions, they turned right at
the first intersection, right again up a poorly marked route
that led northwest. Only when they were well away from
Krasvin's lands and the outer environs of Camrioca did
Buncan finally relax.

Neena had been heaping insults on her brother ever since
they'd fled the estate, but had quickly succumbed to exhaustion and fallen into a deep sleep. They'd paused long
enough to stretch her lengthwise across her saddle, Snaugenhutt's broad back and short stride being sufficient, together
with her own belt, to ensure that she wouldn't fall off.

As he ambled down the trail Snaugenhutt hummed some
obscure martial ditty to himself, occasionally breaking into
outright song. Listening to him sing was almost as interesting, Buncan thought, as watching him fight. Of Krasvin
there was no sign, despite his reputation. Buncan hoped the
fire had burned his backside bald.

They stopped in the town of Poukelpo for provisions
before entering the Tamas Desert. Poukelpo was little more
than an outpost, full of tired, slightly disreputable types
unable to make a go of it in the more prosperous lands to
the south and east. While Gragelouth haggled over the price
and quantity of their supplies, Buncan inquired as to the
meaning of the desert's name and was informed that the first
person known to have entered and returned alive had been a
legendary kangaroo rat name of . . .

"Tamas," Buncan finished for the speaker.

"Nope," said the scruffy tamandua. "The rat's name was
Desert. Funny coincidence that." He shrugged. "I've no
idea where the 'Tamas' comes from."

It was a not altogether illuminating explanation.

There was still no sign of pursuit. Either they had
outdistanced it, or else Krasvin was still too befuddled or

discouraged to mount any. Buncan began to think that they'd seen the last of him and his aberrant drives.

"Not surprised." Snaugenhutt looked up from his feeding. "No one's gonna follow us into the Tamas. Nobody goes there for any reason."

"He's right." Viz fluttered out of the way as the last of the gurgling water casks was slung across his companion's commodious back.

Buncan shaded his eyes as he let his gaze wander out past the edge of the little community. Heat shimmered above distant canyons and mesas. According to what he'd overheard and been told, they were about to enter a region of unknown dangers and great uncertainty. It seemed that he and the otters were to be regular visitors to such lands.

"How long will it take us to cross?"

"Impossible to say." Gragelouth looked over from where he was supervising the loading. "My inquiries have failed to produce a consensus on the desert's extent. Everyone seems to agree that there *is* an end."

Buncan smiled thinly. "That's gratifying."

"It is said that eventually the tablelands and sand give way to wooded mountains profligate with game and good water, but none are certain as to the actual distance." As always, the sloth accepted his chosen fate quietly. "However far it is, however long it takes, we must cross." He pointed north with a heavy paw. "That way lies the Grand Veritable."

Or a veritable lie, Buncan thought. He shrugged inwardly. They'd come too far, had overcome too many obstacles, to turn back now. Besides, he'd always wanted to see a real desert. As for the water-loving otters, they were apprehensive but game.

There was no need to worry about Snaugenhutt. Fit and completely sober for the first time in years, the rhino was ready to fight mountains.

No one bade them farewell as they ambled out of Poukelpo. The townsfolk had seen too many people charge bravely off into the Tamas, never to return. They went about their daily business in the manner of all desert dwellers: with care and deliberation.

The days did not strike Buncan or his companions as particularly hot. This was more to Snaugenhutt's benefit than anyone else's, as he was doing all the work and lugging armor to boot. He plodded methodically northward, able to tolerate the heat so long as they rested during the hottest part of the day.

The otters busied themselves catching fresh lizard and snake to supplement their stores, while Gragelouth strained to see ahead, using his experience to select the most likely route since there were no paths or roads through the desert. Neither Buncan nor the otters ever disputed his choices. The merchant was the seasoned traveler, not they.

Several days out from Poukelpo they found themselves passing among towering, twisted formations of reflective colored sandstone. This was country, Buncan mused, to delight the eye if not the feet. Snaugenhutt's thick, horny footpads were not troubled by the crumbly rock underfoot, and his passengers were as feathers to him. They made steady progress.

That was why it was such a surprise when he began to sway unsteadily.

A concerned Buncan leaned out and forward. "Something the matter, Snaugenhutt?" Behind him his companions strained to hear.

Viz had been scouting a little ways ahead. Now he returned to query his friend. But Snaugenhutt wasn't listening.

"Everybody off," the tickbird said abruptly. "Off, off!"

They complied; the otters with inherent grace, Buncan awkwardly, Gragelouth with so much deliberation that he barely made it before the rhino keeled over onto his side. Supplies went flying as their indestructible mount let out a vast moan. He lay there, groaning and burbling, eyes rolling back in his head as his legs feebly kicked and pawed at the dry air.

His passengers gathered to stare at their stricken companion. Viz settled on Buncan's shoulder. To his great relief the tickbird did not seem panicked.

"What's wrong with him?" he asked worriedly.

"I think the shock finally wore off."

"The shock?" Neena frowned. "Wot shock?"

"Recall our fellow traveler's condition at the moment we

were about to storm the Baron's domicile,'' a suddenly comprehending Gragelouth suggested. ''It was only an unexpected fall from a great height which returned him abruptly to consciousness. That has finally worn off.''

''Wot's worn off?'' Squill made a face. ''You talk in riddles, merchant.''

''I am saying that he has been functioning under the impact of that moment ever since. Until now.'' The sloth dispassionately considered the unsteady heap of sudden insensibility. ''It has finally worn off.''

''Got that right,'' agreed Viz with feeling.

''But it's been days,'' Buncan pointed out. ''How is that possible?''

''I did not think it was possible for any living being to get that drunk, either.'' Gragelouth shrugged.

Squill found himself a soft patch of sand beneath the shade of a wind-polished boulder. ''Looks like rest time, mates.''

''Not hardly.'' Buncan moved to unlimber his duar. ''We've got to sing away the last of his inebriation.''

''Wot, now? 'Ere?'' The otter indicated the towering buttes, the peculiar spiny plants, the tiny but highly active reptile scuttling into a hole. ''Why not just wait for 'im to sleep it off?''

''That could mean days,'' Viz informed him. ''I've seen it take that long.''

Gragelouth considered the sky. It was cloudless, intensely blue, and while not burning, decidedly less than comfortable. ''Better not to linger in such a place. I, for one, am not of a mind to wait if it can be avoided.''

''Come on.'' Buncan plucked experimentally at the strings. ''It shouldn't take much of a spellsong. We're just going to cure a delayed hangover, not transform birds or call up unwilling whales.''

Neena sidled over to her brother. ''Wot are you afraid o', slime-breath? Me, I don't want to squat 'ere drinkin' up our water an' waitin' for the Gut-that-Walks to get over 'is beauty sleep.'' She kicked at him, and he scurried to avoid her foot. Buncan noticed that she'd done her best to reapply her makeup, though it was considerably less florid than when they'd started out. The streaks of color that flowed back from her muzzle were not as bright or well-defined as before.

Why she felt the need to wear makeup into a trackless desert was a question only another female could answer.

"Let's leave it up to the one who knows him best." Buncan turned to the tickbird.

"Help him if you can," Viz replied. "He'll dehydrate lying out in the sun like that."

"Why is he kicking and moaning?"

"D.T.'s," the tickbird informed him curtly, adding, "You don't want to know what a drunken rhinoceros hallucinates."

Buncan nodded, found himself a comfortable rock to sit on after first making sure it was not home to anything small and fast that was inclined to bite him on the butt, and settled the duar across his knees. For a change he could enjoy improvising. This time their lives weren't at risk. They were only trying to help a friend in distress.

"Got no time to waste in this place
Got to move on, got to find our space
'Tis a race
We're in, so you 'ave to feel better
Get over your trouble, get to somewhere that's
wetter
Shit, you ain't sick
You're in the thick
O' the trick."

Neena tracked the musical line easily, chivvying her brother into a reluctant harmony. It was good to hear the two of them singing together again, Buncan thought, after the successful but erratic sorcery he had perpetrated with each of them individually.

He relaxed as the by now familiar silvery cloud began to take shape alongside the moaning rhino, growing thicker and more pronounced with each note, each rapped rhyme. It would be interesting to see what form the cure would take. Would it be visually intriguing, or simply straightforward and functional?

It took the form of a grotesque, misshapen outline stained green and yellow that laughed horribly out of the side of slavering, rotting jaws.

Furthermore, it was not alone.

Horrid multiples of the initial phantasm were taking shape all around them, half stolid, half invisible. Noxious ichor dripped from wicked, curving claws.

"Stop it," wailed Gragelouth. "Make them go away!"

"Go away?" Frantic, Buncan didn't know whether it would make things worse to cease playing or keep on. Judging by their dismayed expressions, neither did the otters. "How can we make them go away? We're calling them up!" Something stung him on the cheek. Hard.

"Sorry." Viz was apologetic. "I had to get your attention. You're not calling these things up. *He* is." A wingtip indicated the moaning, twitching Snaugenhutt. "They're what he's seeing. I know, he's described his D.T.'s to me before. Your singing is just making them visible, giving them substance." The tickbird's voice was hard. "Of course, I'm not experienced in such matters, but it seems to me that if you just quit cold you're liable to leave something like these things hanging around."

Something that smelled like rotting flesh on burned toast was shuffling toward them, fungoid arms extended, eyeballs dangling from the ends of raw, frayed strings. It was still only half solid, and Buncan forced himself not to run.

"If we keep singing," he muttered even as his fingers continued to draw music from the duar, "we're liable to make it worse."

"We got no choice, mate," Squill called to him. "I ain't goin' nowhere with these drunken imaginin's taggin' along. 'Ow can I meet any ladies with somethin' like this 'angin' off me bloomin' shoulder?"

The specter that had chosen to focus on Buncan hovered nearby, not quite corporeal enough to make actual physical contact. He shuddered. There was entirely too much of it as it was.

If they stopped singing and playing it might simply fade away. If Viz was wrong. Except that thus far the tickbird had usually been proven right.

If their music could give substance to someone else's nightmares, surely it could also give them the boot? He caught the otters' attention as he changed keys.

Brother and sister modified their lyrics. Sure enough, as they did so the loathsome shapes began to dissipate.

"Not fair," gibbered something with six arms and a spastic proboscis.

"Just getting ready to suck some brain," groaned another. It took an intangible swipe at Squill with a glistening, translucent tentacle. The blow passed right through her.

The more the swiftly deteriorating D.T.'s complained, the less the unconscious Snaugenhutt moaned and kicked. As with most alcoholics, he couldn't conquer his problem until he faced it. Only this time, the otters and Buncan were facing it for him. Literally.

A concatenation of rotting fangs and putrefying eyeballs swam up in Buncan's vision only to seep past and vanish. It turned out to be the last of the discomfiting visions. As it evaporated Snaugenhutt slumped into peaceful rest, breathing in slow, steady heaves like an armored bellows.

"That ought to do it." Viz couldn't sweat but looked like he wanted to.

Buncan slumped, his fingers numb and sore. "He's still asleep."

"Aftermare," the bird informed him. "Might last an hour, maybe a couple. No more." He let out an elated chirp. "Guaranteed. You did good."

"Thanks. I think." Thoroughly worn out, Buncan felt like a nap himself, but decided to hold off. Snaugenhutt's nightmares were still too vivid in his own memory.

Also, some of them might still be hanging around with nowhere else to go, and after what he'd seen of them so far he didn't want them popping up in his own dreams.

CHAPTER 17

WHEN THE RHINO AWOKE THAT EVENING, HE WAS FULLY rejuvenated and ready to roll. To his surprise, none of his companions exhibited comparable enthusiasm. So he was compelled to wait while they spent the night in the shelter of the eroded boulders, wondering how they could be so exhausted when he felt relaxed and thoroughly refreshed.

Snaugenhutt's nightmares had departed for more congenial dreams, and everyone slept comfortably. After a quick breakfast, they remounted their bemused but now fully recovered four-legged ferry and pressed on deeper into the Tamas.

The landscape grew ever more fantastic, presenting towers and turrets of stone that had been carved by angry wind and impatient water into a surfeit of fanciful shapes. Fragile fingers of layered stone reached hundreds of feet into the sky, while rivers of broken rock flowed in frozen riot down the slopes of brooding, flat-topped mesas. The blaze of mineralized color ranged from pure white to a deep maroon that reminded Buncan of fine wines he'd seen for sale in the shops of Lynchbany. Black basalt and gleaming obsidian striped the lighter stone like collapsed veins in the bodies of fallen giants.

They passed beneath a wall of solid peridot, the intense green volcanic gemstone afire with inanimate life, and had to avert their eyes from the glare.

Squill stared until the tears ran down his cheeks, and not only from the light. "Wot a site! A determined bloke could winkle out jewels 'ere for a century without dentin' the supply. Ain't that right, Gragelouth?"

The merchant nodded. "It is certainly a remarkable deposit."

"Remarkable? 'Ell, it's bleedin' unique."

"Mining's hard work, Squill." Buncan shifted his backside against the unyielding iron. "You're allergic to hard work, remember?"

The otter pursed his lips. "Oi, that's right. For a minute there I'd forgotten." He went silent as Snaugenhutt picked a route between a pair of brittle sandstone spires.

They stopped for the night by the side of an arroyo. A small stream sang through its twists and turns, running clear and cold over slick sandstone slabs. There were several deep pools, one of which provided the otters with an opportunity for a noisy swim.

All the talk in Poukelpo had been of the desolate, unforgiving Tamas and its endless stretches of windswept rock and gravel. So far the actuality had been both greener and wetter. They'd found water not once but several times, and their casks were as full as when they'd started out.

Maybe, he dared to muse, after all the trouble they'd had in places where they'd expected none, they might now have an easy time of it in the one region where difficulties were anticipated.

While the Tamas had proven itself unexpectedly benign, it was still far from an inviting place. Not only hadn't they met a soul since leaving Poukelpo, there was no indication that anyone else had passed this way at any time in the recent past. There were no tracks of riding animals, no casually cast-off detritus of civilization, not even the chilled embers of an old campfire. They were truly alone.

The arroyo gave way to a spectacular, sheer-walled canyon that wound north. Gragelouth was good at analyzing the topography ahead, and they had the benefit of Viz's wings. Each time the merchant decreed a change of direction, the tickbird would soar ahead to confirm or deny the wisdom of his decision. Invariably, the sloth chose correctly.

Buncan marveled openly at this talent. "Years of traveling by oneself sharpens one's sense of direction, cub."

"It must, because I'd get us good and lost in these chasms and gorges." He scrutinized the sandstone ramparts. "How much more of this do you think there is?"

"That I cannot tell you." The sloth scanned the high rim of the canyon they were traversing.

"So far it's been a lot easier than I expected."

"Yes." The dour-visaged merchant almost, but not quite, grinned. "Something must be wrong."

"Nothin's wrong, mate." Squill lay flat in his seat, his incredibly limber body curled so that his head rested on his hips. "Our luck's changed, that's all. 'Bout bloody time, too."

The canyon continued to grow both deeper and wider, until it seemed as if any passing clouds must surely stumble over its lofty rim. Here and there isolated pinnacles thrust their peaks into the sky. Their appearance was deceptively frail. Though it looked as if the first random gust of wind would topple them, still they stood, silent and immutable sentinels, the only witnesses to the presence of the diminutive creatures on the canyon floor far below.

Armor clinking, Snaugenhutt splashed through a shallow tributary of the cheerful stream they had camped beside the night before. On the far side he paused and knelt to slake his thirst. Sensing the chance for a quick dip, the otters dismounted and disrobed in one smooth, flowing motion. Buncan settled himself in a comfortable hollow in the rocks, while Viz hunted for water bugs along the shore. With great dignity, Gragelouth slid from his seat and set about washing his face and hands.

Buncan lay back and contemplated the sky. Not such a bad journey, not now. He glanced lazily to his left, then to his right. And blinked.

Something was coming down the canyon toward them. It was big, bigger than Snaugenhutt. Much bigger.

In point of fact, it reached a third of the way up the canyon wall.

He scrambled to his feet. The object most nearly resembled an inverted cone, its top being much broader than the base on which it scooted along the ground. As it drew nearer, the faint whisper which had first caught his attention had risen to a dull roar. The otters had scrambled clear of the pool and were throwing themselves into their clothing. Viz had rushed to his armored perch atop Snaugenhutt's forehead, while Gragelouth edged close to the rhino's protective bulk.

The merchant was anxiously examining the base of the canyon walls. "Shelter. We have to find shelter."

"Don't worry. I've seen bigger whirlwinds in the Chacmadura country," Viz told him. "Everybody hunker down close to Snaugenhutt. I don't think it's strong enough to move him." He glanced to left and right. "I don't see any caves, merchant. We might as well stand our ground."

"Easy for you to say." Gragelouth clung determinedly to part of the rhino's armor as the introverted storm bore down on them. "You can be caught up in such a phenomenon,

thrown skyward, and simply cast free while the rest of us
would suffer a prolonged and possibly lethal descent.''

Snaugenhutt turned his snout into the oncoming whirlwind and braced himself against the rocks underfoot. The
storm collected gravel and unfortunate insects, swapping
them for twigs and fragments of other plants it had picked
up elsewhere. Its roar was loud but not overpowering.

Buncan hugged the rhino's comfortingly massive flank,
squinting into the flying debris. The disturbance would pass
over them quickly and they could be on their way.

He was feeling quite confident until he saw the second
whirlwind.

It entered the gorge from the opposite end, as if sniffing
along their track. Much larger and more intense than its
predecessor, its concentrated winds reached three-quarters
of the way up the canyon walls. Instead of a muted, mottled
gray, it was an angry black. Instead of twigs and leaves,
entire trees could be seen spinning and snapping within its
tubular core. As it bore down on them, it lifted huge sandstone boulders as if they were pebbles and flung them aside.

Gragelouth saw it too. "Most unusual to encounter two
such atmospheric phenomena at the same time. I fear for
our safety." He rubbed at his eyes. Flying sand was starting
to become a problem. "Perhaps they will bypass us, slam
into one another, and cancel themselves out.''

"Crikes." Squill waved downcanyon, past the original
whirlwind. "There's *another* one!''

"And another," shouted Neena.

A new pair of whirlwinds came corkscrewing up the
canyon in the wake of the first. Somehow they maintained
their individuality despite bumping into one another and off
the sheer canyon walls. As the travelers turned they were
not surprised to see additional whirlwinds of varying shapes,
sizes, and colors filling the upper end of the chasm from
side to side, crowding in behind the black giant that had first
raised their apprehensions.

There was no way out now, nowhere to run. Both ends of
the gorge were completely blocked. Buncan pointed to a
cluster of prodigious boulders that lay heaped against the
nearest wall. One had been reduced by wind and water to a

high, sweeping curve, a frozen, buff-colored wave. While no all-encompassing cavern, it did promise some shelter from the onrushing winds.

"Over there!"

Snaugenhutt put his mass in motion, wishing loudly for the half-barrel of hard liquor they didn't have with them. Once beneath the arc of stone, they arranged themselves as compactly as they could behind the rhino's armored bulk. Flecks of mica sparkled within the rock as they waited to see what would happen when the two onrushing clusters of wind slammed into each other. Would they simply pass around or through, or would the opposing cyclonic forces tear themselves to pieces?

They got their answer when the first two whirlwinds to enter the canyon paused in their advance and turned toward the mound of boulders. Highly concentrated gale-force winds sent dust and sand flying and muddied the surface of the small stream that flowed through the canyon.

"I saw them first." The voice of the smaller vortex was a breathy rush of syllables. Somehow Buncan wasn't surprised. He'd often listened to the wind moaning and howling in the treetops of the Bellwoods, and if it could howl and moan, why not also speak?

"Not so!" The larger, far more intimidating storm seemed to bend in the middle to peer down at them. "It was I who first sensed their presence."

"What does it matter?" wondered a third from behind the first two. Wind had set Snaugenhutt's armor to clanging. It tore at the travelers' clothing and hurled specks of dust into their eyes, making them blink and squint. Averting his face, the rhino locked his knees and held his ground.

Buncan had to shout to make himself heard. The canyon was filled from side to side with pushing, shoving storms, each violently roiling the air around it, each competing with its neighbor for a place to set its turbulent foot. The din was overpowering.

"It matters to me," replied the first whirlwind. "I saw them first, so they're mine." The second bumped up against it, but the smaller storm held its air. Storm currents contended tumultuously and suspended objects were wrenched from one brawling eddy to another: whole trees, chunks of rock, bits of plant matter, even live animals flashing dazed expressions.

"I didn't know whirlwinds fought among themselves," Buncan muttered.

"Fought, 'ell." Squill pressed against Snaugenhutt's armor, one paw clamped determinedly over his hat. "I didn't know the bloody things could *talk*."

"Not all of them. Only the educated ones."

Buncan and Squill turned to the merchant, who was now sitting with his back pressed against the curving stone.

"How did you know that?" Buncan asked him.

"Because I have encountered one such previously." Gragelouth was trying to shield his eyes with his hands. "It stole my entire inventory. Extracted everything from my wagon and wrapped the contents about its exterior for all the world like a demure maiden draping herself in the finest linen. It was a small whirlwind, no more than ten times my own height, and utterly amoral. They're very curious and, as I learned to my dismay, highly acquisitive.

"I first realized it was capable of communication when it complimented me on my choice of merchandise. Though this revelation allowed me the opportunity to argue for its return, for all the good it did me I might as well have been remonstrating with these rocks. I was told to consider myself fortunate that it did not have the resources to accumulate *me* in addition to my goods." He gestured at the vast, howling storms. "I do not think it necessary to point out that these are strong enough to do so."

"So they collect objects for fun?" Buncan asked.

"Not for fun." The explanation was supplied by a modestly decorated maelstrom which had managed to slip in close past the two angry combatants. "We are simply bound to collect things. It's what we do."

How did you conduct a conversation with something that had no mouth, no eyes, no face, no features of any kind save those acquired objects held suspended with its body? While Buncan wondered, Neena inquired.

"You mean you go lookin' for stuff intentionally?"

"We do. Then we meet several times a year at a

predetermined rendezvous like this canyon to swap swirling stories, gusty gossip, and found objects.

" 'Ere now," Squill protested angrily, "I ain't no 'found object.' "

"You are so an object," explained the unrepentant eddy, "and you've been found."

"So those two?" Buncan indicated the quarreling minicyclones.

"Want to collect you," their interlocutor explained. "Each is claiming right of initial perception."

"We object," the huddled Gragelouth announced. "We are intelligent beings and we have our own priorities."

"Oh, you wouldn't be collected permanently," the whirlwind moaned. "After a while the novelty of you would get old. With time even the most diverting acquisitions lose their attraction. For example, I'm thinking of trading this."

A petite offshoot of the central vortex protruded horizontally from its parent's flank. Clasped unsteadily within this gyrating pseudopod was a cracked but still intact ceramic bathtub. Buncan was relieved to see that it was unoccupied.

"Collected this on the other side of the world not three months ago. Beautiful, isn't it?" There was unmistakable pride in the whirlwind's voice. The airy pseudopod contorted, the bathtub rotating along with it.

"See, the white finish covers both sides."

"Very pretty." Buncan made sure he had a firm grip on his precious duar. It was still too early to panic. Thus far they'd only been threatened verbally.

"Even a short stint as ornaments would hinder us in our own search," Gragelouth pointed out.

"Don't intelligent people have a say in whether they're collected or not?" Viz stayed hunkered down behind his little shield. Even a casual gust of wind could sweep him helplessly to his doom.

"That's a question of ethics," the whirlwind replied unhesitatingly. "As a force of nature, I'm not required to have any. And by the way, our existence isn't an easy one, you know. Life isn't all open fields and low-pressure centers. Maintaining one's appearance and posture in calm air is a real struggle. You don't know what's it like to be tightly wound all the time. Collecting helps us to relax.

"Being a found object's not so bad. We take care to sweep up food and water for the ones that are alive, and you get to do a lot of free traveling."

"Excuse me if I decline the 'onor," said Squill. "I never 'ad me 'eart set on pukin' me way around the world."

"Why haven't you taken the opportunity to suck us up while those two are fighting?" Battling the wind, Buncan clung with one hand to Snaugenhutt's heavy armor.

The vortex skittered backward, unintentionally pelting them with sand. "I'm not into living creatures, myself. Too much work to keep them alive. I prefer inanimate objects. But you might as well resign yourselves. Once those two have settled things between them you're going to be collected, voluntarily or otherwise."

"We cannot allow that." Gragelouth was insistent in spite of their situation. "We seek the Grand Veritable."

The whirlwind spun a little tighter and its voice rose. "I've heard of that. There's nothing to it. No reality. It's a story, a rumor. Nothing more than a tale with which to amuse a fresh breeze."

"That is what we seek to determine. Not to minimize the honor of being deemed collectible, but we really cannot spare the time."

"Good luck convincing *them* of that." Reabsorbing its esteemed bathtub, their drafty interlocutor retreated.

Another maelstrom took its place, rotating proudly. "Want to see what *I've* collected?"

"I don't think so," replied Buncan slowly.

"Ah, c'mon." It spun very near. "See?"

A spiraling torus was thrust toward them. Buncan flinched but held his ground.

An old woman hovered within the blustery extrusion. She was clad entirely in black. Long, stringy hair hung from beneath her pointed black hat, and her narrow, pinched face was dominated by a huge hooked nose at the end of which reposed a hairy wart of unsurpassed ugliness. The folds of her skirt billowed around the broomstick she straddled.

"Lemme guess," said Neena. "You *do* collect intelligent creatures."

The cyclone hummed. "You got it."

"Hey, you!" The old woman shouted toward them. "Can you get me out of this? I'm late for a whole batch of appointments."

"Sorry, madame," replied Gragelouth politely. "We are preoccupied with troubles of our own."

"Yeah, well, I've heard *that* before. It's just that I've been stuck inside this damn thing for longer than I care to think. Sort of flying in place, if you get my drift."

"'Ow'd you 'appen to get trapped in there?" Neena studied the old woman with interest.

"Didn't get trapped, young water rat. Got collected. Last thing I know I was heading south past Topeka air control, minding my own business, and the next I'm swept up in this thickheaded hunk of air." She shook her head in disgust. "That's what I get for evesdropping on cockpit conversations instead of paying attention to the regular FAA weather updates."

Buncan didn't quite know how to respond. "Uh, how are you doing in there?"

"Well, the food ain't too bad, and the view's interesting. Could be worse, I reckon. I expect I'll get out of here soon enough. *Then* she'll get it!" The torus retracted into the body of the whirlwind.

"Who'll get it?" Neena wanted to know. But with a hideous cackle, the old woman disappeared skyward.

"You never know where you're going to find things when you travel between worlds," the storm informed them.

"Whirlwinds can travel between worlds?" Buncan asked.

"With ease. Molecular diffusion beats jogging any day. The aether's more permeable than most people think. You just have to pick your spots."

"Sounds like rot squared to me." Squill scratched his forehead.

A bulge in the whirlwind's side provided them with a temporary view of a small elephant with extraordinarily large ears. "You wouldn't *believe* where I picked this up,"

the storm told them. Before they could take a closer look,
the airborne pachyderm vanished into the dark depths.

The vortex which had first approached them interrupted
the display. "Looks like those two have finally got their
coriolis forces aligned." Leaving distinctive tracks in the
sand, the garrulous pair retreated.

Their place was taken by the two wailing storms which
had been battling over right of perception: the large, charcoal-
gray, intimidating spiral and its smaller but equally pugna-
cious counterpart. They roared and bellowed within a
handsbreadth of each other as they confronted the travelers.

The smaller inclined its crown toward them. "We've
reached a settlement."

"We have," boomed the other as flying rocks crashed
against one another within its flanks.

"Look here." Gragelouth adjusted his attire. "We have
some conclusions of our own."

"Silence!" A blast of wind sent the sloth stumbling.
Buncan and Squill caught him under his furry arms.
"Collectibles should be seen and not heard. Besides, we're
not going to hurt you. Physical damage would reduce your
display value."

For some reason this revelation did not make Buncan feel
especially grateful.

"We've decided to divide you among us. I get the large
armored quadruped and its small flying companion. The rest
of you will go with C's*." The smaller whirlwind advanced
slightly.

"You're not splitting us up." Buncan draped a possessive
arm loosely over Snaugenhutt's neck.

"You have nothing to say about it," growled the larger
storm. Behind it, the assembled cyclonic forces murmured
their approval. They completely filled the canyon, obscuring
the sheer stone walls and the sky beyond. Amidst these
howling and bellowing gales the cluster of boulders held by
Buncan and his friends was an island of calm.

No avenue of escape presented itself. Even if one had,
Buncan knew, they couldn't outrun the wind.

"If you'll just organize yourselves into two groups,"
hissed the smaller whirlwind, "this'll be a lot easier for

everyone." Buncan felt a persistent gust nudging him to his right. He fought against it as best he could, trying to dig his heels into the sand.

"We haven't got time for this." He steadied the duar against his waist and began to play.

The otters hadn't been idle. They'd used the delay to prepare themselves. Clinging tightly to Snaugenhutt's armor, they sang out at the top of their lungs.

"Hey, yours make music," rumbled the larger of the two acquisitive eddies. "That's not fair."

"The agreement is made." The second etched small circles in the ground with its foot.

As they squabbled Buncan played on, grateful for the respite. Keeping a watchful eye on the whirlwinds, the otters harmonized maniacally.

"Yo, y'know, we got us a real problem here
There's some winds in the air gonna cost us dear
Need somethin' to stiff 'em
Stifle 'em, kick 'em
Knock 'em for a loop and stuff 'em
Down in a crack, gotta break their back
Take 'em apart or cram 'em in a sack, Jack
If y'know what we mean."

Something began to take shape between the wind-battered travelers and the bickering storms. The magic was working, but Buncan's elation was muted. Instead of a familiar silver-gray mist, something black and ominous was forming.

It started as a softly mewing spindle-shape hardly large enough to bully a pebble. As the otters rapped on it grew larger, until it was the size of a bedpost, then a lamppost. Tightly wound as an anxiety attack, it swelled and expanded, a coal-black shaft screwing its way skyward.

In seconds it was large enough to divert the attention of the equivocating whirlwinds. The smaller suddenly refocused its attention.

"Are you doing that? Look at it, just look!" It spun in uneasy circles. "Stop it. You've got to stop it." This expression of concern from that which had just threatened them naturally inspired Buncan to play faster, the otters to improvise even more enthusiastically.

The agitated whirlwind shifted toward them, its intentions clear. Buncan braced himself for the shock of gale-force gropings.

They never came.

The squabblers had waited too long. By now the spellsung black spindle was enormous. Punctuated by intermittent bolts of dark lightning, its howl was deafening.

As the whirlwind darted forward, the spindle cycled to intercept it. A sound not unlike a breathy grunt filled the air as the approaching vortex was knocked backward. Trees, rocks, chunks of debris flew from its flank as it momentarily lost shape.

"Never seen a whirlwind throw up before," the immovable Snaugenhutt observed.

As the rotating black spire they had called forth continued to mature, Buncan wondered if perhaps the otters oughtn't to tone down their lyrics a little. But he couldn't stop playing long enough to make the suggestion, and in any event the specter they had conjured was now making too much noise to be heard by anyone.

The now gigantic malign cloud seemed composed of dense black smoke. Lightning continued to flash from its fringes, and the sound it made stiffened the small hairs on the back of Buncan's neck. Gragelouth cowered against the curving sandstone while Viz clung desperately to his iron perch.

Meanwhile the otters, motivated now by a sense of malicious mischief as much as a need to defend themselves and their companions, rapped on, ignorant of what they had wrought but delighted at the effect it was having on their erstwhile abductors.

"*Tornado!*" screamed the dazed whirlwind, collecting itself as best it could after the blow it had taken. Staggering wildly, it skittered off down the canyon.

The panicked cry was taken up by the rest of the boreal convention as, pushing and shoving, they scrambled to escape. Mass confusion ensued as collections and isobars slammed into and sometimes through one another. Fleeing from the restrictive walls of the canyon, the frenzied storms scattered frantically to . . . well, to the four winds.

By this time the invoked tornado towered higher than the greatest of the previously assembled whirlwinds, an inverted black cone that sucked at the sky. Its power was palpable, its bellowing like that of a runaway waterfall. Squill and Neena could hardly hear themselves sing, much less each other.

As they looked on it pounced on a retreating vortex and tore it apart, sending its collection of rubble flying in all directions. Where a moment earlier there had been a healthy whirlwind in flight, in seconds only a scattered cluster of desultory breezes remained. It was an appalling display of meteorological ferocity.

Far higher now than the canyon walls, the black spindle pawed angrily at the ground as if searching for additional victims. It spun back and forth, daring any organized wind to approach.

In shifting to the middle of the chasm, the noise had been reduced to just less than intolerable levels. Snaugenhutt glanced back and up at Viz.

"What's a tornado?"

Clinging to its perch, Viz shook his head. "Beats me, Snaug. But at least it's on our side." *For the moment,* the tickbird thought.

Save for the apparition they had called into being, the canyon was now clear of breezy intruders. Buncan let his fingers fall from the duar. The otters ceased their rapping as Squill moved to loosen one of the water casks.

"I have never seen or heard of such a thing." Looking down, Buncan saw the awestruck merchant staring at the awesome cloud. "What a weapon it could be."

"Oi," commented a relieved Neena, "think o' wot it could o' done to that bastard Krasvin's 'ouse. Splintered it and sent every one o' them up the dirty bugger's arse. Impaled 'im on 'is own—"

"We get the picture, Neena." Buncan carefully checked his duar for damage from flying gravel.

The tornado whipped across the little stream that ran down the center of the canyon and in an instant sucked it dry. It displayed no inclination to pursue the fleeing whirlwinds.

Gragelouth plucked tentatively at Buncan's sleeve. "A most useful conjuration and demonstration, but do you not think that it is time to make it disappear?"

Viz peeped out from his armored howdah. "Yeah. Make it go away, Buncan." The tickbird faced the now aimless storm warily. "It's making me nervous."

"Right. Squill, Neena?"

Squill nodded as his sister slaked her thirst. "Righty-ho, mate. Give us a minim 'ere." When Neena was sated she recorked the cask and settled herself close to her brother. Each put an arm around the other's shoulder as they leaned their mouths close. Whiskers tangled.

"Done your job and done it well
Blew 'em all away like a storm from Hell
Now's the time to leave
Time to go on your way
Hey tornado, wot you say?
We say, you gots to go away and maybe come again
Some other day, okay?"

With a violent twist, the black spire abandoned the creek bed and started toward them.

Eyes wide in his gray-furred face, Gragelouth retreated until his back was once more pressed against the sandstone arch. "What are you doing? Make it go *away*."

The otters rapped faster and Buncan's fingers flew over the duar's strings, but the savage storm continued its deliberate, turbulent advance until it was almost upon them. In the face of that terrible wind Buncan had to fight to stay on his feet, while the otters now clung to each other in deadly earnest. Even the massive, defiant Snaugenhutt was brushed backward several feet.

This storm, Buncan sensed, would not delicately collect them, would not care for and pamper them. It would smash them as thoughtlessly and thoroughly as it had the unfortunate whirlwind it had overtaken.

Behind him he heard Gragelouth screaming frantically. "Make it go away, spellsingers! Make it go away! Oh what a tangled web we sloths weave!"

The sorrowful lament wasn't intended as a suggestion, but the otters jumped on it just the same.

> "Wind it up and tie it tight
> Lock it down like sleep at night
> Bind it fast and make it helpless
> Got to see it doesn't eat us
> Don't want to make it angry at me, at thee
> At anyone we see
> Just have to put it away for a while
> Time to do it fast, and for sure in style."

The propulsive vortex was almost upon them when its outer edges began to kink and snap. As the tornado halted, Buncan sensed a distinct feeling of puzzlement. It began to groan as if it had bones, embarking on a succession of violent convulsions. Tumultuous winds continued to buffet the watchful travelers, but they came from all directions now, confused in their approach and aimless in their passing.

As they stared the tornado folded in on itself. Disorganized streaks of black wind coiled in all directions. The storm contracted and spasmed, knotting and reknotting until with an audible groan the entire towering structure keeled over to slam into the canyon floor, sending a cloud of dust and sand flying.

Buncan averted his face until the cloud had begun to settle. When he looked back he saw the tornado lying prone, twisting and humping helplessly in a futile attempt to loosen the thousands of knots into which it had tied itself at the behest of the otter's spellsong.

A benumbed Gragelouth sought to gather his wits. "Astonishing, but we had best depart before the treacherous phenomenon ascertains a solution to its current predicament."

Neena took a deep breath. "I'm all for that, guv. That were a near thing."

With a prudent eye on the bound tornado, they took turns mounting Snaugenhutt, who as soon as everyone was aboard trotted off up the canyon, careful to maintain a circumspect distance between himself and the enraged but impotent maelstrom.

As they finally exited the steep-sided chasm, Gragelouth
turned in his seat to peer back the way they'd come. There
was no sign of the beknotted tempest.

"That is what I try to do to my competitors," he informed
them somberly. "Surely it will free itself eventually?"

"I'd think so." Buncan scanned the mesas and plains
ahead. "Hopefully, before that happens we'll have put
plenty of distance between us."

The merchant settled himself back in his seat. "Of
course, if it were to pursue us you three could simply bind it
within itself again."

Buncan felt his duar bouncing lightly against his back.
"Don't count on it, merchant. So far we've been pretty
lucky with our spellsinging, but Jon-Tom always said something about sequels never being as good as the originals. I
guess that's just a natural component of sorcery. So if it
comes after us we might have to try something else, and it
might not be as effective. I'd rather make speed."

"I suspect I have more confidence in you, young human,
than you do in yourself."

" 'Ere now, guv," said Squill, interrupting without hesitation, "I've got plenty o' confidence, I do. Feel free to
compliment me."

Gragelouth half-bowed in the otter's direction. "My trib-
ute was intended to include all."

"Well, then." Squill pushed out his lower lip. "See that
it stays that way, guv."

An otter, Buncan mused, was the only creature he knew
of that could strut sitting down.

CHAPTER 18

THEIR ENHANCED CONFIDENCE DID NOT MAKE THE TA-
mas any smaller or do anything to mute its rising temperatures. They took to resting and sleeping for long stretches

during the middle of the day and trying to make up the time lost at night.

"Oi, guv'nor." Squill clung cheerlessly in his iron seat. Even the bright feathers of his cap drooped listlessly in the heat. "'Ow much more o' this blasted country is there?"

Grageclouth shifted his attention from an unusually tall pinnacle. "No one really knows for certain. In that the good citizens of Poukelpo were being truthful. But our progress is steady. I would not think the crossing would require too many more weeks."

"Weeks!" barked Neena. Her mouth hung open and she was respiring in short, rapid pants. "I don't know if I can take many more *days* o' this."

"Do you wish to turn back and perhaps meet up with our cyclonic friends again?"

"No fear o' that, guv." Squill straightened slightly in his saddle. "They've been scattered, they 'ave."

"Getting a little tired myself." Snaugenhutt punctuated his complaint with a frustrated snort. "This armor isn't getting any lighter."

Viz hopped down from his perch to bend over and peer into the rhino's eye. "Quit complaining. If you're thirsty there's plenty of water. Or is it something other than water you're worried about?"

"Put a beetle in it, bird. I'll stay clean."

"'Aven't 'ad a swim in days. Otters like water, not sand." Neena's expression turned dreamy. "Big river, good friends, plenty o' fish to catch. This bleedin' Grand Veritable better be worth all this trouble."

"More than that," her brother added reproachfully, "it 'ad better exist."

"Do I detect a certain waning of enthusiasm?" Grageclouth murmured.

"Wanin', 'ell," Squill groused. "It's on bloody death's door, it is."

Buncan winced as Snaugenhutt hit a couple of bumps while loping down a dry ravine and back up the far side. "I don't know about the two of you, but I couldn't turn back now if I wanted to."

"Why not, mate?" Squill asked him.

"Because it would mean admitting defeat." The duar bounced lightly against his back.

The otter blinked. "Wot the 'ell's wrong with that? Anybody offers me a sack o' fresh crawfish, I'll admit defeat right now, I will." Raising both arms melodramatically, he implored whatever gods might be watching. " 'Ere you! See, I admit defeat! I embrace it, I do. Now, 'ows about somethin' fresh to eat?" He held his arms aloft for another minute before lowering them.

"Gods must be busy. Strikes me as 'ow they're always busy."

"We're not turning back." Buncan was firm.

"Ain't we? 'Ows about we put it to a vote, wot?" He glanced back along Snaugenhutt's spine. "All those in favor o' turnin' back raise a 'and." He thrust his own skyward.

When it was not seconded he glared goggle-eyed at his sister. " 'Ere now, wot's this? You were complainin' more than all the rest o' us put together."

A chagrined Neena turned away from him. "Well, I been thinkin' about wot Bunski there said about admittin' defeat, an' 'avin' to explain it to Mudge an' Weegee an' all, an' I just ain't so sure it's a good idea to give up just now."

"Is that bloody right?" Her brother's exasperation was plain. "When is a good time, then?" When she didn't reply he added, "So you're in favor o' continuin' with this madness?"

"I didn't say that. I . . . I abstain, I do."

"Say wot? You can't bleedin' abstain."

Her whiskers thrust forward belligerently. "I just did."

Buncan reflected that only a couple of otters, sustained by their remarkable agility and superb sense of balance, could manage to engage in a serious tussle on the back of an ambling rhinoceros without falling off. At least things were back to normal.

As always, the scuffle concluded without any serious damage having been inflicted to either side. Squill settled back in his seat as though nothing had happened.

"Cor, mate, 'ow about we try to spellsing up a nice, cool pool. Pick a likely-lookin' depression in the rocks an' make a job of it?"

"I don't think so."

"Blimey, where's the 'arm, Buncan? Just enough for a quick swim. Wouldn't take much o' a spellsong."

Buncan looked back at him. "I said no. We've been pushing our luck all along. We might need a spell like that for drinking water, and as I've said from the beginning, harmonic replication's a pain."

Squill took mild affront. "Ohhhh, 'replication,' is it? Who's been studyin' behind me back?"

Buncan returned his attention to the route ahead. "You don't need a swim."

"The 'ell we don't! 'Tis our natural right, it is. 'Tis in the bleedin' tribal constitution."

"Well, your constitution's suspended until we leave the Tamas." He made an effort to soothe his irritated companion. "Don't think about it. If Gragelouth's right, we'll be out of this soon."

Squill was not mollified. "Cor! If 'Gragelouth's' right."

Their frustration was muted by the country through which they were passing. If anything, the towering formations grew increasingly more impressive, infinitely varied in silhouette and color. Gigantic buttes rose from the desert floor, their flanks sculpted into fantastic shapes by eons of patient wind and water.

Acutely aware of the uncomfortable situation, Gragelouth made an effort to divert the otters from their discontent. "You two need to get your minds off our present condition. See those cliffs?" He pointed to the abraded walls of a dark volcanic plug which rose from the earth like a dead tooth. "Notice how the edge resembles the profile of a human face?" His fingers moved. "That rocky projection in the center is the nose. The brow rides higher, while beneath the nostrils are—"

Squill cut him off. "At the moment I'm not interested in anythin' that looks like a bleedin' 'uman." His gaze burned into an indifferent Buncan's back.

The merchant refused to be discouraged. "Very well. Look at that eroded pinnacle off to our right. Does its outline not resemble that of a porcupine?"

Squill was reluctant to turn and look, but when his natural

curiosity got the better of him he was surprised to discover that the merchant's sense of the surreal was keen. He perked up slightly.

"Bugger me for a blistered bobcat if you ain't 'alf right, gray-face. It do right look like a member o' the spiny tribe."

Neena found herself drawn into the game in spite of herself. Anything to alleviate the endless boredom. It became a contest to see who could read the most outrageous or unlikely identities into the deeply worn rock. Her identification of a pile of rubble as a crouching kudu was surpassed by Squill's insistence that an isolated butte looked exactly like an armored mouse.

Before long everyone was finding recognizable shapes and forms in the passing scenery. More than anyone would have believed possible, the merchant's game was helping to pass the time. As for Gragelouth, he was better at it than any of them, explaining that it was a pastime he'd been forced to indulge in on many a long, lonely journey.

The game was resumed in earnest the next morning, the merchant having drawn up a means for keeping score. Points were awarded for accuracy, imagination, and frequency. Snaugenhutt was pointing out what he asserted was a hawk hidden among a sandstone overhang when the silence of their surroundings was broken by shouts from the dry riverbed ahead.

Everyone strained to see, but it was Viz, hovering high above, who first matched the sound to a possible source.

"Armed riders, on large bipedal lizards. They're all hooded, so I can't make out their tribes. Outlines are indistinct."

"How big?" a concerned Gragelouth inquired.

"Riders no larger than the otters. Snouts protruding from the hoods. Light-colored whiskers. I see some tails. Long and fur-covered, mostly light brown." The tickbird glanced meaningfully at his companions. "They're coming this way."

Snaugenhutt took a deep breath. Espying a large boulder, he headed toward the natural barrier. "Better get ready for company." No one argued with him.

As the rhino positioned his backside to the stone the otters drew their bows, making sure arrows were at the ready.

Buncan laid his sword across his lap as Viz settled onto his armored perch atop Snaugenhutt's forehead. Gragelouth sought to find a use for his fingers, and failing that, nibbled nervously on the pointed tips of the thick, heavy claws.

Their progress marked by the cloud of dust kicked up by their mounts, the riders advanced until they were within spear-throwing distance. Spreading out, they formed an unbroken line in the shape of a crescent in front of the stolid Snaugenhutt. There were enough of them to block any attempt at flight, not that the rhino could have outrun the speedy lizards even over flat ground.

As the dust settled, Buncan and his companions were able to get a good look at those confronting them. The riding animals pawed at the ground with nervous energy, bright green eyes shining alertly, small sharp teeth glistening in their jaws. Leather bridles and reins were intricately tooled, as were individual saddles and other tack.

As their mounts settled in place, several of the riders adjusted their hoods. It was the widely traveled Gragelouth who finally identified them.

"Meerkats."

"I don't know that tribe." Buncan was intrigued by the creatures.

"An uncommon one. The eyes and snouts are unmistakable. They are fabled desert dwellers. I myself have encountered them only once before, in far more civilized circumstances than these."

Though the meerkats were in the majority, there were also a couple of ground squirrels among the riders, as well as individual representatives of several other desert-favoring tribes. Buncan tensed as one of the riders slowly advanced, an elaborately whittled spear cradled in his short but powerful arms. A beaded cloth quiver lashed to the riding lizard's right flank held half a dozen similar implements.

Wide, dark eyes inspected them carefully. The mouth seemed frozen in a perpetual half-sneer. "More interesting than most travelers we see. From whence do you hail?"

"From farther than you can imagine." Buncan was as startled as anyone to hear Gragelouth speak up. "From beyond the Tamas, beyond Poukelpo, beyond Camrioca, and even the river Sprilashoone.''

"That far." The rider did not sound impressed. "Well, never let it be said that the Xi-Murogg denied hospitality to travelers in their country. If you will follow us back to our village, we would be pleased to exchange tales and share victuals with you."

Buncan hesitated. "We're kind of in a hurry."

"To refuse hospitality is to insult not only me but all the Xi-Murogg." As the rider spoke, his fellow villagers shuffled their weapons: everything from javelins to small, one-handed crossbows to hooked knives and swords.

These nomads were not likely to scatter in panic at a charge from Snaugenhutt, Buncan reflected. Tough and determined, they were fashioned of far sturdier stuff than Krasvin's retainers. Had they numbered half a dozen or less, maybe, but there were nearly thirty of them.

Perhaps all they did want was the company of strangers. Certainly they didn't encounter many travelers out here. It was also possible they might know the fastest and easiest route out of the desert.

"You lead and we shall follow." Gragelouth had apparently reached the same decision.

The hooded one bowed slightly. "Graciousness is unto a shield in the desert. I am Chi-churog, First Rider of the Xi-Murogg people. It will be my honor to welcome you into my house." He turned and sent his lizard trotting northward. The line of riders parted to let him pass.

Squill leaned forward, whispering. "I don't care for this, mate."

"Gragelouth's doing the right thing. What else can we do?"

"Run like 'ell an' make a fight of it," the otter replied.

"No." Human and otter turned to face the merchant. "Their mounts are too quick. They would run us down. We may yet have to fight, though I am putting my faith in tact and diplomacy. But this is not the place to do it. Let us sound them out first."

"Bloody 'ell. I'm outvoted again, ain't I?"

"Afraid so." Buncan turned to speak with Viz, leaving the otter to sulk in his seat.

Escorted by the Xi-Murogg, Snaugenhutt trundled along behind Chi-churog as they crossed a series of crumbling gullies. Turning right up a smooth-surfaced slope, they passed through a high, narrow cleft in a sheer rock wall. This penetrated the solid stone for a respectable distance before finally opening onto a sizable box canyon.

High-peaked tents dyed in a panic of colors and patterns were scattered about the high ground. Some were striped vertically or diagonally, others were checked, a couple sported polka dots of alternating hue. Most clustered around the spring-fed, reed-fringed pool that occupied the depression in the center of the canyon. The colorful, nonthreatening view somewhat offset the realization that there was only one way out of the sheer-sided stone amphitheater.

It was a natural fortress and an excellent place to camp, Buncan reflected as they rode in. Squill's reservations vanished as soon as he saw the pool. When the otters' request was made known to Chi-churog, he amiably and without hesitation granted them permission for a swim. They didn't hesitate, doffing their attire with admirable speed and plunging into the delightfully cool pond without delay. A number of villagers gathered silently to watch the lanky visitors sport within the clear waters.

Buncan was feeling much better about their situation. The overtly cheerful tents, the neatly tended and surprisingly extensive irrigated fields, Chi-churog's friendliness, all combined to suggest a comparatively peace-loving people who armed themselves only out of need to deal daily with the exigencies of a harsh land.

Only when he had dismounted and gone for a stroll later among the tents did he see the expertly mounted, carefully cleaned bones.

They decorated more than one dwelling, and there were too many of them to write the grisly displays off as a familial aberration. None boasted of reptilian origins. A horrified Buncan identified the bleached white skulls of two large cats. Another hut was crowned by a bear's skull. What a bear had been doing roving the Tamas he couldn't imagine; he knew only that the unfortunate ursine's wanderings had ended here.

Had these wretched travelers perished from heat or exhaustion out in the unforgiving desert, or had they been deliberately slain and brought here? He was beginning to fear that Squill had been right and they should have made a break for freedom the instant they'd been confronted by the nomadic outriders. Too late now. A glance was enough to show that the only way out, through the narrow cleft by which they'd arrived, was well-guarded.

Yet the skulls mounted like trophies didn't square with the extensive fields of painstakingly tended crops. Dedicated agronomists didn't slaughter strangers, and the extensively tilled land was proof that the Xi-Murogg were not roving bandits. What was going on here?

Females and older males were tending to the fruits and vegetables, while the younger meerkats, together with an occasional kangaroo rat, jabbered amusedly at the lightning-fast antics of the otters. Others prodded and poked at the massive Snaugenhutt. His thoughts churning, Buncan rejoined his friends as they emerged from the water and proceeded to dry themselves.

"I bid you join me in my domicile." Chi-churog led them to what was by far the largest tent in the village. It wasn't quite large enough, though. The Xi-Murogg leader explained apologetically.

"I am afraid there is not quite enough room for your great friend." He gestured at Snaugenhutt.

"No sweat. I'll wait here." The rhino licked thick lips and crossed his front legs. "Something to drink would make me feel less left out."

"Your acumen is to be commended. Rewarded it will be." Chi-churog spoke to one of his people in a strange dialect. The villager thus addressed nodded his understanding and hurried off toward another tent.

Woven mats covered the spacious floor. Large pillows fashioned of fine material stolen or bartered for lay scattered strategically about. Chi-churog promptly crossed his short legs and sat down. Sleek female meerkats appeared from behind a cloth divider to proffer water, some kind of lukewarm desert tea, and platters of produce doubtless freshly picked from the fields Buncan had seen.

Old enough to be interested in more than vegetables,

Squill let his eyes track the progress of the lithe feminine forms. "Well now, this 'ere's more like it!"

"It pleases me that you approve." Chi-churog gestured with a broad sweep of his hand. He had removed his robe, to reveal his bright white-furred form clad in shorts and some kind of diaphanous shirt. He was a handsbreath or so shorter than the otters, and considerably smaller than Buncan.

The visitors settled themselves against the soft cushions. Delighted to feel something against its backside besides rock or lightly padded iron armor, Buncan's body betrayed his unease. It was almost impossible not to relax.

Chi-churog accepted a long smoking stick from one of the females and waved it casually. "Now, then, tell me how you come to be in the lands of the Xi-Murogg? It must be some matter of great importance to have brought you, as you have said, so far from your own homes."

Before either Buncan or Gragelouth could respond, Squill was off and running. Omitting certain unflattering details, vastly embellishing upon others, he regaled the attentive leader of the Xi-Murogg and his equally rapt harem with a story of unsurpassing skill and gallantry, occasionally even remembering in an off moment to insert a brief word or two about his five companions.

"Bloody rotten stinkin' egotist of a sibling," Neena muttered under her breath.

Squill blinked, turned to her. "Say wot, sister?"

"I was remarkin' that you're your father's son." She smiled pleasantly.

"That's a fact." Squill resumed his oral epic.

Evening pressed down on the box canyon when he finally finished. Their host seemed pleased, and the travelers had consumed a prodigious quantity of fresh fruits and vegetables, as well as several delicious prepared varieties which had been transformed through drying, steaming, broiling, and other means of efficacious preparation. Within Chi-churog's tent unabashed contentment reigned among hosts and guests alike.

To the otters' astonishment, one polished wooden platter was even heaped high with dried fish.

"There are caverns nearby," their host explained, "cut

by water and populated by colorless, blind fish.'' The meerkat smiled. ''But not tasteless, I assure you. Their flesh is tender and succulent and forms a welcome addition to our diet.''

It finished off the otters' suspicions as neatly as if they'd been pared away with a sharp knife. Even the always leery Gragelouth was compelled to admit that their welcome had been all that could have been hoped for.

Tiny belly bulging, Viz glided into the tent to land on Buncan's shoulder. He'd taken a moment to relieve himself. After belching delicately, he whispered into the human's ear.

''Keep your expression bland and don't let on that I'm telling you anything, but we're in trouble.''

Buncan smiled as he waved off a fruit-laden female. ''How do you mean?''

''Want to take a guess? It's Snaug.''

This time is was harder for Buncan to maintain his composure. ''Don't tell me they got him drunk?''

Viz's beak was all but cleaning Buncan's ear. ''They must've done it when I was in here with the rest of you. I don't know if they did it deliberately or if he got a taste of something that appealed to him and asked for more. Snaug's a hard one to say no to. Not that it matters. The important thing is that right now he's lying flat on his side, out cold to starboard, snoring like a ventilation shaft from hell. I don't think he'll be able to stand up 'til morning, much less run.''

''What's that you say?'' Chi-churog leaned forward, and Buncan remembered having read something about meerkats having exceptional powers of hearing. ''Your great friend is already asleep?'' The village leader burst out laughing in a series of sharp, squeaky barks, similar to but higher-pitched than that of the otters. ''He should rest well tonight, then. As will you all.

''Tomorrow we will have the Ceremony.''

With studied diffidence Buncan slid the duar off his shoulders and laid it across his knees, making a pretext of checking the tightness of the strings. He tried to sound nonchalant. ''What ceremony?''

''The Ceremony of Fertilization.'' Chi-churog glanced at

the roof of the tent. "Tomorrow night the moon will be full. We need to ensure that our fields will be also."

Buncan untensed, his muscles relaxing. For a moment his natural suspicions had gotten the better of him. "What is this Ceremony of Fertilization?" However it was performed, he mused, it sounded anything but threatening.

"You have seen our fields."

"Wonderfully kept they are, too." Gragelouth was at his obsequious best.

Chi-churog accepted the compliment with a nod. "We are proud of what we have wrought from the Tamas. Our fields do more than sustain us; they provide us with the means to live well in a place where few others can even survive. We tend them as if our lives depend on them, which they certainly do. The Xi-Murogg wandered the Tamas for many years before finding and settling in this place. Since then we have cared for the soil of this canyon as if it were our own flesh. We have ample labor, and enough water. Only one shortage complicates our work."

"I wondered about that," Gragelouth admitted.

What are they talking about? Buncan mused. Though he'd been following the conversation closely, he felt suddenly lost.

Chi-churog stared evenly at Gragelouth. "You are perceptive, traveler. Many successful seasons have thinned and weakened this earth. Rain carries some nutrients down from the surrounding rim, but it is not nearly enough. Our springs run clear and clean, which in this case is less than helpful. We make use of the dung of our riding and pulling animals, but even this is limited in the results it can achieve.

"Therefore, whenever the occasion presents itself we miss no opportunity to lavish upon our precious sustaining fields whatever additional fertilizers may become available."

Gragelouth smiled demurely. "If you would like to add our personal by-products to your efforts we will be happy to accommodate you, but except for what Snaugenhutt can produce I fear you will be disappointed."

Chi-churog put the stub of his second smoking stick aside. "You underestimate yourself, sloth." He grinned, his black nose twitching. "Crops do well on dung, but better by far on blood and bone."

At which point Buncan knew exactly what had happened to the bodies of the original owners of the mounted skulls he had encountered earlier.

CHAPTER 19

WITH SPEED NO ONE IMAGINED HE POSSESSED, GRAGElouth sprinted for the exit and straight into the arms of the half dozen guards waiting outside. Buncan wrestled his duar into position while Squill and Neena lunged for their weapons.

The meerkats and rats and ground squirrels were too fast. They poured into the tent and swarmed the travelers, too many for the otters, too quick for Buncan. Viz made a dive for the doorway and flew straight into a waiting net. Squill managed one good sword stroke, slicing an overanxious meerkat from groin to armpit, before he went down under five or six assailants. Without Snaugenhutt's aid they didn't stand a chance in close quarters, and Snaugenhutt was apparently indisposed until morning.

They wouldn't have until morning.

It was all over in less than a minute.

It wouldn't have mattered if the otters had fumbled for lyrics instead of weapons. The duar was quickly wrenched from Buncan's fingers. Not because the Xi-Murogg had any idea it possessed unique powers, but because it was large and well made and if properly wielded could conceivably bash in an unwary meerkat's skull. Which was just what the furious Buncan wanted to do, except that his hands and feet were being rapidly and expertly bound.

Anyone who could bind an otter to the point where it couldn't move, much less free itself, knew how to handle ropes and knots, he reflected. If Squill and Neena couldn't get loose, he knew he'd only be wasting time and energy trying.

In moments the travelers had been reduced to so many impotent bundles flopping futilely on the mats. Gragelouth was trussed so tight he couldn't move, while Viz's wings had been secured to his sides and his feet bound at the ankles.

Satisfied, their confident assailants left them to gaze longingly at their weapons and worldly goods, which had been tossed in an indifferent pile in the center of the tent. Viz hung upside down from a cross-pole, bemoaning his fate.

"First trussed, next dressed?" From his ignominious position he glared at the contemplative Chi-churog.

The village leader winced at the affront. "We are not cannibals. We do not eat intelligent beings. Do you think we of the Xi-Murogg are uncivilized?"

Squill would have replied, except that Neena shot him a look threatening sudden death if he so much as opened his mouth. Under the circumstances it wasn't much of a threat, but her brother kept silent anyway. Not, Buncan thought, that any otterish invective could make their situation any worse.

Chi-churog continued. "You will be drained of blood. This is not an unpleasant way to die. One drifts first into unawareness, then sleep, and finally death."

"Yeah?" said the incorrigible Squill, unable to remain quiet for more than a minute. " 'Ow about you give us a demonstration, guv?"

The village leader did not deign to respond. "Afterward your bodies will be pulverized and ground to powder. During the height of the full moon you will be sown upon the fields of the Xi-Murogg. This is an honorable passing. That of which your bodies are made will contribute to the production of food and to the continued health of new, young individuals."

"You can't rationalize it," Viz chirped from his inverted position. "It's cannibalism by any name."

"It is not." Chi-churog was unmoved. "Your passing will inspire new life."

"Because we're bleedin' unlucky enough to 'ave arrived just before the full moon," Neena muttered.

Chi-churog strolled over to peer down at her tightly bound form. "Blood and bone can be preserved between ceremonies. A full moon simply provides better light for the process of sowing. The presence in the night sky of a new moon, or a half-moon, would not have altered your fate.''

"Gee, I feel much better now," she said sardonically.

Chi-churog stretched. "It is time to rest, but not here. If you moan and scream and disturb our sleep, it will be necessary to gag you as well. I would rather not do that. Your last night should be as comfortable as possible. Within reason." He departed in the company of two guards. "I go first to check the ropes on your large friend. He is several fields' worth of fecundity unto himself."

A single meerkat was left to watch over them. Given the condition of their bindings, even one guard seemed superfluous, Buncan thought. They had been tied with fiendish invention. He could barely move his fingers, let alone a hand. No chance of working the heavy leather thongs against one another behind his back. His legs were bound at the ankles and knees. If he struggled too much, he'd probably fall over onto his side.

At least he was able to rest his back against one of the tent poles. Squill and Neena had been left on their sides, facing the center of the tent. Their bindings were secured to pegs hammered into the floor. They couldn't even turn over. Like Buncan, Gragelouth had been favored with a sitting position. In addition to the usual thongs, leather mittens had been fastened over his hands and feet to make sure he could not make use of his heavy, albeit closely trimmed, claws. In his upside-down position Viz was less than helpless. Their captors were taking no chances.

This is it, then, he mused. *I'm gonna die not in glorious battle against some wicked sorcerer or Dark Forces, trying to rescue some beautiful girl in distress, or while taking possession of the Grand Veritable, but as fertilizer for a fruit tree.*

Along with their swords and the otters' bows his duar rested in the pile alongside the guard, who sat bored and cross-legged in the middle of the tent. Hoodless, he leaned back against the tent's centerpole, cleaning his claws with the point of a stiletto while sparing them only the occasional cursory glance.

It was extremely frustrating. Ungagged, Squill and Neena

could rap all they wished, but without the unique accompaniment of the duar their efforts would come to naught. He tried working his wrists against one another and had about as much success as he expected, which was to say none.

As the night progressed, the steady stream of complaints from the two otters began to slow. There being nothing else to do, they tried spellsinging anyway, producing such a stream of rhymed invective that it seemed certain the guard would respond. Save for an occasional tolerant smile he utterly ignored them, refusing to be provoked by Squill's inflammatory prose. Why should he be, Buncan thought, when all six of them would be so much ground meal by this time tomorrow?

So bored was the meerkat that from time to time he actually dozed off, only to snap awake again after a slumber of several minutes. It was a promising development they could take advantage of only in their imaginations.

With the onset of nightfall a steady, polyphonic chanting had begun deep within the village. It was accompanied by small drums, finger cymbals, and rattling gourds. Some sort of formal invocation, Buncan mused, to whatever gods of the soil required musical propitiation. Though it was now past midnight, there had been no letup in the droning concert.

When it terminated, he suspected, so would he and his friends. He wondered how long it took to drain a body of blood.

A glance through the open portal revealed no sign of emerging daylight, though he could only guess at the actual hour. Jon-Tom had brought back from the Otherworld a device he called a watch, though Buncan couldn't understand why it wasn't called a time. It was a portable clock. Half of him wished the gadget was presently encircling his wrist so he could know the exact hour, while his other half wanted to remain ignorant. Morning would come soon enough.

Sorry, Dad. Sorry, Mom. This isn't how it was supposed to be. The world, he thought, could be very uncooperative.

Not the guard, though. He'd drifted off again, his head drooping onto his right shoulder. Buncan struggled mightily with his wrists and succeeded only in exhausting himself. If anything, the leather strands seemed to grow tighter, threatening to cut off the circulation to his hands. The otters were half asleep themselves, while Viz emitted soft whistling snores from the cross-pole from which he hung.

So he was more than a little surprised when a voice behind him whispered anxiously, "Get ready."

Buncan turned his head to scrutinize the merchant. "Get ready? Get ready for what?"

"Why, to spelling, of course. To work your magic." He shifted his attention. "You! Squill, Neena."

"Miphhh . . . what?" Squill looked up sleepily.

"Wake your sister. Prepare a spellsong."

The otter blinked, sparing a glance for the dozing guard before returning his attention to the merchant. "Come off it, guv. We can't do no spellsingin' without Buncan's duar to back us up."

"I am aware of that. I am about to free you all."

Neena was now as awake as her brother. "With wot? Kind words an' good intentions?"

"Be still," the sloth whispered, "and watch."

Gragelouth sat bound securely, his claws contained, his arms tied behind him. He was neither as strong as Buncan nor as agile as the otters. It should have been obvious to any observer that he was completely helpless.

Except . . . he was not as thoroughly bound as his captors believed. Possibly in their triumph they had simply overlooked it, or perhaps they had never encountered a representative of Gragelouth's tribe before. Sloths had powerful, highly visible claws, and these the Xi-Murogg had rendered useless.

But they had forgotten to do anything about his tongue.

Long, flexible, and prehensile, it curled out of the merchant's mouth as he leaned forward, straining against the post. It crept down his chest, crossed his waist, and reached the top of his pants. There was a gentle click as it nudged one of the fake jewels which decorated the buckle of his snakeskin belt. The guard stirred, and everyone held their collective breath. The meerkat rubbed his snout, twitched his whiskers, but didn't open his eyes.

As soon as the guard had settled afresh, Gragelouth re-returned to his work. With the click the front of the buckle had popped open, to reveal a hidden compartment containing a well-traveled, experienced merchant's emergency supplies: a miniature vial of energy-giving honey-based concentrate, another of poison, a couple of valuable jewels . . . and a small, all-metal blade. At the sight, it was all the otters could do to contain themselves.

The guard slapped at a fly, turning his shoulder to the center tent post. Exerting himself to the limit, Gragelouth felt of the blade with his tongue. Delicately the end of that sensitive organ curled around the short hilt. Buncan winced sympathetically, but the merchant never faltered.

Gripping the blade, Gragelouth removed it from the open buckle. Neena lay nearer than Squill or Buncan. Steadying himself, the merchant rocked to his left until he fell over on his side. Buncan inhaled sharply, but the sloth held on to the blade. Extending his tongue to the limit (which was greater than Buncan would have believed possible), he passed the tiny knife into the otter's waiting fingers.

"Don't drop it, you silly twit." Squill squirmed against his own bonds, a bundle of pure, restrained energy.

"Shut up, broom-face." A pause, then a husky whisper of triumph. "Got it!"

Gragelouth retracted his tongue, licking his lips as he smiled gently at Buncan. "That was something of a strain."

"Why didn't you tell us?"

The merchant shifted against the floor, unable to sit back up. "What, and have one of you cubs perhaps give it away? Besides, I honestly did not know if I could reach the buckle, bound as I was. I am not one to raise false hopes."

"Hurry up!" Squill admonished his sister.

Her fingers worked the blade back and forth. "Want me to drop it? Then chew your whiskers and leave me alone." Squill went silent, but it required a distinct effort of will.

The guard dozed on, oblivious to the silent struggle taking place practically under his nose.

What seemed like hours passed. Finally Neena's arms gave a visible twitch and her hands came around in front of her. She barely paused long enough to rub circulation back into her wrists before starting on her leg bindings. The work went faster now that she didn't have to worry about dropping the knife.

Once free, she tiptoed silently around the inner edge of the tent to come up noiselessly behind the guard. Buncan gave a little jerk as she used the knife. The unpleasant business quickly concluded, she immediately set to work on the thongs binding Gragelouth.

"Oi!" her brother exclaimed. "Wot about me?"

"You can just lie there for a minim, mister always-in-a-hurry." Squill glared at her and gnashed his teeth, but quietly.

The merchant was soon loose. Avoiding her brother, who tried his best to bite her on the leg as she stepped past, she set to work on Buncan's bonds. Only when he and Viz had been released did she at last turn to Squill.

Buncan nudged the motionless guard with a foot as he strapped on his sword. The thick woven mat soaked up most, but not all, of the meerkat's blood. "Where'd you learn how to do that?"

She didn't look up from her work. "From me dear ol' mum. She always told us that academics should be grounded in a good practical education."

As soon as he was free, Squill favored his sister with a threatening glare. But instead of assaulting her he limped over on tingling legs and kicked the dead guard square in the face. Blood spurted.

Buncan frowned. "There's no need for that."

The otter smiled thinly up at him. "Cor, I know that. I just did it for me own personal pleasure." As he drew back his leg for a second kick, Buncan stepped in front of him.

"C'mon. We're a long ways from being out of here."

Squill hesitated, then nodded and hurried to salvage his own belongings from the pile.

Viz was stretching his wings, fluttering into the air and then landing to rest. "We can't leave without Snaug." The tickbird shook his head dolefully. "I can't believe they got him drunk. He'd been doing so well."

"Doubtless he thought he could handle it." Gragelouth was philosophical. "A common misconception of those overly fond of the bottle. Do not be too hard on him."

"Maybe they didn't get him drunk." Buncan slipped the duar over his shoulders. "Maybe he was drugged."

Viz brightened. "I hadn't thought of that. I made the obvious assumption."

"We all did." Buncan stroked the duar in anticipation. "We're not going to be able to just walk out of here, free Snaugenhutt, and ride out through the break in the rocks. Too many guards and chanters around. But right now surprise is ours. We'd better make good use of it."

"Spellsinging, yes," said Gragelouth enthusiastically. "But what form should it take?"

Squill stepped forward. "Leave it to Neena and me." His eyes flashed.

Buncan's fingers strummed the double set of strings. At the center, something fiery flared. The otters murmured one very angry sentence.

A globe of reflective flame leaped from the duar's nexus, floated like a bubble across the interior of the tent, and burst against the far wall. Concentric ripples of silver fire expanded outward from the hole in the wall like ripples in a pond. Gragelouth looked delighted.

"My, but aren't we incensed?"

Squill and Neena stood side by side, fingers entwined, bobbing in time to Buncan's music. This time no grins were in evidence as they sang. Viz settled expectantly on the merchant's shoulder as they followed the highly focused human and otters outside.

Not far away Snaugenhutt lay on his back, still clad in his armor. His feet thrust into the air, front and rear securely bound at the ankles. Heavier thongs crisscrossed his exposed belly, binding him to the earth.

Viz glided over to land on the ground next to his associate. The tickbird turned his head sideways as he examined his friend and companion.

"How you feeling?"

The rhino looked away. "They offered me a drink. Some kind of fermented lizard milk or somethin'. I was thirsty."

"Maybe a bit too thirsty?"

Snaugenhutt's voice was uncharacteristically muted. "Maybe. I don't have that much. There must've been something in it." Buncan had to admit as he continued to strum the duar that the rhino did not sound drunk.

The music and conversation alerted a startled guard who was sleepy but not asleep. The ground squirrel barked a challenge in Viz's direction. Viz ignored him as he spoke to the merchant.

"Hey, Gragelouth! You can help here." The sloth waddled over and began applying the blade of his larger knife to the rhino's bindings.

By this time the agitated guard was yelling for help. Sleepy, half-clad figures came stumbling out of nearby tents. Buncan and the otters ignored them. A lambent, silvery mist now all but obscured his busy fingers.

Chi-churog emerged from a large tent opposite the recumbent Snaugenhutt. The First Rider of the Xi-Murogg reached back as someone within handed him a curved sword. He waved it over his head as he started toward the escapees.

"You have ruined the timing and dishonored the Ceremony! Now we will have to wait another day."

Viz rose and darted at the meerkat, easily avoiding the sword stroke aimed in his direction. "Sorry, rat-face. We're out of here."

Chi-churog paused as armed males gathered around him. "Am I to be moved by your serenade? Your story did not impress me. I, Chi-churog of the Xi-Murogg, am not one to be frightened by the desperate warbling of inept troubadours."

"Who's inept?" Buncan shouted challengingly. The otters were no less irate.

"Stomp 'em in the ground, cut 'em to pieces
Kick 'em in the 'ead, make 'em all dead
Grind 'em into powder so their fields can be fed
With their own blood, hey
Turn it to a flood, say
Turn the ground to mud, yea
Let Snaugenhutt trample
Everyone who tries to flee
Start with that one as a bleedin' example!"

But Snaugenhutt's thongs didn't fray and dissolve. No invisible, impenetrable wall materialized to protect them from the now fully awake and furious villagers. No enraged dragon or other powerful defender appeared to challenge their approaching captors.

As Chi-churog and his mob of heavily armed villagers lurched forward, long snouts twitching, eyes full of murder, Buncan began to feel concern. Playing faster did nothing to alter the status quo, nor did the most violent imprecations the otters could improvise.

"For this outrage," Chi-churog declared, "the traditional butchering will proceed simultaneously with the collection of blood. This so that you may see for yourselves as you die with what skill our females wield the ceremonial knives. Consider it a special honor which . . ."

That's when the ground began to shake.

Well, not to shake, really, but to tremble, as if the earth itself had been agitated by the otters' lyrics. Buncan considered slowing the music, but he had to keep up with Squill and Neena, who were spinning insults and threats as fast as they could think of them. Maybe, he thought, he should have been paying more attention to the content of their rap than to the approaching Xi-Murogg. How dangerous a condition could they conjure? He wailed away grimly at the duar.

By now the surface was shaking sufficient to bring Chi-churog and his people to a halt. A poorly posted tent collapsed nearby, sending its dazed occupants stumbling out into the night. An apprehensive Gragelouth plied his knife as fast as he could. Snaugenhutt's front legs were free, and he and Viz were working frantically on the back pair.

The tickbird kept glancing worriedly in all directions. "Hurry up, merchant. Something's happening."

"I am as aware as you." Gragelouth sawed at a stubborn thong.

"This spellsinging?" Viz fluttered above his friend. "They have it under control, don't they? They know what they're doing, don't they?"

"More or less."

"More or less?"

"It seems to be something of a hit-or-miss proposition. The sorcery always works. It is the results that are unpredictable."

As if to punctuate the merchant's observation, the earth

promptly gave a thunderous belch, tossing the sloth to the ground. Feet freed, adrenaline pumping, Snaugenhutt rolled forcefully to his left, ripping the pegs that held the thongs across his belly out of the dirt. He stood erect, shaking himself like a dog after a swim. His iron scutes clanged violently, sounding the bells of the Church of the Contumacious Rhinoceros.

More furious than frightened, Chi-churog made an effort to advance over the quivering ground. His people followed reluctantly, their initial enthusiasm waning fast. They'd advanced several paces when they halted in their tracks.

Buncan turned to look over his shoulder. The sun was lightening the eastern sky, but it wasn't the sun that rooted Chi-churog's followers in place. It was something that had appeared between the village and the sun.

Two towering buttes looked down into the box canyon. Both were shuddering violently, enormous boulders and slabs of sandstone sloughing from their sides. Buncan remembered how as they'd progressed through the Tamas he and his friends had made a game of finding shapes and outlines and faces in the cold rock.

It was apparent now that they hadn't imagined those creations.

As more and more stone slid from its shoulders, the outline of a gigantic armored ape became visible. Spikes and blades projected from its burnished armor and a fringed helmet adorned the low-browed skull. Slowly, ponderously, it uncoiled from the crouching position in which it had been trapped for untold eons. An ax the size of a small town dangled from one immense hand.

The second butte collapsed to reveal a great cat of unidentifiable lineage. Its armor differed dramatically from that of the ape but was no less awe-inspiring. As one huge paw thrust a short sword skyward to pierce a low-hanging cloud, the liberated giant let out a roar that reverberated like thunder across the canyon.

Not only was the sight sufficient to send Chi-churog and the rest of the Xi-Murogg fleeing in panic, it was plenty impressive enough to intimidate Buncan as well. Not having enough sense to be afraid, the otters sang on.

Buncan removed his fingers from the duar and waved at them. "Hey, guys, I think maybe that's enough." The otters ignored him, utterly focused on their rap. Beyond the sheer sandstone walls, monstrous ape and gargantuan cat were turning curious, unnatural eyes toward the faint sounds emanating from the bottom of the box canyon.

Buncan slung his duar across his back and grabbed each otter by the neck, using force instead of reason to choke off their singing. "I said *that's enough*." He indicated the two titanic figures. "Let's *go*."

Clutching its ax, the ape was leaning over the canyon wall for a better look. As the edge crumbled beneath immense hands boulders crashed into the fields below, smashing fruit trees and threatening to bounce into the village itself. Wailing Xi-Murogg dashed in all directions, not knowing what to do. The riders who moments earlier had been intent on spitting Buncan and his friends were now desperately trying to control their spooked mounts.

"Whoa," said Squill as Buncan dragged him and his sister toward the waiting Snaugenhutt, "I told you those rocks looked like a monkey."

"You did not," Neena objected vociferously.

"Not *now*." Buncan shoved them halfway up the rhino's capacious back. As soon as he followed them and before he was even settled in his seat, Viz chirped into the hairy ear he was holding.

"Now, Snaug! Let's move!"

With a nod and a snort the rhino turned and rumbled out of the village, heading at an inspired gallop for the cleft in the canyon walls. No one tried to stop him. Once he got up to speed, nothing short of a natural disaster could.

Only a terrified and completely frustrated Chi-churog took a swipe at them with his sword as they hurtled past. The blade shattered on Snaugenhutt's armor. Their last view of the First Rider saw him hopping up and down amidst the confusion of his panicked village, hurling imprecations in their wake.

A few rocks fell from the rim of the chasm as Snaugenhutt barreled through, but they missed the riders on his back. Of the armed Xi-Murogg who normally guarded the way out there was no sign.

As they emerged into open desert Buncan allowed himself a sigh of relief. "That's it. We did it, we made it."

Snaugenhutt was slowing. "Don't count your retirement money yet, human."

Off to their left the armored ape stood tapping his massive ax against an open palm the size of a small plateau. The rising sun glinting off his red armor made him look as if he was on fire. Nearby, the sword-wielding giant cat stood surveying the landscape, its pointed ears scraping the clouds.

Moreover, they were no longer alone.

Snaugenhutt came to a halt. As far as they could see, perhaps a third of the buttes and mesas of the Tamas were coming to life, each one revealing and releasing a different soldier from some long-forgotten war of the titans. One by one they sloughed off their ancient shackles the way a sleeping human might shed a cosmetic mudpack, rising to their feet and stretching mightily in the warming sun. The noise of ton upon ton of cracking, crumbling, falling rock was deafening.

Snaugenhutt's head swayed from side to side, searching. "Which way?"

Gragelouth cupped his hands to his mouth to make himself heard. "Northwest, Snaugenhutt! Ever to the northwest!"

Viz pivoted on his perch atop the rhino's head. "Why?"

The sloth shrugged. "That is where we must go, and under the circumstances it seems as good a way as any."

Viz nodded, relaying the instructions to Snaugenhutt. The rhino resumed his heavy-footed lope, heading down a slope in the indicated direction.

As he jogged along, rock spilled from the butte on their immediate right. Something with three heads emerged, unlike anything Buncan had ever seen or heard described. Four legs supported the squat body, and a barbed tail the size of an oceangoing ship whipped reflexively back and forth. Each hand held a club the size of Clothahump's tree.

Espying them, the monstrosity let out a bellow and reached down with a third hand that blotted out the sun as it descended. Even though Snaugenhutt accelerated to his maximum speed, Buncan saw there was no possibility of avoiding those immense fingers. They would smash them flat or pluck them from the ground as easily as he would a flower. Gragelouth was mumbling something under his breath, the otters held each other, Viz bravely elected to perish with his old friend, and Buncan simply shut his eyes.

He felt something massive but controlled patting him gently on the head. Opening his eyes, he saw that the hand was similarly caressing his companions.

It withdrew, and the apparition straightened. Its subsequent bellowing could, with difficulty, be comprehended.

"FREE! FREE FOR THE FIRST TIME SINCE BEFORE TIME!" The barbed tail lashed a gully in the ground as the entity's three heads inclined to stare down at them. "I WHO HAVE KNOWN NOTHING BUT TIME NOW SAY THERE IS NOT ENOUGH TIME WITH WHICH TO THANK YOU FOR YOUR SONG."

Squill grinned nonchalantly. "Well, you know 'ow it is, guv. We just like to sing."

"Yeah, 'e's a real altruist, me bro' is." Buncan threw Neena a warning look. Naturally she ignored him.

All around them, as far as they could see, the liberated giants were embracing. Some were crying pond-sized tears. Others clapped long-petrified acquaintances on the back, sending booming shock waves rolling across the plain.

"I wonder how many have come this way before and remarked on the outlines in the rocks," Gragelouth murmured, "never dreaming it was not their imaginations at work but their perception."

Since it was apparent they were not about to be crushed into paste, Snaugenhutt saw no harm in slowing to a walk. Shielding his gaze against the rising sun, Buncan spoke to the specter.

"What will you do now that you're free?"

The three heads replied in chorus. "WHY, RETURN TO WHERE WE CAME FROM, OF COURSE. IF IT STILL EXISTS."

An utterly unexpected voice bellowed behind them. "I'll kill you all. I am not afraid of anything, be it god or mortal!"

Squill turned in his seat. "Well, I'll be double-buggered. Look who's comin'."

Waving his sword defiantly above his head, Chi-churog, First Rider of the Xi-Murogg, was galloping in pursuit, urging his nervous blindered mount onward while screaming defiance.

"Illusions!" they heard him howl. "You have manufactured illusions to fool my people! You have disturbed their minds, but you do not fool me! I will cut your heads off. I will have you roasted alive over the cooking fires. I will . . . !"

The armored ape reached over and down. An enormous thumb descended. Chi-churog barely had time to look up and emit a single startled squeak before he was turned into a dark smudge against the earth.

"Bloody effective illusion," Neena observed demurely.

None of Chi-churog's fellow villagers seemed inclined to mimic their chief's action. There was no sign of any further pursuit.

Extending arms the length of rivers, the great creatures linked hands (and in one instance, tentacles) across the Tamas. Ancient warriors of a forgotten titanic land, paralyzed gods of another place and time, whatever they were, they suddenly began to ascend slowly heavenward. Final vestiges of their long earthly imprisonment, a few clinging rocks and boulders tumbled from their sides, plunging to the ground as they drifted up through the clouds toward the intensifying sunshine. As they rose they diminished in size until they looked almost normal, then minuscule, finally vanishing entirely into an all-encompassing sky. Dust still rose from the enveloping rock they had shed.

For a long time no one said anything. There was only the sound of dust and rock settling, and Snaugenhutt's heavy breathing.

"I wonder where they came from," Buncan eventually murmured after the rhino had resumed his march northwestward. "Gragelouth?"

The merchant shook his head. "Who can say? The world is full of wonders. Too many times we look right at them and recognize only their shape and not their reality. It took your necromancy to restore life to those." He nodded skyward. "To find wonders one must first know how to look."

"An' sing," Neena added. "You 'ave to know 'ow to sing."

Gragelouth conceded the issue. "Perhaps the next time we require assistance you could be a tad less motivated? The next apparitions you conjure might turn out to be less grateful."

"Not to worry, guv." Squill was bursting with confidence. "We know exactly wot we're about, don't we, Neena?"

"Oi, to be sure." She looked back over her shoulder at the sloth. "You can relax, merchant. We're goin' to escort you safely to this 'ere Grand Veritable, an' nothin' better get in our way, wot?"

Gragelouth pursed his lips. "The assurance of ignorant youth. There are forces at work in the universe you cannot begin to comprehend." He raised his eyes to Buncan. "You are clever, and far more important, I think, lucky. But you are not your fathers."

"I don't pretend to be." Buncan checked to make sure the duar was secure against his back. "And you know what? I'm glad. Jon-Tom's music tends to get a little old-fogeyish sometimes. You need new music and new words to make new magic."

"Wotcher," agreed Squill.

Peering ahead, Buncan thought he could just make out a line of hills. Where there were hills there might soon be mountains, and that would mean cooler temperatures, more water, game, and shade. The end of the Tamas.

Gragelouth wagged a proverbial finger at him. "Sometimes the old magic is best. This is known."

Buncan replied without turning. "I won't dispute that because I can't, merchant, but I will say this. Where both music and magic are concerned, you have to go with what you feel."

CHAPTER 20

SEVERAL DAYS OF EASY MARCHING SAW THEM LEAVING the desert behind, as Buncan had hoped. They climbed into

scrub woodland where the first brave but scraggly trees
tested the fringes of the Tamas. Following a route that led
steadily upward, they soon found themselves tromping through
real forest.

But it was like no forest Buncan or the otters had ever
seen. Instead of growing close together the trees were
spaced widely apart. Their leaves were long and thin, their
consistency oddly stiff. Bark peeled in narrow strips from the
trunks, which were varying shades of white or red instead of
the familiar brown. Certain species pulsed with a dull,
thrumming sound that echoed persistently inside Buncan's
head, as if a tiny fly had become trapped in his inner ear.
Dense clumps of bushes played tag with the trees and each
other, leaving plenty of open space for Snaugenhutt to
traverse.

From the valley of a small river which sank rapidly into
the sands of the desert they ascended to rocky slopes and
thence to more densely vegetated rolling highlands. The
trees were remarkably polite, none pressing too closely
upon its neighbor. As they continued to climb, more familiar
growths made their appearance, but the verdure was still
dominated by the strange white-barked trees of the low-
lands. Day and night the alien forest boomed softly around
them.

Buncan pointed to one especially dominant specimen. It
thrummed deeply and he could feel as well as hear the vibrations. "Gragelouth, do you know what that's called?"

The sloth regarded the growth. "No. In all my travels I
have never seen the like of these trees before."

"Nothin' like 'em in the Bellwoods." Neena was standing erect in her seat, effortlessly maintaining her balance
despite Snaugenhutt's rolling gait. "Looks like you could
go up to one an' strip the bark off in a few minutes."

"Yet the peeling appears to be a natural phenomenon.
Most striking."

They were following the crest of a steep-sided, winding
ridge. Neena gazed longingly at the river which tumbled
playfully through the canyon below. Already the foothills of
the Tamas had become unnamed mountains. The way was
growing increasingly rugged.

Small reptilian game was plentiful, and the numerous streams which tumbled down the rock faces drilled pools which yielded tasty freshwater crustaceans. There were fruits and nuts to be gathered, most unfamiliar but many edible, and plenty of forage for Snaugenhutt. The bounty of the land allowed them to be parsimonious with their supplies.

So relaxed were they that they reacted with equanimity to the sudden appearance of the wombat and thylacine in front of them. The squat, heavily built wombat was clad in light-brown cloth. He carried a poorly ˙fashioned spear and wore leather armor only around the waist. There was nothing protecting his head, or legs, or for that matter, his expansive gut. A wide-brimmed hat flopped comically around his head.

The thylacine was more formidably armed, both naturally and artificially. Unlike his companion, he looked as though he knew how to use the long pike he carried. Beneath his extensive brass armor expensive silks gleamed brightly, and the helmet he wore boasted a narrow vertical strip of metal to protect the topside of his long snout. Reflections of the skill of some accomplished cobbler, his well-fitted sandals were laced all the way up to the backs of his knees.

"Now what have we here, Quibo?" The thylacine spoke without taking his eyes off Snaugenhutt.

"Bushwhacked if I know, Bedarra." Dark eyes peered up at them from beneath the brim of the oversize chapeau. "Where might you lot be headed?"

Buncan leaned to his right to peer past Snaugenhutt's armored frill. "Northwest." He nodded forward. "Be easier if we don't have to go around you."

The singular pair didn't move. "Did you hear that," the thylacine said to his companion. "They're goin' northwest." The wombat grunted as the thylacine turned back to the travelers. "What business would you be having up there?"

"Not that it's any o' your business," said Squill, standing in his own seat, "but we're searchin' for the Grand Veritable."

"Grand Veritable." The thylacine leaned against his pike

and scratched behind one ear. "Never heard of it. Would it by nature be necromantic?"

"You've 'it on it, guv." Behind the garrulous Squill, Gragelouth rolled his eyes. Keeping a secret around the boisterous, boastful otters was like trying to conceal Snaugenhutt in a side pocket.

"What might this Grand Veritable be?" the thylacine inquired.

Squill smirked at him. Otters were professional smirkers. "That's wot we aim to find out."

The thylacine nodded and yawned, displaying an astonishing hundred-and-eighty-degree gape. "I don't suppose you'd know that the monastery of Kilagurri also lies to the northwest?"

"No, we wouldn't," Buncan replied. "Is it something we should know about?"

The thylacine straightened, his tone darkening. "You expect us to believe that? Everyone knows Kilagurri." He gestured with the pike. "Better get off your mountain. Now." Next to him the wombat lowered his spear.

Squill and Neena promptly drew and notched their bows. They exhibited no particular haste. The notion of these two interfering with the progress of the heavily armored Snaugenhutt was laughable.

Buncan was more cautious. He'd learned from Jon-Tom that any obviously outnumbered and overmatched potential opponent who refused to yield ground was either a complete fool or knew something you didn't. He wasn't positive about the wombat, but he was pretty sure the thylacine was no fool.

Snaugenhutt glanced back at his riders. "Want me to turn 'em into roadkill?"

"Not just yet." Buncan leaned forward and whispered. "What do you think, Viz?"

The tickbird was leaning against the side of his armored howdah, his feet firmly clamped to his perch. "I think there's more to these two happy hikers than meets the eye." Instead of watching those confronting them, he'd been studying the surrounding forest.

The thylacine gestured with the point of the pike. "Let's go, friends. Climb down."

"We're considering your request,"' said Buncan. "So far we don't find you very persuasive."

"We can fix that." Putting two fingers to his extensive lips, the thylacine blew a short, shrill whistle.

Subsequent to a premonitory rustling the woods disgorged a host of armed creatures who immediately surrounded the travelers. Despite his concern, Buncan was amazed that so many had managed to remain hidden for so long. Many of the tribes represented were unknown to him except through his studies. All were armed to varying degrees, but while their number was impressive their appearance was decidedly motley.

This was no formal military force, he concluded. Even if they were bandits they weren't putting up much of a show. But there were an awful lot of them, and there was no mistaking the determination in their faces.

He picked a couple of wombats and one other thylacine out of the mob. There were also koalas, several platypi (one of whom flaunted a gold ring through its leathery beak), a couple of monjons who'd woven wicked-looking metal barbs into their tufted tails, a trio of spear-carrying emus, similarly equipped cassowaries, diminutive possums wearing dark shades to protect their sensitive eyes against the daylight, and at least one squadron composed entirely of dingoes. But the majority of the ragtag force was made up of wallabies and kangaroos representing more than a dozen subtribes. Buncan counted fifty individuals before giving up.

One rarely encountered any representatives of these tribes in the Bellwoods, he reflected. Remembrance of those temperate, accommodating woods brought a sudden and quite unexpected tightness to his throat. He and his friends were very far from home: from the warm confines of the dimensionally expanded tree by the riverside, from his own room, from his other friends, and from his mother's exotic and sometimes overspiced cooking.

Now was not the time to succumb to the foibles of resurgent adolescence, he reminded himself firmly. He was now an experienced adventurer and spellsinger, and he'd damn well better act like one.

By this time more than a hundred armed males and females surrounded Snaugenhutt and his companions. An equal number of arrows and spears and pikes and swords were pointed in their direction. While there was no doubt that the rhino could break through the encirclement, it was equally certain that a shower of weaponry would fall on him and his passengers. With what kind of accuracy it was difficult to say, but many of the wallabies and roos looked agile and fast enough to bound right onto the rhino's retreating back and if necessary engage Buncan and his comrades in hand-to-hand combat.

"She's right, then!" declared a deep, booming voice. A huge russet-tinged roo as tall as Buncan hopped out of the foliage, leaped effortlessly *over* the wombat and thylacine, and landed with a thud an arm's length in front of Snaugenhutt. Wearing only light snakeskin armor, he stood gazing thoughtfully up at Buncan, apparently utterly indifferent to the fact that with a quick lunge Snaugenhutt could impale him on his horn and fling him into the nearest bush.

A spiked earring dangled from the roo's right ear. A strip of leather bristling with steel spikes ran from his forehead, down between his ears, and all the way down his spine to his heavy tail, the tip of which had been fitted with a double-sided wooden club. This gave an occasional, ominous twitch.

In his right hand the roo held a double-sided war ax. Both feet were shod in some kind of socklike material. Upward-pointing hooks flashed at the toes. Like the rest of his companions the speaker, Buncan reflected, was not dressed for casual conversation. Haphazard and disorganized, they were clearly not military, and they were overequipped for mere banditry. What was going on in these far-off, strangely vegetated mountains?

"I'm Wurragarr." His war ax flashed in the sun as he strained to peer past Buncan. "You're a curious lot. Not from around here, that much is clear."

"We're from a lot farther than you've ever been," Neena informed him.

"I won't argue with that, shiela." He returned his attention to Buncan. "Myself, I'm a simple blacksmith. Don't get around much. But the good folk of Nooseloowoo have invested me with the responsibility of leadership, and I aim not to let them down." He jerked a thumb in the thylacine's direction. "Heard you tell Bedarra and Quibo you were heading northwest. Kilagurri lies to the northwest."

Buncan fought to contain his exasperation. "Look, we don't know what's going on here, and we've never heard of this Kilagurri place. We're on a quest of our own, and we're just trying to stay out of everybody's way."

The roo was insistent. "What's your business in the northwest?"

"Didn't you hear that too? We're looking for the Grand Veritable."

"Never heard of it."

"We told your friends. We don't know what it is either. That's what we're trying to find out." He hesitated. "It's said to be the source of great power and great danger."

The roo nodded contemplatively. "Can't say about power, but we've plenty of danger here to go around." He turned and pointed with the ax. "You continue on the way you've been goin' and you'll for sure find it."

"That's our business." *Beter to keep up a bold front*, he thought, *than show any weakness*. "We've been dealing with trouble ever since we left home."

"Bloody right," said Squill.

"So if you'll be good enough to let us pass," Buncan continued, "we won't trouble you any further. I don't know what your business is with this Kilagurri, but it has nothing to do with us."

"Kilagurri has to do with everybody," insisted an armored quokka from the edge of the mob. A mutter of agreement spread through the assembled.

Squill gestured with his bow. " 'Ere now, you lot, we 'aven't got time for this. Me sister and me 'uman friend 'ere," he put a paw on Buncan's shoulder, "are bleedin' great spellsingers, we are. If you don't make way there, we'll show you some real power. Turn you into a flock o' gabbin' geese, or toads, or make all your 'air fall out, or maybe dump you in each other's pouches." Otters were not particularly adept at threatening glares, but Squill gave it his best shot.

"Spellsingers!" Wurragarr's brows rose. "Now that's interesting." Turning, he called into the crowd. "Windja, Charoo, Nuranura!"

Three stocky birds lifted clear of the mob and soared over to land on a fallen log to the quokka's left. Each was slightly larger than Viz. They wore uniform scarves of black striped with yellow, but no headgear. Their plumage was white with black highlights, and their thick, pointed bills looked too heavy for their bodies. Buncan had never seen anything like them. Except for the outrageous beaks they might well have been oversize kingfishers.

As they settled down on the branch, murmuring among themselves, a pair of small wallabies hopped forward. One carried a pair of short wooden sticks inscribed with arcane symbols and drawings, while his companions held an intricately painted wooden tube hollowed at both ends. It turned in upon itself at least three times. An attempt to duplicate the duar's systemology of mystical intersecting strings? Buncan wondered.

Wurragarr gestured with quiet pride at the waiting group. "As you can see, we have our own spellsingers. So don't think to intimidate us with music."

"We're not trying to intimidate you, or anybody," said Buncan patiently. "We're just trying to get on our way."

The thylacine stepped forward and snarled softly. "You lot don't look much like sorcerers to me. You look like a bunch of cubs too lazy to walk." Laughter rose from those close to him.

"Who's a cub?" barked Squill angrily.

"Squill." Buncan turned in his seat.

The otter was not to be denied. "Just a small demonstration, mate. To show these buggers wot we can do to 'em if they ain't polite."

Gragelouth leaned to one side. "Perhaps an exhibition of a *very* minor nature might serve to facilitate our departure?"

"Haven't said you could leave yet," Wurragarr reminded them.

"Just going to sing a little song." Buncan unlimbered the duar, scowled warningly at the otters. "Nothing hostile."

Neena smiled brightly as she and her brother began to improvise.

"'Ere in the woods 'tis peaceful and calm
Wouldn't wanna hurt it by droppin' no bomb
Just want to go, yo, go on our way, hey
Say how pretty it is
Look at the blossoms, let Viz
Lead us away, hey."

There. Surely that was harmless enough, Buncan mused as he rested his hands.

Nothing happened. Then Snaugenhutt let out a violent sneeze as a bouquet of exquisite purple orchids began to grow from his nostrils.

"Hey! Knock it off." He shook his head violently, but the spray of blooms developed rapidly until they formed a small carpet that drooped from his snout.

Viz surveyed the thaumaturgical horticulture thoughtfully. "Kind of mutes the intimidation factor."

Snaugenhutt shook his head again and flowers flew in all directions. "Yeah. This'll really strike fear in the hearts of our opponents."

"Quit complaining." The tickbird hopped down the length of the rhino's head until he could bend over and inhale deeply. "This is the best you've smelled in years."

Buncan's brows drew together as he frowned at the otters. Neena lifted both paws noncommittally.

"You wanted nonhostile, Bunscan; you got nonhostile."

"That's just a sample," Squill declared warningly. "Weren't even strainin' ourselves. We can call up thunderclouds, earthquakes, all the aspects o' bleedin' nature. The forces o' the universe are ours to command, they are." Buncan glared at him, and the otter smiled innocently.

"Not bad." Wurragarr glanced at the wallabies and kookaburras. "Show 'em, mates."

The birds essayed a few experimental trills. Then the

one in the middle nodded and the nearest wallaby began
rhythmically clapping the sticks together.

"Whacksticks," Wurragarr explained for the benefit of
the interested travelers.

"What's whacksticks?" Buncan wanted to know.

Wurragarr grinned. "If the magic doesn't work, you can
always whack your enemy over the head with 'em."

The other wallaby put his mouth to the top of the painted
tube and began to blow. A low throbbing tone not unlike
that made by the booming paperbark trees emerged, only
deeper and with variations. It sounded not unlike Snaugenhutt
after an especially bad night.

"That's a didgereedon't,"the roo informed them as the
three kookaburras began to harmonize. Their song had the
quality of ancient chanting.

"Deep within the earth moves
The great spirit Oolongoo.
The great worm of legend.
Vast is his power
Irresistible his strength
Powerful his crushing jaws that—"

"I could use a worm about now," blurted the bird on the
end, putting a crack in the refrain. Immediately, his companions stopped singing and began to giggle.

Wurragarr made a face. "Put a cork in that, Windja."

The kookaburra wiped its beak with a wingtip, its breast
still heaving. "Sorry, Wurragarr." He nodded to the wallabies.

They resumed their playing. Buncan sensed the slightest
of vibrations in the air.

"Oolongoo we call
And Nerrima of the sky
Who drops down upon our enemies
Slays them in their sleep
Rips them to shreds..."

"And pees in their beds," added the second singer,
folding his wings across his chest and collapsing in hyster-

ics. His companions held on to their dignity for approximately another half second before joining him. The two wallabies ceased their playing and looked helplessly at the big roo.

Burned by that overbearing marsupial glare, the spell-singers tried a third time. This time their laughter was sufficiently infectious to spread to the motley assemblage behind them, with the result that the entire band threatened to dissolve in uncontrolled mirth.

A disgusted Wurragarr watched as tears tumbled down the kookaburras' cheeks. Two of them fell off the dead log on which they'd perched and rolled about on the grass, holding their sides. The third lay prone, pounding desperately on the log with both wingtips as his guffaws grew steadily weaker. The vibration which had so briefly disturbed the plenum vanished.

"Dag." Wurragarr noticed Buncan watching him. "That's the trouble with kookaburras. This lot really can spellsing, but they also can't take anything seriously. Not sorcery, not our present desperate situation, nothing. They'd laugh all the way to their own funerals. But they're the best we've got. Somehow they're going to have to counteract the necromancy of the monks of Kilagurri." He glared at the embarrassed but still-giggling trio, who were slowly picking themselves off the ground.

"As for you lot," he said, turning back to face Buncan, "you don't strike me as the type who'd ally themselves with the likes of Kilagurri." He stepped out of Snaugenhutt's path. "Go on your way." The thylacine made as if to protest, but the roo waved him down. "No, Bedarra. Despite their strangeness, I'm convinced these travelers know nothing of our problems here. We've no right to involve them and ought t'let them pass in peace. If they run into trouble near Kilagurri they'll have to deal with it themselves." He stared evenly at Buncan.

"You've been warned. I and my friends are absolved. We can't worry about you. Our own sorrows are too great."

"Now hold on a minute," Buncan began. Squill leaned forward to jab him in the ribs.

"Wot minute, mate? You 'eard 'im. Let's get movin'."

Buncan turned in his seat. "I just want to find out what we may be getting into."

"We ain't gettin' into nothin'. We're gettin' past it."

Ignoring the otter's protests, Buncan dismounted and walked up to Wurragarr. "What is this Kilagurri, anyway?"

The thylacine's jaws parted, showing sharp teeth. "I don't think you should tell them anything. What if you're wrong and they are in league with the Dark Ones?"

"I'm convinced they're not, Bedarra. For one thing, they could ride to safety now yet this one chooses to stay and ask questions. Minions of the monks would grab the first opportunity to flee. For another, can you imagine the Dark Ones recruiting anything like those two to their cause?" He indicated Squill and Neena, who were bickering vociferously atop Snaugenhutt's spine.

Viz left his iron perch to settle on Buncan's shoulder. "My friend and I are well-traveled, but I've never heard of this Kilagurri either."

"Maybe you're not as indifferent as you make out." Wurragarr regarded human and tickbird thoughtfully. "I accept that you're sorcerers, even if so far you've only proven that you're sorcerers of the flowers." Behind him, Quibo and several others chuckled. The brooding Bedarra didn't crack a smile.

"We can do more than conjure flowers," Buncan told him. "A lot more."

"I won't deny that we need all the help we can get." The roo indicated the trio of kookaburras, who were still recovering from their bout of hysterics. "I'd hate to have to depend on that lot in a critical moment." Those of his companions-in-arms within earshot murmured their agreement.

"Even if pretty flowers represent the apex of your wizardry, we could use whatever kind of help you could provide. It's clear from the armor worn by your great friend and the ready bows of your water rats that you travel prepared to fight. I won't say that your presence among us would turn the tide."

"Hold on," said Buncan. "I just asked to know what's going on. I haven't said anything about helping."

"Fair dinkum, stranger." Wurragarr encompassed the

mob with a sweep of his free hand. "We're all dwellers in this same land, in these hills and mountains. We and our ancestors have lived here in peace and harmony, more or less, since before memory.

"Most of us are farmers or simple townies, or craftsfolk like myself. We ask only to be left alone to live our lives in peace. We've never had any trouble with the monks . . . until a little more than a year ago.

"The monastery of Kilagurri sits in a small, steep-sided basin high above the valley of Millijiddee. It's not a place for those who'd contemplate the goodness of the world. Prior to a year ago we had little or no contact with those who dwell within. Then something changed. Kilagurri has become home to those who thrive on evil machinations. Bad doings, stranger.

"Travelers who pass close tell of frightful noises issuing from within. Tormented screams and unnatural voices. Though curious as to the source of these sounds, they hurry on. One can't blame them.

"From time to time several of the monks will descend to shop in Millijiddee Towne, or have something fixed they cannot repair themselves. Nowadays all good folk shun them as well as their business." The roo was leaning on his thick tail as he spoke.

"Not that we haven't had trouble with 'em before." The wombat wagged a thick finger at Buncan. "Used to be little things. A blight on some greengrocer they thought had cheated 'em. A sprained leg that took too long to heal. Consumptive farm animals. Nothing like what's been happening recently. Nothing like it."

Wurragarr took up the refrain. "Just over a year ago, unnatural clouds were seen to gather above the monastery. Bolts of lightning struck within, yet there were no fires, no sign of damage. The Dark Ones began to play with great forces. What little we've been able to learn of their doings fills us with fear. It's clear that the monks are intent on some vast evil.

"A truce used to exist between the common folk and the monks. They've broken that with their detestable doings.

Nothing was left to us but to try and put a stop to them permanently, before they can go any further."

"Go any further with what?" Viz asked him. "Snaugenhutt! All of you, you'd better come and listen to this." The rhino nodded, ambled over. The crowd retreated to make room for him.

Wurragarr turned and peered into the assemblage. "Mowara! Where's Mowara?"

A pinkish-white avian fluttered out of the crowd to land without ceremony on the roo's left shoulder. In addition to a light blue-and-green-checked scarf, a mother-of-pearl anklet flashed from his left leg.

"Mowara's actually been inside the monastery," Wurragarr informed them. "He's the closest thing we have to a spy. He's taken a big risk."

The galah nodded. "They pluck birds up there. Seen it myself." He shuddered, feathers quivering. "Horrible. You should see their new guards. Great awful things, all claws and fangs and beaks."

"Mowara confirmed the stories we'd been hearing," Wurragarr went on. "Confirmed them, and worse."

"Too right, mate."

Their spy was old, Buncan thought. His eyes were dulled with age and his beak worn. His attitude suggested the first stages of senility. Or maybe he was just a little crazy. Could he be believed? Wurragarr seemed to trust him completely.

"People have been abducted," the roo was saying, "and taken to the monastery." His voice was grim. "Lately the monks favor cubs and infants, those of travelers and out-landers as much as local folk. Most are never seen again. But there have been a few escapees. Mowara confirms what they've told us."

"Seen them at work, the Dark Ones." The galah stretched his aged wings significantly. "Heard them talking. Saw *things*."

"Cor, wot sorts o' things?" Neena inquired. In front of her, Squill affected an air of bored indifference.

"Saw them," the galah insisted. *"Tampering."*

"Tampering with what?" Buncan wanted to know.

The bird leaned forward, and his eyes bulged. "Nature. The Dark Monks, they're tampering with Nature itself."

CHAPTER 21

"I DON'T UNDERSTAND," BUNCAN SAID CAUTIOUSLY.

"Who does, who does?" Pink wings flapped urgently. "The Dark Ones don't understand either, but that doesn't stop them. The forces of life, the threads that bind it together, that's what they're stuck into up there on that mountaintop. Weavers they think they are, but all they can tie are knots, nasty knots." Though there was no need to lower his voice, he leaned forward and whispered.

"Used to be just irritating, the monks were. Not no more. Want to control it all now. Not just the hills and valleys. All of it. The whole world.

"I've heard them speak words, words I don't understand. Nobody understands them, including the Dark Ones. But they use 'em. Words of somber power, traveler. Words unknown to the monks until a year previous."

"What sort of words?" Gragelouth slowly dismounted. "I am quite facile with words."

"Not these, mate, not these. Words like . . ." The galah struggled to remember. He was old enough, Buncan mused, that his memory was no longer his servant but a constant irksome challenge.

Squill whistled derisively. " 'Ell, there ain't no bloomin' mystery words."

"Desoxyribonucleic acid!" the galah abruptly blurted. "Peptide chains! Molecular carbon. Heterocyclic compounds. Enzymatic cortical displacement." He blinked.

It all sounded like nonsense to Buncan. But organized nonsense. Necromantic or not, organized nonsense could be dangerous. Maybe Clothahump could have made sense of the galah's ravings. Buncan couldn't, nor could Gragelouth.

"Cross-nuclear chromosomal ingestion. Forced immune

system rejection repression.'' Mowara was gesturing wildly
with both wingtips. "They use these words to commit
iniquities. To make things.''

"What 'things'?" Buncan pressed him.

"New things. Outrages. Horrors.'' Even Bedarra was
subdued as the bird rambled on. "New kinds of *people*.''

Neena's expression reflected her confusion. "How can
you make new kinds o' people?''

"By combining them. I saw them, I saw them myself.''
His voice fell again. "They take a wallaby. Then they take a
lynx. Tie 'em up and put 'em in a cauldron. Pour foul-
smelling liquids over them. Then the Dark Ones come out,
the monks in charge. They chant the words.'' Buncan could
see that the galah was all but overcome by his own memories. But the bird pressed on.

"Vapors cover that cauldron. You can't see. The Dark
Ones chant louder. Now you hear the *sounds*.'' Again he
shuddered. "The chanting fades away. So does the smoke.
And that poor wallaby, and that poor lynx, they're gone.''

"Gone?'' Gragelouth swallowed.

"Gone, departed. Something in their place. Some *things*.
One useless, dribbling and drooling, gone. The other, a
combining. Legs of a wallaby, eyes of a cat. Tail of a
wallaby, claws and teeth of a cat. Ugly, nasty, evil. No mind
of its own anymore. Does what the Dark Ones tell it.''

"What do they do with the unsuccessful half?" Neena
was unsmiling.

Mowara stared at her. "What do you think?" She didn't
push him to elaborate.

"That was a good one,'' the galah insisted. "Seen worse.
One head, three eyes. One body, six legs, all mixed up.
Two tails. Two heads. Horrors. Lose their bodies, lose their
selves. Lose their wills. Belong to the Dark Ones now. Do
their will.''

"But *why*?" Buncan demanded to know. "It's the worst
thing I've ever heard of. To take two healthy, happy individuals and do that to them . . . it's worse than the stories I've
been told of the Plated Folk.''

"Sounds bloody ridiculous to me.'' Squill looked bored.

"Does it now?" The galah gazed up at the otter with such

unexpected intensity that Squill blinked involuntarily. "Wouldn't think so if you'd seen some of the things, some of the things I've seen. Mole-rats merged with gazelles. Koalas all mixed up with hawks. Numbats with fish fins."

"But what can it all be for?" Gragelouth wanted to know.

"Not sure. Heard the Dark Ones wanted to make people more beautiful. At first. That doesn't justify the tampering, no sir. They had some successes. Got ideas, got corrupted. Started trying to make guards and warriors, servants. Beauty can't never compete with power." His feathers quivered. "Destroy the results they don't like. Can't change 'em back."

"When we first questioned the disappearances, they denied knowing anything," Wurragarr explained. "Then they insisted only criminals and maladroits were taken, or travelers who tried to break into the monastery and rob them. We stopped believing their denials when our own young started disappearing."

"Sham, all sham," the galah insisted, "to cover their activities. We know them now for what they are. Been corrupted, yes they have. By the Dark Forces. Maybe too much testosterone. They use that word a lot now."

Wurragarr indicated the anxious, determined faces gathered close. "Many of those here have lost children. They don't even know if they're still alive, or in their original form. But they want to find out. They *have* to find out." The roo's eyes were level with Buncan's. "Human infants have also been taken."

"Even if any o' this piffle is for real," said Squill challengingly, "what makes you think you can do anythin' about it?"

Wurragarr's tone didn't change. "We will, or die trying."

"Fair dinkum," growled Bedarra, gripping his pike tightly.

The roo took a step back. "We won't see any more of our cubs vanish from their beds, or disappear from our towns and farms. We won't watch them turned into creatures their own parents wouldn't recognize."

"So you're goin' to storm this bleedin' monastery." Squill glanced back at his sister. "Sound familiar, Neena?

Why does I 'ave a feelin' this'll be a tougher nut to crack than a certain Baron's walled mansion?''

"It will be difficult," Wurragarr admitted. "The monastery is located high in the mountains, in a narrow basin. A wall protects it from the front, and the cliffs on both sides are extremely steep and difficult to scale. There are no trees above the wall, and cover is scarce. Therefore we must attack from the front. There are two springs in the basin behind the monastery itself. They can withstand a long siege.

"But there will be no siege. We all of us have trades to practice, crops to plant or bring in, families to look after. We can't afford to be long at this work. So we must attack and shatter the main gate, the only gate." He gestured with the ax. "Then we will put Kilagurri to the torch, and incinerate the evil it contains." An inspiring cheer rose from his companions, echoing through the paperbark woods.

Buncan hesitated, uncertain how to respond. "I don't know what to say, Wurragarr, except that we have our own priorities."

"Bloody right we do." Squill gazed down importantly. "We've come a long way, and we ain't about to chance no dangerous detours here."

"We're searching for the Grand Veritable and we've a ways to go yet," Buncan added.

"Tell 'em, Bunc," Squill said with a whistle.

"So if you want what help I can give, it's yours." He extended a hand.

"Right, we've . . ." Squill broke off, goggling at his friend. "Say that again, mate?"

"It's what Jon-Tom would do," Buncan explained.

Squill was beside himself. "Well, it ain't bleedin' wot Mudge would do!"

The roo ignored the fuming otter as he shook Buncan's hand. "We can use every extra fist, mate. I'm sorry we misinterpreted your presence here at first."

"No, no, you didn't misinterpret anything'!" Squill was waving wildly, looking to his companions for support. Neena gave a little shrug and smiled beatifically.

"What about the rest of you?" Wurragarr let his gaze

rove over the travelers. "The workings of the Dark Ones threaten you as much as us. If they are not stopped in our country, who knows how far their scourge might spread? Maybe even beyond the Tamas."

"I'm in." Snaugenhutt gave a little shake that set his armor to jingling lightly. "Could do with a good fight. Don't remember too much of the last one I participated in."

"Same here." Viz and Mowara exchanged acknowledgments by simultaneously dipping their beaks.

Buncan eyed the merchant. "Gragelouth?"

The sloth was reluctant to commit himself. "Squill's observations are like a battered bowl: It leaks, but still holds truth. We should be on our way."

"I know, but there's greater truth in these folks' misery. We could maybe make a difference here." He indicated the three now abashed kookaburras. "I don't see how we can deny them our help."

"Ask me," growled an indignant Squill. "I'll show you."

Buncan looked past him. "Neena?"

"'Tis an awful lot you're askin', Bunkles."

"You really think Mudge would have ridden on by?" She squirmed uncomfortably. "Don't you want to be better than that?"

"Don't you want to bloody well live?" Squill asked him.

Buncan glared at his friend. "We survived Hygria. We survived the Sprilashoone and Camrioca. We saved Neena from Krasvin and crossed the Tamas in spite of the Xi-Murogg. What does that tell you, Squill?"

"That we're temptin' bloomin' fate, mate."

"Are we spellsingers or not?"

"You sure got Jon-Tom's talent." The otter sighed. "Why'd you 'ave to go an' get 'is bleedin' sense of duty as well?"

"I'm not going to argue with you anymore." Buncan turned away. "You don't have to come."

"Cor, wot are we supposed to do?" Neena put hands on waist. "Go on by ourselves, then? Without 'im?" She pointed at the reluctant merchant. "'E's the only one who knows the way.

"We three needs to stick together, we do. We can't make magic without you, and you can't make it without us."

"I can still use my sword," Buncan reminded her.

"You? A swordsman?" She let out a series of long whistles.

He ignored the insult. "I don't like the circumstances either, Neena, but part of the reason I'm here is to participate in worthy adventures like this."

"Is it now?" said Squill. "Then why'd we 'afta come all this blinkin' way? You coulda got yourself killed right back 'ome. There's plenty o' them in Lynchbany would do the job for free."

"As I told you, I'm a blacksmith by trade." Wurragarr spoke quietly. "Not a soldier. None of us are."

"Me 'eart bleeds for you." Squill spat to his right, unfortunately not quite missing his foot. A hundred pairs of eyes and more watched him silently. "Oh, right then," he muttered. "Go on, bury me in guilt. Dump it copiously. I loves it, I'm a glutton for it." He reached back to finger his quiver. "Blacksmith, you think you can make me some more arrows?"

A broad smile creased the roo's face. "We've plenty with us. You can have your pick, so long as you promise to stick them where they'll do the most good."

"Friar Dunkum, or wotever the 'ell you said," Squill mumbled disconsolately.

Wurragarr, Bedarra, and Mowara let Snaugenhutt lead the column as it wound its way through the forest. The path led steadily upward. Unfamiliar evergreens began to appear more and more frequently as they ascended, their branches and needles so evenly spaced one would have thought them fashioned by hand instead of grown. Higher up they could make out the first bare rock faces, naked granite devoid of any vegetation.

"We're not afraid of the monks," Wurragarr explained. "Only the revolting creations that do their bidding. Some are more formidable than others. We have Mowara's description of a numbat crossed with a thylacine. I wouldn't care to meet something like that on a black night."

"If you and your people can handle the fighting," Buncan told him, "maybe my friends and I can come up with a spellsong to counteract their sorcery. Based on our experiences, I think the best thing to do would be to confront them directly. That means slipping us inside. We managed that feat under similar circumstances not long ago, but we were lucky. I don't know if we could do it again."

The roo looked thoughtful. "Mowara's the only one of us who knows the monastery's interior, but he's a flier." He rubbed his chin as he hopped along, easily keeping pace with Snaugenhutt, his tail flicking behind him. "What about it, Mowara?"

The galah timed his shrug to Wurragarr's bounce. "Hard to get out. Might get in. Can you sneak?"

Buncan grinned. "I'm traveling with two otters."

"Wait just a bloody minim, mate." Squill had been listening closely. "You want us to go *inside* this den o' sorcerers an' their offspring an' clean 'em out?"

Buncan looked up at the otter. "Not clean them out. Just keep them from using their necromancy against Wurragarr and his people. Confuse them, tie them down, create a diversion."

"I liked it better when we were throwin' Snaugenhutt around."

The rhino glanced back and up. "Easy for you to say, otter."

"Right. So this time all of us are to act as a diversion. Wot 'appens if the oversize rat 'ere an' 'is mates don't make it in? By my way o' thinkin' that leaves us 'appy sappy diversions 'igh an' dry, singin' our bleedin' 'earts out."

"You get tucked into the Dark Ones and we'll get in," Wurragarr assured him.

"Well, then, there's nothin' to worry about, is there? Wot am I goin' on about it for? Why, there's one thing don't concern me already."

"What's that?" Wurragarr asked politely.

The otter's reply was bitter. "I don't own enough worth makin' out a will for."

"What about aerial guards?" Buncan inquired.

"According to Mowara, that shouldn't be a problem."

The roo hopped easily over a large boulder that Buncan had to scramble around. "They can combine an eagle with a badger, but it still won't fly."

"Planning to attack at night?"

"Yes. We'll strike when the moon is at its highest. Maybe we'll catch them groggy with sleep. Even monsters have to sleep, or so I'd imagine." He didn't sound like he believed it, Buncan mused.

Suddenly he recalled something the roo had mentioned earlier. "You said that the cliffs surrounding Kilagurri were steep and difficult to negotiate. How's Snaugenhutt going to climb them?"

Wurragarr looked away. "Actually, I don't see that your large friend can. We were hoping he would help us assault the gate. Surely you can see that he's better suited to that than alpining?"

"I hear you," said Snaugenhutt.

"Besides," the roo added, "I'd think you'd find it hard to slip him inside unseen, even with Mowara's help."

"It isn't up to me." Buncan looked over at the tickbird. "Viz?"

"The roo's right, Buncan. We'll take this gate, however strong it is. If there's climbing to be done, you'd be better off with an elephant than ol' Snaug here." The rhino did not object to the conclusion.

"I, too, should remain with our newfound friends," Grageloulth declared. The merchant was contrite. "My tribe is not designed for speed. I would not want to delay you at a critical moment."

"Marvelous," said Squill from atop Snaugenhutt's back. "Anything else we need to leave behind? Our clothes maybe? Our weapons? We're already leavin' our bloomin' brains."

"Wot brains?" Neena opined. Squill turned on his sister as they embarked on their favorite pastime of trading insults.

Buncan let his gaze sweep over the valley below. In the distance the lights of a small village were just visible. He returned his attention to the mountain path. "How much farther?"

Wurragarr indicated the lightly used trail they were following. "Another day's march. Are you still ready and willing?"

"We're willing, anyway." Buncan smiled.

"You won't surprise 'em." Snaugenhutt maintained his steady, unvarying pace. "They're bound to see a troop this size coming."

"We know. Our hope is that when we just encamp outside the wall and don't attack they'll think we're settling in for an extended siege. Then we'll get into 'em when they're in bed. You've obviously had experience in these matters. What's your opinion?"

Snaugenhutt considered. "Good a strategy as any."

"Don't let's drown in optimism, wot?" Neena made a face. "Don't it trouble no one else that this whole enterprise depends on the wiles of a senile pink parrot?"

The monastery of Kilagurri was an impressive pile of moss-covered cut masonry situated behind a massive wall of huge, square-cut stones each as big as a good-size boulder. The wall sealed off the basin containing the monastery buildings as thoroughly as a dam. A trickle of water ran from a pair of drainage pipes set in the base of the wall. Heavy iron grates prevented entrance to the pipes, and Buncan had no doubt they were watched at all times. That obvious way in was closed to them. He was not disappointed. The culverts smelled abominably.

The trail they were following continued past the main gate and ended at an impassable waterfall. Trees had been cleared in front of the wall, meaning anyone approaching would be instantly visible to those within. The only way in was through a comparatively narrow gate reinforced with iron bands and bolts the size of his fist. It was a far more impressive and forbidding structure than Buncan had anticipated. He found himself wondering if it would ever yield to Snaugenhutt.

As they spread out among the trees he could see caped figures gathering atop the wall. Wallabies, a couple of koalas, one numbat. By the light of the torches they carried he could see that regardless of species the fur had been shaved from the crown of each head. Cryptic markings decorated each naked skull.

"Hermetic tattoos." Bedarra stood close to Buncan. "We don't understand them."

Occasionally the monks and acolytes atop the rampart paused to converse with one another. More torches were brought and set in empty holders, until the entire wall and the open ground below were thoroughly illuminated. Certainly there was enough light for those within the monastery to watch as the corps of common folk busied themselves setting up camp. None of Wurragarr's people had challenged those inside, nor had the silent shapes on the wall tried to hail the interlopers establishing themselves among the trees.

"Maybe they think we are pilgrims," Gragelouth ventured, "and are waiting for the first supplicants to present themselves at the gate."

"We'll present ourselves, all right." Buncan was studying the steep slope where the mountain met the wall. "But it won't be at the gate."

CHAPTER 22

"THIS WAY." MOWARA WOULD VANISH INTO THE DARKness, then dart back to chivvy them onward. "It's not bad, it's not."

Our second nocturnal sortie, Buncan reflected as he scrambled up the increasingly steep cliff. He dared not look down. Nearby he could hear the agile but short-legged otters cursing steadily.

This, he mused darkly as he fumbled for a handhold above his head, was a smidgen more difficult than being gently set down atop the Baron Krasvin's mansion.

The idea was to climb until they were high above the well-guarded point where the wall met the mountain, scramble forward, and then slink downslope until they were within the monastery proper. A large scaling party would doubtless have been spotted, but just the four of them creeping slowly along might escape the notice of those within, whose attention was sure to be focused on the rowdy mob of angry farmers and townsfolk who were busily establishing camp in the woods.

"We're high enough." Mowara fluttered inches from Buncan's face, pivoting in midair to gesture downward with a wingtip. "Quietly now." Trailing in his wake, they began working their way toward the shadowy structures below. Most were dark, but lights beckoned in a few high, narrow windows. To Buncan's relief, the slope leading into the monastery was much gentler than the one they had scaled outside. There was no sign of any guards. He hoped the monastery's entire defense would be concentrated on the wall.

Neena kicked a rock loose and they all hunched low as it initiated a miniature avalanche. The pebbles banged and bounced noisily off one another for a minute or so before the slide petered out. Silence once more took possession of the hillside. No shouts rang out below them, no torches were waved in their direction. Buncan breathed a sigh of relief as he resumed his downward crawl.

"I can't believe no one's even looked up 'ere." Squill tried to tiptoe around the loose scree. "We're pushin' our luck, we are."

"Not luck, no, not luck." Mowara dipped and darted above their heads. "They have so much confidence in their sorcery, and in everyone else's lack of imagination. Think they're the only ones who can think, they do." He allowed himself a soft derogatory squawk. "Stuff 'em, the pongy sods."

Buncan edged carefully around a steep drop. "Keep in mind that we don't have wings, Mowara."

"No worries, mate," the aged galah cackled. "She'll be right, she will." He left them to scout on ahead.

Eventually he directed them to a spot where the third floor of a large stone structure impinged against the bare rock. In the light of a waxing moon, they followed the galah across the open slate roof past planters filled with sleeping blossoms of unknown type toward an arched doorway of

peculiar design. As they hugged the shadows, Buncan saw
that the portal was framed by numerous bas-reliefs. The
subject matter set his hair on end.

A reassuring distance off to their right they could see the
inside of the wall. Brawny forms dire of aspect were
beginning to join the monks on the parapet. Buncan was
inordinately glad he could not see their faces.

He glanced skyward. They had until first light to do what
damage they could before Wurragarr's people attacked. That
assault would take place whether the infiltrating spellsinging
trio succeeded or not. The country folk had come too far to
turn back now.

We'd better do something, he thought grimly. *They'll
never breach that wall without help.* Not even with Snaugenhutt
leading the charge. The question most profound was: Precisely what could they do?

Improvise, Jon-Tom had always told him. When in doubt,
improvise. Almost as if in anticipation, the duar chafed and
bumped against his back. He found himself wishing he had
the knowledge to grasp the meaning behind the Dark Monks'
mysterious invocations.

"Softly now, groundbound friends." Mowara settled gently
on Buncan's shoulder. "Around this first corner your first
glimpse. You can decide if what is measures up to what I've
said, you can."

Buncan stepped through the open doorway and peered
down the lamplit corridor. Mowara's descriptions had prepared them, but words could only do so much.

Standing guard at the nearest intersection was a creature
with the legs of a wallaby and the squat body of a wombat.
Its profile revealed the face of a dingo in the last stages of
some grisly degenerate affliction. Abortive dull green
wings protruded like diseased eruptions from its shoulders.
It carried a blade the size of an executioner's sword.

"'Ow do we get past *that* freak?" Squill whispered.

"Leave it to me." Neena edged to the forefront. "I'll
dazzle it with me charms an' the rest o' you can sneak up
behind 'it."

"Hey, wait!" Buncan made a grab for her but was too
late. She was already sauntering down the corridor as if she

owned it, in full view of the wallabat and whatever else might happen to come along.

"Shit," Squill muttered. "Get ready."

Neena halted right in front of the guard, who gaped at her. "'Ello, gorgeous. 'Ow come you're stuck in 'ere when all the action's out front?"

Yellow, bloodshot eyes narrowed as they focused on her. Its voice was tortured. "Kill," it rumbled as it swung the oversize blade in a great descending arc.

It cracked the floor where Neena had been standing an instant earlier. "'Ere now! Wot do you think I am, rough trade?"

"Kill," snarled the abomination, lurching after her.

"So much for stunnin' it with 'er irresistible beauty." Sword drawn, Squill was racing down the hallway. Buncan and Mowara had no choice but to follow.

It saw them coming and brought the blade around in a sweeping horizontal arc. Buncan stumbled to a halt, glad that the haphazard creature hadn't been given the arms of a gibbon. Squill ducked lithely beneath the blow and drove his sword up into the ogre's belly, while Neena struck it from behind. It let out a soft gurgle, choking on its own blood, and made a last desultory swipe at the hovering Mowara which the galah avoided easily. The blade tumbled to the floor as the guard clutched at its throat. It fell over, kicking spasmodically. The kicking slowed rapidly, and soon all was still.

The otters stood over the corpse, breathing hard. Mowara fluttered approvingly nearby. "Hope you're as adept with your magic as you are with your swords."

"There were only one of 'em." As he wiped his weapon clean on the fallen guard's raiment, Squill grinned at his sister. "I 'ope we don't 'ave to depend on your good looks to overcome anythin' else."

"Oh, shut up," she snapped. "It were worth a go. At least I distracted it."

Controlling his revulsion, Buncan forced himself to examine the dead guard. "Gross. I wonder who it was originally."

"This is but a tame example of the horrors perpetrated by

the Dark Ones." Mowara was keeping an eye on the
corridor ahead. "There exists far worse."

"Cor, now that's encouragin'." Squill sheathed his weapon.

In truth they were lucky. Once, a troop of unholy grotes-
queries armed with huge battle-axes marched by ahead of
them and they were forced to wait in an alcove until the
guards had passed to a lower level, but nothing actually
impeded their progress.

"Where are you taking us?" Buncan inquired of Mowara
as they cautiously started down yet another set of winding
stone stairs.

"To the axis of all evil," the galah replied. "So you can
kill it at its source."

Buncan found he was more eager than afraid. Whoever
could deliberately pervert honest, wholesome sorcery in
such an appalling fashion deserved whatever Fate bestowed
on them.

Their advance continued unchallenged. Perhaps those
who would normally be patrolling these corridors were
gathering on the wall to confront and intimidate Wurragarr's
people. Whatever the reason he was grateful, and remarked
on their good fortune to Mowara.

"Won't last, it won't." The galah was pessimistic. "The
Dark Ones will realize Wurragarr ain't going to attack right
away. Then maybe they'll think to check their backsides.
Got to work fast, we do." Abruptly he backed wind and
landed on Buncan's shoulder. "We're close now, we are.
Quietly go."

Buncan lowered his voice and tensed. "Close to what?"

"To the secret room. To the place where the Dark Ones
plot their malignancies. The Lair of the Board."

The galah turned into a narrow, low-ceilinged corridor.
"Found this by accident, I did. Hush now: I can hear them
talking."

"Planning their defense," Neena opined.

"Quiet, I said," Mowara hissed.

They slowed, and Buncan saw they were approaching a
small hole in the corridor wall. Light and voices were
visible on the other side. As he eased forward and caught a
glimpse of what lay beyond, he sucked in his breath. It was

a vision extracted whole and uncensored from the fevered imaginings of some seriously ill necromancer.

There were ten of them gathered in the chamber below. All wore the dark cowl of the Kilagurri monk, making it impossible to identify individuals. They sat around a long table of polished wood of a color and grain Buncan had never seen before. It had a sheen more suggestive of glass than honest lumber.

Strange carpeting with a weave so tight and fine he couldn't imagine how it had been loomed covered the floor. The cups the monks sipped from were filled with a dark, bubbling, odorless liquid. Several of those present were scribbling on thick pads bound together at the left edge with loops of thin metal wire.

In the center of the table four boxes set with glass windows faced the four points of the compass. Several dials protruded from the top of each. Wires connected them to a much bigger box in the middle of the table, and also to small rectangular panels that rested in front of each monk. Several of the attendees were tapping hesitantly at their respective panels. Theurgically lit from within, the window boxes displayed shifting, moving images that appeared to respond to the seemingly random tappings of the monks. The master box in the middle whined softly, like a live thing.

As Buncan stared a beautiful female possum entered, tail elaborately wound with green ribbon and held high. Squill whistled softly, inducing his sister to jab him in the ribs. From a ceramic carafe balanced on a tray the servant refilled the monks' cups with more of the steaming dark liquid. They took no notice of her presence.

"Wot sort o' sorceral potion is that?" Neena murmured.

"I've heard them speak of it." Mowara craned his neck for a better view. "From what I've been able to observe, they're all addicted to it. It alters them in strange and subtle ways. They call it 'coffee' and believe it bestows on them special powers, though I've no proof of that. Maybe it's some kind of collective ritual delusion whose social function is of paramount importance. See?"

As they looked on, the assembled monks raised their cups

in unison and mumbled some sort of hypnotic chant, of
which Buncan caught only the solemnly intoned words
"Brighten your day" and the meaningless "caffeine." Following this brief ceremony they returned to their conferencing.
Try as he might, Buncan could detect no change in their
collective demeanor as a result of consuming the liquid.
Any glow or enhancement they felt must be wholly internal.

The windowed boxes were something else, something
tangible. He wondered at the complexity and staying power
of the spell that caused the images displayed therein to
change so rapidly. Often two or more of the monks would
put their heads together and whisper furiously before tapping on the knobby panels. The unnatural activity raised
prickles on his spine.

Listening intently, he thought he could make out some of
the sorceral terms Mowara had mentioned during their first
meeting, words like "haploid dispersion" and "mitochondrial
enhancement." There was frequent mention of the long necromantic term desoxyribonucleic acid.

"They're concocting some great misfortune to throw against
Wurragarr," Mowara whispered. "We have to stop them,
we do. This all has to do with implementing the corporate
plan."

Buncan frowned. " 'Corporate plan'? What's that?"

"I've heard them speak of it often. It's the foundation of
their sorcery, the framework for all the iniquity they work."

Squill made a face. "Sounds like somethin' that should
be stepped on to me."

" 'As a cold sound to it, it does." Neena's whiskers
twitched involuntarily.

"You were right, Mowara." Buncan rolled the shoulder
the galah was perched on, trying to keep the muscles loose.
"This evil does extend beyond your country. It needs to be
stopped here, now, before it can grow and infect other parts
of the world. Or even other worlds," he added, mindful of
Jon-Tom's place of origin.

"Don't want no bloody corporate plan pollutin' the
Bellwoods," Squill muttered darkly. "Wotever it is."

"Look, they're doin' somethin'." Neena nodded toward
the opening.

The monks were rising from their oddly upholstered chairs. The window boxes had gone blank, their glass faces now dark and imageless.

Raising a hand for silence, the figure standing at the head of the table solemnly addressed his colleagues. His words were clearly audible to the quartet huddled in the narrow corridor.

"We shall now vote."

At that command they all threw back their hoods and stood revealed in the steady lamplight as representatives of the same tribe, though many individual clans were represented.

Hares, Buncan realized. They were all hares.

"Why hares?" he found himself whispering aloud. "Why should they be the Dark Ones, the dabblers in evil? Why them?"

"I know. I know because I've listened to them rage, because I've watched their frenzies, I have." Mowara's beak was close by Buncan's ear. "It's because they're sick of being thought of as cute and harmless. Ten thousand years and more of accumulated resentment has pushed this lot over the edge, it has. They're tired of being cuddled and stroked by everyone else. It's respect they want, and they aim to get it through sorcery."

Puzzlement mottled Neena's expression. "But they *are* cute and cuddly. 'Tis the way they were designed. They can't 'elp it, the bloody fools. Would they rather be like the skunk tribe, wot nobody wants to get near? Wot's wrong with this lot?"

"I told you," Mowara whispered. "They're so mad they've gone bad. Collective self-loathing. I think it's one reason why they're so set on creating new creatures, I do. Twisting and warping reality. Their anger has driven them insane."

Buncan found himself staring at the nominal leader of the ten. His fur was predominantly dark brown, with white, unhealthy-looking splotches. With his wild eyes and buck-teeth that had been filed to sharp points, he looked anything but cute and cuddly.

"We will throw the blasphemers back!" he was declaiming.

"Fling them over the falls!" another added enthusiastically.

"This, too, can be incorporated into the Plan." The leader ran a finger along the edge of the strange table. "Once this band of simple villagers has been defeated, there will be none to stand against us in the mountains. We can make servants and slaves of those who survive, and use them as the base for our planned corporate expansion. Mergers and takeovers can then proceed apace." He let his gaze rove over his followers. "All those in favor?"

"Aye!" the chorus of acolytes resounded.

The leader nodded his approval. "See that it is so recorded in the minutes." Lifting both hands, he tilted back his head and closed his eyes. His colleagues did likewise as he intoned The Words.

"Stock manipulation. Insider trading. *Currency exchange.*"

The room grew dark save for a singular greenish glow which seemed to emanate from the ceiling. The assembled monks murmured softly to themselves.

"They've certainly tapped in to something," Buncan whispered. "Some kind of gloom-laden power I've never encountered before." He wished silently that Clothahump were there.

Mowara shifted nervously from foot to foot on Buncan's shoulder. "That's Droww doing the invoking. He's the biggest fanatic of the lot."

The chanting rose in volume and the greenish glow intensified, until with a triumphant shout of *"Leveraged hostile buyout!"* the assembled monks vanished in a cloud of bilious smoke.

Buncan exhaled slowly. "That's very impressive."

"Where've they got to?" Neena wanted to know.

"Not far, not far, if experience is an indicator." Mowara shifted to Buncan's other shoulder. "To the Vault is my guess, it is, to prepare some special poison. Come, and we'll find them." Spreading aged but still competent wings, he fluttered off back up the corridor.

They had to avoid a single, pitiful guard: a transformed sugar glider whose wings hung about her in tatters. A prehensile tongue dangled from the misshapen head of what had once been a graceful gazelle. The sight turned Buncan's stomach.

"Tread softly here." Mowara settled once more onto Buncan's shoulder. "This is the kitchen where decay is prepared."

The corridor opened onto a vast chamber dominated by a lofty bowl-shaped ceiling. Lamps glowed in holders set high on stone walls. They stood on an upper floor looking down into a circular pit within which slablike tables and numerous cages were visible. The tables held much elaborate thaumaturgical apparatus fashioned of glass and metal.

Buncan recognized the monks from the Board room. Hoods back, they were bustling about the exotic apparatus and cages, mixing fluids and measuring powders. Droww stood at an intricately inscribed wooden pulpit which supported a huge, open book. There was also a knobbed panel attached to its own small window. This pulsed with light and unseen schematics. The leader of the Kilagurri monks gripped the sides of the podium while watching his faithful at work.

"There, in the back." Neena gestured insistently at the far side of the pit. "By the Black River itself!"

Buncan let his gaze follow her lead. She was pointing at the last row of stacked cages. These held not deformed monstrosities, not unfortunate travelers, but cubs: the young of numerous tribes. Even at a distance he could make out an infant flying fox and immature osprey huddled fearfully together. Both their wings had been clipped to forestall any chance of their flying to freedom.

Other cages held juvenile roos and platys, possums and tiger cats, dingoes and koalas, along with equally disconsolate representatives of outlying tribes such as small felines, rodents, a black bear cub, and an especially wretched sifaka. It was a panorama of collective misery heartbreaking to see, and for the first time he was glad as well as proud to have offered his help to Wurragarr's band.

There were also two human children crammed into a cage too small for them to stand up in. While he wasn't and never had been a tribal chauvinist, their plight still affected him more powerfully than that of any of the other captives. That was only to be expected, he thought.

An angry knot formed in his stomach. At that moment the

wizard Droww and his fellow hares did not look in the least bit cute or cuddly.

Though he knew sorcery was involved, the mechanics of the physical intermelding baffled him. Aside from wondering why anyone would want to, how could you combine the characteristics of a human child and a flying fox or wallaby? He couldn't shake loose of the question as his gaze shifted to the abominations jammed into some of the other cages.

"What you doing here?"

Whirling, Buncan saw exactly the sort of brute he feared.

Except for the protruding, black-tipped snout it had the face and arms of a young human, but the remainder of the body was wholly roo. Enormous, oversize feet, stout lower body tapering to a narrower chest, powerful tail, high leathery ears; all reminded him more of Wurragarr than his own tribe. The creature regarded them belligerently, a large club easily balanced in both hands, light chain mail hanging from the smooth shoulders.

"Get 'im!" yelled Squill without hesitation. He and Neena were on top of the creature instantly. Buncan was right behind them as Mowara darted back and forth overhead, whistling encouragement.

Buncan wrenched the club out of the creature's grasp while avoiding a kick that if it had connected would have taken his head off. The rooman fought back as best it could, but was no match for the combination of Buncan's strength and the otter's agility. In moments they had it pinned on its side. Neena's face burned where she'd caught a glancing blow from the muscular, madly flailing tail, but otherwise they were all three unharmed. Straddling the prone neck, Squill raised his sword.

"Go ahead; kill me," the rooman mumbled.

Frowning, Buncan raised a hand to block the otter's blow. "Wait."

"Wait?" Squill pushed his hat back on his forehead. "Wot the 'ell d'you mean, 'wait'? 'E'll give the bleedin' alarm."

The trapped creature gazed up out of limpid blue eyes. "Please, just kill me. I want die." To everyone's astonishment, the grotesque entity began to cry. Now even the notoriously unempathetic Squill found himself hesitating.

"Go on," it sobbed. "What wait for? Finish." The eyes closed.

Squill hadn't lowered the sword. "The ugly blighter's tryin' some sort o' bloomin' trick, 'e is."

"I don't think so." Rising, Buncan eased Squill gently but firmly aside. The otter backed off reluctantly.

Given the chance to rise and flee, the rooman didn't move. It just lay there bawling softly like any abandoned kid. "Make quick. Fast, before Dark Ones see what happening."

Buncan looked toward the busy pit, then back to their captive. "They can't see over here. We won't let them hurt you."

"Can't prevent." The rooman's sobs faded to sniffles, and he squinted up at Buncan. "Who you people, anyway?" Twisting his malformed head, he met first Squill's gaze, then Neena's. "You not from around here."

"No, we're not." Buncan retreated a step, giving the creature some room. "We come from a land far to the southeast, farther than you can imagine."

Gingerly, the rooman sat up. "Why? What you do here?" He gestured at Mowara as the galah landed on Buncan's shoulder. "You kind I know. You from here."

"Damn right I am, mate," said the bird huskily. "What we 'do here' is gonna put an end to these monks and their monkeying once and for all."

The rooman's eyes widened. "Cannot do. Cannot challenge the Dark Ones. Will destroy you. They draw strength from other worlds. Too powerful now." He looked around anxiously. "You go now, before they see. I not tell. Not!"

"We saw them at work." Buncan spoke patiently, soothingly, trying to calm the panicky creature. "They're powerful, but it's only sorcery."

"Only sorcery!" The rooman rose, and Squill immediately pressed the point of his sword against the poor creature's ribs. It gazed at him sorrowfully.

"Not tell," he reiterated.

The otter glanced at Buncan, who nodded slowly. Squill

backed off, but not far. His sister hung close on the other side.

"We're spellsingers," Buncan explained. "We've come with Mowara here, the warrior Wurragarr, and many others to try and put a stop to what these Dark Ones have been doing."

"Oi. We were just passin' through with nothin' else t'do." Squill's tone was caustic.

The rooman studied each of them in turn, still unwilling or unable to believe. "You sorcerers too? You fight Dark Ones?"

"That's right," Buncan told him.

"Must do this!" The creature spoke with such sudden violence that Buncan was taken aback. "Must stop them now, or they take over whole world. Everyplace and everyone and everything. Stop them now!"

"That's what we aim to do, mate." Mowara fluffed his feathers.

"Their style of sorcery is new to us," Buncan noted, "but it is only sorcery. As the great wizard Clothahump has said, 'Any magic which can be propounded can be countered.' " Neena gave him a sideways glance, and he looked slightly embarrassed.

The rooman's human fingers worked nervously against one another while the thick tail switched back and forth. "Been here long time. Sometimes I listen, learn things. Not so dumb. Not! Droww first to make hateful breakthrough and learn words of corruption. First makes plan, then recruits others. Starts small, with bugs. Puts wings of one on body of other. Fish next.

"I remember when both my turn. Originally two me. Now one you see. Other . . . throw away." His voice was momentarily choked. "Not sure which me, me. Not sure which throw away. Me lucky. Many times both throw away. Sometimes make things hard even for Dark Ones to look at. Much screaming." He was silent for a long moment.

"Me 'success.' " The word was uttered with enough sarcasm to cut oak. "Must serve Dark Ones, all monks. Only life. Rather be dead. Not so easy to be dead. Forget things."

"What's your name?" Buncan asked as gently as possible.

Tortured blue eyes gazed back into his. "Name dead too."

"Well, then, what do they call you?"

"Cilm. Maybe original name of one of two that I was. Maybe not. Matters not." It turned hopeful. "Kill me now?"

"We're not going to kill you," Buncan declared firmly. "I can't do it."

Squill lowered his sword. "Bloody 'ell, I can't do it neither. That's a first."

"You're not responsible for . . . what you are," Buncan continued. "We don't want to hurt you or any of your friends."

"Have no friends." Cilm managed a feeble shrug of his half-human, half-roo shoulders. "None here friend to another. Each our own private horrors."

Buncan nodded as if he understood. "Then help us. I'm asking you to be our friend. Help us to make an end to this."

The rooman looked doubtful. "Dark Ones have so much power."

"You ain't 'eard our power, guv. Wait 'til you 'ear wot we can do."

"Will you help us?" Buncan tried to be insistent without being overbearing.

Clearly resistance was not a concept with which the rooman was conversant. "I not sure. Not . . . know. You not see what Dark Ones do to any who dare fight back." He quivered all over. "Not want to see."

"We can take care of ourselves," Neena assured him with a confidence she didn't entirely feel.

Still the creature hesitated. Then roo ears flicked forward, suddenly alert. "Cilm help. But only if you promise one thing."

"What's that?" Buncan asked curiously.

"If we losing, you will kill me."

Buncan swallowed hard. This was very different from Neena's gallant rescue. There was no glory to be had; only something that needed to be done. He felt no exhilaration, no feeling of anticipation. Only a grim sense of determination.

"All right," he heard himself mutter. It sounded like someone else.

Cilm nodded understandingly. "Must be strong. I beautiful compared to what you will see. Must destroy devices, potions, powders, everything. No more experiments. No more sorcery. No more me's."

Buncan peered down into the pit. "We have friends outside. A small army. They're going to attack Kilagurri just before daybreak. When they hit the wall, that's when we should make our move."

"Too right," Squill murmured by way of agreement.

"Is there a place we can hide 'til then?" Neena inquired.

The rooman considered, then beckoned for them to follow. "Storage place near here. Little used. Window high up. You come."

CHAPTER 23

DESPITE HIS DETERMINATION TO STAY AWAKE, BUNCAN found himself dozing on and off. His intermittent sleep was filled with fractured dreams populated by broken bodies. As soon as one would come together properly it would fall, tumbling over and over, to shatter like glass against the red rocks of the Tamas. Each time he would awaken, only to drift off again.

Finally he awoke to an enclosure that was perceptibly brighter. And no longer silent. A distant clamor could be heard through the single high window. He shook Mowara awake, then Squill. Neena was already alert, conversing softly with Cilm. Following his lead, they moved back out into the corridor.

A hooded monjon was hopping just ahead of them. They trailed a safe distance behind, halting at the overlook as the small marsupial continued down into the busy pit. The Dark Ones were conversing anxiously with one another, their voices louder and considerably more agitated than they'd been earlier. As the travelers watched in silence they left in groups of two or three through the main doorway, until the chamber was deserted save for those who were unable to flee.

"Now." Cilm rose from his crouch and took a long bound toward the nearest stairs. "Before they come back."

Down on the floor of the pit Buncan found himself surrounded by tables laden with arcane apparatus. Sleepy moans emanated from the stacked cages. Tilting back his head enabled him to see the elaborately painted symbols stenciled on the curvilinear ceiling. Despite the rising sun, it was still dark inside. He found himself longing suddenly for the lucid, unpolluted air of the woods; any woods.

On the table in front of him were several constructions that looked like children's toys: unrecognizable shapes consisting of small balls connected together by sticks, globes that split into other globes. Notepads were filled with peculiar hieroglyphics.

A crash sounded off to his right, followed quickly by another. The otters had started in, dumping fluids and powders onto the floor and smashing their containers. Taking out his sword, he began flailing methodically at the toy-models, reducing them to fragments.

At Droww's vacant pulpit he found himself staring at the blank window box. Though he put his face right up against the glass, he couldn't see anything inside. It was an impenetrable, opaque gray. He tapped on the connected panel, but nothing happened. Being ignorant of the requisite magic, he was neither surprised nor particularly disappointed when his fingering failed to enlighten him.

The important thing was to ensure that it could no longer enlighten the Dark Ones. Removing it from its resting place, he raised it high overhead and slammed it to the floor. The shell cracked like an egg, spewing bits and pieces of wire and plastic. With his sword Buncan hacked at the remains, reducing them beyond hope of repair.

Whooping and hollering with delight, Squill and Neena were smashing their way through the surviving apparatus.

Mowara helped where he could, but Cilm was unable to overcome his conditioning. He stood off to one side, not lending a hand. But he observed it all, and his eyes shone.

Powders and fluids mixed on the stone floor, occasionally forming hissing, bubbling patches which Buncan and his friends in their deliberate vandalism were careful to avoid. By now the first uncertain queries were being voiced by the bastard inhabitants of the cages. Buncan wanted badly to release them, but knew the contrivances of the Dark Ones had to be attended to first.

He wondered how Wurragarr and his people were doing outside, not to mention Viz and Snaugenhutt.

The knobby panel was fashioned of some particularly tough material. Putting up his sword, he picked up the rectangle and slammed it repeatedly against a wall until not a knob was left connected to the panel itself. Then he stood on the rectangle and tugged until it snapped in half. He threw the two pieces in opposite directions, looked around, and paused.

"Where's Squill?"

Panting heavily, Neena relaxed her sword arm. She was surrounded by debris. Mowara stood on a table that had been cleared of equipment.

"Don't know." The galah sounded concerned.

Neena flicked her head in the direction of the far stairway. "Said not to worry. Said 'e 'ad a bit o' an errand to run. See, there 'e is now."

Turning, Buncan saw the otter standing at the top of the stone staircase. In his short arms he held the critical metal box from the Dark Ones' conference chamber.

"Wouldn't want to leave an' forget this." Smiling, he heaved the heavy container into the air. It slammed into the stone stairs and tumbled toward the floor of the pit.

To their astonishment, it screamed as it bounced.

"Leave me alone! Don't come near me! Unauthorized access, unauthorized access!" The words were clearly audible above the metallic whangs and bangs as the box bounced down the stairs.

When it finally rolled to a stop, Buncan moved toward it.

Instantly it rose up on four tiny rubber feet and tried to skitter away from him.

"Don't touch me! You have not been properly formatted." The words issued from one of a trio of tiny slots in the box's front. All three were jabbering away simultaneously.

"C drive inactive, C drive inactive... Unauthorized access attempted... Insert a properly formatted diskette.... Entry refused, entry refused...."

"Is that so?" After overcoming his initial surprise, Squill had trailed the protesting contraption down the stairs. Now he deliberately thrust the point of his short sword into the most vociferous of the complaining slots.

He was rewarded with a grinding, whirring sound. The entire sword began to vibrate. So did his arm. When he tried to yank the weapon free the slot clamped down hard on the blade. Drool dripped from the other slots, and Buncan thought he could see tiny teeth lining the interiors.

"Wipe intruder, wipe intruder!" piped one of the free slots.

"You ain't wipin' nothin', you bloody hunk o' accursed tin!" With both hands Squill managed to wrench his weapon free. Raising it high overhead, he began flailing away enthusiastically at the frantic container. Still screeching incomprehensible insults and occasional comprehensible threats, it tried to dodge and, failing that, to bite its tormentor, but was no match for the active otter.

On the other hand, its metal skin was uncommonly tough, and Squill's best efforts succeeded only in denting the smooth surface.

"See the damned thing." Mowara hovered just above Buncan. "Sorcery that complains."

"Let me." Cilm took a flying leap and landed on the box with both huge feet. His weight failed to faze it.

A commotion on the level above drew Buncan's attention. "We're discovered. We've got to finish here and get out." Working alongside Neena, he concentrated on smashing the last of the intact gear. With Cilm's help they were able to upend the largest of the worktables. What remained of the delicate equipment it held went crashing to the floor. Still not satisfied, he took his sword to the fragments while Squill continued to duel with the jabbering box.

"Rebooting required, rebooting required!" As it hobbled toward the stairway from which it had made its ignominious entrance, Squill leaped on its back in an effort to restrain it. Like that of some squat, squarish turtle, its internal mass was sufficient to haul him upward.

"Gimme a 'and 'ere, mates!" he bawled as he clung to the slick metal surface. " 'Tis tryin' to get away!"

"Hold it, Squill!" Searching through the rubble, Buncan found an intact bottle three-quarters full of some pale yellow liquid. Racing up the stairs, he joined Squill in forcibly tilting the box onto its back. Rubbery feet kicked at the air, seeking purchase.

"Unauthorized entry, unauthorized entry!"

While the otter did his best to hold the box steady, Buncan poured the bottle's contents into the largest and loudest of the three mouths. When it was empty he stepped back. A moment later Squill let go.

The box staggered up another two stairs, then stopped and began trembling violently. A distinct gargling noise came from all three slots. This was followed by mechanical retching noises and the regurgitation of several small bits of plastic. One mouth gasped feebly.

"Blind, I'm blind! Where's the See-prompt? I can't find the See-prompt. Maledictions on you all! Abort, reentry, fail. Abort, reentry... fail..."

With a final shudder it seemed to settle down on its tiny feet. Then it rolled over and bounced back down the stairs, to lie silent and unmoving at their base. Descending to stand alongside, a wary Squill nudged it with a foot, glanced over at Buncan. Both human and otter were breathing hard.

"I think it's dead, mate."

Buncan nodded, turned to look upward. The commotion he'd detected was growing louder. "Someone's coming. Mowara?"

The galah flew toward the ceiling, called anxiously down to them. "They come! The Dark Ones come! Beware and be ready!"

A hand touched Buncan's arm and he forced himself not to pull away from its tormented owner. "Remember promise," Cilm said softly.

"I'm not killing anyone. Not yet." Sheathing his sword,

he brought the duar around in front of him. "Squill, Neena!" The three of them put their heads together and in low tones began to rehearse possible defenses, while Mowara squawked and circled overhead. Left to himself, Cilm ripped and tore at the innards of the unmoving box until they lay strewn all over the floor.

"Who dares!" came a bellow of outrage from above.

"They have destroyed the oracle!" Judging from his tone, the second speaker was more frightened than angry.

Hooded figures were gathering on the level above the pit. Buncan was gratified to see that they carried not cryptic sorceral implements but ordinary weapons: swords and knives.

"Get ready," he murmured to his companions. They formed a tight little knot off by themselves.

"Kill them, kill them!" Beginning softly with one of the figures, the chant grew quickly in strength and volume.

The tallest of the hooded ones stepped to the edge of the stairs and shoved back his cowl. Eyes burning, ears twitching, Droww glowered ferociously down at them.

"You will be most agonizingly dismembered, and then I will have the pleasure of transmuting your genes!" His glare was pitiless. The threat had little effect on Buncan, since except for the part about dismembering he didn't have the vaguest idea what the wizard was talking about.

"By the power of the All-Splicing Mage, by the haploid dissolution. By the fecundity of my kind and the fevered twists of their DNA, I call upon the Great Master of Selective Breeding to make an example most hideous of these blasphemers!" Raising his hands toward the ceiling, he began a new chant that was quickly picked up by his followers.

A dark glowing mass formed at the base of the stairs. Low, reverberant grunts and growls began to issue from within.

"Steady," Buncan urged his companions, his fingers taut on the strings of the duar.

Something was moving within the bloodred cloud. As it began to dissipate, a hulking shape half as big as Snaugenhutt emerged. Sloping, hunched shoulders were clad in a studded leather vest. Its short, fluffy tail had been transformed into a nest of spikes, as had the crest that ran down its back. Both ears were ragged and torn, and long fangs hung from the upper lip. One hand dragged an immense wooden mallet along the floor.

"Carrot!" it rumbled.

"No, no!" Above, Droww was forced to interrupt his chant and point at Buncan and the otters. "Rend, tear, immobilize!"

The massive figure blinked uncertainly. "Carrot?"

"Carrot later!" a dyspeptic Droww bellowed. "Rend first!"

Heavy-lidded eyes focused on the unmoving trio. Lifting the mallet in both hands, the mutated hare lurched forward and swung.

Buncan began to play even as he leaped to his right, the otters scattering in the other direction. The head of the mallet dimpled the floor where they'd been standing.

"Hey, gruesome, over 'ere!" From beneath a still-intact table Squill made a face at the apparition, which brought the mallet around and down with a prodigious grunt, reducing the wooden platform to splinters. Squill had long since scrambled to safety.

Droww wrung his hands helplessly. "No, *no*! Be *careful*!"

This request evidently involving elements of subtlety far too fine for the ungainly executioner to comprehend, it paused to blink dumbly up at its master. "Rend careful?"

The delay allowed Buncan and his friends time to regroup. Despite being winded, the otters harmonized splendidly and without hesitation.

"This no place to ignore a dare
Callin' up this thing's 'ardly fair
But that's all right, 'cause we got rap to spare
If you won't fight straight, we won't fight square
Beware
Up there
Better have a care
Better watch your hare
'Cause our fresh hip-hop's
Gonna fix your lop
An' your magic ensnare."

Silvery fog enveloped the mallet-wielding monster. Halting in midswing, it let out a mammoth sneeze (evidently the enchanted mist was ticklish) and, despite the by now somewhat desperate chanting of the Dark Ones, began to shrink. Fangs diminished, feet contracted, head and body dwindled. Only the ears remained resolutely unchanged.

The brute continued to reduce until there stood in its place a diminutive rabbit no larger than Mowara, with ungainly ears that went all over the place. A representative of the lop clan, Buncan thought with a smile as he relaxed his fingers, to end all lops.

Despite the transformation, it still made an effort to comply with its original directive. "Rend!" it declaimed in a high, squeaky voice as it brought its equally shrunken mallet down on Squill's foot.

The otter let out a yelp and danced clear. "You bloody little . . . I'll tie you up in your own ears an' use you for a bleedin' yo-yo!"

"Enough!" The raging Droww flung his arms wide. The other Dark Ones drew away from him.

"'Ear that?" Neena prompted him. Straining, Buncan could make out the sounds of fighting somewhere outside the chamber. He smiled. With the Dark Ones diverted, it sounded like Wurragarr and his people had managed to breach the gate. If they were inside the wall, it was only a matter of time.

"It's over!" he shouted up at the aggrieved hare. "You're finished, Droww. Even as we stand here, our friends are busy cleansing this monastery."

"Except for you," Neena added pleasantly. "You're too bloomin' ugly to cleanse."

"You slew the oracle." Droww's voice was a tormented snarl. "You have destroyed knowledge. Do you know what that means?"

"Yeah, we know what it means." Buncan gave the inert, disemboweled box a kick, and it rattled hollowly. "It means you'll never again be able to use it to foist your perversions on innocent people."

"Perhaps not, but while the knowledge-giver has been slain, the knowledge it has already given remains with us."

He spread his arms to encompass the pit. "All this, yea, even all this, can with time be replaced." He glanced to his left. "We can begin anew, Brothers." A murmur arose from the other Dark Ones as they waited to see what their mentor would do.

He returned his gaze to Buncan and his companions. "But first," he hissed, "we must deal finally and irrevocably with these intruders. Then we will take care of those pathetic country folk outside." The wizard straightened. "You spelling impressively."

"Cor, we ain't 'ardly worked up a sweat, guv. Colloquially speakin', that is." Though Neena knew she was physically incapable of perspiring, she'd often wished she could sample the sensation.

"I tire." Droww let out a measured sigh. "So much to do, so many distractions. It is hard to contemplate greatness when one is always tired."

"It's even 'arder when you're dead." Squill fingered his sword as he favored the wizard with a friendly grin, whiskers arching.

"An observation full of truth, water rat, and one which applies equally to the mundane." Turning to the acolyte on his immediate left, he murmured, "Release the Berserker."

"The Berserker?" the hooded one stammered. "But great Droww—"

"Release it, I say!" He gave the hesitant hare a violent shove. "I will establish control."

Hearing a moan, Buncan turned to see the rooman backed up against the wall. "What's this 'Berserker,' friend Cilm?" But this time their ally was unable to reply.

An instant later the chamber echoed to the sound of wood splintering as a mighty physique came smashing through an upper-level door. Fragments of wood spilled over into the pit. Buncan waved away sawdust and tried to focus.

A much smaller shape came gliding rapidly toward him. "Viz!" On the level above, Buncan could see Snaugenhutt peering down at them, a satisfied smile on his homely face. Bits of door teetered on his broad back and his armor was badly dented, but he appeared otherwise unharmed. In his wake the sounds of fighting doubled in volume.

"We're through," declared the tickbird, hovering overhead. "They're giving up all over the monastery."

Buncan turned to stare back up at the master of the Dark Ones. "It's all over, Droww. The 'simple' folk you despise have overcome your creations. Make it easy on yourself and surrender now."

Droww appeared not the least concerned. The wizard was looking not at him but to his right, toward the dark portal that sealed off the far end of the pit.

"Not only is it not 'over,' human cub, it has not yet begun. Your immature mind is not capable of envisioning the end product of informed and inspired genetic manipulation. Indeed, you are not even aware of the forces of which I speak. It therefore falls to me to enlighten you. Pay close attention. It is the last thing you will ever learn." His laugh was like a rotting jellyfish: soft, unpleasant, redolent of decay.

"When you have been dismembered, it will be my pleasure to recombine you. I will fashion from your remains several simpering, crawling things, the lowest of the low. You will live in constant pain, begging for death, an example to any and all who would dare consider defying the sanctity of Kilagurri."

Squill pointedly blew his nose into a sheaf of papers he'd picked off the floor. "That's quite a speech, guv, but it ain't relevant, 'cause you're gonna be 'eadless real soon now." Gripping his sword tightly, he started toward the stairs.

A distant rumble made him stop.

Everyone looked curiously, uncertainly, toward the shuttered portal that was now the focus of the wizard's attention. Suddenly a high-pitched shriek that scraped the upper limits of audibility echoed from behind the opaque barrier.

Buncan shivered in spite of himself. Nothing screamed quite like a dying rabbit.

Droww pushed out his lower lip. "Pity. It would seem that in the course of carrying out his duties Brother Jeurrat did not move quite quickly enough."

It wasn't so much a rumbling, Buncan thought restively, as a ponderous heavy breathing that was coming nearer and nearer. He thought of the bellows constantly at work at the Lynchbany Smithy's. No cheery, animated sparks accompanied the approach of this sound. It resonated with prodigious threat.

Neena glanced at him. "Buncan?" The seriousness of the situation was reflected in her calling him by his real name.

He kept staring at the blocked portal, mesmerized by something he could only sense. "I don't know. Something big."

Droww held his ground, but his colleagues commenced a slow retreat, murmuring nervously among themselves.

"Something wrong, spellsinger? Come, give us a tune! Something jaunty and brisk. Have you never crooned a Berserker before? Is not music supposed to soothe?" His arms and hands were jerking about, tracing edgy spirals in the air.

As Wurragarr's people pressed their offensive deeper into the confines of the monastery, the constant buzz of hand-to-hand combat in Buncan's ears diminished but did not cease. He knew now that was only an echo of a sideshow. The outcome of the entire undertaking would be decided any minute, here in the ruins of the monks' laboratory. Mowara and Viz looked down from above, while Snaugenhutt paced fretfully on the upper level. Cilm was nowhere to be seen, the rooman having fled precipitously. Otter to the left of him, otter to the right of him, Buncan waited for whatever was coming.

And something was coming. Of that there was no doubt.

It did not crash through the heavy barrier, nor smash it violently aside. It simply bit through the gate as if it were fashioned of paper instead of iron-barred timbers, then contemptuously spat the crumpled wood and metal aside.

Buncan considered the apparition. It was not quite as big as Snaugenhutt. Its aspect, however, was enough to strike terror into the hearts of heroes yet unborn.

Great muscles bunched like skin-wrapped boulders beneath the humped shoulders. Two sets of widely spaced, sharp-pointed horns protruded from atop the skull: one facing forward, the other inclined forward and up as if standing ready to reinforce the murderous effects of the other pair.

Except for its excessive muscularity, the rest of the body

was unceremoniously ungulate: umber-hued short-haired coat, tufted tail, four legs terminating in cloven hooves. Only the head seemed grafted and greatly enlarged. It was that of a highly specialized canine grown to obscene proportions. Docked to those massive shoulders, it appeared neckless. Bulging red eyes sweating damp murder sought quarry, while the powerful jaws worked spittle from thick lips. From the hidden throat came an abyssal, squalid gurgling as if the creature were masticating a cud consisting of the tormented remnants of previously consumed souls.

Of all the corrupt crossbreedings and odious recombinants the Dark Ones had brought forth, of all their vile manipulations and stirrings of Nature's most personal and private depths, this was their monument most foul. Body of a mammoth steer, skull of the most relentless of fighting canines. Teeth and horn, jaw and hoof.

The pit bull–bull shook its head and spat out a sticky iron bolt. Buncan heard it go *ping* as it ricocheted off the stone floor. Then it glanced up, searching, until it fastened on the long-eared figure of Droww. The intimidating skull dipped respectfully.

"Master, thy servant awaits."

Droww looked quite pleased. But his finger quivered as he pointed. "Tear 'em up . . . but not beyond hope of restitching."

The skull rose and turned. A humorless smile split the timber-crunching jaws. "With pleasure, Master. It is what I love to do." It started toward the opposing staircase.

Buncan and the otters were already retreating, scrambling up the wide stone steps. As he ascended, Buncan was once again unlimbering the duar.

"C'mon, guys. A song, some lyrics; let's get with it!"

"Wot d'you think I'm doin', Buckles?" Neena glared at him.

Droww was laughing delightedly to himself, his acolytes having by this time retreated to a far corner. There they huddled fearfully, their eyes panicky beneath their hoods.

"No song will save you now, young tunesmiths. Nothing will save you now! No power on or off the earth can stop the Berserker!"

"Maybe not, but I'm about to give it one hell of a try!"
By the time the monster mounted the final step, Snaugenhutt
had mustered an impressive head of steam.

He plowed into the surprised pit bull–bull with tremendous force. The creature stumbled and slid backward several
steps. Then it gathered itself, eyes raging, and lunged with
incredible jaws agape.

Displaying unexpected agility, Snaugenhutt dodged. Unnatural horns dipped and shoved. The points did not penetrate the rhino's thick skin, but the muscles behind that
stabbing blow could not be resisted. Snaugenhutt's feet
scrabbled for purchase at the edge of the level overlooking
the pit. With a twist of its great head, the pit bull–bull
actually lifted the rhino off the floor and tossed him to his
right. The distance was short, but it was enough to send the
helpless Snaugenhutt over the side.

With a sound like two symphonies colliding at high
speed, the rhino struck the floor of the pit. The concussion
sent bits of armor flying in all directions. He lay there on his
side, kicking convulsively.

"Snaugenhutt, Snaug! Get up, load! Quit treading air!"
Beating atmosphere, the tickbird tried to rouse his companion.

"Viz, look out!" Buncan yelled frantically.

With a loud *whump!* immense jaws slammed shut as the
pit bull–bull snapped downward. The monster bit only air as
Viz darted neatly aside and continued to beseech his fallen
friend.

"Come on, move it! You ain't dead. Quit acting like it.
We *need* you."

Snaugenhutt was indeed still very much alive, but the fall
had stunned him. He lay blinking and kicking. It would be
necessary for him to recover his senses before he could
recover his feet.

The interfering rhino disposed of, the pit bull–bull sought
other prey. Advancing deliberately, it tried to trap Buncan
in the nearest corner, perhaps realizing he would be easier to
catch than the more nimble otters. Holding the duar out in
front of him like a talisman, Buncan retreated, knowing that
while he might be able to dodge the creature, he couldn't
possibly outrun it.

"Let's go," he called to the otters, who hovered nearby. His fingers cajoled harmless melodies from the dual sets of strings. "Words, I need words!"

"We're bloomin' tryin', mate!" In an attempt to distract the creature, Squill darted across its line of vision. The otter's presence barely registered on the brute's senses. It was utterly focused now. The young human first, then ample time for the others.

Scampering dangerously close to sharp forehooves, Neena was likewise ignored. She and her brother exchanged harassed whispers, while Buncan grimly tried to decide which way he was going to have to jump.

On the other side of the pit the rest of the Dark Ones had begun to edge forward, encouraged by their leader's apparent control over the Berserker. Hesitantly at first, then with increasing enthusiasm, they began to voice their support in the form of an ascending, unified chant.

Squill and Neena, too, had finally begun to sing.

"Push 'em back, push 'em back,
Wayyyyy... back!
Back in the 'ole where he can't be seen
Over the line, back through the wall
Back so far that the big becomes small
Stop him right 'ere, if you know what we mean.
Gots to do a number an' fix this scene."

Even as he played wildly, Buncan was shouting at his friends.

"What kind of spellsong is that?"

Squill made a face as Neena agonized over a second verse. "Cor, mate, she's the best we can do for now."

Bits and pieces of shattered glass and twisted metal began to rise from the floor of the pit. Sprouting glowing wings, they soared upward and flung themselves recklessly against the advancing form of the pit bull–bull. Every one bounced harmlessly to the floor, some to flap futilely against the stone, others to be ground to dust beneath ponderous hooves.

Even the crumpled operating table lurched into the air. On leathery wings of lambent green it soared as high as the ceiling, only to fold its sails and dive straight at the pit bull–bull's skull. A smaller creature would have been killed by the blow, and even Snaugenhutt stunned, but the monster simply twisted and caught the plunging chunk of enchanted furniture in its massive jaws. A single, powerful snap reduced it to kindling.

"Give up!" Droww was yelling from the far side of the pit. "The Berserker is immune to your simple tunes. An all-encompassing veil of ignorance protects it. It doesn't understand sorcery, it doesn't understand spellsinging, it does not comprehend even the rudiments of thaumaturgy, and therefore cannot be affected by them. Its entire development has gone to muscle. Only the sound of my voice penetrates its thick mode of bone to reach the brain beneath."

The otters changed their song. Evanescent effervescent dust rose in clouds from the floor with the aim of obscuring the creature's vision, but they only made it sneeze as it lumbered on through, shaking its head irritably from side to side.

Buncan was running out of room almost as quickly as he was out of ideas. Spellsinging seemed ineffective against this ultimate invention of the Dark Ones, and he said as much to his companions.

" 'Tis got to work." Neena strove frantically to improvise still-fresher lyrics. " 'Tis always worked for Jon-Tom an' Mudge, an' it 'as to work now."

"I'm not Jon-Tom!" Buncan slid to his right. The pit bull–bull edged sideways to match his movement.

"Then by the Aardvark's Spittle, think o' somethin' your sire would never think of!" Squill challenged him.

Easy to say, Buncan reflected tiredly. Hard to do. Exhaustion was creeping up his legs. His fingers were growing numb, and he knew that the otters' throats had to be raw from rapping at the tops of their lungs. Nothing they tried had any effect on the relentless specter. One snap of those preposterous jaws, one diffident bite, and he and his friends would be reduced to soggy pulp. That was assuming they managed to dodge the twin sets of horns and . . . .

He brightened as the lyrics flashed on him. It had worked once before. Though using the same or similar lyrics in a second spellsong was dangerous, they were about out of options. What did they have to lose? He made the suggestion.

Neena squinted hard, trying to watch him and the advancing mountain-with-teeth at the same time. "Pardon me presumption, Bookoos, but ain't this an inappropriate time for baby babble? We need strength, we need power, we need . . ."

"Something different, like your brother said. The lyrics have power. We just need a different take on them." The wall was very near now. He saw himself kicking and twitching, impaled on one of those formidable horns. "I'll start it off, and you and Squill copy. Just listen to the words and . . ."

With a roar that shook dust from the rafters, the pit bull–bull lowered its head and charged.

"Scatter!" Buncan threw himself to his right as horns slammed into the stone wall and steel-trap jaws crushed the air where he'd been standing an instant earlier. The monster was much faster than anything its size ought to have been. It skittered sideways to block any further retreat, realizing it had its quarry trapped. This time it didn't even bother to lower its horns.

Off in the distance he could hear Viz yelling at Snaugenhutt to pull himself together, but the rhino couldn't help now. He'd taken his best shot at the creature and barely budged it. It was all up to the others and to Buncan. In a quavering voice he began to mouth the lyrics he remembered from childhood, the lyrics which had worked so well for him and his friends not so very long ago. Only . . . different, this time. Even to his ears it sounded like a lamentation.

Squill and Neena could be as quick with their wits as they were with their feet. Having sung the song once before, it was easy for them to rework the simple refrain.

Indifferent to the music, the pit bull–bull glanced from otters to human, trying to decide which to annihilate first.

As he listened to the otters, Buncan had to admit they had managed to inject a truly anguished quality into their singing. This time around, the same lyrics were full of sorrow and pathos, of sadness and poignancy. His playing was slower,

their vocalizing was slower, and together they generated an
aura of ineffable sadness that pervaded the entire chamber.

No luminous clouds coalesced within the room, but the
duar pulsed a rich, dark blue, utterly reflective of the music
Buncan skillfully coaxed from the dual sets of intersecting
strings.

" 'Ow much is that doggie in the window, yo?
The one with the waggly tail, y'know?
'Ow much is that doggie in the window, bro'?
It looks so sad, gotta be mad
Wrong head on its body, it's gotta be bad
Poor old thing, 'tis all alone
Nothin' else like it anywhere
Like to throw it a bone
But I hate to stare
Someone oughta care, it needs to rest
Be best, be safe, don't wanna berate
But that anger you need to stick in a crate
And relax, take a pill, chill
Take some time your own dreams to fulfill."

The spellsong was full of anger (it was rap, after all), but
also loneliness and yearning, a yearning after stability that
particularly escaped one inhabitant of that chaotic chamber.
It expressed desire and want for the unobtainable, for
half-forgotten dreams. Back on his feet at the bottom of the
pit, Snaugenhutt too was caught up in the harmonic web of
melancholy Buncan and the otters wove. No one within
listening range remained unaffected. Even some of the Dark
Ones unwillingly found themselves drawn to bygone memories.

Sweating profusely, Buncan played on, watching the pit
bull–bull as it glared down at him.

It took a defiant step forward . . . and paused, bastard ears
pricked forward. Spears it could disregard, arrows it could
shrug off, swords it could shun, but it could not ignore the
music. As Buncan stared, the fiery eyes seemed to dim and
glaze over. The dark red tongue, a slimy hunk of drooling
meat, slipped out the side of the powerful jaws and hung
dangling from the misshapen mouth.

As the mountain-with-teeth sat back on its hindquarters and began to pant contentedly, an unmistakable if slightly obtuse canine smile spread slowly across its hideous face. As the otters continued to improvise, this was shortly replaced with an expression of great sadness framed by tears as profound emotions penetrated the benumbed berserker brain. The great jaws no longer snapped hungrily. Eyes half shut, swaying slowly in time to the music, it continued to listen and absorb and be affected.

Amazing the results thoughtful modifications to a simple tune could have, Buncan mused.

By the time they embarked on their fourteenth improvised stanza, the great creature was lying on its belly, eyes closed, that nightmare skull resting peacefully on crossed forehooves. For the first time in its tormented existence, it was at peace. Every now and then it emitted a distinct, soft whimper and wagged its composite tail.

Exhausted but quietly exultant, the otters terminated their most recent and final refrain. Buncan's fingers plucked conclusively at the duar. Except for the futile howls of the sorcerer Droww and the echo of distant fighting, it was silent in the chamber. The soft snores of the soundly sleeping pit bull–bull drifted contentedly ceilingward.

Enraged and frustrated beyond reason, Droww wrenched a saber from one of his startled acolytes and rushed around the rim of the pit to confront Buncan. His duar secured, Buncan stood his ground, awaiting the charge with his own sword drawn.

The sorcerer made a pretense of swinging his weapon, then leaped into the air and struck out with both enormous feet. Buncan proved more agile than his opponent expected, but then, he'd spent years tussling with otters. At the last instant, he ducked. Droww sailed over him . . .

. . . to land with both feet, hard, on the head of the softly dozing pit bull–bull.

Awaking with a snort, it instantly espied the cause of the interruption of the first sound sleep it had ever enjoyed, and growled warningly.

Fumbling with his robes, Droww stumbled to his feet and thrust a shaky finger at Buncan. "Kill him. Kill all of them!

Start with that one. Don't worry about preserving body parts for recombination. Shred him slowly. Pick him apart.''

The pit bull–bull rose to all four feet. Buncan began backing away slowly. But it did not come for him. It did not move at all.

Droww whirled and waved both arms emphatically. "What's the matter with you? Obey! Comply! By the gnarly DNA, I command you! By the genetic bonds and Mendelian Progression, by diploid dupes and haploid hopes, I order you to do my will!" Snarling deep in its throat, the ungulate ogre was slowly advancing on the irate sorcerer, pressing him relentlessly toward the edge of the pit.

"Stay back!" There was confusion in Droww's voice and, for the first time, a hint of fear. "I will have you respliced!"

Two of Wurragarr's people, an ax-wielding bandicoot and a sword-armed ringtail, stood entranced in the far doorway. The other Dark Ones likewise looked on in fascination and horror, unable or unwilling to interfere. Mowara and Viz rested on Snaugenhutt's back, while the otters had moved to stand next to Buncan.

Droww glanced over his shoulder. He could probably survive a leap to the pit floor below, but an angry rhino awaited him there. Snaugenhutt was nearsighted but not blind. His attention was fixed eagerly on the retreating sorcerer. One heavy foot pawed expectantly at the stone.

The long-eared wizard turned back to his grandest experiment, his greatest achievement. "Stop, I say. You will come no farther." With a threatening snarl, the pit bull–bull took another step forward.

Despairing at the uncooperativeness of an indifferent universe, the sorcerer whirled and leaped for the pit, preferring to take his chances with the aggressive but awkward rhinoceros below. He never got the chance.

Lightning-fast jaws lunged and snapped. With a crisp, piercing *crunch*, Droww vanished into the mouth of the being he had caused to come into existence. A couple of cursory chews, a prodigious swallow, and just like that the sorcerer was gone. A few bones, a little blood, some shredded robes clung to the pit bull–bull's lips: meager legacy for so much evil.

Buncan glanced at his friends. "I think it's time for us to leave."

The massive misplaced canine skull swung 'round to peer in their direction. Then it leaped . . . not toward them, but across the wide gulf that was the pit, clearing it easily. It was an astonishing demonstration of physical prowess. As it landed heavily on the far side, the remaining Dark Ones scattered for their lives. The offspring of their inimical interference pursued energetically.

Snaugenhutt mounted the steps that led out of the pit, whereupon they all conferenced with the two fighters who had arrived moments earlier. Resistance within the monastery had begun to break down. As soon as word reached the remaining defenders that Droww had been killed and the pit bull–bull was on the loose and looking to revenge itself against its former masters, it would doubtless collapse.

The bandicoot and ringtail rushed out to inform their companions of what had transpired within. As soon as the information reached Wurragarr, he ordered a general pull-back. The victorious but spent farmers and craftsfolk retreated through the shattered gate to the fringe of the forest, leaving the terminal cleansing of the monastery to the rampaging pit bull–bull.

Overcoming their initial distaste, they eventually welcomed the grotesque but pitiable Cilm into their company, as they did all those refugees from the abode of the Dark Ones who made it out alive, repenters and innocents alike. Within the high walls terrible screams and piercing shrieks attested to the remorseless activity of the pit bull–bull as it revenged itself against its creators. Fires were beginning to break out among the stark structures as lamps and torches were toppled in the ongoing frenzy.

"What'll happen to the canine-thing?" In the flickering light Snaugenhutt's bulk looked as if it had been hewn from granite. Gragelouth stood nearby, talking trade with a casual cus-cus.

"I don't know." Buncan leaned against the rhino's flank for support as he stared at the engulfed monastery. "But I don't think it'll come after us. Maybe it'll stay with, live within the ruins. Maybe it'll remember the song we sung it and be comforted a little. Eventually I hope it'll make peace with the people who live around here. After all, it was one of them once. Several of them.''

"What if it doesn't, mate?" Turning, Buncan saw Wurragarr approaching. Bedarra and Quibo accompanied him. "What if it comes out looking for a fight?"

Buncan stood away from Snaugenhutt's side. "Where are those happy fliers, your spellsingers? And their accompanists?"

"Too happy by half." Wurragarr gestured at Bedarra, who disappeared into the woods. The thylacine returned moments later with the three kookaburras and their attendant musicians. Looking anything but jovial, the heavy-beaked birds landed on a convenient branch nearby. They had witnessed sufficient slaughter to mute even their normally irrepressible sense of humor.

Settling himself cross-legged on the ground, Buncan cradled his duar against his waist. "I want you all to pay attention. The tune is not difficult, nor are the words. Squill, Neena?"

Looking bored, the otters lay down next to him. "Not again, mate?" Squill picked at the grass.

"This shouldn't take long." Buncan turned back to his attentive audience. "If the monster emerges, and is hostile, this is the spellsong you use against it." He began to play. With notable lack of enthusiasm, the otters supplied what words they could remember.

Deep within the blazing monastery a visceral, pitiable howl rose above the dry crackle of burning wood and the crash of collapsing timbers.

CHAPTER 24

ALL NIGHT THE FOREST RESOUNDED TO THE EBULLIENT cries of abducted children and unlucky travelers being reunited with their families and friends. At Wurragarr's insistence, food and fresh clothing were shared with those unfortunate individuals who were the offspring of the Dark Ones' experiments. Such joyous reunions helped everyone to put aside their memories of the carnage which had taken place behind the scorched walls of the monastery.

Gradually empathy supplanted revulsion as Cilm's fellow mutants were welcomed into the fellowship of the country folk. Despite their often horrific appearance, all had been normal at one time. While their former lives could not be restored to them, they could be made comfortable within the limits imposed by their condition. Amid scenes of great heartache, all were promised a place to live in quiet and safety for the balance of their unnatural lives.

Once safely down the mountain a great weight seemed to lift from the little army's collective shoulders. That night saw a celebration the likes of which Buncan and the otters had only imagined from Mudge's often exaggerated tales. Buncan made friends with a human girl his own age, while Squill and Neena exuberantly partnered up elsewhere. Neena opted for the companionship of a handsome young tiger cat from a far valley, while Squill found himself in the company of a black-furred, bare-tailed, robustly built young female of a tribe he didn't recognize.

"I'm a marsupalian devil, mate," she informed him in response to his query. He lowered his eyelids along with his voice.

"I'll bet you are, luv," he replied suavely.

Songs of thanksgiving and reconciliation filled the forest.

The following morning the travelers gathered around a hastily erected stone firepit whose blackened contents still smoldered from the revelry of the night before. Seated on a half-burned log on the other side, Wurragarr and Bedarra listened respectfully to their newfound friends' exotic tale of travel and tribulation. Around them the woods bustled with farmers and tradesfolk readying themselves for the long march back to their homes.

"We can't tell you how grateful we all are." Wurragarr indicated the old galah, who perched comfortably on the big roo's right shoulder. "Mowara's told us about what happened inside. Seems clear that without your help we wouldn't have stood much of a chance against the mucky sods."

"You're bloomin' right there." Squill allowed himself a broad smile until Buncan jabbed him in the side. " 'Ere now, mate," the otter protested. " 'Tis true."

"Haven't you two ever learned anything about tact?"

Squill whistled sharply. "Learned about tact? From *Mudge*?"

Buncan pursed his lips. "I see your point." He turned back to their hosts. "We were glad we could be of help. As the offspring of great adventurers, we had no other choice."

"I seem to remember—" Squill began, but Gragelouth cut him off.

"Perhaps in your gratefulness you might do us a good turn?"

"Anything within our power to grant is yours," Wurragarr replied magnanimously. "We owe you more than our lives."

Gragelouth ran two fingers through the thick gray fur of his forehead. "As you know, we seek an undefined, uncertain something which may or may not actually exist. It is known as the Grand Veritable."

"Yes, I remember you mentioning it before," said Wurragarr. "Go on."

"I think we are closing on it, but we still have a ways to go to the northwest." The sloth looked up at the shadows which loomed in that direction. "We must go higher still into these mountains. While supplies would be welcomed, a guide would be more useful still."

Wurragarr and Bedarra exchanged a glance before the roo returned his gaze to the travelers. "We've left behind families who need to know that we've triumphed and survived. All of us have obligations at home: businesses to attend to, crops to plant or bring in, children to raise." Turning with a slight hop, he gestured into the distance.

"No one I know travels into the high mountains. There's nothing there except cold and rock. To the east, yes; to the south, yes; to the north, occasionally in winter. But never to the west or northwest. That may change now that the Dark Ones are defeated. Or it may not. The high mountains are home to many shadows which we simple country folk are not inclined to pursue.''

''There, you see!'' Gragelouth's tongue darted in and out reflexively as he turned to his companions.

''Proves nothin', guv'.'' A disinterested Squill lay on his back, picking his teeth with a sharpened twig.

Bedarra yawned, displaying his incredible gape. ''There are stories of some who choose to explore that country. They go in search of jewels or precious metals. They never return.''

''Bedarra's right.'' Wurragarr turned back to them. ''Nothing good has ever come out of those mountains. I'd prefer not to think of you, our good new friends, going up that way.''

''Nevertheless, that is our goal.'' Gragelouth was apologetic.

The roo nodded slowly. ''We will give you all we can in the way of supplies, but you won't find anyone who'll go with you. We're not adventurers or great sorcerers like you. I myself have a farm to tend to. Sorry, mates.''

It was silent around the corpse of the fire. ''We shall simply have to proceed on our own, then, as best we can,'' Gragelouth said finally.

''Now 'ow did I know you were goin' to say that?'' murmured Squill sarcastically.

They accompanied the ragtag but victorious army until a tumbling stream pointed the way up toward a likely-looking pass. There ensued many emotional farewells, replete with hugs and kisses in which Buncan and the otters participated enthusiastically while Gragelouth stood shyly aside. Wurragarr and his companions reiterated their promise of shelter and succor anywhere in the fertile valleys and hills beyond... should the travelers return this way, though that unhappy thought was not voiced.

''I wonder what finally happened to the pit bull–bul?'' Buncan mused as they began their ascent.

''Died in the fires.'' Snaugenhutt climbed slowly, carefully. ''Pitiful critter, but a hell of a fighter.''

''Maybe it got away,'' Neena suggested. ''Found itself a cave or somethin'.''

''Maybe.'' Buncan's attention was on the rugged peaks that lay before them. ''If it did, we could run into it again.''

"Let's hope not, Bikies." She was scampering along the edge of the stream, an eye out for edible crustaceans. "I ain't sure I could sing any more verses o' that bloody cub song o' yours, no matter '*ow* strong its magic."

As they climbed higher, the last of the paperbark trees gave way wholly to evergreens. These in turn grew stunted, becoming no more than bushes, until at last there was only hearty low scrub and grasses eking out a living amongst the wind-scoured boulders and scree.

Streams like molten quartz cascaded in musical falls down steps of schist and gneiss, while strange insects buzzed busily about the vegetation that invariably gathered at the base of each water drop. The blue of the sky was deeper here, the gray of the rocks more brilliant, and always they walked in the shadows of recent encounters. Curiosity and Gragelouth drove them on.

As the days passed, Buncan began to wonder if they would cross the top of the world and start down the other side. Rumor was a powerful bait, but it was not irresistible. Old doubts never put entirely to rest began to trouble him as they crossed ridge upon ridge, climbing ever higher. Whenever he felt assured, Squill was always there to put fresh doubts in his mind.

Snaugenhutt swerved to go around a large dark-brown bush when the growth, with unexpected alacrity, rose up on two legs, extended an absurdly small head on the end of a long, curved neck, and stepped out of their way. The travelers regarded it with astonishment.

"What are you?" Buncan asked as they halted.

Bright blue eyes blinked. An enormous feathered body balanced deftly on the pillarlike legs. Clawed, splayed feet looked strong enough to rip the guts out of any presumptuous attacker. For such a formidable body to terminate in so tiny a head was unavoidably comical. The creature was all out of balance, Buncan thought. It looked like a runaway adjective.

"Wot the 'ell are you?" Neena asked with typical otterish subtlety.

"I'm a moa," the giant flightless bird explained politely. "Who are you? Not many visitors up this way."

"Your kind is new to us." Gragelouth eyed the bird with the same sort of look he would have bestowed on a gold coin that had suddenly gone transparent. "Not in all my travels have I ever seen anything quite like you, though you are clearly kin to the tribe of ostrich."

"There aren't a lot of us," the bird explained.

"No moa, huh?" Neena ignored the glare Buncan threw her. "Sorry, Bunkles. Couldn't resist."

"You should learn to."

"I'm used to jokes." The moa had a melancholy voice. "All of us who survive up here are. The world has left us behind." A huge wingtip indicated the surrounding, snow-clad peaks. "This is the Country of the Recently Forgotten."

"As opposed to the Land of the Often Overlooked." Gragelouth ventured a thin smile. "I have traveled that region, but not this one."

"Here dwell creatures who have surrendered the future to others. Myself included." It let out a heartrending whistle. Buncan was instantly sympathetic, and even the hardened otters were moved. How could one not feel sorry for something Nature had designed to look like a bad joke?

"I didn't mean to make fun of you," Neena said when that whistle of lamentation had finally perished among the side canyons. "Well, actually I did, but right now I rather wish I 'adn't."

"That's all right. I expect to be extinct any day now anyway. In the meantime, it's nice to meet others, any others. I haven't seen another moa for nearly a year. No, not many of us left. For all I know, I might be the last of my kind. There are a lot of lasts up here, living out their tribal heritage. Before long, only our memories will be left."

"Well, ain't this the cheery interlude," Squill grumbled.

Gragelouth studied the absurd bird. "I don't suppose that you have in your considerable wanderings heard anything of a Grand Veritable?"

Long eyelashes fluttered. "Oh, that old thing. Yes, I know of it. I even know where it is."

Buncan felt a surge of relief and elation. Maybe they weren't going to have to hike to the top of the world after all. Their quest had a destination.

If the flightless bird could be believed, the Grand Veritable was more than mere rumor.

"Well, what is it, what is it like?" The excited merchant fought to control himself. Which, in Gragelouth's case, did not require much effort.

"What does it *do*?" Neena prompted the moa eagerly.

The tiny head dipped to one side. "I wouldn't know about that. When you're facing imminent extinction, you don't really have much interest in peripherals. You'd have to ask the Guardian."

A catch, Buncan thought suddenly. As Mudge was so fond of saying, there was always a catch. Though he had to admit he wasn't really surprised. If anything as fabulous as the Grand Veritable actually existed, it was only natural to expect it to have some kind of guardian.

Well, they'd overcome whirlwinds and bandits and inside-out rivers and a pit bull–bull. "What's this Guardian like?"

"Not too big?" Gragelouth essayed a hopeful smile. "Willing, perhaps, to let us have a look?"

"I wouldn't think so." The moa was unencouraging. "He's very testy."

"Is he also one of the Recently Forgotten?" Buncan inquired.

The moa nodded. "Personally, I'd like to see him become one of the Completely Forgotten. Him and all his tribe." Feathers riffled as the bird gave a visible shudder. "He's bad company. You don't want to provoke him."

"If we were foolish enough to want to," said Gragelouth slowly, "how might we go about it?"

The moa let out a regretful whistle, like the lowest note of a pipe organ. Turning, it gestured with both beak and wing.

"Continue on your present course. Before long you will come to a branching of this stream. Follow the branch. Though it appears to run straight into a sheer mountainside, track it upward. The Veritable is housed in a cave that is also home to the Guardian. You can confront him if you wish, but I wouldn't try it. He'd probably eat me."

"Eat you!" Gragelouth gaped at the moa. "The Guardian is one of the cold-blooded?"

"No, he's as intelligent as you or I. But we of the

Recently Forgotten retain ancient instincts and habits that have been largely abandoned by the rest of the world. Oh, he'll think about it before he eats you. Maybe even have a moment of regret. But he's not called the Guardian for nothing. He's up there to keep the Veritable away from inquiring minds. Been doing so for as long as the Veritable's been there, I imagine.''

'' 'Ow did this wonder get 'ere?'' Neena wanted to know. ''In a shower o' stars, or via some sorceral sublimation?''

The moa shrugged. Feathers went everywhere. ''I have no idea. I'm not into necromancy. Some say it arrived on a pillar of blue flame, others that is was delivered in the beak of the Maker herself. The story I personally give the most credence to says that it just fell out of a stormy sky one day and bounced a couple of times before coming to rest in a puddle of muddy water. When some Wise-Ones-Who-Shall-Go-Unnamed found out what it could do, they stuck it in the cave and assigned a Guardian to it. Successive Guardians have kept watch over it ever since.'' A huge wing rose and fell.

''Like I said, it doesn't much interest me. When you're on the verge of extinction, little things like Guardians don't bother you. Obviously you feel otherwise. I wish you luck.''

Buncan smiled sympathetically. ''We wish you luck as well.''

''And I,'' Snaugenhutt rumbled. ''I know what it is to be alone and abandoned.''

''Not by Nature, you don't.'' The moa turned and strode off downstream, singing softly to itself. They watched until it had disappeared.

''Shame,'' Neena murmured. ''A handsome creature, if a bit oddly proportioned. Did you note the blue o' its eyes, an' 'ow the sun reddened its plumage?''

''Maybe he'll find another moa,'' Buncan suggested, ''and they'll have lots of little moas.''

'' 'Ow many moa does it take . . . ?'' Squill began. In a somber mood, Buncan cut him off sharply.

They followed the cheerful little tributary up into a dense thicket of low scrub, Snaugenhutt plowing easily through the tightly interwoven branches and trunks. Much of the vegetation they were now encountering was of a type unfamiliar even to the widely traveled Gragelouth.

Truly this was a place of the Forgotten, Buncan reflected. He pondered what the Guardian would be like even as he wondered if he ought to be afraid, then decided he was too tired. Whatever it was they would deal with it, as they had dealt with every other obstacle which had crossed their path. The duar bounced lightly against his back.

Topping yet another in a seemingly endless series of natural granite steps, they found themselves standing on a small flat plateau. Cliffs rose steeply to left and right. Ahead additional steps led onward and upward, but the stream did not tumble down them. Instead it curved leftward against a raised shoulder of rock and terminated at the base of a narrow waterfall. A small clear pool shimmered at the rocky intersection of stream and cascade. To the right lay a dark, yawning void in the cliff face, a black blot on the otherwise unmarred granite.

Dismounting from Snaugenhutt to give him maximum room to maneuver, they approached the cave with caution. A thick, musky smell emanated from within.

"Let 'im come." The rhino pawed at the gravel. "I'm ready for anything."

"Sure you are." Viz bobbed atop his iron perch. Like the rest of Snaugenhutt's armor, it was slightly the worse for wear from the fall the rhino had taken inside the monastery of the Dark Ones. "Just don't get carried away. We may be up against something more powerful here than the minions of the Baron, or even the crazed horrors of the monastery."

"You watch your butt and I'll watch mine," the rhino rumbled.

Buncan peered hard but saw nothing. The depths of the cave were veiled in blackness. He took courage from the fact that the opening wasn't very large, and that it was unlikely any inhabitant would be larger than its egress.

After a querulous glance at Gragelouth, who could only shrug helplessly, he turned back to the black and called tentatively. "Hello in there? We're travelers from a far land. We've come a long way to see if there really is such a thing as the Grand Veritable, and we were told you had charge of it.''

Silence most profound greeted this declamation. After a pause, Buncan tried again.

"Listen, all we want at this point is a look, to see if the damn thing's real.'' This time, an echo of silence.

Emboldened, Squill sauntered right up to the entrance. "Me, I always said there never were any such contrivance. 'Tis all piffle, an' so's any bleedin' Guardian.''

"I am not piffle," declared a voice from within. A very deep voice. A voice most carnivorous, of a timbre and resonance that inspired in the otter an urge to precipitous retreat.

"Nice goin'," muttered his sister as they huddled together against Snaugenhutt's bulk.

Buncan too had retreated, but not as far. He started to draw his sword, instead swung the duar around in front of him. "We must have a look. We've come too far and endured too much to just walk away now. At least grant us proof of the Veritable's existence." *And maybe an explanation of what it is,* he added silently.

"Go away!" The Guardian's speech was half snarl, half cough, all menace. "I'm in a truly foul mood today. Provoke me, and I'll come out."

" 'Tis bluff.'' Buncan looked sharply back at Neena. "I've 'eard about these 'orrible 'guardian' things all me life. Monsters that are supposed to watch over secrets an' treasures an' the like, wot? If they ain't just gossip they're always overstated. Why d'you think this one ain't showed 'isself? Because there ain't much to 'im, that's bloomin' why. They all rely on their reputations, they do."

"I dunno." Buncan turned back to the cave. "Just a look, that's all we want!''

"Blood of my liver, you want to steal it!" came the sonorous reply. "Frankly, that'd be all right with me. I'm sick of this job. But my job it is, and I'm bound like all who preceded me to perform it to the best of my ability. So don't make my day any more difficult, okay? Just leave."

For one entrusted to watch over the Source of All Knowledge and the Fount of Limitless Power, this Guardian sounded quite reasonable, Buncan thought. While he had not acceded to their request, he had already deigned to converse with them.

"I'm sorry, but for the reasons I've already mentioned we can't do that."

"Can you describe the Veritable to us without coming out?" Gragelouth inquired.

"Yeah, give us a 'int," barked Squill. " 'Tis it animal, vegetable, or mineral?" He winked at his sister.

A thunderous roar amplified by the natural bellows of the cave rattled the ground like a seismic tremor. Small rocks tumbled from the cliff side.

"SO BE IT UPON YOU! DON'T SAY YOU WEREN'T WARNED!"

As Buncan stumbled frantically backward, blazing green eyes centered on something huge and tawny exploded toward him.

CHAPTER 25

IT WASN'T AS BIG AS THE PIT BULL—BULL, HE THOUGHT as he threw himself to his left, nor as horrifying as some gramarye wraith, but it looked quite capable of butchering each and every one of them without pausing to take a breath, including the massive Snaugenhutt.

Its headlong charge carried it well past the diving Buncan. Gravel and dust flew from beneath its clawed feet as it landed and spun, gathering itself for a second, better-timed attack.

Because of its color and general shape, Buncan at first thought it a lion. But there was no mane, the skull was longer and decidedly flattened, the ears were positioned differently, and the forelegs were more muscular at the shoulder. More startling still, it walked on four legs instead of two and wore no clothing or decoration of any kind, both hallmarks of the civilized. Certainly a throwback, yet one capable of speech and rational thought.

It was hard to contemplate what all this might mean, because he found himself mesmerized by the pair of incredible, backward-curved canines which protruded downward from the roof of the Guardian's mouth. Each was fully half the length of the otters' short swords and looked just as sharp. When the Guardian yawned, its gaping upper and lower jaws formed a nearly straight line. Among all the other creatures Buncan knew of or had ever encountered, only the thylacine Bedarra could duplicate the feat, and his admittedly impressive teeth were no match for the ivory scimitars of this brute.

It glared at them. "On your own heads be this. Who'll be the first to die?"

"Actually none of us are in any particular hurry," squeaked Gragelouth from his position behind Snaugenhutt's protective rump. The rhino shook himself, rattling his armor, and lowered his head. If this creature could place a bite between the iron plates, Buncan knew, those great incisors could sever the rhino's spinal cord. Or his jugular.

As for himself or Gragelouth or the otters, those powerful jaws could snip their heads clean off. Only Viz was comparatively safe.

His fingers were tense on the duar, and he could see that Neena and Squill were ready to rap. But could they sing fast enough to save themselves? The creature's initial charge had taken only seconds, and it was clearly infinitely more agile than the pit bull–bull. He'd been lucky to dodge it once. He doubted he could do it again.

"What do you call yourself?" He struggled to maintain a brave front, and incidentally give the otters more time to improvise some lyrics. "Of what tribe are you? We've already spoke with one who calls this the Country of the Recently Forgotten."

"That's right, remind me." The Guardian pawed at the gravel, his head weaving from side to side. "I haven't mated in nearly a year, and that doesn't make me any less irritable."

"I know how you feel," mumbled Snaugenhutt even as he angled his horn.

"This Guardian is of the tribe of the sabertooths, since

you're unable to puzzle out that simple fact, and I warned you.'' It raised one paw (at least it was capable of that much learned behavior, Buncan reflected) and pointed toward the cave. ''In there lie the bones of those who came before you and lingered to disturb my rest. They are well gnawed. It will be good to have a fresh supply to crack.''

''Surely you cannot seriously be thinking of eating us,'' Gragelouth protested. ''That would be uncivilized in the extreme.''

''I lay no claim to civilization,'' The lunatic canines gleamed in the mountain light. ''Do I look like a vegetarian to you? I eat whatever comes my way, whether it's capable of intelligible conversation or not. I don't discriminate between idiots and geniuses. They all taste the same going down.''

Suddenly the Guardian winced, eyes squinting tight. Throwing back its head, it let out a deep wail. Squatting on its haunches, it ignored them as it proceeded to howl mournfully at the sky.

Some sort of pre-attack ritual chant, Buncan thought as he and the otters took the opportunity to retreat all the way to Snaugenhutt's side. At least now the sabertooth couldn't single them out. At which point the utterly unexpected occurred.

Gragelouth started forward, hands extended.

A disbelieving Neena yelled to him. '' 'Ave you gone mad, merchant? Get back 'ere before you're fish meal!''

''Cor, let the silly twit sacrifice 'imself if 'e wants.'' Squill sniffed disdainfully. ''Maybe 'e'll give the toothy blighter a bellyache.''

The sloth glanced over a shoulder. ''I am not about to sacrifice myself, and I am quite frightened out of my wits. It is only that when you travel as widely as I do and see as much as I have you acquire all manner of odd information. While observing our assailant just now, I imagined I saw something specific.''

''Right,'' agreed Neena. ''Waitin' death.''

''Something besides that.'' As he continued to advance, the sabertooth ceased its dirge and lowered its gaze.

"A volunteer for the first course. That doesn't happen very often."

Gragelouth halted just out of immediate claw reach. "Your pardon, father-of-all-fangs, but prior to your consuming me might I have a closer look at something? A final favor, if you will."

The sabertooth's expression narrowed, which, given his already low sloping forehead, have him the look of a piqued executioner. "A look at what? I've already told you that you can't see the Grand Veritable. I'm guarding it."

"Not that; something more personal. Just now, when you had your head back singing, I thought I noticed something."

The great carnivore eyed the sloth warily. With a single swipe of one great paw he could easily tear out the merchant's throat. Therefore, there was no need to hurry.

"Just what is it you want to see?"

Gragelouth raised both hands over his head. "I am unarmed."

The Guardian scrutinized the proffered limbs thoughtfully. "You will be shortly."

"I mean that I have no weapons." The soft-voiced merchant would not back down. "These others are here at my instigation."

"I thank you in advance for supplying so large and diverse a meal." In no great hurry now, the sabertooth lifted a paw and examined its claws.

"Having come this far in search of a dream, I cannot turn and run, I cannot back down without an answer. Do you understand?"

"I understand that you will tickle sliding down my gullet. Could you not have shaved first?" Glowing green eyes glistened in deep-set sockets.

"All I wish," said the sloth as he warily lowered his hands, "is to have a look inside your mouth."

The Guardian's eye ridges rose. "You'll see that soon enough."

"You do not understand. It is one small portion that intrigues me." He had moved closer, and Buncan saw that no matter how effective a spellsong he and the otters might mount, it would not be in time to save the merchant.

"A peculiar last request. Peculiar enough to be granted."
The sabertooth stretched its incredible jaws wide. "Indulge
yourself. I'll let you know before I bite."

"Thank you." Gragelouth stuck his head forward and
down, twisting to one side to stare at the Guardian's upper
palate. Buncan and the others held their breath. "Ah, there.
Just there." His expression knotted sympathetically. "That
must hurt something terrible. It is no wonder your disposition is so befouled." He withdrew.

Instead of lunging forward, jaws agape, for the fatal bite,
the sabertooth eyed the squat sloth uncertainly. "What can
you know about it?"

"I can see it. Upper left canine. It goes right down into
the socket. How long has that tooth been bothering you?"

"What makes you think it bothers me?" The Guardian let
out an anticipatory snarl.

Gragelouth spoke a little faster. "As I said, one acquires
many odd bits of knowledge in one's travels. It is bothering
you, is it not? Did it not just cause you shooting, throbbing
pain?"

"Don't speak of it! You . . ." The Guardian suddenly
winced. "Yes, it hurts. The pain is like a running fire in my
brain."

"For how long?"

"Soon after I ate a pair of exotic dancers who lost
themselves in these mountains. A human and a cat, they
were." He looked downcast. "They tasted harmless at the
time."

"Ah." Gragelouth nodded knowingly. "One must take
care not to consume too many sugary tarts."

"The pain comes and goes, but each time it returns it's
worse."

"I thought as much."

Unable to overhear the conversation clearly, Squill raised
his own voice. "Oi, gray-bottom! Wot's the bleedin' story?"

"He has a cavity," Gragelouth explained. "A hole in one
front tooth."

"No wonder 'e's in such a bad mood," Neena declared.
" 'Avin' a chopper like that, you can only imagine the
toothache it would give."

"I'd rather not," said Squill.

"And I can't," Viz added.

Buncan moved to join Gragelouth, ignoring the otters' warnings. "I'm sorry to hear about your problem. What if we could fix it for you?"

The Guardian growled at him. "You can't 'fix it' for me. No one can fix it for me." As Gragelouth took a well-considered step backward a huge paw reached out to land on his left foot, preventing him from retreating any farther. The murderous skull drew close and green eyes blazed into the merchant's own. "*No* one."

"Not wishing at this point in time to incite you any further, I must still point out that my friends may be able to do something for you. Though young, they are purveyors of exquisite necromancy. Spellsingers."

For just an instant, the sabertooth hesitated. "Spellsingers?" The restraining paw did not move, but the eyes rose to peer past the trapped sloth. They settled on Buncan. "Is what this furry snack says true?"

"It's true. How do you think we got this far if not with the help of powerful sorcery?"

"I don't know. Blind stupidity?" He lifted his paw, releasing Gragelouth's tingling foot. Knowing better than to try to run, the merchant implored the glowing Guardian.

"At least let them try. If they fail, you can still run us down one by one."

"Spellsinging . . . I don't know," the sabertooth brooded. "What if they make it worse?"

Buncan took another couple of steps forward. "Is that possible?"

Gragelouth was once more bending to peer into the Guardian's gaping mouth. "It appears to be eating into the root. If you do not have it taken care of very soon, you will lose the entire saber. I suspect you will not grow another."

"You'll look bleedin' 'umorous with only one o' those stickers 'angin' out o' your trap," Squill commented.

The Guardian threw the taunting otter a murderous glare, then winced as fresh pain shot through his upper jaw. When he finally spoke again he was much subdued.

"Can you really help me?"

"We can't make any promises." Buncan spoke slowly, cautiously. "Sometimes the magic doesn't work, and often it takes paths we didn't envision. Furthermore, most of our spellsinging has been defensive in nature. We've never attempted anything quite so . . . constructive. We've only tried to do what was right, without hurting anyone or anything."

"Yeah," added Squill energetically. "Moral shit like that, wot?"

The Guardian nodded his understanding. "I will let you try. No tricks now, I warn you! I am nearly as quick of mind as feet, and I won't hesitate to shred the first one I suspect of something sly. But if you can mute the pain even a little, if you can help me, I would . . . I would be grateful."

Fighting to restrain his excitement, Gragelouth inquired delicately, "If we can fix the problem permanently, will you let us see the Grand Veritable?"

The sabertooth's green gaze shifted back to the merchant. "If you can fix this so it doesn't hurt anymore, ever, I'll give you the damn thing!"

The merchant's face broke out into a wholly uncharacteristic wide smile.

"Right," muttered Buncan. "Let's do it."

He huddled with the otters while the others, including the tormented sabertooth, waited expectantly. Torn between a natural desire to rend and tear, which he was obligated to do, and a desperate need to alleviate the worsening pain in his jaw, the Guardian sat silent as a house pet and waited.

Before long the human confronted him again. "We're ready." When the Guardian didn't respond he nodded to his companions.

The rhythm was gentler than any they'd employed previously, coaxing rather than challenging, soothing instead of belligerent. No problem with that. Rap was adaptable. They'd just never had the occasion to speak softly before.

"Ain't no gain without no pain
But the pain, in the main
She's a tiresome refrain, the bane
Of existence
Do we make sense?

Got to chuck it out
Shouldn't have to shout
That it's plain that the pain
Is on the wane an' on its way out."

As they played and sang, a small silvery cloud, a miniature of those which formed so often when they spellsang,
drifted from the duar's nexus to the Guardian's mouth. It
swirled gently about the infected tooth, taking on multiple
forms and shapes: now a small pointed instrument, now one
through which glistening white liquid flowed.

An expression wondrous to behold slipped over the
sabertooth's face like a cleansing wrap, an expression not
there seen since it had been a cub. Though only the corners
of his mouth curved upward, there was no mistaking the
contortion for what it was: a smile.

As the silver radiance faded, the heavy paw which had
temporarily pinned Gragelouth rose to feel gingerly of the
area around the left saber. The merchant dared to inspect the
sensitive region yet again.

"The dark gap appears to be gone."

"It *is* gone!" Emitting a roar of pure delight, the Guardian leaped into the air, turned a complete somersault, and
landed effortlessly on all fours. The light in his eyes burned
as brightly as before: Only the motivation had changed.

Neena considered the sabertooth thoughtfully. "Mate,
you really ought to learn to walk on your 'ind legs, proper
like."

The Guardian nodded. "I know that's how it's done these
days, but I'm one of the Forgotten, or soon-to-be. Many of
the old ways are still mine. I'm comfortable with them." He
rubbed his jaw. "More comfortable than I've been in some
time."

"Let him be," Snaugenhutt advised her. "Some of us
just ain't inclined to walk vertical."

"I keep my word." The sabertooth pointed toward his
cave. "It's just inside. Don't want to trip over it in the
dark."

Buncan turned to gaze at the cave. After all they had been
through, it seemed impossible they'd actually achieved their

goal. More important, if the Guardian was not lying, it
seemed that there was actually a goal to achieve. The Grand
Veritable was real. Real *what* remained to be seen.

"You've done so much for me," the sabertooth was
saying. "Wait here and I'll bring it out to you." Springing
from the rock on which he'd been sitting, he loped into the
cave.

Buncan waited; they all waited. Even Gragelouth, who
had to restrain himself from following the Guardian into his
lair.

"Can't be very big," Neena observed. "Not if the cat
can drag it out all by 'imself."

"Maybe 'tis a pink diamond the size o' 'is 'ead," Squill
commented hopefully.

"Or a wand." Now that they were actually about to
encounter the mysterious source of legends, Buncan recalled
the odd mixture of disdain and apprehension with which
Clothahump had treated the subject. "No matter how innocent or harmless it looks, we need to be careful with it."

" 'Ell, you worry too much, mate." Squill twisted completely around to groom his tail. A human attempting the
same move would have to dislocate his spine. "Wotever it
is, it ain't 'urt this 'ere kitty-cat none. I'd say 'e's 'ad plenty
o' time to play with it, and if it couldn't cure 'is bloomin'
toothache, then I says there can't be much power in it."

"Perhaps it is possessed of a different sort of power."
Gragelouth's gaze was fixated on the cave mouth.

All speculation aside, there wasn't one among them who
wasn't surprised when the sabertooth finally reemerged with
the object held firmly but respectfully in his mouth.

"Well, I'll be orificed." Neena sat down right where
she'd been standing. A puzzled Snaugenhutt simply smiled
and shook his great head, while Viz let out a series of
bemused whistles.

"What's *that*?" A wary Buncan bent for a better look as
the Guardian carefully placed the object on a smooth-
surfaced boulder.

"The Grand Veritable," the sabertooth replied. "It's
what you wanted, isn't it? What you traveled all this way to
find?"

"Righty-ho," said Squill, frowning at the subject under discussion, "but wot *is* it? Wot do it do?"

"Do?" The Guardian was openly bemused. "Why, it doesn't 'do' anything. It just is. Truth, that is. The Grand Veritable is truth, just as its name implies. That's what the Ancient Ones who set my kind to watch over it said."

Gragelouth sat down heavily, moaning. "Solipsisms. All this way come, all this distance traversed, great dangers and perils overcome, for *that*."

The rejuvenated sabertooth growled. "Don't underestimate it. Truth is the most valuable of all commodities . . . and the most dangerous."

Squill gave the object a tentative kick. It did not react. "Don't look so dangerous to me."

The Guardian grinned. "You can't hurt the truth that way."

Gragelouth put one hand to his forehead. "What good is truth to me? I'm a merchant, a trader. You can't sell truth."

Neena let out a derisive bark. "Why not? I thought the stuff were always in short supply."

The sloth looked up at her. "Truth's an intangible. I do not deal in intangibles."

She knelt next to the object. "Looks kind of . . . broken."

"I assure you it's not." Bright green eyes studied Gragelouth. "I owe you much. Had I eaten you, there's no telling how long I'd have continued to suffer. So you are a merchant in 'tangible' things? I know about merchants. I've had several for dinner. There exists a base for the Grand Veritable. Maybe you'd find it of more interest than the Veritable itself."

The sloth blinked slowly. "I do not understand."

"Come and have a look-see." The sabertooth started toward the cave. So despondent was Gragelouth that he followed without thinking.

Time passed while Buncan and the others studied the Grand Veritable closely. Their examination left them no less baffled than when the Guardian had first presented it to them.

A voice shouted from the lip of the cave. "Hoy, Snaugenhutt! Come give us a hand here, would you?" The

rhino shrugged and ambled over. As it developed, the
assistance of Buncan and the otters was required as well.

Deeply graven with cryptic inscriptions, the ancient pedestal was as tall as Neena. Poured in the shape of a pyramid
with the top sliced off to form a resting place for the
Veritable, it was so heavy it required their combined efforts
to wrestle it into place on Snaugenhutt's back, where they
secured it with leather straps. Still, Squill worried about it
falling off on their return journey.

"No need to concern yourself on that matter." Gragelouth's eyes were shining. "I will ride alongside and see
to its stability."

At least, Buncan mused, they wouldn't have to worry
about it blowing away. The pedestal was fashioned of solid,
absolutely pure gold. The purest gold, Gragelouth breathlessly
informed them, he had ever seen. A gold that was not of
this world, but was recognizably gold nonetheless.

"No revelations," he commented, "but for all that, a
most profitable journey. Yes, most profitable."

" 'Ere now." Squill was quick to protest. "Wot makes
you think that bit o' furniture's all yours?"

The merchant looked hurt. "You came seeking adventure.
Surely you have had that in quantity. You also have the
Veritable. The wizard of whom you spoke should find it of
considerable interest. Each of us has gained what we came
for. Do not think to deprive me of *my* dream, however base
you may find my motives."

"Take it easy," Buncan told him. "We don't want your
gold."

The otters gaped at him. "We don't?" they chorused.

"Gragelouth's right. We've gained more from this journey than mere gold could buy."

"But," Squill sputtered, "maybe just a little mere
gold . . . ?"

Buncan had turned away from him and back to the
Veritable. "I still don't see how this thing embodies or
represents truth."

A frustrated Squill gave it another kick. "It don't embody
nothin' but garbage, Buncan. Me, I'd rather 'ave a share o'
the gold."

Buncan knelt next to the large, rectangular metal box and ran his fingers over the surface. There were glass-covered numbers with little arrows pointing to them, round knobs and buttons, and a large window beneath which a paper scroll was prominent. A narrow metal pointer thrust halfway up the height of the scroll, which was in turn divided by innumerable little black squares, and a black rope that ended in a twin-pronged knob of some kind protruded from the rear of the box. The exterior was somewhat the worse for wear, but intact at the corners and seams. Of one thing Buncan was certain: The Grand Veritable was indubitably a device necromantic.

"Be careful," the Guardian warned him as he fiddled with the knobs and buttons. "It's enchanted."

"It's manure," groused Squill. Because of his long torso and short arms, he had to bend almost double in order to thrust his hands angrily into his pockets. He leaned over Buncan's shoulder and shouted at the bruised and scratched box.

"Go on, then; show us somethin'!" Stepping around Buncan and ignoring his protests, the otter picked up the container and shook it firmly. It made quite a bit of noise, as if there were a number of small bits rattling around loose inside. Disgusted, he let it drop unceremoniously. "Some source o' ultimate power!" he griped. "A smidgen overrated, wouldn't you say?"

"Like most wondrous rumors." There was a hint of sadness in Neena's voice.

"Maybe we just don't know how to make it work?" Buncan suggested.

"A spellsong?" Neena eyed the box uncertainly.

Buncan looked doubtful. "How to begin? We don't know what it's capable of or what it can do, if anything. So how do we design a song?"

"Why sing to that hunk o' junk?" Squill had turned his back on the sorry-looking Veritable. "Might as well sing to the trees, or the sky. The 'truth' is that we've come all this bloomin' way for nothin'. If the bloody thing ever did do anythin', it don't no more."

"Where's your sense of vision, of higher motives?" Buncan challenged him.

Squill squinted up at his friend. "I'm an otter, mate. We don't 'ave a sense o' vision or 'igher motives. We 'ave *fun*. Gold aids an' abets that. Junk don't."

"Come on, Squill. Which would be more valuable to you: the truth, or a little gold?"

The otter made a truly appalling face. "Let me get back to you on that, mate."

Disappointed, Buncan turned back to the object of controversy. "Maybe Clothahump and Jon-Tom can do something with it." Bending, he carefully raised it off the rocks. It was heavy, but not unduly so.

"You don't mean you're goin' to take up ridin' space with that thing?" Squill was more outraged than angry.

"It's my space. I'll make room for it." With those few remaining straps which hadn't been used to secure the pedestal, Buncan set about tying the Grand Veritable to Snaugenhutt's back.

They left the sabertooth on his mountain, turning somersaults and yelping with joy as he snapped at trees, rocks, and whatever else struck his fancy, biting for the sheer joy of being able to once again bite without pain.

CHAPTER 26

THE JOURNEY HOME PROVED FAR EASIER AND FASTER than it had been coming out, for they knew which areas to avoid and which to stick to. This time they encountered no caucusing whirlwinds or animate mesas. They crossed the Sprilashoone downstream of Camrioca and its doubtless still-seething Baron Krasvin. By the time they reached the Muddletup Moors they found its brooding atmosphere almost invigorating, so near were they to home.

After what seemed like an age (but if you think carefully

about it was really not so very long as all that), they found themselves again in the bright and friendly confines of the Bellwoods, heading south. Timswitty provided civilized comforts for a day and a night, and then it was on to Lynchbany, passing to the west of Oglagia Towne. There they parted company with Gragelouth, leaving him to see to the melting down of his beloved gold into more manageable form.

Upon greeting her long-absent, wayward son, Talea alternated hugs and kisses with blows of such ferocity that it was uncertain as to whether she would love or beat him to death. Squill and Neena received similar attention from Mudge and Weegee (bear in mind that otters can deliver attention of both kinds at twice the rate of the fastest human).

When everyone's respective offspring had recovered from their shower of affection and concurrent beating, there was a formal gathering at Clothahump's tree. As the wizard's dimensional expansion spell had not been designed to accommodate individuals of Snaugenhutt's bulk, the rhino waited outside, placidly cropping the fresh grass.

The rest of them assembled in Clothahump's central workshop, Viz sharing a perch and whispered conversation with the wizard's famulus, Mulwit. The Grand Veritable rested, a mute and battered enigma, on the wooden workbench. Jon-Tom and his hard-shelled mentor regarded it thoughtfully.

"So this is the Grand Veritable. *The* Grand Veritable." Clothahump rubbed at his lower jaw, cautiously nudged the box with a finger. When it didn't go off he prodded it again, harder. There was no reaction. "I admit it doesn't look like much, but then, the truth rarely does."

"Ought to be in Lynchbany," Squill mumbled rebelliously, "sharin' out the gold with that greedy sloth."

"Be glad you returned with your lives." Jon-Tom glared at the young otter, who dropped his eyes.

"Should 'ave you sheared," said Weegee, " 'til you look like a naked mole-rat. That'd be fit punishment for the worry you gave us."

Indifferent to this ongoing display of domestic bliss, Clothahump continued to prod and examine the mysterious device. But it was Jon-Tom who finally spoke up.

"I think there's one thing I can say with some certainty."
Everyone looked to him. "It's definitely a mechanism from
my world."

"I suspected as much but wished to hear you confirm it."
The wizard adjusted the glasses which rode on the forepart
of his beak. "Do you have any idea as to its intended
function?"

Jon-Tom looked thoughtful. "According to what the kids
have told us, it's supposed to be, or to represent, truth. In
my world we have a machine called a polygraph. When I
was a law student I got to see several. This is an old model,
but I'm pretty sure that's what it is." He hesitated. "Though I
suppose it could be a seismograph, or some other kind of
'graph.' It's pretty beat up."

"The Guardian said it was enchanted," Buncan informed
them.

"Enchanted or not, the apparatuses I'm familiar with are
far from perfect. All too often they fail to reveal the truth."

At that the box gave an unexpected twitch. Jon-Tom
glanced quickly at Clothahump. "You nudged it again."

The wizard took a step backward, shaking his head.
"Didn't."

Shimmering softly, the black cord rose into the air like an
awakening cobra. The pronged knob turned slowly to face
first Clothahump, then Jon-Tom. Slowly it scanned the rest
of the room, weaving slightly from side to side. The guts of
the machine were now pulsating a soft, luminous yellow, as
though something vital had sparked to life within.

"I *always* tell the truth," a voice announced through a
tiny grid inset next to the glass-protected scroll. Buncan
could see that the long metal needle or pointer was quivering.
With indignation? he wondered.

"Then you are some kind of polygraph?" Jon-Tom inquired
hesitantly.

The knob (which Buncan later learned was called a
"plug" but which still looked like a snake's head to him)
pivoted to "face" the senior spellsinger. "I am the Grand
Veritable. I am the Truth, and I never lie."

Jon-Tom scratched behind one ear. "You're a damn sight

more voluble than any polygraph I ever saw. How'd you come to be here?"

"I don't know. Truth travels everywhere. I remember a great storm, being studied and inspected, being transformed, enhanced, and enchanted, and finally ending up on a high place outside a cave. There I've slept for some time, until your offspring brought me hither."

"What is your purpose?" Clothahump, Buncan noted, was treating the device as if it were some kind of highly poisonous reptile.

"To relate the truth, the whole truth, and nothing but the truth."

Squill let out a barking laugh. "Cor, this may turn out to be a bit o' all right after all! If only that merchant knew wot he'd passed on in favor o' a pile o' gold."

"It wouldn't matter. He's quite content." The Veritable's plug swung 'round to confront the startled otter. "He wouldn't know what to do with me. He is a merchant, after all."

"I know what to do with you." Clothahump kept a wary eye on the pulsating device.

The plug turned to him. "No, you don't. That's a lie. You continue to believe that I'm mortally dangerous, and hide that truth from your friends."

Everyone turned to look at Clothahump, who sputtered and harrumphed uncomfortably. Jon-Tom sought to cover his mentor's embarrassment.

"Why haven't you spoken before now?"

"No one addressed me, no one questioned me. But you," and the plug darted sharply in the spellsinger's direction, "insulted me, and I felt I had to defend myself. When all one has to offer is the truth, one can't sit silently aside and let it be besmirched."

Clothahump peered over the top of his glasses at his young human colleague. "Are all such devices in your world this forward?"

Jon-Tom shook his head. "Usually they're speechless. But then, in my world I couldn't make magic with my singing, either. I acquired certain abilities when I stepped over here. Maybe the same is true for machines. It seems to be for this one, anyway." He considered the enchanted polygraph. "Unless it's lying, of course."

"I never lie," the Veritable insisted. The plug drooped. "Sometimes I wish that I could. There are so many floating about unexposed. Lies, that is. Never enough time to deal with them all."

"*If* you're telling the truth," Jon-Tom reiterated.

"Couldn't we try it out?" Neena suggested. "On each other?"

"I do not know," Clothahump said slowly, "if that is such a good idea. As I have been trying to point out all along, the truth can be a dangerous thing."

"And that's no lie," the Veritable declared. "You're very perceptive, turtle."

"I am the greatest wizard in all the worlds." Clothahump spoke quietly and without a hint of boastfulness. It was significant that the Veritable did not contradict him.

"I've got an idea." Sudden excitement suffused Squill's face. " 'Ow's about we take this 'ere yappin' box into town?"

"That is not a good idea either." Clothahump hesitated. "Still, under carefully controlled conditions, the experience could be enlightening. For everyone."

Buncan looked to his father. "You can always spellsing any problems away, Dad."

"Uh, yeah, right," Jon-Tom mumbled.

The Veritable piped up without prodding. "That's a lie."

Talea glared at the box. "I wonder if the spell under which you're enchanted could survive a few well-placed sword strokes."

The plug stiffened. "You can't cut down the truth."

"I'm not sure I like the idea of a machine that's smarter than me," Jon-Tom opined.

"I am not smarter than you," the Veritable declared formally. "That, too, is the truth. I just call 'em as I see 'em, and I'm always right."

"Every time?"

The cord nodded. "Every time."

"Pity we can't unplug you for a while."

"You can't turn the truth on and off like water, spellsinger."

He frowned at the machine. "You don't need to analyze everything I say."

"Sorry. It's what I do. Call it a job-related compulsion."

Jon-Tom stared at the box for a long moment before turning to his mentor. "You're right, Clothahump. You were right before the kids found this thing, and you're right now. It's dangerous as hell, and we've got to get rid of it."

Buncan and his friends immediately protested. They found an ally in Mudge.

" 'Ere now, mate. Let's not be 'asty. It strikes me that somethin' which can tell truth from fiction and never lie itself ought to be worth a bit o' money."

"A fortune," agreed Clothahump readily.

"Then why get rid o' it?" Squill and Neena had moved to stand next to their father. Weegee looked on and tapped one foot threateningly.

"Because it is unbelievably dangerous. Because truth kills." He glanced up at his colleague. "An appropriate spellsong might be best, Jon-Tom. Send it away. Far away."

"Wait a minute, now!" Mudge ignored Weegee's warning glare. "I've somethin' to say in this."

"So does we." Squill huddled close to his father, sister, and Buncan.

Jon-Tom eyed his son. "You side with them in this?" Buncan nodded stiffly. "Well," the spellsinger sighed, "it's not the first time we've disagreed."

"Then let it be as you wish." Everyone looked in surprise at Clothahump. "I wash my hands of it. Experience is the best instructor, and evidently I am not. Jon-Tom?"

The spellsinger glanced uncertainly at Talea, then back down at his mentor. "If you're going to have nothing more to do with it, then neither will I."

"Good!" Mudge stepped forward and put his arms around the device, then hesitated. "Are you goin' to stop us from takin' it out o' 'ere, mates?"

"Not at all." Clothahump had turned away and was busying himself with his equipment. "Do with it what you will. Just keep it well away from my tree."

"Oh, that we'll do, sor!" With Buncan's help the otter began wrestling the mechanism toward the doorway. Squill and Neena trailed behind. "Beggin' your pardon if we also keep all the money we're goin' to make with it."

Talea and Weegee stood together in the doorway to watch the three otters and one young human disappear down the extended hallway. Mudge's mate glanced worriedly back over her shoulder.

"Great Clothahump, do you think they'll be all right?"

The wizard sniffed. "I am too old to argue with children, but I sincerely hope so. Where the inimitable truth is involved, who can say what might happen?"

The two ladies, one gray of fur, the other red of hair, were not comforted.

The next day, the expectant confidants sauntered full of anticipation into Mudge's favorite Lynchbany watering hole. Espying several acquaintances at a central gaming table, the otter wandered over and sat down nearby, making convenient seat of the unprotesting Veritable. Buncan, Squill, and Neena hung by the bar, sipping what liquid the bartender would provide them, and watched.

An elegantly clad and coiffured weasel pushed back his dealer's cap and gestured at the box. "What's that, friend? Some sort of magical device?" His playing companions chuckled over their cards and dice.

"Some sort," confessed Mudge with a smug smile.

A husky badger frowned as he tugged at his black leather vest. "You been dealing with that turtle again?"

"Actually, mates, me pups an' their friend brought this little toy back from a far-distant land, recent-like." He nodded in the direction of the bar. Neena waved back prettily.

"Nice-looking girl you got there, water rat," commented the weasel approvingly. He was sucking on a stick saturated with keep-awake.

"Just keep your bleedin' paws an' mind on the cards, Sucrep," said Mudge warningly. "I've always suspected you o' unhealthy goin's-on." Reaching down, he patted the Veritable fondly. "In fact, this little box is about to answer me a question I've been wonderin' about for years."

The smirking weasel attended to his dealing. "Why you can't get it up anymore?"

"Somethin' not quite as personal. Mind if I buy in?"

Sucrep readily shifted to one side. "Your money is always welcome at this table, Mudge. Especially since you leave so much of it here."

The game continued as before, coins changing their position in front of the various players according to the flash of dice and cards. Beneath Mudge, the Veritable was silent. Mudge won some and lost some, but as was usually the case his luck attended more frequently to the latter than to the former.

A kinkajou emitted its eerie, high-pitched giggle as he collected a pot. "Thet box mey be full of megeek, but et hesn't mede you a beeter kerd pleyer."

"That's true," declared the Veritable suddenly.

Amidst general laughter Mudge leaned over and glowered at his makeshift metal pew. "I don't recall askin' for your opinion just yet. Whose side are you on 'ere, anyway?"

"You know what side," the Veritable replied calmly.

"Can it do anything besides talk?" asked a heavyset hog curiously.

Mudge straightened and forced himself to smile. "It tells the blinkin' truth. Always. Every time."

"Interesting." A wolf clad in rough muslin peered over his cards. "So it will tell us if you are cheating." He leaned forward. "Tell me something, box."

" 'Ere now." Mudge half rose in his seat. " 'Tis my device! I'll be the one to ask it any bloody questions."

"Sit down and shut up, river rat," said the wolf dangerously. "Box?"

"I am the Grand Veritable," announced the device stiffly.

"Right then, Grand Veritable. Has Mudge here been cheating on us?"

"Not today," the Veritable declared positively.

"Oh well, then." The wolf relaxed and studied his cards.

"See there?" Mudge permitted himself a sneer of self-satisfaction. "I've never cheated on you, Ragregren."

As soon as he said it, he was sorry.

"That's not true." The Veritable was inexorable.

The wolf blinked. "What's that?"

"Nothin', mate. Nothin'. See to your cards." To the Veritable the otter hissed, "Turn your bloody self off until I ask for you!"

"Sorry. The truth doesn't work that way. Once you call it up, it just sort of sticks around."

"I asked what was said." Putting his cards aside (face-down), the wolf rose, an imposing figure on the far side of the table, and again addressed the box. "Grand Veritable, when has the river rat cheated us before?"

"I can only tell the truth," the grid declared apologetically. "I cannot read the future or the past."

"I never cheated you, Ragregren! The damned thing's confused."

The burly wolf was staring at him hard. "You just told us yourself that it couldn't lie."

"I can't," added the Veritable for good measure.

"Then you have cheated at this table before." The wolf pushed his chair back.

"I bloody well 'ave not!" Mudge was sputtering wildly. "You . . . 'tis you who've done the cheatin'!"

"Don't try to worm your way out of this, river rat. I'm not the one who's been cheating here."

"Not today," declared the Veritable cheerfully.

The wolf froze. "What's that?"

"You've cheated before, but you're not cheating today. Actually, the one who is cheating today is that hog over there."

"I *beg* your pardon?" said the hog. He shrank back in his seat as both Mudge and Ragregren turned to glare at him. "There must be some mistake."

"You've been winning an awful lot today, Bulmont," the wolf muttered suspiciously.

The hog drew himself up. "You've no right to accuse me just because I am a better dice thrower than you, Ragregren."

"But you're not a better dice thrower," declared the Veritable.

"My dice are clean," the hog protested.

"Indeed they are," agreed the machine.

"Ah, you see?" Bulmont looked greatly relieved.

Mudge nudged his seat with a sandaled foot. "Explain yourself, not-so-Grand Veritable."

"It's quite simple. The weasel who calls himself Sucrep always deals appropriately to the porcine one. Therefore, the individual Bulmont need not worry about his dice, because his cards are correctly loaded even before he can throw. I suspect that at an appropriate time the two will split the hog's winnings."

Sucrep said nothing. He didn't have to. The look on his face as the keep-awake stick fell from his lips was revelation enough.

"The cursed container lies!"

"I do not," replied the Veritable quietly. "Check beneath the table where he sits. There is a hidden compartment containing the requisite additional cards."

With a roar the wolf lunged. Displaying the agility for which his kind was noted, Sucrep dove beneath the table. Bulmont made a frantic attempt to sweep up the last pot, only to be bowled over chair and all by the infuriated badger. The kinkajou reached for the coins, froze as Mudge's stiletto slammed into the table between two of the fruiteater's slim fingers.

The otter grinned thinly. "I think we'll divide up this pot a bit differently, wot?" The kinkajou nodded slowly, then brought his other hand up and around. It held a bottle, which shattered against Mudge's feathered cap.

"Oi!" yelled Squill. "Dad's in trouble!" Together he, Neena, and Buncan rushed to join the fray. With a sigh, the bartender ducked down behind his heavy wooden barrier.

"You'd better stay out of this, Buncan!"

Startled at hearing his name, Buncan paused and looked around for the speaker. When the admonition was repeated, he saw that its source was the now sinister metal box.

"Why?" he demanded to know as he prepared to fend off any attackers. By this time the tavern existed in a state of utter pandemonium.

"Because you're not half the fighter you think you are."

"What are you talking about? I'm as good as the otters or Jon-Tom."

"No, you're not. You're liable to get yourself killed. And that's . . ."

"The truth; I know, I know." Confused and uncertain, he hunkered down beneath the table.

" 'Ello, mate."

He was startled to see his friends folded up nearby. "You two too?"

Squill nodded. "We thought it best to take the bloody thing's advice. It 'asn't been wrong so far. Besides, me mum'd 'ave me arse if I let Neena be 'urt in some bleedin' bar brawl."

"Why worry about her? She's a better fighter than you," announced the Veritable helpfully.

"Don't act the mechanical twit," groused the otter. "When we're wrestlin' I always win."

"That's right," agreed Neena.

"She lets you win," said the Veritable.

"I do not!" Neena glared at the box but wouldn't meet her brother's querulous gaze.

"That is a lie," stated the Veritable with quiet aplomb.

"I'll show you who's the better fighter!" In an instant, and for the first time in some while, the two otters were rolling across the floor, locked in each other's antagonistic embrace.

"Let 'em fight," Buncan muttered wearily. "When they've had enough, I'll spellsing them apart."

"You cannot spellsing," observed the Veritable. "You can only play the duar."

"Well, at least I can do that better than anyone," Buncan replied irritably.

"You cannot. Jon-Tom is better."

Buncan's eyes widened. "*I'm* better. He's said so himself."

"He flatters you to build your confidence."

Buncan rested his chin on his knees as he turned away. The brawl surged around him. An astonishing mixture of roars, bellows, squeaks, yelps, and howls reverberated the length and breadth of the tavern. "I need the otters' singing now, but if I keep working at it I'll be able to spellsing all by myself someday."

The Veritable was relentless, but not insensitive. It spoke

softly. "You will never be able to spellsing by yourself, young human."

Buncan turned sharply. "Why don't you just shut up for a while, okay?"

"Truth is always in great demand," the Veritable whispered, "for everyone except ourselves."

A chair slammed into the table over his head. Being fashioned of honest wood, it did not break, unlike the wineglass which shattered like thin ice on the floor nearby. Eventually Buncan spoke again.

"I'm beginning to understand what Clothahump was talking about."

"No, you're not. You're too young to understand. You're just poking around the periphery. The meaning of truth is not so easily grasped. You seriously overestimate your perceptual and analytical capabilities as well as your martial skills and duar playing."

"I didn't ask you for criticism."

"Just truth. Only truth. Always truth. Hurts, doesn't it?"

Another chair came sliding by. It still contained its most recent occupant, who was in no condition to escape its confines. Buncan leaned out from beneath the table for a better look.

"We need to get you out of here before one of these happy, mature adults tries to make off with you. Though at this point I'm not so sure I'd fight anyone to keep you." He quickly saw that Squill and Neena would be no help, still intent as they were on pursuing their most recent sibling altercation.

From the time they'd entered the tavern less than an hour had elapsed, and in that brief span a little truth had reduced a placid establishment and its contented patrons to bloody chaos.

The path to the front door was blocked by battling customers. That was where the police would enter anyway. Dragging the Veritable by its cord, he worked his way around behind the bar and found himself in the company of its owner, a corpulent pangolin. Semiprecious stones and sequins sparkled among his scales.

"My beautiful gaming room!" he wailed.

"You have to help me get out of here." Buncan hugged the Veritable close.

"No, you don't," the grid informed the tavern owner cheerily. "It's not necessary."

"Shut *up*." Though he doubted it would do any good, Buncan slammed a fist down on top of the device. It made him feel better.

"What's that?" The pangolin was eyeing the Veritable with sudden interest.

"Nothing," Buncan growled. "A toy."

The pangolin looked uncertain. "I can't imagine what started this."

"He did," declared the Veritable. "He and his friends. Three otters."

The proprietor's voice rose. "So! You are the offspring of that tree-dwelling spellsinger, are you not? Wonderful! I can sue for damages. The wizard's guild shall hear of this!"

"Watch yourself," said Buncan warningly. "You can't sue a spellsinger."

"Of course you can," chirped the box.

This time Buncan gave it a swift, hard kick. It rolled over and came to rest right side up. The radiance within was as strong and implacable as ever.

"You can't get rid of the truth that easily, my young human friend."

"How about if I dump you in the deepest part of the river?"

"Won't work. The truth has a tendency to cling."

"Truth, eh?" The pangolin looked delighted. "Then I *can* sue a spellsinger for damages?"

"Yes. But you wouldn't want to."

The narrow-faced insectivore entrepreneur blinked. "Why not?"

"Because you've been running a crooked house here all along."

"I, crooked? What are you saying?"

"All these 'decorative' mirrors. In the walls, in the ceiling." The plug stiffened, the prongs pointing upward. "Some are made of one-way glass. You have agents in the crawl spaces above them, spying on the games below. They report to your own plants among the players, who adjust their games accordingly. A large portion of their illegal winnings goes to the house. To you. They skim just enough off the legitimate games so that none of your patrons become suspicious.''

"Fiend-in-a-box! Accursed furniture of the Nether Regions!" The enraged owner searched wildly for a weapon.

"Easy to curse the truth!" shouted the Veritable as Buncan hefted it in his arms and rushed toward the back of the tavern in hopes of finding an exit. "Hard to deal with it!"

A large bottle of amber liquid exploded against the wall to his left as he dumped the Veritable into a garbage chute and dove through behind it. It deposited both of them atop a fetid mound of quite indescribable foulness in the alley behind the establishment. Struggling to his feet, he stumbled free of the rancid hillock and gathered the Veritable in his arms.

"Which is the safest way to go?" He glanced wildly to left and right, scanning both ends of the alley.

"To your left." The Veritable spoke without hesitation.

As he staggered off in the indicated direction, Buncan rounded a corner and found himself face-to-face with Ragregren, the wolf who'd been at Mudge's table and who was largely responsible for initiating the melee inside. Blood trickled from a gash on his forehead and one ear dangled loose, having been bitten almost completely through. His rustic attire was in disarray, stained with liquor and blood only partially his own. One paw gripped the amputated leg of a chair, and he was breathing hard.

"You!" he rumbled darkly. "You and that, that unmentionable *thing* are the cause of this!" With a cry, he charged, holding the chair leg over his furry head.

Buncan ducked, and the makeshift club smashed into the wall behind him. "I thought you said this was the best way to go! You lied!"

"I never lie," said the Veritable primly. "My hearing is most excellent. I overheard the owner giving directions to his minions. They lie in wait at the other end of this passageway, and would most certainly have killed you had you gone that way. This one is merely likely to just beat you up.''

"You can count on it!" Ragregren raised the club over his head and brought it down sharply. Unable to reach his sword, Buncan attempted to block the blow with the only shield at hand.

The club struck the Veritable. Buncan braced himself for the impact, but surprisingly there was none. No shock, no recoil. The chair leg fragmented into splinters, the splinters disintegrated and became sawdust, the sawdust sifted to the ground as evanescent yellow glitter.

"Violence will never break the truth," the Veritable declared positively. "Submerge it sometimes, blanket it sometimes, but destroy it, never."

Buncan pursed his lips. "Neat trick."

"Damn your eyes!" the wolf howled. "Damn you and your accursed device!" He whirled and ran down the alley in search of another weapon.

Buncan waited until Ragregren was out of sight. The distant echo of battle still resounded inside the tavern. "Is it safe to go on now?"

"Yes."

"No, I mean *really* safe?"

"Really safe. Insofar as I am able to judge the truth of the situation."

An inquisitive crowd had gathered outside the tavern. They evaporated wordlessly when a wagon full of uniformed skunks, civet cats, and zorillas arrived. The police would quickly put an end to the conflict, Buncan knew.

Among the hastily retreating spectators, one face stood out. He ran toward her, waving feebly.

"Mariana! It's me, over here!"

She didn't slow until they met behind a general store. One didn't want to be anywhere in the vicinity when the police began their work. Her expression fully conveyed her reaction to his appearance.

"Buncan? What happened to you?" She nodded in the direction of the tavern. "What's going on in there?"

"I don't know."

"A lie," said the Veritable.

Ignoring the observation, she peered curiously at the machine. "What's that?"

"Never mind. Have you any transportation?"

"My riding lizard, but . . ."

"Can I borrow it? Just for a short while." He glanced nervously back toward the tavern, where shrieks and screams indicated that Lynchbany's finest had set to work among the miscreants inside. "I have to get out of town fast." He held up the Veritable. "This is something the great Clothahump and my father need to deal with."

She wrinkled her nose and took a step back from him. "My lizard's not with me. I walked into town."

"That's a falsehood. It's close by."

Her pretty face twisted as she glared at the box. "Are you calling me a liar?"

"Of course. It's my job."

She spoke as she continued to back away. "What is this, Buncan? Some kind of depraved necromancy propounded by your father and that ridiculous turtle he works with?"

"No, no, it's nothing like that," he implored her. "It's something I found, Squill and Neena and I."

"Those *otters*. No wonder." She hesitated. "Maybe you're not responsible, then. I guess . . . I guess I could do something."

"You've got to help me, Mariana. You know how deeply I feel about you."

"Lie," burped the box.

"It's not! Mariana's a good friend."

"Another lie." Buncan gazed at his loquacious burden in horror. "You just want to get into her pants. You've been dreaming of it for years." With great difficulty the mechanism managed to inject something like an electronic leer into its artificial voice.

Mariana gaped at the Veritable, then up at Buncan. "You bastard! I thought you loved me. And here I've been saving myself for you."

"Lies, lies, lies," the box chorused happily. "You've already slept with more of this young human's friends than he could imagine."

Buncan swallowed hard. "Mariana, can this be true?"

"Of course it can be true," declared the Veritable. "I just said it was, didn't I?"

"Damn you!" Buncan raised the machine over his head, intending to smash it to the pavement. But when he looked to Mariana for approval she was already gone, lost in the crowded streets. Slowly he brought the box back down.

Then he started running, grim-faced, through the throng and toward the edge of town. As he ran, the Grand Veritable provided a running commentary, as it were.

"That one there, the large man, has a vial of poison in his pocket that he intends for his mate's lover. And that one next to him is—"

"Be silent!" Without much hope but not knowing what else to do, Buncan slapped a hand over the grid.

"Sorry," the muffled voice of the Veritable replied, "but I'm starting to feel really good. Warmed up. There are so many suppressed truths about that need telling."

"I don't want to hear them!"

"Yes, you do."

"Please," Buncan mumbled as he flew along, "have some pity."

The Veritable's voice was like the wind off a glacier. "There is no pity in truth. Like most people, you fear it."

"And with good reason," panted Buncan as he raced toward the forest.

CHAPTER 27

SOMEHOW HE MADE IT TO THE FAMILIAR, TRANQUIL glade. Jon-Tom and Clothahump weren't present, but a perplexed Mulwit let him in and made him comfortable while they waited.

"I tried to warn you," said Clothahump when he and Jon-Tom finally returned, "but you would not listen to me." He took a deep breath, expanding his carapace. "Hardly anyone under a hundred ever listens to me."

"Mudge never listened to anyone, me included." Jon-Tom peered anxiously into his exhausted son's sweat-streaked, grime-laden face. Behind them the Grand Veritable once again reposed quietly on the workshop bench, a picture of mechanical innocence.

Buncan wiped dirt from his eyes. "I never realized how dangerous the truth could be."

"Civilization is not founded on absolute truths," Clothahump declaimed importantly, "but only on those the majority of people can deal with, and those are precious few."

"Truth," the Veritable observed.

"Nobody asked you," Jon-Tom growled. Buncan kept a watchful eye on the device, as though at any moment the twin metal prongs on the plug might metamorphose into actual, dripping fangs.

"What are we going to do with it?" Jon-Tom asked his mentor.

Clothahump considered the temporarily quiescent device. "Try to magic it away, I suppose. I will make an attempt. Should that fail, perhaps a spellsong would be in order."

"Yeah!" Buncan sat up quickly. "I could . . . !" He went silent at the look on his father's face.

Clothahump's magic shook and twisted the tree, and drew curious storm clouds overhead. Lightning and thunder failed to impress the Veritable, which sat unmoving atop the workbench. When the turtle eventually admitted defeat, Jon-Tom drew upon his memory for his most powerful spellsongs. These likewise had no effect. Finally he even let his wayward son have a go at the duar while he sang in place of the absent otters, all to no avail.

"You can't wish away the truth." The Veritable spoke up only when it was clear they'd finally thrown in the thaumaturgical towel. "Not all your spells or sorcery can make it disappear. Nor is it so easy to dump in a river," it added pointedly.

"We must get rid of it somehow." The wizard looked sternly at Buncan, who was appropriately contrite. "I tried to warn you about bringing it back. Most people already have all the truth they can stand. More, in fact."

"That's so," agreed the Veritable.

"It induces the ill-equipped, which is to say most folk, to fight among themselves. It destroys families, whole communities. It starts wars."

"That's not my fault," said the device. "I don't make truths. I only report on them. You can't blame me if people prefer comfortable prevarications. Why, if everyone told the truth I'd be out of a job, and damn glad of it."

Jon-Tom looked beaten, but no more so than his mentor. "What do we do now?"

"Leave it here. Isolate it within this tree. Keep it away from everyone else. I have lived several hundred years and can handle the truth better than most. We must all do our best to ignore it."

"You can't isolate the truth, and you can't ignore it," declared the Veritable.

Eyes glittering, Clothahump approached the mechanism. Beneath that wizened, unexpectedly energetic gaze the plug drew back. Maybe the truth couldn't be eliminated, but it could occasionally be cowed.

"We can but try." The wizard beckoned to Jon-Tom. "Come, my friend. We will consult the texts and see what can be done. If anything more *can* be done."

That night a lithe, muscular shadow approached Clothahump's tree. Numerous spells protected the wizard's home, but this particular intruder had prepared well for his nocturnal excursion. Proceeding directly to the object of his intentions, he swathed it in a large canvas bag and tossed it over his shoulder. Mulwit, who ought to have detected the thief, unaccountably slept through the entire intrusion.

In a distant riverbank Mudge and Talea lay entwined in a manner no humans, no matter how flexible, could have duplicated. Having recovered from the fracas at the tavern, a spent Squill and Neena gently whistled away the night in their own beds. Side by side in a tree somewhat less ensorceled than Clothahump's, Jon-Tom and Talea alternately hugged covers and one another, while down the woody hallway Buncan tossed and turned uneasily in his sleep.

So the thief got away clean, to rejoin his colleagues in the depths of the Bellwoods.

"I told you I could do it!" Triumphantly, the coati unbagged his prize. In the dim light his companions eyed it appreciatively.

"Truly you are the greatest among thieves, O honored Chamung," the raccoon murmured. His ringtailed companion concurred.

"I *knew* that if we waited, and watched, and bided our time, the opportunity for revenge would come!" The bandit leader's teeth glinted in the light that fell between the Belltrees. "Those cursed interfering youths! I would have slit their throats, but the tree was empty save for the dotty old wizard and his apprentice. With them I have no quarrel." He nudged the Grand Veritable with a foot.

"Now we have this: the booty they journeyed so far to acquire. I learned of it during a brawl at Nogel's Tavern in Lynchbany, and subsequently laid my plan. They cost me my band; therefore I take their prize. Life is just!" His voice fell to a conspiratorial whisper. "Do you know what this magical device does?"

"Uh-uh," admitted the ringtail, wondering simultaneously if he was being set up.

"It reveals the truth. All truths, apparent or hidden. With this I will raise a great army. Beginning with Lynchbany, we will lay waste to the Bellwoods. The forest will run red with blood. Not even a great wizard can stand against the truth! I will bathe in his scraped-out shell, and sleep on the tanned skins of those three cubs, and those of their relations, and their friends. In payment for the humiliation I have suffered, their skulls will be impaled on the gables of my home!" Exhilarated and breathing hard, he struggled to unwind.

"Come, my loyal companions. It is time to begin." They moved into deeper forest, heading toward town. "I will share my victory with you, as I have always shared our spoils."

"Speaking to that," chirped the Grand Veritable unexpectedly, "it is a statement which contains several blatant untruths."

"No one queried you, box," snarled Chamung.

When he looked up, it was to find that his two remaining warriors were eyeing him speculatively.

* * *

Not too many days later a thrashed, defeated figure limped into the distant town of Malderpot, having been chased from one town after another. His clothes were in rags, one ear and several teeth were missing, and his formerly resplendent tail had been singed down to the bare skin.

The hidden chime tinkled as the door to the small shop closed behind him, shutting out the steady rain. Beneath one arm he carried a scratched and battered, but still intact, metal box from which issued a steady, undying saffron glow.

As the visitor warily shoved back the hood of his cape the shop's proprietor, a slightly inebriated muskrat, emerged from behind a curtain. Though he had been drinking steadily to keep out the cold, sufficient faculties remained to him to reveal that the coati had been through a difficult time. The muskrat perked up. Here was an individual in the final stages of physical and mental dissolution. In short, the source of a possible bargain.

The walls of the little shop were covered with strange objects, its shelves lined with tightly capped jars full of noisome organics. Mysterious devices and stuffed reptiles hung from the ceiling, dangling at the ends of strong wires.

"Thimocane, you have to help me." The coati's voice was shaky, and his speech was interrupted frequently by hacking coughs. "I am told that you are a wizard."

"I used to engage in shorcery," the muskrat admitted freely. "Now I shimply buy and shell. I'm short of shemiretired, you shee. But if you'd like to buy me a case of good liquor..."

"Later, later." The coati glanced nervously over a shoulder, as though even on a rotten night like this someone might be after him. Or some thing. "I can't buy you anything right now, or even pay for your services. I'm utterly broke."

The muskrat raised both paws. "Then I don't know what you're doing here. I'm no charity."

"Please!" The coati all but collapsed on the narrow countertop. "You've got to help me! If you don't I will surely die ... or go mad."

"That's the truth," announced the box beneath his ill-kempt arm.

Intrigued, the muskrat stood on his tiptoes and leaned forward. "Now what have you there, traveler?"

"For All-Tails' sake, don't listen to it! Don't pay any attention to it. Pretend it's not there." The coati's expression verged on mania, the muskrat thought.

"You can't do that." The light within the box throbbed. "You can't ignore the truth."

"The truth?" The muskrat was shobering fast. "What does it mean, the truth?"

"It detects lies and gives the truth." The coati was almost sobbing. "Always. Whether you ask the truth of it or not." Water ran down his long snout and dripped from his black nose. "That's all it does, is tell the bedamned truth."

The muskrat nodded discerningly. "Now I undershtand your unfortunate condition, shir."

"Can you help me?" the coati whispered weakly.

"Not I. This ish a matter for greater shkill than ever I posshessed. But I know of another who might. A wizard of great shkill and experience. He dwells far to the shouth of here, a turtle named—"

"NO!" screamed the coati with sudden force. "I can't go to him, though I almost would. You see, I stole this from him."

Again the muskrat nodded. "Are you sure he didn't curse it on you? I cannot believe from what I have heard of hish reputation that thish Clothahump would be sho foolish ash to deal with anything sho dangeroush."

"Well, he did. I did steal it from him." A little (but just a little) of Chamung's old arrogance crept back into his voice.

"Ah. And you owe your present shituation to forces he has shent in purshuit of you?"

"No," mumbled the coati miserably. "It's all the fault of this damnable device. I don't have the skill to manage it. I don't know that anyone does."

"Maybe you should get out of my shop." The muskrat began to edge surreptitiously toward the curtain. "If the great Clothahump was sho afeared of thish thing that he allowed it to be shtolen, then it is far beyond my shimple shkills to mashter."

"You're my last hope." Chamung was begging again. "I can't go on. I've tried abandoning it, leaving it behind, even throwing it into a deep ravine. It follows me wherever I go: sleeping, eating, everything."

"Once you get attached to the truth," the box declared, "you can't just walk away from it."

"You see to what pitiful state I, the great Chamung, king of thieves, am reduced."

"You're certainly in a bad way." The muskrat interrupted his retreat.

"Truth," quipped the box.

"There may, just may, be one way." The shopowner was considering the Veritable thoughtfully.

A flicker of life brightened in Chamung's eyes. "Anything! I'll do anything."

"There are tales of a passhage. A means of travel between our world and another. Rumors, gossips, hearshay. If you could enter that passhage and leave this infernal apparatus on the other shide . . ."

"Yes, yes?" the coati prompted him.

"It ish true that you cannot abandon the truth. But it is shometimes posshible to give it away."

Chamung turned violently on the Grand Veritable. "Well? Does the small fat one speak the truth?"

"He does," the box reluctantly admitted.

Upon a promise of a lifetime of devoted servitude (which covenant the muskrat thoughtfully had the Veritable verify), the small wizard (semiretired) mounted and led an expedition far to the south of the river Tailaroam, beyond the Lake Region and the Morgel Swamps. There, after a long and most arduous journey, they succeeded in abandoning the Grand Veritable in the far reaches of a certain cave.

Many days passed in retracing their difficult route until the coati was convinced the curse of truth had been lifted from him, and true to his promise he remained in the service of the shopowner until the day he died, of an excessive imbibulation of a certain high-proof booze.

* * *

In the lightless pitch-black recesses of that singular cavern the Grand Veritable languished, barely active, until one day a pair of children much younger than Squill, Neena, or Buncan stumbled upon it. They wore old blue jeans and carried waterproof flashlights, for the cave was often full of water at that time of year.

Being well-trained children, they did not touch the box but instead brought their grandfather to see it. He was accompanied by their guide, who promptly pushed his hard hat with its carbide lamp back on his head and scratched at his receding hairline.

"Don't recall ever seein' that in here before. Damn teenagers is always dumpin' their trash around." The old man tilted his head back, blinking as drip water splashed in his eye. "Must've fallen down through a sinkhole or natural pipe."

The other man played his light over the device's metal exterior. "Wonder what it is."

His eldest grandson spoke up. "If it doesn't belong to the people who own the cave, Grandpa, does that mean we can keep it?"

"Well, Ah dunno." He looked at their guide.

The old man shrugged. "Looks like junk to me. I'd be beholden to you if you'd get rid of it for me."

The visitor nodded, bent to examine the battered machine more closely. "Looks like some kind of measuring device. See heah." He wiped grime from the large glass plate. "Hey, you know what? This is an old polygraph." He chuckled. "Something Ah sure don't need in *my* business."

"Is it broke, Grandpa?" asked the other boy.

"Ah'm sure it must be, dumped heah like this in the wet and dark. But it's almost an antique. Spruced up, it might be kind of fun to put in the office. Sure to get a few laughs from the staff."

He was a big man, even for a Texan, and with the guide's assistance was able to wrestle the device over to the main trail and back to the cavern's entrance.

When the prize had been loaded in the back of the visitor's minivan and the children were in the tiny store buying candy, the guide couldn't help querying his guest. After all, it wasn't every day he escorted a private party into the far reaches of the cave.

"If you don't mind my askin', mister, just what is it you do?"

"Ah'm a state senator," the big man replied, his distinguished appearance only slightly muted by the dirt streaking his face. "From down neah Corpus." He patted the muddy metal box fondly. "Can you imagine the kick my colleagues will get from seein' this in mah office?"

"A lie detector in the Legislature?" Seeing that he was to be allowed in on the joke, the guide permitted himself an easy, agreeable chuckle. "Good thing it don't work, ain't it, Senator?"

The big, white-haired visitor smiled. "Now, suh, don't believe everything you read in the papers, especially the local ones. Most o' those ol' clichés aren't anythin' moah than that: clichés. There's a many good folk workin' up in Austin, an' a good bit o' truth an' honesty prowlin' the halls o' yoah state capitol."

Unseen by either man, the box in the back of the minivan began to glow ever so softly.